Sabelle's mind spun with thoughts, emotions warring with one another: She loved Justin . . . She should be resisting him . . . She would . . . She couldn't . . .

But then she heard him whisper in his familiar husky timbre, "I want you, Sabelle. As I've wanted no other woman, I want you!" And she was lost, lost beyond help, or hope, or prayer.

The pent-up hunger they'd shared in the library was back again, in full measure. They clung together greedily, their mouths crisscrossing in a frenzy of passions too long denied, whetted by their growing awareness—and increased knowledge of each other. . . .

St. Martin's Paperbacks Titles
by Veronica Sattler

PROMISE OF FIRE
A DANGEROUS LONGING
SABELLE

SABELLE

VERONICA SATTLER

ST. MARTIN'S PAPERBACKS

SABELLE

Copyright © 1992 by Veronica Sattler.
Excerpt from *Gypsy Lord* copyright © 1992 by Kat Martin.

Cover photograph by Nancy Palubniak.

ISBN: 0-312-92600-6

Printed in the United States of America

St. Martin's Paperbacks edition/May 1992

10 9 8 7 6 5 4 3 2 1

To Glynis Littlewood, *animal lover* **extraordinaire**,
And to *Maggie (who knows who she is)*—*my thanks.*

V.S.

⊰Prologue⊱

London, 1792

"**YOU FAITHLESS BITCH!**"

Fourteen-year-old Justin Hart froze as he recognized the angry voice of his father reverberating through the closed drawing room doors. Then, when he heard a responding voice, he felt his breath catch in his throat, nearly choking him, and his face grew deathly pale; this was his mother's voice, and it was filled with rage.

"Bitch, is it? And *faithless!* Why, you hypocrite! The tongues of the Court gossips have grown *numb* with tales of *your* conquests over the years, Your Grace! How *dare* you castigate *me* for such! What was I to do whilst you went slinking off after every available skirt, like a dog for a bitch in heat? Sit home and twiddle my thumbs? *Nay!* What's good for the gander is good for the goose, I say!"

Young Justin took a faltering step backward, his hands jammed at his ears. It was a futile attempt to shut out the strident sounds that were, in the space of a few horrible moments, wiping out every notion he'd ever held about his parents. Wildly, his spinning brain tried to ascribe some sense, some explanation, to the unmistakable evidence, which was continuing to bombard him now from beyond the closed doors. Somehow all was not well with the marriage of the two people he adored more than anyone else in the world. How, in God's name, was this possible?

But even as he shook his head and felt hot tears sting his eyes, no answer came. Vanessa and Derek Hart were still shouting furiously at each other, and his whole world was crashing down around his ears.

It had been a safe, sure, and often beautiful world that had surrounded him during his fourteen years as the only child and heir of Derek Hart, seventh duke of Haverleigh, and Vanessa, his beautiful duchess. Raised with all the wealth and privilege an English dukedom could afford, Justin wanted for nothing. His clothes had always been the finest; his lodgings—whether here in London at the Hart town house, or in his private chambers at any one of the family's five country estates—were grand enough to house any prince of the blood; he had a multitude of servants at his beck and call; and his education at the hands of private tutors had been even better than princely, for wasn't he, this very morning, off to Oxford, where he would read in literature, history, *and* the classics?

There weren't many other sons of noblemen who could boast so broad or fine an education. Indeed, few of them even thought of attending Oxford or Cambridge, whilst he, Lord Justin Hart, had every expectation of taking a first in each of his declared areas of study.

This scholarly preparation had been the idea of his mother—the same mother whose vituperous recriminations were now resounding from the drawing room. But his father had agreed to it when, at the age of two, his young son had presented him with evidence that he had taught himself to read—in Latin as well as English—from some of the books in the ducal library.

He'd basked in the love and approval Vanessa and Derek had sent his way over the years as report after shining report had come in from his tutors: At four he had mastered Cicero; at five, he'd translated Caesar's *Gallic Wars;* at eight, Euclidean geometry had become mere child's play for him. And with each glowing account, his mother had smiled the famous smile that Gainsborough had captured so well in the portrait that now hung over the mantelpiece in that wretched drawing room, but just for him—just for Justin! And his father! Why, his father had beamed, he'd been so proud.

Oh, Justin might not have seen that much of the two of them over the years—no children of their class did. Titled parents were deeply enmeshed in the social obligations their positions demanded; they were far too busy to see to a fledgling lord's day-to-day routines. But Vanessa and Derek Hart had made it a point to have dinner one evening a week with their brilliant son since the time he was barely out of leading strings; they had discovered early on that he could carry his own in convivial, adultlike conversation at the dinner table. And on each of these cherished occasions, young Justin had felt his love and esteem for his parents grow; they had presented themselves as an ideally devoted and loving couple who doted not only on their precocious offspring, but on each other, as well.

How could he have been so wrong?

Unable to bear the torrent of verbal abuse, Justin swiped angrily at the tears coursing down his cheeks and whirled about, heading for his chambers. There, his valet awaited his final instructions for seeing his baggage sent on to Oxford; Justin would see this done and leave—just as fast as he was physically able.

"Justin . . . ?"

The boy halted at the softly uttered phrasing of his name and raised troubled silver-gray eyes to the tall, slender figure of his tutor, standing at the end of the hall. A look of chagrin passed briefly over his youthful face before he banished it with a frown; Thomas Long was the last person in the world he wished to discover him like this—in pain and reduced to tears by what he'd overheard. What they'd *both* overheard, he realized with a growing sense of horror; for the furious exchanges within the drawing room were continuing, their angry tones leaving no doubt as to what was causing Justin's distress.

"What is it, Thomas?" asked the boy curtly. He was trying mightily to still the trembling of his voice as he addressed the tutor by the familiar form they'd long ago agreed on. In his mid-twenties, Long was not much older than his charge, and during the five years they'd known each other, the two had established a relationship more like that of older brother to younger, than mentor to pupil.

"Why aren't you waiting for me in the carriage?" Justin spoke testily, pretending he hadn't needed to raise his voice to be heard above the din in the drawing room. "It *was* where we agreed to meet, wasn't it? Or have you decided not to accompany me on the journey after all?"

Thomas Long gazed at the stoically rearranged features of his charge's handsome face and felt his heart go out to the boy. *Damn them anyway!* he thought furiously as his glance darted briefly to the closed doors. *Why couldn't they have contained themselves long enough to see the lad off this morning? Where was all their patrician self-control?*

But Long knew the answer to that. They all did, the various servants and retainers of the duke's vast household; they'd been secretly involved for years in keeping from the child any knowledge of the true state of his parents' troubled marriage. Because the duke and his wife were largely absentee parents, it had been easy enough for the staff; they'd loved and cared for their young master enough to form a kind of unspoken conspiracy to protect him from the ugly truths about his parents.

Young Justin, therefore, had an idealized image of the duke and duchess. He'd been prevented from seeing the elder Harts for what they actually were—a pair of selfish, spoiled children who, like many of their set, were bound together in a loveless marriage. They had not shared a bed in years, and each had taken lovers in that time.

But, like the rest of the staff, what Long also knew was that last night, things between the duke and duchess had come to a head. Last night Derek Hart had actually *caught* his wife in the act of adultery! Of course, it was an act he had long been aware she engaged in, as he had himself; but he had chosen, for the sake of the façade they presented to the *ton*—as well as their son—to ignore it. But last night Vanessa, duchess of Haverleigh, had gone a step beyond the pale: She had taken her lover *into their marital bed!* And His Grace, for all his penchant for deliberately looking the other way, had finally been unable to ignore his wife's infidelity. His "honor" would not permit it. Indeed, his *family's honor* forbade it!

But what of the boy? Thomas asked himself as he examined the carefully schooled features. *Was it necessary to uphold the family honor at the expense of this? Was the boy's pain worth it?*

Carefully, sensing Justin's unwillingness to share his pain, Long extended his hand in a comforting gesture. "Justin, lad, I—"

"Spare us any further waste of time this morning, won't you, Thomas?" Justin spoke abruptly, moving quickly away from the tutor. He turned toward the grand staircase at the end of the entry hall. "And kindly see to it that our baggage is properly secured, once I've sent it down with the footmen," the boy continued. Then he strode resolutely toward the stairs.

It was a dismissal, and Thomas knew it. His charge had always been a charming, carefree youngster, full of kind words to the staff and quick to laugh or smile. But on certain rare occasions, as when his displeasure had been aroused, he had evinced the cool, implacable look he wore now; and then none who knew him had any trouble seeing the budding evidence of the powerful duke he would one day become: There was a core of steel beneath that boyish façade, and woe to any who ran up against it!

Sighing, the tutor watched the boy's long-legged frame ascend the stairs. With a last, irritated glance in the direction of the drawing room, he headed for the carriage.

Half an hour later the grand, well-appointed carriage was threading its way through the late-morning traffic of London's fashionable West End. The day was heavily overcast, with a darkly lowering sky; the air outside, oppressively dank as well as dirty. There were numerous infusions of soot and smoke billowing from London's chimney pots as its citizens tried to ward off the chill.

Thomas Long wrapped his cloak more tightly about his thin frame in an effort to keep from shivering, just barely succeeding as he studied the boy sitting across from him in the carriage. The expression on Justin's face hadn't changed since they'd left the town house. Their departure had been marked by nothing more than a tersely scribbled farewell note, which the boy had handed to one of the footmen from the carriage—almost as an afterthought. Since then, the youthful visage had been set in cold, implacable lines, its features harsh and unyielding.

Yet Thomas suspected the emotions residing beneath the surface of that stony exterior were anything but cold. The boy had a deeply passionate nature; he'd seen him moved many times by a particularly stirring piece of verse or passage of prose they'd come across in their studies.

The trouble was that this time his emotions had been triggered by something far more real and devastating than one of literature's purple passages; this time his sensitive young feelings had been mangled by something entirely too close to home . . . *or within his home,* Thomas amended wryly.

'Tis all the fault of that damnable institution they call marriage! the tutor went on angrily to himself. *That loveless, ineffectual contract that binds two people together for a lifetime, regardless of how they feel about each other!*

The duke and duchess of Haverleigh weren't bad people, the tutor mused as he continued to watch the carefully composed features of the son they'd just succeeded in disillusioning—and hurting in the worst possible way. Actually, when regarded separately, Derek Hart and the beautiful bride he'd taken for reasons that had to do exclusively with lineage, title, and wealth were each quite likeable people.

The tall, aristocratically handsome duke was one of the most charming, personable men Long had ever met. He was admired and respected by servants and peers alike, exhibiting a keen wit, an easygoing manner that immediately put people at ease in his company, and a generosity that was well known by all with whom he associated.

As for his duchess, Vanessa Hart . . . besides being one of the foremost beauties of her age—"an incomparable," the Fleet Street wits called her—she was a woman possessing a lively intelligence that she was clever enough to hide when out among the *ton* (where brains were never considered an asset in a female), but which she used quite effectively in running the half-dozen complex households belonging to her husband.

But the travesty they called a marriage had brought out the worst in them; and now, as was perhaps inevitable, Long thought with increasing ire, its effects had filtered down to their son.

Another glance at the boy's hardened countenance confirmed this in the tutor's mind, and he suddenly felt a need to do something to break through that feigned indifference, to defuse somehow the hurt he was certain it hid.

"My lord . . . Justin . . ." he began carefully, the plan he'd just hit upon barely formed in his mind.

The boy's thickly lashed, striking eyes moved from the drab, fog-banked streets he'd been studying outside to regard him coolly. "Yes, Thomas, what is it?" His voice matched the remoteness in his eyes.

Long reached into the portmanteau that rested on the seat beside him, pulling out a slim, well-thumbed volume. " 'Twould seem we're in for at least another hour and a half's ride, judging by the traffic, so why don't we put it to good use, eh? I thought we might delve into some leftovers from our studies, lad."

There was an arching of one raven-colored brow while the boy glanced at the volume in his hands.

"Nothing like a bit of food for thought from one of the better minds of our age, eh?" the tutor went on. "Ah, here we are! 'Tis one of those poems we never got around to discussing when we were on Blake a week ago, Thursday. You recall, surely? We were interrupted in our discourse when—"

"I recall the reason," Justin said abruptly, "as well as the verse." He eyed the leather-bound volume in his tutor's hands for a moment longer, then met Long's imploring gaze and heaved a resigned sigh. "Very well, Thomas, begin the lesson."

Long stifled a sigh of relief and withdrew his reading spectacles from a breast pocket. "The one called 'London' would seem an appropriate place to begin," he said. He adjusted the spectacles on his thin, aquiline nose, brushed a lock of sand-colored hair off his forehead, and began to read:

I wander thro' each charter'd street
Near where the charter'd Thames does flow,
And mark in every face I meet
Marks of weakness, marks of woe.

In every cry of every Man,
In every Infant's cry of fear,
In every voice, in every ban,
The mind-forg'd manacles I hear:

How the Chimney-sweeper's cry
Every black'ning Church appalls,
And the hapless Soldier's sigh
Runs in blood down Palace walls.

But most thro' midnight streets I hear
How the youthful Harlot's curse
Blasts the new born Infant's tear
And blights with plagues the Marriage Hearse.

Long lowered the book and looked hopefully at his pupil. "A rather startling metaphor, that at the end, don't you think?"

Justin regarded him levelly, not taken in for a moment by Long's obvious ploy. For one thing, they'd been through it all before—William Blake's preoccupation with society's corrupt values, the rottenness he saw beneath officialdom's adherence to institutions such as the Church, or the marriage vows—and, Justin added wryly to himself, Thomas Long's preoccupation with *Blake!* Why, the man was close to being obsessed with the notion that marriage killed the joys of love, and in Blake he'd found a kindred spirit.

Well, my friend, Justin thought, *you and your favorite poetic genius may well be right, but I'll be damned if I'll let myself be drawn into some gut-spilling dialogue of that no-tion and how it's come to roost in my own—ah, God! Father! Mother! How could you have lived such a lie with me all these years?*

Using every ounce of self-control he possessed, Justin quelled the pain roiling inside him and addressed his mentor evenly, with a casual shrug of his shoulders. "I prefer his reference to the chimney sweeper's cry, Thomas. It reminds me of another poem of Blake's. You know it . . . 'The Chimney Sweeper' . . . ?"

And using the gift of perfect recall he'd been born with, Justin began to quote:

A little black thing among the snow,
Crying "weep! weep!" in notes of woe!
"Where are thy father and mother? say?"
"They are both gone up to the church to pray.

"Because I was happy upon the heath,
"And smil'd among the winter's snow,
"They cloth'd me in the clothes of death,
"And taught me to sing notes of woe.

"And because I am happy and dance and sing,
"They think they have done me no injury,
"And are gone to praise God and his Priest and King,
"Who make up a heaven of our misery."

Justin smiled thinly when he'd finished. "You see, Thomas, the chief value of Blake's works, as I've begun to view them, lies in their ability to underscore the brutal nature of life—the hardness and cruelty of it, especially in this wonderful modern age we live in."

Long looked at him, at the newly emerged cynicism he saw in those silver eyes, and wanted to weep. The boy had missed his point entirely—or deliberately chosen to ignore it, he realized suddenly. He drew a breath, preparing to tell him as much, when, at that moment, there arose a loud hue and cry from the street outside, and they both leaned toward the window to see what had caused it.

"Make room! Make room, I say!" came a gruff voice from the midst of a crowd they could see gathered outside the carriage.

Then they felt the vehicle plow to a halt while numerous voices raised the noise level of the street to an angry din.

" 'E's dead, 'e is!" shouted one.

" 'Ere, give over and lay th' pour mite down!" they heard another cry.

As Justin and Thomas glanced at each other in bemused inquiry, they felt the carriage rock slightly, and then the door opened and their carriage driver's apologetic face poked through.

"What is it, Cranston?"

"Er, a bit of a delay, milord." The older man glanced over his shoulder at what now appeared to be a swiftly gathering mob thronging the street outside. " 'Pears there's been an accident of some kind, milord, an' I daresn't move the 'orses wi' them all standin' about, gapin' an'—"

"See if you can determine what's happened, then—and how soon it will be before we can be on our way," Justin ordered.

"Aye, milord."

Cranston turned into the crowd and disappeared; but when, after several minutes, he hadn't returned, the curiosity of the carriage's two occupants got the better of them, and they climbed out to investigate.

A few moments later, Thomas Long was wishing devoutly that they hadn't. The accident Cranston had mentioned involved a young chimney sweep. His sootblackened, emaciated little body lay still, stretched across the cobblestones.

But it was the look of pure agony on the child's charred features which had Thomas reaching for his handkerchief and wretching as he and Justin listened to a bystander's bitter explanation of how the boy had died.

"Th' sweepsmaster shoved 'im inter 'at 'ot chimney, 'e

did, milords," said the coarsely dressed stranger. "Sent 'im ter an 'orrible death right up there." The man gestured to a rooftop where smoke could be seen billowing from two of its blackened chimneys. "It ain't human, whut these sweepsmasters 'ave become, milords. Gawd, I kin still 'ear th' wee mite's screams!"

"Dear God," murmured Long as Cranston approached and quickly verified the stranger's story. Shaken and trembling, he allowed the carriage driver to assist him back into the carriage while a silent Justin followed.

Moments later they were again under way, and Thomas forced himself to take several deep, calming breaths before turning to Justin, across from him.

The boy's face was as cold as stone.

"That poor, wretched child, Justin!" the tutor managed in shaken tones. "Did you see—?"

"I saw."

"Justin, for the love of God, lad, didn't what happened back there—"

"I suspect that God has little to do with it," Justin went on emotionlessly, his gaze on the grimy rooftops outside the carriage window. "In fact, my dear Thomas, I seriously doubt whether God—if there is a God—even recalls we exist."

He turned toward his companion then, and Long shuddered at the pitiless look in the silver-gray eyes.

"As I was saying before, Thomas," Justin continued, "we live in a cruel, hardened world . . . hardened, indeed. . . ."

And without another word, he returned his gaze to the window.

❧ Chapter 1 ❧

Surrey, England, 1812

SIR JONATHAN BURKE STUDIED THE ELFIN features of his granddaughter with amusement. The delicate, heart-shaped face of Lady Isabelle Corstairs wore a charming, childlike scowl while she scanned the members of the hunt party preparing to set off on the chase. If he hadn't been so entertained by her blatantly obvious censure of the pastime enjoyed by her parents' guests, he might have joined her in scowling.

For the truth was that both he and the seventeen-year-old Isabelle—or Sabelle, as she was called—had no taste for this bloodsport of the aristocracy. Indeed, they both abhorred it, animal lovers that they were.

The smile on Sir Jonathan's lips broadened as he considered the similarities between himself and this child he had raised practically single-handedly. It was no accident that Sabelle thought as he did on most important matters. He had recognized in her a kindred spirit almost from the time she was out of the cradle; and even now, all these years later, he thanked God and his lucky stars that his frivolous daughter and the society-minded earl she'd married had been too busy, too preoccupied with the social obligations of their set, to spare much time for their only offspring.

And so the upbringing of little Sabelle had fallen to him, and if it constituted selfishness on his part to be glad of this, Jonathan had long ago come to terms with the occasional stab of guilt. The child was such a sunny, joyful little minx, a free spirit who made the best possible use of the independence his rearing had encouraged.

Growing up on his estate, which neighbored that of the earl and his daughter, Sabelle had enjoyed a freedom unheard of among even the sons of the aristocracy, let alone its daughters.

He pictured her there, barefoot and carefree whenever the weather allowed, and when she was not in the schoolroom, of course. (Oh, yes, there had been academics, for Sir Jonathan believed in educating the mind as well as the body and the spirit—even in a female offspring—if she had the mind for it, which Sabelle had: She was as bright as a brand-new shilling!) Sabelle had had the run of the place, and, more often than not, she was to be found in the woods, trailing after the gamekeeper and drinking in his lore. If she was not there, she was down at the stables, helping the head groom break in a new horse—but gently . . . always gently, with all the love and kindness her grandfather insisted on for animals under his care.

And if some of the servants or tenants on his estate considered her a wild thing, part wood sprite and part nymph—a half-magical creature who ran with the deer in the park and could actually *talk to horses*—well, who was he to tell them otherwise? The fact remained that Sabelle was that rarest of creatures, a young woman allowed to be herself and who, as a result, was *truly happy*.

Of course, she wasn't all that happy at this moment! He glanced about him, at the men and women in full hunt regalia, pink coats and top hats brilliant under the bright, cloudless autumn sky, and he knew a moment of anger to match Sabelle's. What right had these preening bluebloods to dress themselves in such peacock finery when they were about to engage in a bloody ritual that was more worthy of a barbaric tribe than of a culture which considered itself a paradigm for the civilized world? How dare they strut and parade themselves so, when the object of their morning's pursuit was the violent death of a poor, innocent animal!

As these thoughts ran through his mind, Sir Jonathan's benign features did indeed begin to resemble his granddaughter's, and at that moment the girl looked up and caught his scowl.

"Good heavens, Grandfather, you oughtn't frown so! Mother says 'twill give you wrinkles!" Sabelle exclaimed. Then, noting the myriad crisscrossing of lines on the beloved face—and recalling Jonathan's proud assertion once that his wrinkles were to him "a badge of honor, and every one of them honestly earned"—she broke into a peal of laughter at the ridiculousness of what she'd uttered.

Meeting her sea-green eyes and hearing the self-directed laughter, Sir Jonathan exchanged his scowl for a grin. The ability to laugh at oneself had been among the first of the human values he'd taught her, and he was not about to let his approval go unnoticed!

But at that moment someone let loose the foxhounds from their kennels, and the small black, white, and tan animals charged into the courtyard with such a clamorous baying that they drowned out all human voices for the next several minutes.

It wasn't until the master of hounds had settled them down somewhat that Sabelle and Sir Jonathan could resume their conversation; when they did, their heads were bent closely together.

"There's that miserable Sydney Alsop," Sabelle was saying as she gestured behind her with the riding crop her mother had forced her to carry. "I wish he hadn't been invited!"

Sir Jonathan threw the young lord in question a brief glance, then answered her in his customarily mild tone. "It could hardly be avoided, my dear. He *is* the son of a neighboring peer, you know."

"Yes, I know," Sabelle replied angrily. "An earl's son who beats his horses and—"

"Not anymore, he doesn't, my dear. You forget that when I purchased that poor, abused stallion from his father last week—at *thrice* what the poor animal was worth, as you know—'twas with a full accounting of what you'd witnessed the son doing to his father's fine horseflesh. *And* with the stipulation that Lord Alsop see to it that Lord

Sydney never be allowed near his animals again until—and only *if*—he'd been made to mend his ways."

"Ah," said Sabelle, "then—"

"Do you see the sour expression his young lordship wears on that weakchinned face of his, my girl?" Jonathan went on. "I shouldn't be half surprised if it was put there by the task his father assigned him"—Jonathan grinned—"of mucking out stalls in his stables!"

Sabelle's brows shot up with astonishment, and then she burst into a fit of giggles.

"Shh!" her grandfather cautioned, hard-put to contain his own mirth.

But they both knew this was not the first time they'd shared some joy, not to mention an overwhelming sense of satisfaction, at the comeuppance someone who'd abused an animal got through their efforts. In fact, the pair of them had, for years, been secretly involved in saving poor, mistreated animals from various cruelties. Dozens of helpless dogs, cats, horses, and other beasts had been bought or stolen away from abusive owners by Sir Jonathan and his granddaughter.

Moreover, it was this very rescue work which had induced Sabelle to endure this morning's hunt. Initially, when the earl and countess of Rushton, her absentee parents, had swooped out from London to announce they were hosting a hunt weekend and had then insisted she attend, she'd thrust out a rebellious lower lip and informed them politely, but firmly, that she would do no such thing: It was against her moral principles!

Of course, her refusal had caused such a shocked, indignant response from her parents, not to mention the terrible row that followed, that Sir Jonathan had been summoned; the elder Corstairses had demanded, then and there, that he explain himself "over the terrible mismanagement of Isabelle's upbringing," as Lord Cecil Corstairs had put it.

"Indeed, Father," Lady Corstairs had echoed, "we see now that you have created a willful, disobedient little hoyden who behaves in as ill-bred a fashion as she looks! (The subject of Sabelle's penchant for dressing like a barefoot village lass or worse, in castoffs from one of the stable lads, had long been a bone of contention between Marjorie Corstairs and her widowed father; but Jonathan had finally circumvented this by coaxing Sabelle to "slip into something seemly" whenever her parents were due to arrive on one of their rare visits to the country.)

On the occasion of Lady Isabelle's insubordination regarding the hunt party, Sir Jonathan's quick thinking had again circumvented a domestic disaster at the Rushton estate: He'd convinced Sabelle to go along with her parents' wishes, even to the point of dressing—as she was now—in a proper riding habit styled for the hunt, by promising her that their secret objective of the morning would be a rescue —of the *fox!*

Near the stables, standing unnoticed in the shadows, was a large, burly man wearing rough country clothes, and beside him, his alert gaze trained on Sabelle, stood an immense shaggy hound. Michael Kelly was Sir Jonathan's trusted groom; and Brendan, her Irish Wolfhound. Michael, Jonathan, and Sabelle had once rescued the dog from a bullbaiting impressario who, when he found Brendan too gentle to be induced to attack on command, was going to shoot him. (They also rescued the bull that day!)

Michael and Brendan were to figure heavily in today's rescue of the fox.

"Look, Grandfather," said Sabelle after their laughter had subsided. "See how Brendan keeps his eyes on me? He senses something's afoot, I vow, and is waiting for me to give the command."

"Hmm. . . ." Sir Jonathan's blue eyes held a merry twinkle. "I rather think he's noticed your attire—how you're so properly turned out in formal hunt dress like any respectable English miss—and is trying to decide if he recognizes you!"

"Humph!" Sabelle slanted him a look of mild reproval. "You wouldn't mock me so, sir, if it were *your* feet trussed up in these torturous riding boots after spending the summer barefoot! Why, I've a good mind to—"

"Your pardon, milady," interrupted a footman wearing the bright green Rushton livery. He bowed to Sir Jonathan. "I've been sent by his lordship to tell you he wishes a word with you, milord."

Scowling as he usually did when being addressed as a lord when he was, as he was fond of telling all who knew him, merely a humble baronet, Sir Jonathan grumbled something unintelligible. With a glance at his groom and the dog, and then a parting look at his granddaughter which said "Be careful," he turned and went off in search of his son-in-law.

Sabelle sobered instantly at the wordless admonition. She was well aware of how important it was that she play her own part in the rescue without mishap. It was imperative that she separate herself from the hunt party without being noticed before circling around to rendezvous with Michael Kelly and her wolfhound. At a prearranged spot she would change into the clothing of a country lad before continuing with their plan; and this, too, was of utmost importance, for Sir Jonathan had insisted that she not embarrass herself or her family by being recognized, should anything go awry.

But nothing will go awry, she mused to herself with a secretive smile as she quickly reviewed the details of their plan in her mind. *Michael is always careful—and capable!—while dear Brendan is perfectly trained to—*

"Ah, there you are, my dear!" a familiar voice interrupted. Sabelle broke off her reverie to see the trim, fashionably dressed figure of her mother walking toward her.

Lady Marjorie Corstairs was a strikingly beautiful woman in her mid-thirties, and as she approached her daughter, it was easy to see which of her parents the girl favored. Petite and fine-boned, the countess had the same honey-gold hair, although Lady Corstairs's appeared darker, for it had never been allowed to develop the flaxen streaks supplied to Sabelle's tresses by hours under the summer sun. Where her daughter's eyes, which tilted similarly upward at the outer corners, were the aquamarine color of the sea, Marjorie's were merely hazel; but the youthful, heart-shaped face was the same, as was the straight, delicately boned nose. Anyone glancing at the pair for the first time might have taken them for sisters.

On the other hand, an astute observer, someone who might look discerningly into the hazel eyes of the one and then into the blue-green depths of the other's, was likely to notice a major difference between these two: Where Marjorie Corstairs's expression normally held a bland, vapid look indicative of an unremarkable intelligence, her child's flashing, sea-green glance told quite a different story. It signaled a spirit that was far too bold, too bright and inquisitive, to be deemed proper in a well-bred young lady.

Moreover, to say that Lady Corstairs was unaware of the difference between them would have been to label her a total dunce, which she was not. Therefore, as she came to stand before her daughter, she at first gave a silent prayer of thanks that Sabelle had been obedient enough to submit to the attentions of her mother's ladies' maid this morning. Then she threw Sabelle an admonishing look before saying, "I've been searching the grounds for you, Sabelle, and here you are all along! Well, no matter, for I've found you at last, and . . ."—Marjorie took a deep, fluttery breath and glanced upward to her immediate right—". . . there is someone I should like you to meet."

It was only then that Sabelle noticed the man beside her. He was tall—taller than any other man there, a good three inches over six feet, she guessed—and he was *devastatingly handsome!* The black à la Titus curls covering his well-shaped head marked him as a perfect Corinthian of the first water, and the lean, perfectly chiseled features of his face were so arresting that Sabelle was initially reduced to staring at him in open wonder—until she perceived the blatant look of arrogance he exuded.

"Your Grace," her mother was saying, "allow me to introduce my daughter, Lady Isabelle." The hazel eyes focused on Sabelle's upturned countenance and in bewilderment noted the suddenly rebellious look. "Sabelle," she went on reprovingly, "make your curtsy to His Grace. This is Justin Hart, the duke of Haverleigh!"

As Sabelle sank dutifully into a wobbly curtsy—she wasn't used to such a movement, and the damnable high heels of her brand-new riding boots almost rendered the action impossible—she found herself seized by an overwhelming sense of antipathy toward the man. She wasn't sure why this was so—perhaps it was his cool silver eyes, perhaps the pantherlike leanness of his tall, well-muscled frame, or perhaps the towering impression of confident male arrogance—but she not only discovered an instant dislike for Justin Hart, she also had the astonishing sensation that—*Oh, but this was silly!*—she was actually a little *frightened* of him!

"M'lady . . ." the duke murmured in a deep, resonant drawl as he took her small, gloved hand when she rose from the curtsy. But a lazy, mocking smile curved his handsome mouth when he spoke, giving Sabelle the impression that he'd taken note of her inadequate curtsy—and the irritating certainty that he found her lack of polish amusing!

Lady Corstairs, too, had caught the mockery in his reaction and was suddenly damning herself for being so foolish. Why, oh why, had she introduced her daughter to one of the *ton's* most sought-after bachelors so early on, before Sabelle had even been readied for her formal introduction into society—her Season?

But the child had looked so *promising* today, so fresh and lovely—*and well groomed,* thanks to the Abigail's skills! And here was His Grace, one of the wealthiest, most powerful, and certainly the handsomest of men in the peerage, turning up at their hunt when he hadn't at all been expected. (It was well known that His Grace disdained attending three out of four social functions to which he'd been invited!) She could hardly be faulted for succumbing to the desire to see a match between her only daughter and this most eligible of bachelors!

And Lady Corstairs was highly aware of just how eligible Justin Hart was. Now thirty-four, he'd succeeded to the Haverleigh dukedom some years earlier; his father, Derek

Hart, having died (of an alcohol-diseased liver, some said) in '01, and his mother, shortly thereafter (bleeding to death from a miscarriage darkly rumored to have been an abortion of a lover's child). He was therefore vaguely mysterious and immensely attractive on all counts, though he did, unfortunately, have a well-established reputation for breaking hearts and shunning marriage. "Hart the Heartless" was just one name he was called by the *ton*. But this and the slight limp with which he walked these days—courtesy of the Napoleonic wars, having been wounded in March, under Wellington at Salamanca—only added to the glamour of his appeal. There wasn't a mother among the *ton*, with an eligible daughter, who didn't dream of somehow ensnaring the handsome rogue for her darling offspring.

"I should perhaps explain, Your Grace," said Marjorie hastily, largely in hopes of steering the conversation to safe territory before that look in her daughter's eyes could materialize into something antagonizing. "This is Lady Isabelle's first formal hunt and therefore, ah, a trifle irregular. She hasn't had her Season yet, you see, though we were thinking, what with the Little Season about to commence. . . ." Marjorie's words trailed off and she gave a nervous little laugh as she noted how intently the duke's silvery gaze focused on her daughter.

"Ah," said the duke, his eyes scanning Sabelle's pertly upturned face, "but things not done strictly by the book can often make life more interesting, can they not? Tell me, Lady Isabelle, do you frequently engage in the, ah, irregular?"

"When the situation warrants it, Your Grace." The sea-green eyes were direct and bold as they met his, and noting this, Lady Corstairs smothered a groan. Well-bred young ladies lowered their lashes deferentially when conversing with their superiors—or with gentlemen to whom they'd just been introduced. They did *not* gaze forwardly back at them as if daring them to say something they might argue with!

But to the countess's surprise, Justin Hart's mouth

quirked with greater amusement as he responded. "And does this hunt party warrant it, m'lady?"

Sabelle's eyes flashed green fire before she turned and coldly surveyed the scene about them, stonily taking in the eagerness of the hounds, the excited chatter of the gentry as they prepared to mount—all the color and spectacle that filled the courtyard. She turned back to Justin.

"Fox hunting, Your Grace, is a pastime I find *highly* irregular when I consider the nobler possibilities to which the human spirit might aspire. It is, as I see it, a barbaric sport designed to make inferior Englishmen feel a spurious superiority. Indeed, I abhor it and am here today only out of duty to my parents, who view it differently."

This time Lady Corstairs's groan was audible, while Justin's brows rose a fraction before he countered in a tone that never wavered. "Then perhaps, m'lady, it is a sport which should exclude the presence of willful, ill-bred children who would instruct their betters from the book of their own ignorance."

Both Sabelle and her mother gasped at the biting setdown, but before either could voice a further reaction, the master of the hunt interrupted with a call to mount up. It was all the invitation Sabelle needed to remove herself from the arrogant duke's presence. Barely nodding in his direction, she murmured something she hoped might pass for an excuse to her mother, turned, and stormed off in search of her mount.

Lady Corstairs stood speechless, in shock over this disastrous encounter she'd so foolishly set into motion. After several awkward seconds she managed to mumble an apology for her daughter's "youthful impetuousness," and then excused herself. But as she turned to leave, she heard the duke murmur beneath his breath something which sounded suspiciously like "impertinent chit!"

Justin's amused gaze followed the retreating figure of the daughter rather than her mortified mother. His Grace was suddenly struck with a thought that was at odds with his previous comments about Sabelle. Noting the gentle, sensuous sway of her hips as she moved, Justin all at once realized her slender, graceful body was anything *but* child-like! Amazed, he realized he could actually feel a stirring in his loins!

He knew he'd already noted an unconscious sensuality residing in the sea-green depths of those incredible, thickly lashed eyes. And he'd not been immune to the promise in the finely sculpted lines of her face, either; it gave every evidence of attaining a level of exquisite perfection, once the brat matured.

But in the next instant, as he recalled Lady Corstairs's ingratiating apologies on behalf of her daughter, Justin made up his mind to dismiss all thoughts of the wench. He'd had more than enough of anxious mamas thrusting their unwed, tedious daughters at him. Indeed, he clearly recognized the countess of Rushton's ambitions, and he had no intention of encouraging her—or her cheeky little offspring!

❧ Chapter 2 ❧

SABELLE EDGED HER CHESTNUT HUNTER carefully around the lake, keeping the mare within the shadows of the trees lining its western perimeter. She longed to urge the horse into a canter, for the baying of the hounds in the distance told her they'd picked up the scent of their quarry; nonetheless, she held the chestnut to a sedate trot, knowing there could be surface roots of trees and other dangerous obstacles hidden beneath the carpet of oak leaves that layered the ground, and she would never risk injuring the mare through such carelessness.

Finally she spotted through the trees the little-used path which her grandfather's gamekeeper had once shown her. With a sign of relief, she turned the mare's head into it and increased her pace. Russet leaves beneath the hunter's hooves scattered as she cantered; but there was still an abundance of greenery on the trees, it being early September, so Sabelle had to strain her eyes to see ahead of them. She finally decided to trust the horse's instincts to get them safely to the other side, and in a few minutes she was rewarded: There, as they broke from the cover of the oaks, sat Sir Jonathan's closed carriage with Michael Kelly at the reins and the great hound, Brendan, beside it.

"Have ye eluded them, then, colleen?" Michael asked as he jumped down to take her reins while Sabelle slid gracefully from the sidesaddle.

"Of course, silly!" Sabelle gave him a saucy wink as she

hurriedly opened the door to the carriage. "Most of them were fat and slow, with abominable seats, and those who weren't were too preoccupied with their bloodlust to give any thought to their hosts' *unblooded chit* when she lagged behind."

As he watched the door slam behind her, Kelly suppressed a shudder. At the end of a successful hunt, an "unblooded" rider—one who'd never been in on the kill—was "honored" for having crossed that barrier by being smeared with the dead animal's blood. Michael had witnessed such a blooding once as a young man on the Irish estate of his first employer, an English earl who owned lands in both countries. The earl's twelve-year-old son had been the one blooded, and as his personal groom, Michael had been present and watched while the bloodthirsty little *Sassenach* had grinned fiercely through the whole disgusting business.

The next day Michael had given his notice.

And only a few poverty-threatened weeks later, he'd been lucky enough to run into Sir Jonathan Burke—of Anglo-Irish stock, to be sure, but an Anglo who didn't believe in fox hunting and who felt the same reverence for living things as did Michael. That had been nearly twenty years ago, and Michael had never regretted going to work for the man—or gaining his friendship.

And now there was the young lass who had his loyalty as well, Michael mused as he finished stripping Sabelle's mare of her sidesaddle and replaced it with one for riding astride. Of course, she could be a handful sometimes, what with her quicksilver little mind that was always darting about, looking for wrongs to be righted—especially if they involved her beloved four-footed creatures, and—

"Here we are!" chirped the young lass he'd been pondering as she bounded out of the carriage. "How was that for excellent speed?"

Michael, who was six feet tall, grinned down at what appeared to be a young stable lad in breeches, his hair hidden by a groom's cap that looked only a trifle bulky and completely hid the flaxen-streaked curls stuffed beneath.

"Not bad . . . not bad at all, at all, colleen." Kelly eyed her archly while scratching his thatch of unruly red hair in thoughtful consideration. "Ye make a fairly fetchin' lad, I'm thinkin', so ye'd best take care none o' the village lasses—"

At that moment a movement from Brendan caught their attention; the great, shaggy, reddish-brown head lifted to alertness while the hound's dark, almond-shaped eyes searched the distance.

Instantly, Kelly dropped his teasing banter, all business now as he cupped his hands to give Sabelle a boost into the saddle. "Hurry, darlin'," he urged, "but mind ye, be careful! Let Brendan lead the way, and don't return until 'tis safe."

Sabelle nodded, her small head turned in the same direction as the hound's while Michael performed a final tightening of her saddle girth. Then, at the big groom's command of "Go, Brendan—search!," they were off, the great galloping strides of the wolfhound setting the pace with the small figure atop the mare a few yards behind.

Sabelle guessed, from the direction the dog was taking, where they were headed. She had learned the terrain while growing up, and she had a fairly good idea of the places a fox might go when run to ground. She and Kevin, Michael's cousin and Sir Jonathan's gamekeeper, had trailed and observed enough foxes through the years for her to learn their habits, for one thing; for another, she and her grandfather had spent the past several nights studying some old maps he'd had of the Rushton acreage, and they'd carefully gone over all the spots a poor, besieged fox would seek refuge. Then they'd laid their plans.

So when Sabelle saw Brendan heading for the stream with its little waterfall and the steep, rocky outcrop above, she smiled.

This fox is a clever one, she thought to herself. *It's heading for one of those caves among the rocks, perhaps hoping to lose its scent to the hounds by crossing the stream. Aye, clever . . . I'll wager it's a vixen!*

The fox was, indeed, a vixen, a cunning old canine that

had escaped numerous seasons tracked by scent hounds in the way Sabelle surmised, but the hardy little creature hadn't dealt with a *sighthound* before. The wolfhound tracked his quarry with his eyes, and so it wasn't long before Brendan's keen vision caught a flash of red among the rocks. Seconds later he was climbing gingerly toward one of the hidden caves marked on her grandfather's map.

Now came the hard part. While she waited nervously on her mount near the waterfall, the sounds of baying hounds growing uncomfortably near, Sabelle could only hope Brendan would remember the most difficult part of his training: to forgo his own natural instinct to kill, and merely *retrieve* the fox without hurting it! They'd practiced the procedure often enough using some half-tame rabbits Kevin kept for this purpose, but this was the first time the wolfhound was being asked to rescue a truly wild quarry, and a frightened, wily fox at that!

Seconds ticked by; and Sabelle had to force herself to remain calm. The baying was perilously close now, accompanied by the eager shouts of hunters in the distance, and she felt a trickle of perspiration slide down her back, despite the coolness of the morning.

Then, at last, she saw them—the huge, reddish-brown figure of the dog emerging from the rocks with the immobile, brighter red form of the fox suspended from his jaws. . . .

Oh, God! thought Sabelle as she noted how still the fox seemed. *I hope he hasn't killed it!*

Brendan's tail wagged steadily as he approached his mistress, and Sabelle heaved a sigh of relief. There, staring out at her from between the wolfhound's gently clamped jaws, was a pair of bright, shiny black eyes set in a triangular face that looked for all the world like that of a befuddled old woman!

"The poor thing's probably in shock," Sabelle murmured to herself after praising the dog. But in the next instant there was little time to speculate further; the foxhounds had reached a spot somewhere beyond the bend, and Sabelle could hear their excited baying. Issuing a quick command to the wolfhound, she whirled her horse about and headed back. But she was wise enough to lead them through the stream for several dozen yards before leaping to dry land and disappearing from sight.

Justin Hart drew up his mount and gazed with disbelief at the scene of confusion about him. The foxhounds were running in haphazard circles about the stream and its waterfall, their confident, excited baying of minutes before reduced to a ridiculous whining. And their human cohorts were faring no better; they behaved like addlepated twits, to Justin's way of thinking.

Several were shouting outrageous accusations at the mystified hounds. Others were sputtering in indignant, redfaced bluster at their companions as they clambered about the rocks or rode about, tangling with the hounds.

"Damme if I ain't moonstruck!" cried one. "Could have sworn—"

"Moonstruck!" exclaimed another, an overweight matron whose scarlet face testified to the exertion the hunt had cost her. "Why, you old ninnyhammer! I'd wager more on the mulled wine you drank before we left!"

"Oh, stuff and cap it, you two!" shouted their companion. "Fact is, the dumb beast's given us the bye and bye! What in hell are we to do now?"

Justin almost laughed at the ridiculous, undignified poses they took, waving their fists at one another and behaving for all the world like a lot of spoiled children who'd had their toy taken away from them.

But then his glance fell on his host and he sobered. Lord Cecil Corstairs was standing off to one side, looking as if he were about to cry. Justin decided to do what he could to help him, though not from any humanitarian motive; the earl of Rushton led a strong political faction in the Lords, and at the moment Justin needed the votes he controlled to secure a piece of legislation he favored. Indeed, it was the reason he'd accepted the countess's invitation to this tedious affair in the first place!

The silver eyes narrowed as he scanned the terrain, then

grew purposeful. He urged his horse downstream, away from the squabbling guests. Something odd was afoot, he reasoned, as he kept his military-trained eyes on the ground along the banks of the stream. Foxes simply did not vanish without a trace!

Several minutes later his efforts bore fruit when he spotted some fresh, huge canine paw prints along the far bank. He knew they could only belong to the enormous dog he'd noticed near the stables. Soon picking up the hoofprints of a lone rider as well, Justin gave a grunt of satisfaction: These were heavier than the dog's prints and made the tracking even easier.

It wasn't long before the trail led him through a stand of oak; he neared the edge of the trees and reined in, keeping well hidden among the shadows.

On a country lane separated from the trees by a grassy clearing, he spied a closed carriage driven by the big, red-haired fellow he instantly recognized as the man who had been with the giant hound. And there, beside the vehicle, was a slim lad dismounting from a chestnut mare that looked somewhat familiar as well.

Taking care to remain hidden among the trees, Justin watched with increasing incredulity as the big man and the lad coaxed the huge hound from the other side of the carriage—where he'd been hidden from Justin's view until now—and succeeded in retrieving a stunned, but nevertheless very much *alive*, fox from his jaws!

Hardly believing what he was seeing, he watched them stuff the bemused animal into the boot of the carriage; he also couldn't help noticing this was done with considerable gentleness and care.

Then, as the lad made for the carriage and prepared to enter it, all Justin's perceptive instincts, honed by years of military training, came to the fore, and he froze.

What in hell—?

His mind seized on the gentle swaying of the lad's hips, the unconscious grace of their movement, and suddenly he knew: *He'd seen that walk before!*

Smiling smugly to himself, he settled down to wait and

was not surprised when Lady Corstairs's impudent daughter emerged from the carriage a few minutes later, dressed in her hunt clothes. He saw her gesture toward the mare, which had wandered close to the stand of trees where Justin was hidden, nod at something the red-haired man said, and wave him off.

The carriage and its purloined contents rumbled away, with the wolfhound, after a command from his mistress, trotting behind; meanwhile, Lady Isabelle went to retrieve the mare.

At the girl's sharp whistle the chestnut raised its head, then moved obediently toward her, and Justin found himself giving the chit a begrudging nod of respect: Her animals were well trained—he'd say that much for her!

After watching the carriage disappear, Sabelle turned toward Brandy, her mare, and prepared to mount, not such an easy thing when one was wearing those abominable skirts—and when one was not very tall to begin with! Finally she spied a large rock near the edge of the clearing and led the mare toward it.

She had just stepped atop the rock when a movement from the shadows caught her eye, and she whirled toward it, losing her balance in the process. In the next instant she felt herself land smartly on her derriere in the grass.

A low rumble of masculine laughter met her ears, and she jerked her head sharply upward. There—oh, God, of all people!—was the duke of Haverleigh emerging from the trees.

"You!" she cried, furious that the arrogant duke should have come upon her while she was in such an undignified position. Glaring up at him, she made an effort to rise, her fury at the same instant giving way to anxious concern: What if the wretch had seen more than just her humiliating fall? What if he'd witnessed—

"My dear Lady Isabelle," said Justin, barely containing his laughter, "do allow me . . ."

He reached his hand toward her, and when she refused it, he grasped her forearm and lifted her effortlessly to her feet.

"There you are, m'lady," Justin continued smoothly, "safely on your feet again and none the worse for wear." He ran his eyes thoroughly over her slender form, noting the bits of grass clinging to her skirts and the way the prim little riding hat she wore was slightly askew. But most of all, he saw the murderous look in her eyes. "Ah, unless, perhaps, we were to consider the affront to your, um, dignity . . . ?"

Sabelle bristled at the mocking tone and the smug, infuriating grin on his handsome face. "My *dignity*," she fumed, "would have suffered *nothing*, had you not startled me out of a year's growth, *Your Grace!* Just what were you doing out here? Hovering in the shadows, *spying* on people?"

A mocking gust of laughter met her ears, and when Sabelle sought to wrench her arm away from the strong fingers, his hold on her merely tightened.

"What am *I* doing out here?" Justin queried. He jerked her forward until she was standing so close that she could smell the distinctly masculine scent of him; it was a combination of shaving soap, leather, tobacco, and clean male sweat, though how she was aware of these particulars, she couldn't have said.

"That's odd," Justin went on snidely. "I was just about to ask *you* the same question." His silvery gaze immobilized whatever parts of her weren't already so, held by his hand locked about her arm. "Just what is your game, Lady Isabelle? Was your life in the country so tedious that you invented that little exercise in *theft* to relieve your boredom?"

"Theft!"

"Yes, theft! You *stole* that fox!"

"I stole nothing! I merely res——"

"Or was it the masquerade which was so appealing, hmm?" Justin's gaze went to her hair, which, as she now began to struggle to free herself, was pulling loose from its pins and falling about her shoulders; then he eyed the riding hat, which had begun to tip crazily to one side. "Were you so utterly bored with these proper ladies' clothes you wore that you had to invent that stupid little subterfuge for a change?"

With his free hand he whisked the hat off her head and flung it aside. "Is that what this was all about, m'lady?"

Sabelle gazed at him in stunned silence—for about two seconds. Then, uttering a shriek of outrage, she drew back her small, booted foot and delivered a swift kick to his shin.

But the duke, his lower legs encased in stout leather riding boots, reacted with nothing more than a narrowing of his eyes as he inquired insultingly, "I wonder, my dear, which is the *real disguise*—ragamuffin's . . . or *lady's?*"

"Oh!" cried Sabelle, stung by the barb, despite the fact that she'd never before cared much about her appearance being ladylike. In fact, she'd often accepted the ribbings she'd received from the stable lads she borrowed clothes from with good-natured grace. So why this arrogant man's comment should have affected her so, she couldn't begin to explain; nor could she explain the other effects he was having on her: His nearness, as he hovered so close, was making her feel strangely weak in the knees, and there was an odd tingle coursing down her spine as he continued to regard her so intently with a strange light in those silver eyes.

In sudden panic, she redoubled her efforts to free herself from his grasp, pushing at his broad chest with her free hand. She cried out in dismay when he merely caught it with his own. Now he held both her wrists.

Justin was quickly becoming aware that, whatever he'd intended when he first confronted the little hoyden, it had somehow escalated into something more. The chit was an undisciplined, willful little brat, to be sure, but a very *beautiful* brat! And as he allowed this fact to register, he made note of the unbridled look of sensuality about her. She had flashing sea-green eyes, and the soft contours of her mouth seemed made for kissing. Moreover, the ripe, lush curves he perceived beneath the clothes he'd mocked her for wearing beckoned with an innocent allure he hadn't expected. In truth, all at once he found himself growing hard against her struggling form. If he did not succeed in bringing himself under control—

At that moment a sharp bark intruded, and they both looked up to see the wolfhound galloping toward them.

It was the excuse Justin needed to extricate himself from what had become an untenable situation. Abruptly he set Sabelle away from him, releasing his hold on her.

This seemed to satisfy the wolfhound only somewhat, however. Brendan's gait slowed to a canter and then to a trot as he neared; but a warning rumble issued from his throat, and he eyed the duke fiercely as he came to a halt. Placing himself between his mistress and this tall man who'd dared to lay a hand on her, Brendan was hardly something the duke could ignore.

"Call off your hound, Sabelle." Justin's tone was the same he'd used to command the men under him in the field.

Irritated by his use of her informal name, Sabelle nevertheless found herself responding to the command in his voice.

"Stay, Brendan," she said. "Good dog." Glaring at her adversary, she stomped over to retrieve her hat. She cast a damning eye on its battered contours, whirled about, and stepped to the rock where Brandy waited patiently.

As if daring him to stop her, Sabelle darted another look at Justin. He stood where he was, looking, she thought, more arrogant than ever. She hurriedly mounted, and from the superior feeling afforded by her height in the saddle, she decided to take the offensive.

"I would suggest you tell no one about what you saw here today, Your Grace. If you were to do so, who knows, but that you might then suffer the wrath of this great hound in earnest!"

Justin's brows rose a fraction at her audacity, but he smiled and sketched a wide—and very mocking—bow. "Far be it from me, m'dear," he said in tones dripping with sarcasm, "to tell the secrets of a"—his eyes scanned her disheveled form with insulting slowness—"um . . . *lady?*"

Barely managing to control her fury, Sabelle forced herself to remember that her primary objective right now should be to escape the man's presence. Her arms and wrists still throbbed from his viselike grip, reminding her that she was no match for him physically. And although she'd issued the threat of Brendan's protection, in reality she knew she would never ask the great hound to deliberately hurt another living creature—even if it was an insufferably arrogant duke! So, gritting her teeth, Sabelle whirled the mare about and called to Brendan to follow. But as she headed for the lane, she could hear the unmistakable sound of mocking laughter behind her.

❖Chapter 3❖

SABELLE AND HER GRANDFATHER STOOD BE-side a horse paddock on Camelot Downs, Sir Jonathan's vast country estate. Inside the enclosure a young, dark bay stallion resisted all the efforts of Michael Kelly to approach him; Kelly had been trying patiently for the better part of an hour to get near enough to attach a lunge line to his halter.

The big Irishman spoke softly to the animal, all his movements slow and careful; yet every time he came within a few feet of the stallion, the bay would roll his eyes fearfully, rear up, and swing aside to canter to the far end of the paddock. After several more minutes of this, Kelly heaved a sigh and turned with a helpless shrug toward the pair who watched.

"I'm sorry, sorr," he said to Jonathan, "but I don't believe we'll be gettin' any further with 'im t'day. The memory o' that abuse he suffered at young Alsop's hands is just too fresh. It'll take some time before he comes round, I'm thinkin'."

Jonathan nodded. "Just continue with what you've been doing, Michael. Time and patience are what it's going to take." His eyes moved to the bay, who was standing in the far corner, nervously pawing the ground as he eyed the groom. "What a shame," Jonathan murmured, "what a rotten shame!"

Kelly collected the lunge line and left the paddock, sending Sabelle a smile before he disappeared into the stables.

Sabelle returned the smile and waved, then turned to her grandfather.

"I didn't want to tell you while dear Michael was still trying so hard, Grandfather, but I spent a few hours watching Storm yesterday, and I have an idea. . . ." She placed her foot on the lower rail of the fence in front of them and began to climb. "I might just be able to bring Storm around, you see, if I can only—"

"*Sabelle*. . . ." The warning tone in Sir Jonathan's voice checked her movements.

"Oh, please don't worry, Grandfather. I'll be careful." She smiled down at him, then continued climbing until she was perched on the top rail, the heels of her boots hooked on the one below it. In the far corner the stallion eyed her with a mixture of apprehension and curiosity, but he'd ceased pawing the ground.

"You see," Sabelle continued as she slowly withdrew something from the pocket of her breeches, "what I noticed yesterday was that Storm shied unrelentingly whenever Michael or any of the stable lads came near him. . . ."

Jonathan watched as she slowly extended her hand and opened it, producing a lump of sugar and allowing it to rest on the flat of her palm.

"But then," she continued, "one of the kitchen maids happened to come down from the house—with a batch of freshly baked scones Cook sometimes sends the stable help —and the oddest thing occurred." She glanced down expectantly at Jonathan.

"And . . . ?" her grandfather prompted as he noticed the stallion toss his head and take a few hesitant steps forward.

"Well," said Sabelle, keeping the tones of her voice soft and unhurried as her gaze returned to the horse, "Nancy— er, the maid—"

"Yes, yes, I know who Nancy is!" Jonathan interrupted testily. This was not his normal tone, but he couldn't help feeling apprehensive when he saw the stallion begin to advance toward her.

"Yes," said Sabelle, "well, Nancy chanced to walk

straight past the rail where Storm was standing, and, Grandfather, he never moved a muscle! He just stood there, eyeing those delicious-smelling scones as she sauntered by!"

Jonathan frowned. "Young lady, are you trying to tell me that on the basis of a single incident—"

"Oh, no, sir! Not a *single* incident!" She inched her hand slowly toward the approaching stallion while she spoke, her eyes never leaving the animal. "You see, after Nancy and the others left, I ran a—an experiment, I suppose you could call it. I walked slowly past the end of the paddock where Storm was standing—several times, in fact—and he never shied at all! And I wasn't even carrying any treats!"

"I see," murmured her grandfather. He watched, incredulous, as the bay stretched his long neck and sniffed at the sugar in her outstretched palm. Then the stallion tossed his head and backed off a few feet. "So you think—"

"I think," whispered Sabelle, hardly daring to breathe now, when the stallion snorted, but began to investigate her palm again, "it's entirely possible Storm associates the abuse he suffered, mostly with the *kind* of person who was responsible for it—a *man* . . . or *men*, if you will. On the other hand, I also think it's possible he associates kindness —and, perhaps, treats—with *women*. I recalled your saying Lord Alsop had informed you Storm's first owner was a woman, Grandfather, a—"

Sabelle sat absolutely motionless as the stallion gave one more toss of his beautiful head and reached gingerly for the lump of sugar. Then he snatched it away and retreated only a few feet to munch it while his dark eyes seemed to regard her thoughtfully. Sabelle's face lit up with a wide grin.

Jonathan let out the breath he'd been holding and grinned back at her. "Well, you minx," he said with a chuckle, "I cannot say I would have consented to your, ah, experiments yesterday—an abused horse is always dangerous, as you should well know by now—but I cannot deny the results of your efforts." He extended his hand and helped her down from the fence. "Well done, my girl, well done!"

Sabelle basked in the warmth of his approval while they turned and began walking up the path to the eighty-room Tudor mansion. It had, as with all of Camelot Downs, been in the Burke family for more than two centuries. As they walked, Sir Jonathan took the opportunity afforded by Sabelle's jubilant mood to bring up a subject he knew was distasteful to her. But it had to be discussed, and he'd been looking for a chance to broach it ever since the hunt. He decided to approach it obliquely.

"Ah, Sabelle, my dear, have you had any word from your mother since she and your father returned to London?"

Sabelle heard the cautiousness in his voice and assumed he was talking about repercussions from the unfortunate run-in with Justin Hart. She'd told her grandfather of the encounter, but only the basic details of it. Nothing had been mentioned of the way the odious man had made her *feel* during the incident—of how he both frightened her and rendered her all quivery inside at the same time; of how he'd held her so close to his tall, masculine frame that it couldn't have been considered proper; and of the strange light which had entered his eyes while he'd done so!

No, she hadn't explained any of this to Jonathan. How could she have, when she hardly understood it herself? She only knew she sincerely wished she'd never met the duke of Haverleigh. And she hoped never to have the misfortune to encounter him again!

Sabelle framed her response to fit the details he *did* know. "I don't think, from the brief note Mother sent yesterday, that we need have any concerns, Grandfather," she said. "It was filled with only the usual—you know, how I must learn to be less forward and behave like a proper lady . . . that sort of thing. She certainly gave no inkling she'd heard something untoward from the duke, and besides"—she gave Jonathan a flippant toss of her curls—"I gave His Grace much to think about before he'd dare reveal what he saw!"

Jonathan chuckled. He could well imagine his little Sabelle standing up to the arrogant Haverleigh and giving him a piece of her mind!

Then he grew serious. "Actually, Sabelle," he said, stopping her for a moment, "it wasn't Haverleigh I was concerned about when I asked about word from your mother."

But in a roundabout way it is, Jonathan mused wryly. His daughter and son-in-law felt he'd thoroughly botched the job of raising their daughter and said they were giving him one more chance to do right by Sabelle; he would hire whatever tutors and dancing masters were necessary and was to make sure the child would be ready to send to London at the end of the month, when her parents would commence arrangements for her Season!"

But as if that weren't bad enough, Jonathan thought, his social-climbing daughter had confided that she actually entertained notions of a *match* between Sabelle and Haverleigh!

To Jonathan, such a match was unthinkable.

It wasn't that he didn't admire and respect the man. Justin Hart had an excellent *public* character: He had an admirable voting record in the House of Lords, his military career had been a distinguished one, and he was renowned for his brilliant working of the estates he'd inherited.

But Justin Hart was a *rakehell*.

At least where *women* were concerned, Jonathan amended to himself, for he did want to be fair to the man. But this was the very reason he abjured Marjorie's insane idea of a match between the man they called "Hart the Heartless" and his beloved granddaughter. Indeed, when his foolish daughter had informed him of her impetuous act of introducing Hart to Sabelle at the hunt—wringing her hands and bemoaning Sabelle's "disastrous behavior" as she disclosed this to her father—Jonathan had wanted to wring Marjorie's neck!

And then to learn the next day, from Sabelle herself, that she'd had this encounter with Haverleigh—that he'd actually caught her rescuing the fox! Well, the situation was beginning to get out of hand and he'd better do something —about it—at once!

"What I was inquiring about, my dear," he said to Sabelle, "was something I was rather hoping your mother would have been good enough to tell you of in her letter, since it was her idea, but"—he sighed—"I suppose the distasteful business is up to me."

Sabelle eyed him warily. "Distasteful?"

Jonathan sighed again. "They've given me notice to have you ready for your Season, Sabelle."

"My Season!"

It sounded as if she were repeating a vulgarity.

"Oh, my dear, I'm so sorry it had to come to you this way, but you must have known it was inevitable that your parents would see to your coming out." He smiled at her, albeit ruefully, while Sabelle continued to regard him with a rebellious expression on her small, upturned face. "Despite my renaming of this estate when I inherited, you cannot remain hidden away here forever, you know, totally immersed in your idealism as if it were the true Camelot. You are almost eighteen, my darling, and the real world beckons. Also, much as I hate to admit it, I'm beginning to feel I may have been remiss in raising you as I have. The freedoms—"

"Oh, no, Grandfather! Never say so!" Tears began to well up in the sea-green eyes and Sabelle threw her arms about his narrow frame. "You've been the best kind of parent in the world to me, Grandfather! Please, please, don't ever take that away from yourself."

Jonathan's thin arms wound about her shoulders, and he found himself blinking hard to ward off tears. What to do? He knew she wanted none of it . . . the *ton* . . . with its balls, routs—all of those things that comprised a Season. She'd told him so often enough, maintaining her desire to stay forever on this rural estate, indulging in her passion for saving poor, mistreated animals.

But he also knew this was impractical, if not impossible: Sabelle was an important heiress, and heiresses needed husbands . . . and then offspring. And Jonathan was aware he could not live forever. What would happen to her after he was gone? No, in the final analysis, Marjorie and Cecil were right: It was necessary to ready Sabelle for her ultimate role in life—marriage and motherhood.

But he would play his own part in the affair, he thought with a sudden spurt of determination; Sabelle might have to submit to the husband-hunting ritual they had planned for her, but there was no reason it had to be the road to misery. Marriages occasionally turned out happy, even for members of the bloody upper crust, and perhaps, just perhaps, *he* might be able to make that difference for Sabelle. Yes, by God, and that's just what he would do!

Taking her gently by the shoulders, he looked down into her forlorn little face and smiled as a plan came to him. If he deliberately *told* her about Marjorie's outrageous notion of a match with Haverleigh, perhaps the child would become incensed enough to accept the idea of pursuing alternative game. He decided it was worth a try. . . .

"*Whaat?*" cried Sabelle when he'd dropped the bombshell. "A match between me and that—that conceited, arrogant—oh, it does not bear *thinking* on!"

"Of course not, my dear," Jonathan countered. "Haverleigh is the last person in the world for you." *Or for any young innocent who values an unbroken heart!* "But think for a moment, Sabelle. What is the best way to thwart your mother's ill-conceived designs?" He glanced hopefully at her.

But Sabelle was in no mood to respond to subtleties. "I'll have it out with them at once! I—I'll ride down to London tonight and tell Mother. . . ." Her words trailed off and died when she saw Jonathan shaking his head at her.

"To get what you want, you must learn to play your opponents' game, dear child," he told her. "And you must play it better than they do!"

"Oh . . ." said Sabelle, "and how do I do that?"

Jonathan smiled. "Listen to me, Sabelle. I'm afraid the cards are on the table: There is no way you can avoid this wretched business they call a Season. Your parents are set on it. But you needn't go along with *all* their plans! I shall do as they've asked and hire some people to help. There's a young Scotswoman I know who might prove just the thing as your ladies' maid. We'll send you to London well prepared at the end of the month, but hardly with the intent of ensnaring Justin Hart! No, never Justin Hart!

"You'll go along with your parents' plans," he continued, "but with just the opposite in mind: to meet as many *other* eligible young men as possible—gentle, caring men, I'm sure, any number of which might prove far more suitable than that ra——Ah, shall we say *unseemly* gentleman?"

Sabelle looked dubious. "*I* should find it far more suitable to have *no* husband at all!"

Jonathan grimaced. He might have known this would prove no easy task. He'd raised Sabelle to have a mind of her own, and, by God, she could be stubborn!

He decided to sweeten the pot.

"Now, now, my dear, this isn't getting us anywhere," he said gently. "You must be willing to face reality, you know. But I do have an idea that might make this whole beastly business worthwhile for you. . . ."

Intrigued, Sabelle waited for him to continue, and Jonathan smiled as he caught the look of interest in her eyes.

"I suggest," he said as he took her arm again and continued walking, "that you go to London as your parents wish, but with one important difference: *I* shall accompany you."

"*You,* Grandfather? But it's been years since you last set foot in—"

"Ah, but this is for something *important,* my dear! Indeed, the underlying purpose behind our *joint* visit is something *far more interesting and important than your Season!* Now, listen carefully. . . ."

❖Chapter 4❖

ON A WARM EVENING, A FEW DAYS LATER, Justin Hart stood in the main assembly room at Almack's and ran his gaze disinterestedly over those gathered there. There was a look of boredom on his handsome features which had changed little during the course of the evening, not even when he was greeted by various persons he knew. Of course, he always behaved with impeccable politeness during these exchanges, bowing courteously when introduced to a newcomer. He even masked his disdain when, more often than not, these turned out to be young, unattached females accompanied by their hovering mamas.

Forced by the limp he'd acquired after Salamanca to abstain from dancing, the duke found himself wondering why he'd even bothered to attend tonight's cotillion. But a glance at the snowy-haired old dowager who now approached him reminded him that he knew the answer to that: Lady Strathmore had practically ordered him to attend, and while she had no real power over him, his maternal grandmother had a habit of getting her way with people; and notwithstanding the fact that Justin often proved the exception to this, tonight was one of those times when she'd persuaded him to accede to her wishes—damn her anyway!

"Is that frown especially for me, Your Grace, or are you practicing for the next hapless young woman with the misfortune to be making your acquaintance?" Lady Strath-more's tone was light, but the look she sent her grandson from beneath forbidding brows was censorious.

"Only if she turns out to have all the wit and sparkling conversation of those to whom I've already been introduced," came the duke's sarcastic reply.

It was the dowager's turn to frown. She hadn't dragged her tired bones out of her comfortably appointed town house on this Wednesday night to satisfy a need for her own social aggrandizement; it had been for the express purpose of seeing Justin through some societal interactions which had been sorely lacking in his routine before she'd come along. And here he was—the young rogue—practically throwing it in her face!

Millicent Strathmore's presence in the duke of Haver-leigh's life had been all but nonexistent during his formative years. She had rigidly disapproved of her daughter's marriage to Derek Hart, and, even more, of the life-style they'd maintained after the wedding, with its infidelities and unhappy consequences. Her own marriage, while not deliriously happy, had been generally harmonious and certainly free of immoral dalliances. But when she'd warned Vanessa of Derek Hart's libertine bent, her daughter had pooh-poohed it, seeing only the duke's good looks and his grand title and wealth. She had persuaded Lord Strathmore to give his consent, despite his wife's disapproval.

And so, over the years Millicent had kept her distance, though this had been more difficult once the child had come along. But Lady Strathmore was nothing if not firm in her principles; she almost never recalled a decision once it was made, not even a difficult one, fraught with doubts.

But then Vanessa had died, and—whether out of guilt or some sudden need to be of use—she had then taken it upon herself to move back to London to keep an eye on the grandson she feared might turn out like his father, especially without the right person to advise him on conduct befitting a duke of England.

As it had turned out, it hadn't been a moment too soon. Though a conscientious peer and landowner, with a fine voting record in the Lords and several prosperous estates to his credit, Justin, she'd learned, was less than fastidious about the company he kept. Drawing all kinds of women to him like bees about a honey pot, with his dark, arresting good looks, he was fast becoming known as a rake. Of this, she could not approve. Indeed, as she so regularly informed him of late, he should be thinking of settling down—of marrying and providing the dukedom with an heir!

But His Grace seemed as disinclined to seek a proper wife as those scandalous friends of his, men who were little better than the women he seemed to prefer—the opera singers and actresses, and worse! Who'd ever heard of a peer of his standing associating with the likes of radical poets and pamphleteers? Lord Byron, indeed! He might be a nobleman, he might be lionized by the *ton* for his literary endeavors, but to her George Gordon was just a crude, upstart opportunist seeking to capitalize on a so-called talent no self-respecting lord would call attention to! The fact that her grandson ran around in his company—as well as that of unspeakable radicals like Percy Shelley and Leigh Hunt—made Lady Strathmore's blood rise. Oh, she needed to keep a persistent eye on Justin, she did, indeed!

But she also knew she must temper that persistence with less than the heavy hand she was by nature inclined to wield; press the boy too hard, and she was in danger of arousing his stubbornness and losing him altogether!

It was with this in mind, then, that the dowager erased the frown from her face and sought to lighten Justin's mood.

"Look there, Your Grace," she said, gesturing with her fan toward a handsome woman who was coming their way. "Our patroness this evening, and I'll wager you two guineas she'll not quit until she wins a smile from that handsome mouth of yours!"

But Justin's mouth was already curving amiably as he saw Lady Jersey approach. Unlike some of the more unbending, snobbish patronesses of Almack's—Lady Castlereagh, for example, who was known as the *grande dame* of them all—he rather liked Jersey and got on well with her. Of course, he was one of her favorites among the *ton,* as were his friends Lord Byron, and Brett Westmont, the duke of Ravensford; and such favoritism went a long way toward making these tedious evenings bearable.

"Better a handsome mouth than an ear-bending one!" said Lady Jersey, picking up on what she'd overheard. "I've just succeeded in escaping with mine intact, before it was bent like a pretzel by that half-deaf old windbag, Lord Ponsonby." The patroness rolled her eyes and gestured discreetly with her fan toward an old gentleman who could be seen across the room, talking into the ear of a young man with a pained expression on his face.

Justin chuckled while his grandmother hid a smile with her fan.

"How are you this evening, Your Grace?" Lady Jersey inquired after exchanging greetings with the dowager.

"At present," replied Justin, darting a glance at his grandmother, "quite possibly two guineas poorer than I was a moment ago."

Lady Jersey looked bemused until Lady Strathmore hastened to explain: "I'd just finished wagering this young rascal such a sum that you could induce him to smile, my lady."

"Ah . . ." said the patroness, "just so. I'd been wondering about that impassive expression you've been wearing all evening, Your Grace. It was perilously close to brooding, which, I'm sure you'll agree, is more our friend Byron's domain."

Justin flashed her a grin, revealing two deeply slashed grooves that were male dimples. "Actually, m'lady, George is far better equipped to affect such a pose than I. He has the pale, wan complexion for it, you see, as well as his famous 'underlook,' and I dare say he uses these most effectively. They send all his female admirers groping for their hartshorn."

Lady Jersey allowed herself a small smile. She nodded as the duke offered his arm and gestured in the direction of the refreshment tables, indicating he would escort the two women there.

"Nevertheless, Your Grace," Lady Jersey told him with a brief glance at the leg that caused his slight limp, "you cannot deny the similarities between the two of you, with regard to the attractions they hold for the ladies. With that limp, you shall soon be out-Byroning Byron!"

Justin barely managed to check a grimace at this remark, but his grandmother was less successful. Lady Jersey noted the disapproval in the slate-gray eyes.

"His Grace, at least," said the dowager in tones that no other would have dared use with the socially powerful patroness, "does not waste his valuable time with *scribbling*, Lady Jersey!"

It was the patroness's turn to hide a smile with her fan. No, she thought to herself, Justin Hart did not write poetry or the like, probably because he had the good sense to realize he'd not been endowed with the literary genius of his friend Byron. Such a gift, after all, rarely came along more than once in a lifetime. But she did know that the duke had a fine mind—a brilliant one, in fact. He was an exceedingly well read intellectual, and it was this, more than his incredible good looks and dashing image as a military hero, which drew the company of men like Byron, Hunt, and others of the literary set.

"Indeed, Lady Strathmore," the patroness replied, "but in keeping with something you yourself initiated earlier this evening, I should like to wager *you* two guineas that there *are* certain, ah, *distractions* we may credit him with!" She gestured archly in the direction of a tall, stunning brunette who was making a beeline for the duke.

The dowager eyed the beautiful brunette for a fleet second, then allowed her features to relax while focusing again on the patroness. "You'll forgive me, I'm sure, my lady, if I do not accept your wager."

Lady Jersey's brows rose at this, but she refrained from comment as the brunette drew near.

Millicent ran her eyes discreetly over the newcomer as greetings were exchanged. Lady Sarah Cavendish, she was well aware, was Justin's current mistress. The "fair Cyprian," as the *ton* dubbed her, was a beautiful sophisticate whose wit and looks had first drawn Justin to her bed.

But what the dowager also knew was the reason why, of all the duke's mistresses, Lady Sarah had lasted the longest: Like the others before her, this earl's daughter would dearly love to lead Justin to the altar, but she was clever enough to pretend otherwise! Justin had frequently remarked on his mistress's being "disinclined to seek a husband—thank God!" during some of the late-night chats he and his grandmother had. Therefore, while Millicent didn't exactly approve of his dalliance with the brunette, she could allow herself to relax in the face of Lady Sarah's cleverly concealed pursuit; Justin would never wed the chit, and that was that!

She resumed her exchange with Lady Jersey as they watched the striking couple depart to take a slow turn about the assembly rooms.

"It is not that I fail to see that as a distraction, my dear," she said to Jersey, "but I cannot quite regard their, ah, relationship as a waste of my grandson's time, either."

"Oh . . . ?" replied the patroness with a look that told her to continue.

The dowager smiled. "A man of the *ton* will always have his lightskirts, my lady. None but the most imprudent of gentlemen, however, regards a *mistress* as suitable marriage material, as I'm sure you'll agree."

The younger woman nodded. After a glance at the duke and his current favorite as they threaded their way across the room in leisurely fashion, she frowned.

"Ah, yes, Lady Strathmore, I quite agree, but . . . the earl of Grantham's only daughter is no common lightskirt! Why, she stands to inherit—"

"I am well aware of the chit's attractions as an heiress, my lady, but she will never suit! An unsullied, gently reared young lady is the only choice for a peer of the realm."

Lady Jersey gave her an indulgent smile. "I am sure, my Lady Strathmore, that those are the standards you were raised with, but surely you are aware that the times are changing." She gestured airily about them at the host of richly attired ladies and gentlemen moving about the assembly rooms of Almack's. "Why, to today's sophisticated members of the *ton*—"

"A titled lord," Lady Strathmore cut in for the second time in as many minutes, "and a duke, especially, must be sure of one thing above all, Lady Jersey: He must wed with the absolute certainty that the offspring of his union will be truly *his!* And, beautiful heiress or not, given her habits of indiscreet conduct, I hardly think Sarah Cavendish qualifies.

"No, my dear Lady Jersey," the dowager added with a final note of assurance, "my grandson will meet an innocent at the altar, and that is that!"

With a regal nod of her head, Lady Strathmore moved away, intent upon the bowl of punch on one of the refreshment tables.

The patroness watched her for a moment, then turned to look across the room at the tall, handsome duke. A smile hovered about Lady Jersey's mouth as she assessed his undisguised sexuality. *That is that, is it?* she mused as she tried to picture the viril Hart putting up with some weak-kneed virgin in his bed. *Oh, I wouldn't even bet tuppence on it, Lady Strathmore. In fact, I wouldn't bet anything at all!*

❖Chapter 5❖

WHILE THE DUKE OF HAVERLEIGH strolled with his mistress through the glittering assembly rooms of Almack's in London's fashionable West End, that same night, in the far-less savory East End of the city a vastly different social drama was being enacted. The filthy, garbage-strewn waters of the Thames lapped sluggishly against a slimy set of stairs where river barges took on cargo and occasional passengers as a trio of thin and ragged youths made their way along the shadows.

"Mind them steps when ye reaches 'em, Jack," said the tallest of the three in a rough whisper. "Ye might find yerself fishbait, along wi' them kitties!"

A muffled snigger came from his companion as he hefted a bulky sack that had been slung over his shoulder and held it up before the other two, as if for their inspection. "Ain't 'nuff meat on the lot, 'ere, t' feed a rat, Billy, me boy, let alone the fishes!"

His cohorts chortled gleefully in response, but it was an ugly sound, underscored by blatant malice. Then, as the one called Jack swung the sack back over his shoulder, the three again proceeded toward the river stairs. Their bare, grimy feet moved carefully over the slippery cobblestones as curling tendrils of fog drifted from the river, partially obscuring them from view.

But that same fog also served to hide two more youthful figures who waited and watched, crouched beside a heap of rubbish a dozen yards away. And if the fog and the night weren't enough to hide them, their dark garments helped to accomplish this most effectively; for theirs were the clothes of chimney sweeps—soot-covered, black, and spare.

The smaller of the two stiffened as a pitiful mewing escaped the squirming bundle on the dirty urchin's back; it took effort to bite back an angry response, but it wouldn't do to alert the filthy culprits before the two got near enough to accomplish their task. With a silent gesture to the other figure in sweep's clothing, the slimmer, petite one began to move stealthily in the direction of the stairs. Nodding, the taller one followed.

The three youths with the sack were all but invisible when they reached the top of the stairs, for the fog was increasing steadily as it rose from the river. The one with the bundle paused and guffawed crudely at something one of his companions said. He removed the sack from his shoulder again.

And then all hell broke loose.

An angry cry echoed out of the shadows as a small, dark figure hurled itself at the group, hitting them behind their knees and bringing them down simultaneously onto the slippery steps. Outraged cries split the air while the youth with the sack whirled to confront their attacker, only to have the squirming bundle snatched from his grasp by a second figure that seemed to come out of nowhere.

With a cry of rage, Billy lunged for the one who'd grabbed his bundle, but the small assailant was quicker. Springing from a crouch beside the flailing bodies, the attacker went at him with a snarl, and two small, soot-blackened hands gave a mighty shove that sent Billy backward. With a screech of surprise, he found himself catapulted, heels over head, into the stinking river.

But now the one called Jack had regained his feet, and his furious gaze focused on Billy's assailant, dimly visible through the eddying fog. "Stinkin' sweeps!" he cried as he launched himself at the smaller figure in black; but at that moment the taller figure turned just in time from carefully setting aside the rescued bundle and thrust itself between him and the petite one. The unmistakable glint of a blade flashed in one hand.

"No' sae fast, laddies," murmured the one wielding the knife, "or ye'll be tastin' the bite o' me dirk!"

"Blimey!" exclaimed Billy's companion as he, too, regained his feet and halted cautiously before the menacing blade. "A blinkin' Scots sweep wi' a sticker!"

"Aye," growled the Scottish burr, "and one wie the itch t' *use* it on scum that tries t' drown puir, defenseless kittens in the river!"

Billy's furious thrashing could be heard in the water, and the petite sweep emerged out of the fog. There was a long, thorough perusal of the two held at knifepoint and then a contemptuous grunt of disgust.

"I ought to order your filthy throats cut!" said a young voice. "But I'm going to allow my Scottish friend, here, to let you go—on one condition!" the small sweep added. The fearful glances of the captives turned to looks of uneasy relief.

Then they saw this sweep, too, withdraw a dagger and whirl to cover the sputtering form of Billy staggering up the steps from the river. "You!" spat the sweep. "Get along there with your gutter-rat friends!"

Billy snarled, but kept fearful eyes on the dagger as he did what he was told.

"Now," said the small sweep when all three would-be drowners of kittens were arranged before the two who wielded the knives, "some instructions before we let you go. The three of you have been caught tonight attempting to drown helpless kittens, *but these are the last animals you will ever seek to abuse in any way, d'ye hear?*"

There was silence as the fog continued to swirl around them, not quite concealing the looks of sullen contempt on the three urchins' faces.

"I said, did you *hear* me?" came the repeated demand, and as both figures in black moved their knives threateningly, there was a hasty chorus of sniveling assent from their captives.

"Very well," came the response. "Then I have only this

to add: You were not apprehended in your filthy endeavor tonight by chance. You were discreetly observed stealing those kittens from their basket at the smith's shop and followed here by me and my companions—and, yes, there are more than just the two of us.

"But, more to the point, I'm telling you now that if any one of you—or any of your acquaintances—ever tries to harm a defenseless animal again, rest assured that we shall know of it—and then *'twill be our blades which do the talking!*

"Am I understood?"

Three unkempt heads nodded vigorously, eyes still trained on their captors' knives.

"Then make sure you spread the word. And now get your miserable carcasses out of here before I change my mind. *Get!*"

The three bolted, leaving the other two to put away their knives, gently retrieve the bag of mewing kittens, and disappear with their precious bundle, into the fog.

But later that night, and for days afterward, a colorful tale made its way around the streets and alleys of the East End: A pair of mad chimney sweeps—one with a Highland burr and another with the unlikely speech of an uppercrust toff—had harassed poor street beggars out for nothing more than a bit of " 'armless sport."

A few days later, in the Haymarket, a second incident spurred fresh tales of mad and dangerous chimney sweeps. A ragman who'd seen an opportunity to swell his purse had loaded his rickety cart with what he hoped to sell as firewood—logs and branches hastily sawed from a tree which had been felled by lightning outside an inn during a storm the previous night. Working stealthily during the remaining hours of the storm—for such wood legally belonged to the owner of the inn and not to scavengers—the ragman had forced his weary, overworked cart horse out, into the driving wind and rain, to steal the wood while the inn's owner was asleep in his bed.

Hours later, amid the bustle of morning traffic in the

business district, the exhausted cart horse, straining from a load far heavier than it might normally carry, stumbled and sank to its knees before the overloaded vehicle.

"Y' good-fer-nothin' nag!" bellowed the ragman. "Get up! Get up, I say!" And he reached for his whip and began to beat the animal unmercifully, thoughts of a lost windfall feeding his rage.

The animal tried to rise, staggered, and went down again, and still the whip sliced the air. Traffic slowed to a stop about the sorry spectacle. Onlookers scowled and muttered beneath the whistle of the whip. Even hardened hawkers and peddlers shook their heads at such a wanton display of cruelty.

Then, suddenly, a pair of youthful, dark-clad figures emerged from the crowd about the cart. Locked in a wild struggle with each other, these slim, soot-begrimed youngsters hurled furious invectives as they wrestled in the street.

"You took it, you dirty Scot!"

"I dinna!"

"Yes, you did! Give it back!"

"I dinna take yer filthy apple, ye Sassenach scum!"

"Scum, is it?"

Clawing and pummeling each other, the two young combatants shoved themselves against the ragman's cart. This threatened to topple the teetering pile of logs it bore, if not the cart itself.

"I'll teach you to steal from your betters!"

"The only thing *better* aboot *ye* is, ye *better* be gone!"

"Scots swine! Thief!"

A couple of logs rolled onto the cobblestones. Alarmed now, the ragman jumped down from his perch, dropping his whip as he made for the two youths.

"Chimney sweeps—brawlin'!" he growled as he tried to find an opening between two flying pairs of grimy fists. " 'Ere, now, ye filthy little beggars, come away from me cart!"

He cursed and sputtered, looking for an opening in which to collar them. Meanwhile, the growing crowd looked on, some cheering the sweeps, others enjoying the ragman's expression as yet more logs fell to the ground. No one noticed the big man who crept quietly through the jostling crowd and approached the suffering horse standing before the cart.

Several frantic minutes later, much to the ragman's chagrin, the pair of squabbling sweeps lurched into the crowd and disappeared.

"Come back 'ere, ye mizer'ble little beggars!" yelled the ragman. "Ye've tumbled me pile o' logs an'—"

All of a sudden, the man stopped. Then he turned and, with mouth agape, stared at his vehicle.

The horse was gone. In its place, fastened to one of the reins which had been cleanly cut, was a note accompanied by a small pile of coins. When the ragman, who couldn't read, finally found someone to decipher it for him, he learned what it said:

> *These are for the poor horse you nearly beat to death. If you abuse* any *animal again, you will lose it as well, but next time there will be nary a coin left in exchange.*

That night, in yet another part of the city, the pair of sweeps who were fast becoming the talk of the East End crept quietly along a row of barrels and crates piled on a wharf. They were taking great care not to be discovered. Beside them, keeping well to the shadows, padded a huge, shaggy hound.

The cause of their stealth was a man they'd followed for the better part of an hour; they'd dogged him after he left a tavern where one Michael Kelly had learned he was going to the docks to receive a shipment of game cocks. If all went well, Lady Isabelle Corstairs and Jeannie MacDougal, the Scottish ladies' maid who was now her dearest friend, would see to it that the expected shipment of fighting fowl never made it to the bloody cockpits.

The two young women watched and listened as their quarry hailed a pair of men who came toward him out of the shadows. They hardly dared to breathe as they overheard the three discuss the details of the shipment's arrival, scheduled for later that night. Then, as the three men repaired to a dockside tavern to await their shipment, the two women nodded to each other. Silently signaling the hound that Michael had insisted they take along for protection, they turned and made their way quickly back to where Kelly waited. He'd make good use of the information they'd gleaned this night!

Sabelle's eyes shone as she and Jeannie hurried after Brendan, who could be trusted to take them back by the safest route. If things went according to plan, all cockfights in the city would be thwarted for weeks to come! Biting back an urge to laugh out loud, she allowed herself a broad and decidedly wicked grin as she ran alongside her companions. *Ah, Grandfather was right! London was a smashing place to be!*

❖Chapter 6❖

THE MORNING AFTER SABELLE CORSTAIRS BE-
gan to see the benefits of life in London, Justin Hart
stood in the library of the Hart town house doing just the
opposite. Having risen early to go over some correspondence with his secretary, he'd endured that tedious work as
long as he could and then abruptly dismissed the man; he
was finding it impossible to concentrate on the humdrum
duties of his life in the city.

The ache from the slow-to-heal saber wound in his thigh
throbbed insistently this morning, and yet he would have
given much, just then, to be in the field again. Not that he
was one of those who reveled in the carnage of war; he'd
seen enough of the slaughter, heard enough of the screams
of the dying and wounded, to be brutally sober about the
reality of battle. But, dammit, at least, there, he'd see his
actions attuned to a clear-cut, visible purpose! At least on
the battlefield he wouldn't find himself drifting aimlessly
about, seeking meaning where none could be found.
Among the endless and fatuous routs and balls and parties.
Among the sanctified strata known as the *ton*.

His thoughts drifted back to the previous evening, when
he'd taken Sarah Cavendish to the opera and then to his
bed. (Not the huge Chippendale four-poster sitting upstairs in the master suite, of course. He *never* brought any
of his women *there*. Rather, he'd taken her to the small, but
well-appointed lodgings he kept for just such purposes on a

quiet street, just around the corner from St. James's Church, near Piccadilly.) The opera, which ought to have pleased him, did just the opposite, for it had been ill-performed. The lady, whose beauty and wit had always pleased him, had also somehow fallen short of the mark. The trouble was, he wasn't even certain why. Except that everything about his routine in the city seemed to pall lately.

"Dammit!" he exclaimed aloud to the books lined up like silent witnesses along the walls. "What in all hell's wrong with me? Why am I—"

A rapping at the door interrupted his thoughts.

"Enter," he called.

The library door opened, and Stewart, his longtime majordomo, stepped inside. "I beg your pardon, Your Grace, but Mr. Thomas Long is—"

"Oh, Thomas. Show him up, please."

"Very good, Your Grace."

As the majordomo went to comply, Justin found his eyes straying, almost involuntarily, to the Gainsborough portrait of his mother across the room. For some reason he associated his former tutor with the late duchess of Haverleigh; perhaps because his mother had been the one to hire Long initially, and she'd always seemed extraordinarily fond of the man while she was alive.

Walking slowly across the green-and-gold Aubusson carpet that covered most of the library floor, Justin continued to gaze at the portrait. Posed on a garden bench at their country estate in Kent, Vanessa Hart gazed out at the viewer with a languid look in her large gray eyes. She appeared every inch what she then was—a beautiful, well-bred paragon of the upper-class Englishwoman, serene within her station, content with her lot in life.

And yet, if one who'd known her well were to look closely, he could discern something contradictory in those lovely eyes. . . . A hint of . . . what? Pain? Despair, even? Whatever it was, it was something she couldn't have wanted the world to see. And yet, Gainsborough, with that all-too-discerning, subtle touch of the master, had captured it, and—

"She was very beautiful, wasn't she?"

Justin whirled about and saw Thomas Long standing only a few feet away. "Thomas!" he exclaimed. "Dammit, man, there ought to be a law against creeping up on a person like that!"

"Sorry," said Long as the two shook hands. "But I took pity on old Stewart, who's begun to get a bit long in the tooth, you know, and decided to spare him another climb up the stairs to show me in."

Nodding, Justin gestured him toward a pair of comfortable chairs by the fireplace, running his eyes over his old friend and tutor as they settled themselves.

Thomas Long was a fine-boned man of medium height, with a body given to spareness. One might perhaps have termed him handsome, Justin thought, with his shock of sandy hair and pale blue eyes—if it weren't for the almost perpetual look of melancholy he bore! It was so different from those early days, when his blue eyes would shine upon discovering a new poetic image or insight. With his youthful enthusiasm for all things academic and cerebral, he'd had the capacity to ignite in his student an infectious excitement about the world of ideas. Even if that excitement occasionally bordered on the extreme, as, for instance, in his intellectual love affair with William Blake.

But with the passage of time, Long had altered. He was a rather strange sort now, a rabid social radical. Rather than grow intellectually, as Justin knew he himself had done, Long had remained fixated, never going much beyond his early absorption with social critics like Blake. In fact, his preoccupation with the brutal social conditions of the times formed the bulk of all he ever talked about these days—like a singer with a one-note theme. As they sat down together this morning, Justin suspected the topic of conversation would revert to Thomas's obsessive ideas, no matter how much Justin endeavored to steer it elsewhere.

He was not to be disappointed.

They'd just dispensed with Long's inquiry about Justin's war injury, when Justin referred to an article in the *Morning Post*. It had to do with the current lawlessness in the

Midlands, spiked by raids from rebellious workers known as Luddites.

"If it's lawlessness you're concerned about," said Long, "perhaps you ought to be doing what you can to change the nature of the *laws* which inspired those poor devils to riot. And not simply bemoan the fact that violence has occurred as a result. Those poor workers in the Midlands are being sacrificed to enrich the coffers of a handful of fat, parasitic hosiers!"

Justin nearly groaned. He was well aware of the growing civil unrest which had been precipitated by widespread unemployment in the woolen and cotton-spinning trades; it had followed the introduction of shearing frames and power looms by the industry's employers, the country's stocking manufacturers. He was aware, too, of the armed bands of men who, just last year, had begun roaming the countryside, their faces blackened and masked as they met in the night to destroy the hated automated frames and looms that were taking away their livelihoods—and burning the workshops in which they were kept. Called Luddites for a symbolic allegiance to their fictitious "General Ludd," the attackers were highly secretive, remaining faceless and nameless as they struck swiftly and disappeared in the dead of night.

But Justin knew what was coming; they had been over this ground before: Long wanted Justin to use his considerable influence in the House of Lords to stop the Tories' determined persecution of the rebels (they had just passed a bill making frame-breaking a capital offense) by convincing Parliament to address the *source* of the workers' discontent, not the *outcome*.

"Look, Thomas," the duke said with a hint of weariness in his voice, "you know how I feel about such matters. Yes, it's a shame there's violence abroad in the land, and, yes, the world's not a pretty place, but those are the cold, brutal facts, my friend. And I am no shining knight on a white charger to right the world's wrongs.

"So please don't press me to do something I have neither the spirit nor the inclination for. I only brought up the piece in the *Post* because—"

"Yes?" said Long, instantly alerted. "Why *did* you bring it up?"

Justin sighed, running a hand through his hair in agitation. "Because it quoted from a speech Byron made to protest that capital-offense bill of last winter. If you'll recall, I was out of the country at the time—on a little matter involving our problems with a certain Corsican—and wasn't aware of our young friend's eloquent words, albeit for a doomed cause."

"At least George Gordon had the courage to *try!*" cried Thomas.

Justin hid a smile; it was so in character for Thomas, a commoner, to refer to a titled lord by his common name— as if he could level the inequities of birth simply by refusing to use the terminology of privilege.

"Ah, yes," he said. "Trust Byron to fight the good fight, no matter how hopeless—or wildly idealistic! But consider the end effect, my dear Thomas. The article said, among other not-so-flattering things, that the speech was long on rhetoric, but *all too short* on specific recommendations!"

"But that's just it!" exclaimed the tutor, a near-fanatical gleam lighting his eyes. "George Gordon is a mere youngster—only twenty-four years old, for God's sake! Little wonder that he hadn't the seasoning to give his speech substance. But *you*, Justin, are a thirty-four-year-old seasoned veteran—both of the Lords *and* the military, I might add. If *you* were to put your weight behind—"

"Sorry, Thomas, but I'm afraid I can't oblige you."

"Can't? Or *won't?"*

Justin shrugged, a bored look on his face now. "Whatever . . . it amounts to the same thing."

As the silver-gray eyes gazed at him with a remoteness that was all too familiar, Thomas wanted to weep out his chagrin and frustration. He knew that look well. It signaled their discussion was at a close. And he knew as well the source of that remoteness, even though Justin had long ago made it clear that he had no wish to discuss it—ever. The remoteness was a result of years of hardening himself to anything that smacked of humaneness, or compassion, or any matter likely to touch the heart. Justin Hart had truly become the "Hart the Heartless" he'd been dubbed over the years. It had all begun with a single incident, that morning outside his parents' drawing room so many years ago. And he, Thomas, had been there. Seen it begin. He had also been helpless to stop it. *Ah, Justin, how I've failed you!*

But Long collected himself and decided to try one more tack.

"Um . . . I was lucky enough to come by one of Blake's etchings the other day, Justin," he said carefully.

"Were you?" replied the duke. "Well, good for you." Despite the fact that he no longer shared Long's extreme fascination with the poet artist, he was not unappreciative of the fine quality of Blake's engravings and even owned a few himself. "Which was it? What's the subject matter?"

Long smiled. "It's from *The Book of Urizen*. You recall?" Then he began to quote, all the while looking Justin directly in the eye.

> He, in darkness clos'd, view'd all his race,
> And his soul sicken'd! he curse'd
> Both sons and daughters, for he saw
> That no flesh nor spirit could—

At that moment a sharp, two-tap rapping stuck the library door. It cut Long off in mid-quotation, and before either could say a word, Lady Strathmore entered.

Both men rose at once, but Thomas looked annoyed at the ill-timed interruption. Justin, on the other hand, welcomed his grandmother's intrusion; he'd known immediately what Thomas was about and felt relieved to be spared another lecture. His smile was unusually bright as he greeted the marchioness.

"Of course, you know my grandmother?" he said to Thomas.

Lady Strathmore eyed Justin suspiciously. It wasn't like

her grandson to disregard her little breaches of etiquette when they violated his privacy. Normally, he'd be scowling furiously at her for entering his inner sanctum unbidden. Of course, it was not that she did such things very often . . . Well, perhaps every now and then, just to test his mettle and demonstrate that her wishes were important enough to preempt certain boundaries! But it just so happened that this time she had every right to barge in on him like this, and she hastened to tell him so without further ado.

"Your Grace, I apologize for the intrusion, but it was necessary, I fear. Your solicitors will be arriving in less than an hour, and here you sit, still in your morning coat! Have you forgotten their appointment with you today?"

Justin groaned, prompting an I-thought-as-much look from his grandmother.

"Their yearly lecture, you mean!" he retorted sourly. "I pray you will excuse me, Thomas, if I appear less than courteous on the subject, but it is one I dread—and I dare say you will heartily agree."

Thomas threw him a quizzical look.

"It's about matrimony, my dear man. Marriage! Ever since I turned thirty, the Misters Witherspoon and Cromby have, each September, taken it upon themselves to emerge from their dry, dusty offices near Whitehall and make a pilgrimage to my doorstep."

Justin began to pace the carpet, throwing agitated gestures toward the walls and ceiling as he moved.

"And for what?" he asked, before proceeding to answer his own question. "For the express and singular purpose of urging me to grab some blue-blooded virgin and make her my duchess!"

Immediate alarm registered on the tutor's face, but it was Lady Strathmore who broke in.

"Really, Justin, you needn't be so dramatic. For a moment, I almost believed I was at the Drury Lane, watching Garrick! But you know as well as I," she went on, "that your solicitors are only doing their duty—by urging *you* to do *yours!*"

"Duty!" cried Long. "Is it duty to tie a man to a woman for life—and vice versa—in a binding contract that offers little or no hope for their mutual happiness? What duty do you speak of, madam? To the Crown? To the *ton*? What about a man's duty to *himself*? What about *love*?"

Lady Strathmore peered at him from beneath stern gray brows. "His Grace," she intoned imperiously, "must do his duty to the Crown, yes. And to society, as well as to his family—and therefore to himself. It is his duty to all to provide the dukedom with an heir."

Pointedly ignoring Long with this, the dowager turned back to her grandson. "Justin, you are well aware of our concern. Your ridiculous cousin Wilbur is just waiting for the chance to take your place. As next in line, he will, you know, if anything should happen to you. Rumor has it he's to wed, and I shudder to think that he—or any similarly twaddlebrained offspring he's likely to produce—might actually become the next duke of Haverleigh! "Think, Justin! You are on the verge of five and thirty. Your duty beckons!"

Clearly upset, Long threw Justin a pleading look. But this gained him nothing beyond an amused glance, and a shrug of the duke's broad, immaculately garbed shoulders.

It was too much for Long. Mumbling his apologies, he stomped out of the library and left the house.

There was a moment's silence as the dowager's eyes rested on the door which had just closed. "I cannot abide that gloom-mongering creature," she told her grandson. "Never could! Even years ago, he was a strange one."

Justin's brows rose in surprise. "I didn't realize you met Thomas years ago. After all, you were never in evidence during my childhood."

"Don't be a ninnytwiddle!" she snapped, instantly reverting to her usual crusty self. "I was speaking of the day of your mother's funeral, when I arrived to find *you* dry-eyed and sensible, but had to endure the disconsolate mopings of that glumster! Heaven knows, I was as grief-stricken over your mother's death as anyone had a right to be. And so were you, I have no doubt," she added as both her gaze and Justin's drifted upward, toward Vanessa Hart's portrait. "But *we* did not hang our private griefs about like so much laundry, did we, my boy? No, indeed, we did not! And proud I am to say so, for that matter."

Justin offered the barest of nods in response as they both continued to gaze at the portrait.

At last Millicent broke the silence with a softly murmured query. "Is there yet no progress, then?"

Justin shook his head as his eyes scanned the portrait one more time; then he sighed as he turned to the dowager. "And I'm afraid we cannot really entertain much hope. It has simply been too many years, Grandmother."

The dowager nodded, needing no further comment on the topic she was well aware she alone dared raise with the hardened duke. For the subject they so tersely alluded to was the identity of the unknown lover who, years ago, had been behind Vanessa Hart's adulterous liaison, as well as her pregnancy—and the abortion which claimed her life.

On the day following the late duchess's funeral, quite by accident, while sorting through some of her things, the two of them had come upon an unsigned letter from the person who was obviously Her Grace's lover. The letter had ordered her to do away with their unborn child. The author had then callously gone on to provide the time and place for the abortion—and thus her ultimate death.

Now, and during the intervening years, Justin—with his grandmother's approval—was secretly endeavoring to find him; with professional assistance from a group of former Bowstreet Runners they employed as detectives, they were determined to learn the identity of the man they held responsible for Vanessa's death.

Their grim, matter-of-fact exchanges on these efforts from time to time did nothing to reflect their frustrations with their lack of success. Nor did they reveal the emotions carefully hidden. Perhaps, if there had been someone present when they spoke together at these times, someone perceptive, who knew them well, he might have noticed that despite a deeply held disappointment with her, each had loved the woman in the portrait very much.

❖Chapter 7❖

"**D**RAT!"

The rear door to the Corstairses' town house continued to emit an all too noticeable squeak, and Sabelle glared at it while pushing it open far enough to admit herself and her two companions.

"I'll be seein' the hinges get oilin', lass," whispered Michael Kelly as he and Brendan followed her quietly into the darkness of the back pantry.

Sabelle nodded, pausing to listen for sounds indicating there was someone else about.

But all was silent in the small chamber, although, from the kitchen she could dimly make out the sounds of servants moving about, preparing the late supper her parents preferred to take when in London.

She fumbled about on a nearby shelf until she located the tinderbox and a chamberstick she'd left there before she, Kelly, and the wolfhound had rendezvoused in the stables late that afternoon.

As she worked the flint to create a spark, she took a moment to assess their afternoon's work. Dressed as usual for these forays, as a chimney sweep, with Michael outfitted as a sweeps master, they'd gone to gather information on a rumor the big groom had picked up—that a certain idiot nobleman of questionable humanity had taken to setting up an aviary in his London house, wherein he caged and mistreated wild birds. They'd found the rumor to have substance, well enough, for Sabelle had managed to converse with a pair of scrawny sweeps the earl had actually paid (though a pitifully small amount, to be sure) to set traps for swallows and other wild birds they were likely to spy during their excursions over the rooftops of the city.

Now all that remained was for Sabelle and her little group to figure out a way to thwart his lordship's endeavors. Cage those wild free spirits of the skies, would he? They'd see about *that!*

The wick caught a spark, and a soft glow revealed the three of them, prompting a grin from Sabelle.

"Michael," she whispered as she gestured him toward a side door leading to the servants' quarters, "in this light you look positively wicked in those clothes!"

The Irishman returned the grin, then sobered. "Ah, lass, 'tis wicked, indeed, these sweeps masters be! T' be sendin' poor lads t'such hard, filthy work! But 'tis *yourself* stops the eye! Yer lovely, wee face is covered with soot, and yer clothes look like the divil's own rags, I'm thinkin'."

Sabelle nodded, then cast an appraising eye at the hound. "Brendan looks worse than both of us, though. I wish we hadn't had to hide him in that coal bin, but I suppose it couldn't be helped. You'll be sure he has his bath, won't you, Michael? Mother has barely consented to allow him in the house as it is. If she were to see—"

"Niver fear, lass," said the big man as he ushered the dog toward the servants' quarters. "But 'tis yerself had better be hurryin' t'bathe. Fancy what her ladyship would say t' yer own appearance!"

With a grin, Sabelle watched man and hound disappear through the door; then she hurried to the set of narrow stairs at the far corner. These were designed for the use of the servants, allowing them unobtrusive access to the second floor. Sabelle gave silent thanks for such a convenience, for she used them to hurry up to her own chambers unobserved.

"Ach! Lassie, ye'll be the death o' me yet!" exclaimed Jeannie as Sabelle entered her private sitting room. The maid had been pacing the floor, worrying. After all, how long should it take to scout out a rumor? It wasn't as if they were performing the actual rescue today!

"Oh, Jeannie, dear, you worry too much," said Sabelle as she headed toward her bedchamber. She paused and turned to look at her friend. "Um, you didn't have any, ah, problems, did you?"

The "problems" she referred to had to do with the task Jeannie had been given with regard to the afternoon's foray; the Scottish girl had been told to cover for Sabelle if her parents wished to see or speak to her. She'd been prepared to say that Sabelle was exhausted from the previous day's round of visits with dressmakers and hairdressers in preparation for her Season and that she was asleep.

"Ach! Nay, lass," Jeannie replied. The Scottish girl was older than Sabelle by three years, and had been hired for her by Sir Jonathan when they came to London. By the time a week had passed, the two were fast friends, and Sabelle insisted they dispense with her "me ladys" when together in private. Instead, Jeannie called her "lass" or "lassie" much of the time.

"Then, pray, what's amiss?" Sabelle noticed Jeannie's agitation. From beneath the mobcap she wore, several of Jeannie's auburn curls had escaped and were bobbing as the maid shook her head in a manner that was atypical; Jeannie was not one to become easily rattled.

Several years before Sir Jonathan hired the tall, thin Scottish orphan to be Sabelle's companion, Jeannie MacDougal had been a ward of Lady Bessborough's school for penniless and orphaned girls. The school took these indigents off the streets and instructed them in useful skills, preparing them to be laundresses or serving maids and the like. Prior to that Jeannie and her family had fallen into abject poverty after being turned out of their Highlands home by the duke of Sutherland's decision to replace crofters with sheep on his Scottish estates. Near starvation and utterly exhausted, the MacDougals had made it to London, where her father, Angus, had hoped to find work, only to be set upon by a fever which killed the whole family, except for Jeannie.

So the young Highlander had endured a great deal of hardship before her fortunate encounter with Sir Jonathan Burke. But Jeannie was tough and resilient, a survivor if there ever was one, and it would take more than a few "problems" to rattle her.

Jeannie's brown eyes widened at Sabelle's query, and she let out an exasperated sigh. "What's amiss? Hae ye fergotten ye're t' be dinin' wie yer parents t'night? They're expectin' ye downstairs in less than an hour, and look at ye! 'Twill take us more time than that t' scrub ye clean, lass!"

"Oh, damn! I forgot all about the bloody dinner!"

"Aye, I thought as much!" Jeannie hastened after her mistress, who'd made a leap for her bedchamber door. "And I was fresh out o' notions o' what t' tell them. After all, 'twould hardly satisfy them t' say ye were still nappin' at nine o'clock in the evenin'!"

"I know, I know," mumbled Sabelle as pieces of sweep's clothing went flying in every direction. She was normally neater than this, but tonight she had no choice. Her parents had told her yesterday that they were fed up with the various delays she'd managed to achieve with regard to coming out this fall. As it was, the Little Season was already under way, but Lady Corstairs had decided they might stretch things a bit and had selected the end of the first week in November as the date for Sabelle's coming-out ball. But even with this additional time, there could be no more foot-dragging; she would keep each and every appointment they'd scheduled on her calendar—and be prompt about them or suffer the "severest consequences!"

And while she scrubbed her clean, Sabelle asked Jeannie about the afternoon's excursion into the East End. The younger girl answered as carefully as possible, for she knew Jeannie's commitment to their rescue operations was as great as her own. Jeannie was an animal lover, too, as was anyone whom Sir Jonathan and Sabelle had taken into their confidence.

Sabelle informed her that the nobleman whose actions they'd tracked down was one Robert Ormley, the earl of Larchmont. He was fat and chinless, according to the young sweeps. A dandy who wore corsets and whose breath reeked of garlic, he characterized himself as a rare-bird fancier.

"Moreover," Sabelle told Jeannie, "the fat fool keeps dozens of birds in a cramped, miserable excuse for an aviary. And if that isn't the outside of enough, his lordship is so avid for his hobby that he guards the poor captured creatures zealously."

"Is that goin' t' gie us a problem?" Jeannie asked.

Sabelle sighed. "I suppose it could. You see, he keeps the keys to the aviary on his person at all times."

A crafty look entered the Highlander's eyes as she began toweling Sabelle's long hair. "I dinna think that t' be sic a problem, hinny. Jest ye gie me a pair o' guid, braw hairpins and I'll—"

"No, Jeannie," said Sabelle quickly. "I refuse to let you risk your safety in—"

"Ah, hinny, I—"

"No, it's just too dangerous, and you'd be the one taking most of the risk. I won't have it."

"But wha', then, lass? Steal the keys?"

"Exactly."

"And tha' weel no' be dangerous?"

Seating herself by the fire which had been built up to facilitate the drying of her heavy mane of hair, Sabelle gave her friend a long, steady look. "We'll have to arrange things so that it won't be," she said at last. "And there is at least one thing I *can* do: If there's to be any risk-taking, I can at least see that it falls on *my* shoulders—not yours!"

The supper hour that evening found Sabelle arriving downstairs to greet her parents on time, beautifully attired and coiffed. Her gown of pale aquamarine silk was high-waisted in the current fashion; its tiny puffed sleeves in a gauzy fabric dyed to match the silk gave it just enough of a demure touch to counterbalance the sophistication of her coiffure.

The hairdo was one of several she'd been ordered by her mother to try out in private, before her debut a fortnight hence. A mass of shining curls were piled atop her head in Grecian fashion, with numerous tendrils allowed to escape about her face and neck. Altogether, the effect was one of artfully arranged insouciance. Threaded through the main body of curls was a narrow ribbon the exact color of her gown.

When she entered the drawing room where the earl and countess waited, the dialogue that had been in progress between Cecil and Marjorie came to a dead halt. While the elder Corstairs's eyes traveled over the small, slim figure of their daughter as if they'd never seen her before, Sabelle knew that, from the tops of her shining curls to the tips of her aquamarine satin slippers, she had scored a hit.

"My dear child," said Lord Corstairs, being the first to break the silence, "I had no idea . . . How—how very lovely you look!"

"Indeed," said her mother, moving closer to better inspect her offspring's transformation. "Though I had some knowledge of the particulars, I confess I never dreamed how beautiful the finished product would be! Congratulations, my dear," she added as she leaned forward to plant a kiss on her daughter's blushing cheek.

And that was how the evening began. But the real test, the one that was to ascertain the results of crammed instruction by a dancing master Sir Jonathan had hastily hired, came during the supper itself. For it was here that Sabelle's behavior was minutely scrutinized to determine if she was "fit for civilized company": In short, it was to see if she could pass inspection by the *ton*. The Corstairses observed their daughter's every move—from the way she took her father's arm as he led her into the dining hall, to the manner in which she conducted her conversation.

There were times when Sabelle wanted to scream out loud, proclaiming that she was not some prized filly to be set out before them and put through her paces. But she knew that in a way she *was* like a broodmare on parade: The whole purpose of a Season was to show off her assets before the *ton*, with the idea being that she would attract offers of marriage from suitable gentlemen; and marriage was followed by children; and if that wasn't tantamount to being offered for breeding purposes, what was?

So Sabelle held her tongue. And when the long evening at last came to an end, she was rewarded, albeit mildly.

"Well . . . I suppose I shouldn't have expected perfection yet," said her mother somewhat doubtfully.

"Still a bit rough about the edges," her father added, obviously agreeing.

"Hmm," murmured her mother, "true enough, but we still have some time. Thank God I had the foresight to delay the coming out until November! As for now, I shall simply have to make room in my schedule and take her in hand myself. No room for error, you know. The *ton* must have her perfect, or nothing."

"I quite agree, m'dear," said the earl to her mother. "Still, I have complete faith in what you'll be able to do for her."

Finally his eyes drifted to the figure of his daughter, all but forgotten on a settee in the drawing room, where they'd retired after dining. "Have no fear, my girl," he encouraged. "We'll have you up to the mark in time. But you must apply yourself and do as your mother instructs. And you've made an excellent start, hasn't she, Marjorie? She's a real beauty—I'll give her that."

"Of course she's a beauty," said Lady Corstairs, "but now that we've perfected her plumage, our little bird must be taught how to fly properly." She nodded in Sabelle's direction. "Come along, my dear. I'll accompany you to your chambers, and before you retire, I'll set up a list of lessons that we can begin on in the morning."

Sabelle gritted her teeth and followed her mother upstairs, while her father jovially called good night to his "little bird."

But at that moment the only birds Sabelle could bear to think about were the ones in Lord Ormley's aviary—and how she was going to free them!

❖Chapter 8❖

"WEEKS, FOR GOD'S SAKE, AREN'T YOU done with it yet?"

The duke of Haverleigh's valet heaved a sigh as he glanced at the handsome image of his employer in the mirror. "Alas, Your Grace, not quite. But if you'll have the forbearance to hold still for just another moment—Ah! There you are, Your Grace! A perfect 'Mathematical'!"

"Mathematical?" queried the duke irritably; he was close to being out of patience, having had to stand absolutely still for all too many minutes while Weeks perfected the tying of his cravat. It was far more than he'd ever had to suffer for his previous valet, who'd retired, comfortably pensioned by his employer, just last week. But the new man, Joshua Weeks, had been recommended by Carlton House itself. And not wishing to offend his prince-regent, Justin had taken him on; but now he was beginning to wonder if it hadn't been a mistake.

"Indeed, Your Grace," Weeks was saying, "the Mathematical Tie. It is so called because, as you might have observed, it is constructed from a triangle, whose height from chin to neck determines the sharpness of its angles. And, I dare say, Your Grace, the angles we've achieved this evening are very sharp—very sharp, indeed!"

Justin, who'd always been considered impeccably tailored—but in the tradition encouraged by Brummel, whose style was a denial of ostentation, marked chiefly by an ele-

gant simplicity of dress and cleanliness of body and linens—
suddenly had a horrible thought: Was Weeks out to turn
him into a dandy? One of those overdressed, rude, and
disdainful young men whose universe revolved entirely
around the latest word in dress? If so, he'd have none of it,
and Weeks had better learn as much there and now!

"See here, Weeks," he said as the valet held out the coat
of dark blue superfine he'd selected for this evening, "just
how involved are we going to become in this business of
tying arcane cravats? A Mathematical! I never heard of the
bloody thing before!"

"Ahem, ah, indeed, Your Grace," replied the valet, clearing his throat. "But you see, my previous employer, the
marquess of Bradbury, was a stickler for cravats. And so
I've simply been following along those lines, you see. I
know fully one hundred and two versions of the cravat, if
you'll permit me to say so, Your Grace."

"A hundred and two!"

"Indeed, Your Grace. There is, for example, the 'Orien-
tal Tie,' white and of an exceedingly stiff and rigid cloth; or
the 'Napoleon Tie,' violet, with a very lovely appearance,
giving its wearer a languishing, amorous look; and then
there's the 'Mail Coach Tie,' of a single knot, you know,
with—"

"Enough!" cried the duke. "It's sufficient I've had to
submit, this evening, to such folderol—and earn an aching
neck in the bargain! But mark you, my good man, I refuse
to become inveigled into becoming one of those fops who
go preening around St. James's like so many ostriches on
parade. Is that clear?"

"Certainly, Your Grace," said Weeks deferentially, picking up his cue to withdraw when the duke turned his back
on him.

Greatly subdued, the man left the duke's dressing room,
but not before hearing his employer mutter irritably under
his breath, "A hundred and two! Hell's bells! Has the
world gone mad?"

But the door had no sooner closed on the valet than it
opened again, admitting an extremely handsome young

man with dark, brooding eyes and attractive brown ringlets framing his face. With him was Justin's majordomo, who announced, "Lord Byron, Your Grace. Ah, you asked that I show him up as soon as—"

"Yes, yes, thank you, Stewart," said Justin, coming from his dressing room to greet the newcomer. "George! Good to see you! I'd heard you were back in town, but your note this morning was a pleasant surprise, nevertheless. How are you, man?"

The two moved together to shake hands, looking oddly like actors in a rehearsed piece, for each walked with a noticeable limp.

"Truth to tell, my dear Haverleigh," Byron was saying, "I'm more than up for a good dose of licentious living tonight. I've just spent my afternoon at Melbourne House, and while the tea and conversation were excellent, the atmosphere ultimately grew stifling"—he raised his eyebrows pointedly—"if you know what I'm referring to!"

Justin did, indeed, know, as did all of London by now. Viscountess Melbourne, mistress of Melbourne House, ran a fashionable, Whig-oriented social circle there, which included the Regent himself, as well as a large number of distinguished and impressive guests. Visitors loved to gather under Lady Melbourne's roof, for she was a stimulating hostess—handsome, imposing, formidably intelligent, and shrewd in her judgments of people and politics. Her grasp of how the world operated was unparalleled, and a broad variety of her contemporaries turned to her for advice. Chief among them lately was Byron.

But the fly in the ointment was that the company at Melbourne House more often than not these days included Lady Carolyn Lamb, Lady Melbourne's daughter-in-law. Caro had fallen madly in love with Byron following his lionization by the *ton*, when *Childe Harold's Pilgrimage* appeared in March and she had been able to secure an introduction to the young poet.

At first Byron had been receptive to her overtures, for this led him into Lady Melbourne's circle, where the dazzling intellectual exchanges fascinated him. But Caro was a married woman—not that this posed any moral qualms for the author of *Childe Harold*—who didn't appear to know the meaning of discretion, throwing herself at Byron with all the delicacy of a charging elephant. And this *did* irritate her mother-in-law. When it began to suffocate him, it irritated Byron, too.

"I tell you, Justin," the poet was saying, "nothing will make her quit. She has, on some days, sent me *hourly letters!* She has waylaid my coach, then leaned shamelessly in through the window, just to try to get me to talk to her. She has dressed herself in disguises and had herself smuggled into my quarters! She has even taken to waking my friends in the middle of the night, trying to convince them to put in a good word for her with me!"

Reaching for a handkerchief, Byron withdrew it and began mopping his broad brow. "I tell you, the very thought of Caro Lamb makes me break out in sweats! Why can't the chit recognize an end to an affair when she sees one?"

Justin gave him a wry grin. "Because she's still mad for you, George."

"You mean she's mad, period!"

"That, too. But, come, we're giving the baggage far more time than she's worth. Tell me of your work on *The Bride of Abydos* . . . any progress?"

Byron seemed to relax, as he always did when discussing his poetry with his friends. "I think it's finished, though I'll only know when I've laid it by for a spell and then taken it up to examine again. But in the interim, I've begun work on a couple of new pieces. I think I'm going to call one of them *The Corsair*. It's—"

A discreet tapping at the outer door interrupted their conversation, and at Justin's call, Stewart reappeared. "Mr. Percy Shelley awaits below, Your Grace. Shall I—"

"Shelley!" the duke exclaimed. "Now, if this isn't turning out to be poets' corner! Show him up, by all means, Stewart! Show him up!"

"Ah, very good, Your Grace, but I neglected to say that Mr. Long is with him. Shall I—"

"Of course," said the duke, "and send up some brandy."

As the majordomo departed, Justin turned back to Byron. "What kept you out of town for the past week or so, George? Percy just finished another canto of his *Queen Mab,* and it's damned good. He wanted to show it to you."

"I have no doubt it's good," said Byron. "I read the first few cantos. As to being out of town . . . well, let us just say I needed time to put my personal life in order."

"Oh? Is your estate at Newstead Abbey—"

"No, not my estate . . . at least, not directly." The younger man took a moment to adjust his lean frame in the chair where he'd been sitting, then gazed directly at his friend. "You see, Justin, I'm thinking of getting married."

"What?" There was surprise in the duke's voice, but he began to grin. "Why, you sly devil! With all your carrying on about Caro Lamb, I thought you couldn't abide the idea of—"

"Abide what idea?" said a male voice from the doorway. An attractive man in his early twenties strode in, his deepset eyes at once perceptive and intelligent. A step behind was Justin's former tutor, followed by a footman with a silver tray bearing a crystal decanter and four brandy snifters.

"Gentlemen," said the duke, rising from the chair opposite Byron, "you're just in time to, ah . . ."—he paused, eyeing Long's melancholy face—". . . either celebrate or mourn. M'lord, here," he added, indicating Byron, "has just told me he's thinking of getting *wed!*"

There was silence as the new arrivals froze, looks of disbelief on their faces.

Then the sounds of the footman setting down the tray and taking his leave broke the tableau, and Shelley moved forward to peer into Byron's face in exaggerated fashion.

"Egad!" Shelley exclaimed. "He doesn't *look* ill . . . I say, Long, do you think it could be the start of a fever?" He made a grand show of pacing back and forth before his fellow poet, examining him with careful, comic scrutiny. "Something he picked up in his tour of the East a couple of years ago? Has it lain dormant all this—"

"George, *no!*" interrupted Thomas, clearly not the least

bit amused by Shelley's antics. *"You,* of all people—you cannot *mean* it!"

"Ah, but I can," said Byron soberly as he accepted a brandy from their host.

"Can? Or *must?"* queried Justin. He was the only other titled aristocrat in the room and therefore felt he knew a little more about these things, especially as they affected noblemen.

Byron sighed. "A bit of each, I'm afraid. Annabelle Milbank is an—"

"Milbank!" Justin exclaimed. "Isn't she that overly serious bluestocking I met at Melbourne House? The one who came into town to attend lectures on mnemonics and geology?"

"And poetry," Byron added, nodding his head. "The same."

"Oh, George . . ." Justin closed his eyes and wearily shook his head. "Not *that* one, please. She's a humorless, straitlaced—"

"She's also an *heiress,"* countered Byron, "and in case you weren't aware of it, my mother's death last year left me with an estate mortgaged to the hilt. I *must* have an heiress, don't you see?" He grabbed the snifter his friend carried to him and dashed its contents down in a single gulp, while Long's and Shelley's protests began to ring about the room.

"It'll be a disaster!" cried Shelley.

"Marriage is a *curse,"* affirmed Long.

"She'll hamstring you domestically," Shelley added. "And loss of personal freedom can only curtail intellectual freedom."

"You cannot love her," moaned Long, "and even if you did, the marriage would kill it!"

"She'll censor your every move," Shelly told him, "and then your spirit will slowly wither—"

"And die," added Long.

"Hold a minute!"

The commanding voice was Justin's, and the chamber

fell immediately silent as the three gave him their undivided attention.

"Aren't we all forgetting something, here?" the duke asked quietly. "It's George's life, and if he wishes to make a major decision in it—mistake or no—that is his *right*. Who are we to sit in judgment?"

There was another moment of silence; then Shelley said softly, "You're right, of course. But we wouldn't be his friends if we didn't give him some advice we thought might benefit him. I mean—"

"You mean as *you* took *my* advice just last year when I cautioned you against eloping with Harriet Westbrook?" Justin asked gently.

Shelley had the grace to blush. They all knew that not only had Percy's disastrous elopement with the draper's daughter estranged him from his socially prominent family, but the marriage also hadn't worked. At this very time, Shelly's wife remained shut up at home while her husband openly flaunted his relationship with his new mistress, Mary Wollstonecraft Godwin, daughter of the political philosopher William Godwin.

"Forgive me for that, man," said Justin quietly. "But I only wished to point out that sometimes we must make choices which are not really our own to make—or perhaps the reverse: choices which *are* ours to make, which force us into *mistakes we might learn from*. I suspect the latter was yours," he went on to Shelley. He turned to Byron. "While the former comprises George's, here . . ."—his words drifted off before he added softly—". . . and perhaps my own."

"Your own what?" snapped Thomas, instantly alerted.

Justin threw them all a sardonic smile. "Why, my own choice to take a wife soon, Thomas."

"Whaaat?" Thomas grew pale with his reaction, and the room immediately broke out into a hubbub once more. Justin finally succeeded in calming them, casting Byron a sympathetic smile as he spoke.

"However much you social radicals might not like it, men like Byron and myself find ourselves placed under certain restraints not of concern to ordinary men. Like it or not, we were bred to accept certain responsibilities, and, in case I had forgotten, my solicitors saw fit to remind me of them just the other day."

"Of the bloody need to produce an heir, you mean!" Long interrupted morosely.

"Indeed," said Justin, "and before you get on your high horse and tell me to forget providing my family with an heir, let me say, Thomas, it is not so simple. You see," he went on, "my solicitors came to inform me that my cousin Wilbur Hart has not only wed, but that his bride is already breeding! And I needn't tell any of you what that could mean. Wilbur is an unvarnished idiot—a fool in men's clothing! Were something to happen to me before—Ah, hell!" he added vehemently. "I'm sorry, my friends, but the lifetime of work and energy I've put into this family means too much to me to throw it all away on a fool like my cousin. Why, that incompetent ass would ruin the dukedom in no time—and I *cannot* allow that to happen."

"But, Justin," said Byron with a hint of sympathy in his eyes, "surely there's no need for haste. You're a young man yet, and—"

"And these are uncertain times we live in, my friend. I had dinner at Carlton House last night. And do you know what we discussed? Nothing less than Boney's retreat from Moscow, and how the allies ought to be prepared to double their efforts, now that he's been routed."

He glanced down at his injured leg a moment, then back at all three. "I do not deem it inconceivable, despite my injury, which is healing, you know, that I could be called to fight again in the event that a major offensive is launched."

He looked each of them carefully in the eye before setting down his untouched brandy and continuing. "Therefore, I have promised Lady Strathmore that I shall go to the altar with the first agreeable face whose lineage is acceptable, get her with child, and so do my duty."

There was another silence in the room as his friends' faces reflected a variety of reactions: In Byron's, there was a mixture of sadness and respect; in Shelley's, sympathy, if not agreement; in Long's there was clearly shock and anger, and he gave voice to it.

"Justin, are you mad? Have you forgotten all I've— Christ, man, do you not remember the 'Marriage Hearse'?"

Justin looked annoyed. "Of course, I remember, but what I am asking all of you to do is to summon enough . . . kindness, perhaps, to help me *forget! I have no choice, Thomas!* Don't you see?"

"But what of *love?*" cried the tutor. "Justin, surely you cannot think to live your life without love!"

At this there was a wild burst of rueful laughter from Shelley.

"To love," said Shelley, as he raised his brandy in a toast. "His Grace will do as I do—find it outside that cursed institution they call marriage!"

❖Chapter 9❖

FOR SEVERAL WEEKS FOLLOWING THE PRIvate supper with her parents, Sabelle endured a seemingly endless series of lectures from her mother. Tedious and repetitious, they all centered around etiquette and manners and, sometimes, Court protocol; in short, they were a crash course in the behavior becoming to a daughter of the aristocracy and, in particular, one who was about to be formally presented to the *ton*.

Notwithstanding the fact that she had scarcely paid any attention at all to Sabelle while she was growing up, Marjorie Corstairs was relentless in these efforts, for nothing would serve but that her daughter get it perfect. She would arrive in Sabelle's chambers each morning, on the heels of a maid bringing a breakfast tray, and rarely leave her daughter's side until long after the supper hour; then the lamps and candelabra where she chose to wind up those lessons would burn late into the night.

Sabelle endured this with as much good grace as she could muster, focusing her inner thoughts on the one thing that made it all bearable: her latest rescue mission. Because of Sabelle's tight schedule, the task of organizing a plan to deliver Lord Ormley's birds from captivity fell to her grandfather. Sir Jonathan's London town house on Grosvenor Square was only a few blocks away. Using his knowledge of people and places in the city—yes, he'd been away from it for some time, but Sir Jonathan retained a number of key friends in high places—the old man had gathered much information on the goings-on and whereabouts of the earl of Larchmont. He'd learned his habits, his daily routines, the places he frequented, and the like, and passed this on to Sabelle through Michael Kelly and Jeannie MacDougal.

But as to putting a plan into action, Sir Jonathan felt that he was too old to be gadding about at night in disguise; that, he said, was best left to the young people. The actual rescue, therefore, would in all likelihood need to wait until after Sabelle's coming-out ball in early November. They'd just have to be patient.

But as Sir Jonathan should have recalled, patience hadn't always been one of Sabelle's strong suits. By early October she felt their little group had all the information required to set a trap for the earl, steal his keys, and free those poor birds. Reports from a pair of footmen she and Jeannie had hired to spy on the earl at his town house and about town had convinced her they had all his movements down pat. Now all their plan wanted was a free evening for Sabelle to lead the others into action.

But that was the problem. With the impossible schedule her mother had set, she didn't have any free evenings. And then, just as she was trying to inveigle one somehow, word came that Ormley had been called out of the city on some matter regarding his country estate. Frustrated beyond telling, Sabelle gathered her fast-fading patience and settled down to await his return.

Then, just a few days before her coming-out ball, in a rare moment when Sabelle found herself alone in her chambers, Jeannie came bursting into her sitting room with good news.

"Ormley's back!" said the Highlander.

Sabelle cast aside the issue of *The Spectator* she'd been reading and leaped out of her chair with such speed that Jeannie half believed she meant to initiate the rescue then and there.

"Thank heaven!" exclaimed Sabelle. "I was beginning to believe he'd never return, but now—Ah, Jeannie, the timing couldn't be better!"

Jeannie looked doubtful. "Better? But, lass, yer ball's a scarce three days awie, and wha' wie yer mam's—"

"Jeannie," interrupted Sabelle, "do you know what tomorrow is?"

The taller girl paused a moment, looking pensive. "Aye, 'tis the fifth o' November."

"Exactly! The fifth of November," came the grinning reply. "It's Guy Fawkes Day, you goose! And do you know what that means?"

Jeannie may have been born in a humble Highland croft, but she knew of the holiday celebrating the anniversary of what was called the Gunpowder Plot. After all, the unsuccessful plot had been conceived of not only to blow up Parliament, but also to kill King James I, and King James had been a *Scot!*"

"Certainly, I ken," she said. "It means there will be fireworks and high jinks and masqueradin' in the streets. The whole city will be celebratin'!"

"Right," said Sabelle, "and thereby provide us with a perfect cover for our . . . ah . . . activities. Even our disguises will work better. No one will think us anything but revelers abroad in the city!"

"True," said Jeannie, "but will yer mam—"

"Oh, she'll *have* to let me out, Jeannie! Even she cannot protest if I get Grandfather to work on her and we promise that I'll have you and Michael along as protective escorts. And if she balks, I'll remind her of how diligent I've been in my lessons, but that I simply *must* have a few hours of recreation!"

"Perhaps," said the Scotswoman, always the more cautious of the two, "but wha' o' yer plan t' rescue those puir, wee-feathered beasties? We've had nae time t' talk these past weeks. Is't all thought out, guid and proper?"

"It is," said her friend excitedly. She gestured for Jeannie to sit down beside her. "Now, listen closely, Jeannie," she whispered, "for here's what we must do. . . ."

And Jeannie did listen closely, to a plan that involved waiting for Ormley outside his favorite club, which he visited every day at exactly the same time, and then waylaying him (or, rather, Michael Kelly would, for the big Irishman had the strength and the knowledge to do this without really harming the earl physically) and stealing his keys. Then it would be a simple matter, Sabelle told her, of rushing to Ormley's town house and using those keys to free the birds before anyone was the wiser.

"So," said Sabelle as she finished explaining, "what do you think? I know there are a few risks, but none worse than the likes of which we've dealt with before. Do you think—"

Jeannie was shaking her head worriedly. "What is it?" Sabelle whispered. "I thought—"

"I almost fergot t' tell ye, lass, wha' wie yer daft schedule and all. Our spies had a wee bit o' extra information t' impart t' Michael a few days past, and 'tis somethin' I expect cuid change the, ah, complection o' matters."

"What? *Tell* me, for heaven's sake!"

Jeannie took a deep breath. "Guess who's also been seen comin' and goin' at Brooks's at aboot the same hour as Ormley."

"Who?" Sabelle's tone was anxious, yet she couldn't imagine the identity of anyone who could cause such a note of trepidation in Jeannie's voice.

"His Grace, the duke o' Haverleigh, *that's who!*"

"*Oh, no . . .*" breathed Sabelle.

"Aye," said her friend sympathetically, for Jeannie had been privy to the events involving Sabelle's unfortunate run-in with the arrogant duke the day of the hunt. In fact, Jeannie, as her friend and confidante, was the *only* one she'd told about *all* the details of that wretched encounter.

"Damn," murmured Sabelle, *"of all people!* You know I swore to myself I'd never knowingly place myself within sight of that overbearing, odious man again."

"I do," said her friend, still sympathetic.

"But, Jeannie, you know how everything about Ormley's habits points to Brooks's. It's the only place he frequents with complete regularity, never missing a visit unless he's ill or out of town. Why, his visits to his club can be *depended* upon—like clockwork!"

"Aye, but accordin' t' those footmen, the *duke* goes t' Brooks's quite often, too—though no' sae regularly as Ormley."

Sabelle nodded, digesting what she'd learned as she sat quietly for a moment, her eyes focused on her hands as they lay in her lap. At last she raised her eyes to meet Jeannie's, and they were filled with the pure determination and intensity of purpose that accompanied every venture the girls had participated in so far.

"We're going," said Sabelle. "And I won't pretend to you that I'm dismissing the risks. Haverleigh knows me on sight, and I—I cannot deny the man makes me . . . uncomfortable—" She saw Jeannie's raised eyebrows. "All right—he *frightens* me s-somewhat. But, Jeannie," she went on, "whoever said our efforts would always be easy? Or safe? If we'd worried about that, I doubt we'd have accomplished half of what we have. Very well, so there are risks. That simply means we must take extra pains to be careful . . . or perhaps to muster up a bit of extra courage . . . ? Yes, that's it . . . extra care and a bit of courage and we'll be fine . . . you'll see!"

Jeannie nodded, but cautiously; her thoughts, she felt, were best kept to herself. Because for some odd reason, a half-forgotten line of poetry from a fellow Scot came tumbling into her brain . . . something about the best-laid plans of mice and men . . .

The following day, Guy Fawkes Day, 1812, dawned cloudy and exceptionally warm for that time of year, but by late afternoon a brisk breeze had swept in from the northwest, clearing away the clouds and even a great deal of the smudgy air that had hung over the city like a shroud. The thoroughfares and lanes of London, from the widest avenues to the narrowest alleyways, quickly filled with holiday revelers, common folk and gentry alike. As evening set in, fireworks exploded and lit the sky, and celebrants wearing masks and exotic costumes thronged the streets, taking full advantage of the improved weather.

But there were three people in that vast throng who were

taking advantage of the crowds, as well as the weather. Seeming to celebrate on the street facing Brooks's exclusive club were what appeared to be a procurer and his two "ladies of the evening"; it wasn't entirely clear, however, even though all three wore demimasks, whether their attire marked them as costumed revelers or true lowlifes.

In fact, they were neither. The tall, scowling man in a long black cloak with a turban on his head was none other than Michael Kelly, and the reason for the scowl was his obvious dissatisfaction with the choice of costumes of his female companions—Sabelle Corstairs and Jeannie Mac-Dougal. According to Kelly, the nature of the garb Sabelle had managed to put together from bits and pieces of clothing found in trunks in her mother's attic was indecent. "Imagine the shame of it—two fine lasses like yerselves dressin' like common—common . . ."

" 'Doxies,' I believe, is the word you seem to have trouble uttering, Michael," Sabelle had said with a grin; but the big man had refused to see the humor in it and scowled all the harder. So now Sabelle decided to distract him by sending him on a brief errand; she asked him to buy them some sausage rolls from a vendor hawking his wares a short distance away.

Kelly agreed to go, but not before cautioning the two young women to "stay right where ye are and avoid blatherin' t' strangers!" Then, with a final scowl, he went off.

Their disguises might have been indelicate, but Sabelle felt they were also secure, for she'd taken great pains to make them concealing, especially her own. Her hair, which she and Jeannie had hennaed, was piled high on her head in a reddish mass and then artfully decorated with three purple ostrich plumes. Kohl had been used to rim her eyes beneath the mask, and her cheeks and lips were heavily rouged.

Sabelle also wore a cloak, in this case a long satin opera cape. Lady Corstairs had worn it once several years before and then relegated it to the attic for being "too extreme in color"; it, too, was purple. Under the cloak was a lavender

evening gown that hadn't always had such a deep, low décolletage—at least not when the countess had worn it. But
Sabelle and Jeannie had gone to work on the neckline with
scissors, needle, and thread. As Sabelle had said, "Who will
ever believe a streetwalker is what she is if she doesn't show
off her wares?"

Jeannie had followed her example, taking scissors to her
own borrowed costume of bright royal blue silk; but she
had made Sabelle promise they'd conceal their immodest
necklines with their cloaks, not only for decency's sake, but
because Michael would never agree to escort them if he saw
that facet of their disguises!

And so they settled down to wait, though after Michael's
departure, it was up to Jeannie to keep her eyes trained on
Brooks's door with the pair of liveried footmen flanking it.
Of the three, only Sabelle had never set eyes on the earl and
couldn't have known what he looked like, despite the de-
scriptions she'd been given.

Minutes passed, and various well-dressed gentlemen
were seen entering and leaving Brooks's, but none the
young Scotswoman recognized. Then, just as Kelly was approaching with their sausage rolls, Sabelle heard Jeannie
gasp.

"Ach!" exclaimed the Highlander. "If tha' isna the bon-
niest mon I've ever set me een on, me name's not
MacDougal! Ach! But he's a bonnie, braw stallion!"

"Who?" queried Sabelle, scanning the crowd.

"Why, the mon who's just coomin' oot o' Br——Ach! I
dinna believe it! 'Tis *Ormley* wie 'im!"

Sabelle turned and saw a fat, corseted man, who *had* to
be described as chinless, emerging from Brooks's. But then
her gaze was drawn to the tall figure with him, and her
breath caught in her throat. The handsome man with Ormley—the one Jeannie had been exclaiming over—*was none
other than the duke of Haverleigh!*

Robert Ormley couldn't believe his good fortune: The
duke of Haverleigh had actually approached him as he was
about to leave the club and suggested they take a stroll

together! He could scarcely believe it—the elusive Justin Hart, the most sought-after Corinthian of the *ton* (aside from the Regent, of course).

Ormley was well aware that Hart had never done more than offer him the slightest of nods before now, even though they had been schoolmates at Oxford (where Hart had excelled, and Ormley barely made it through; but the earl wasn't allowing himself to think about that right now). At Oxford the tall, handsome son of one of the most powerful dukes in the realm had eschewed the company of all but a small, select group of intimates—poets and scholars, mainly.

Flushing with his sudden and unexpected success in drawing the duke's attentions, Ormley never paused to consider *why* the fabulous Hart was all at once deigning to spend time with him. Like all dull and stupid creatures puffed up with a false sense of worth, the earl of Larchmont foolishly assumed his companion had finally seen the light —that he'd somehow become aware of what he'd been missing out on all these years and had come to Ormley for a bit of stimulating companionship.

And Robert was not about to disappoint him, for certainly he could guess what kind of sport might entertain His Grace. After all, wasn't he called Hart the Heartless? And didn't that imply a vast, yet impersonal, indulgence in the female sex?

Clearing his throat importantly, the earl left off his commenting about the fine weather and the gaiety of the crowd of celebrants they passed. He placed a hand on Justin's excellently tailored sleeve and indicated they should halt a moment.

"See here, Haverleigh," he said with more familiarity than he'd ever have dared before, "enough of this small talk. The whole town's out for some fun and excitement tonight, so why should we be any different, eh?"

He paused and arranged his features into something approximating a leer as his eyes scanned the passersby, several women in particular.

Then, his voice lowered suggestively, and he threw Justin

an arch look. "I know of a tavern a distance from here, Your Grace, where a bit of privacy may be found in the upper chambers. And there's an enterprising waiter there with a good eye for . . . ah . . . a certain kind of companion. What say you? Up for some sport?"

Justin had to restrain himself from pulling away as he felt Ormley's hand on his sleeve. God, but the man was repulsive! Not only did his breath reek of garlic—or was it onions tonight?—but the earl of Larchmont stood for everything he hated about the *ton*. Vain, weak, and intellectually dense, Ormley was as foolish and unappealing internally as he appeared externally, with his flabby, corseted physique and bland, colorless features.

And look what the vapid fop had suggested! Justin almost laughed into his chinless face. Go all the way to the Shakespeare's Head to pick up a pair of trollops? Didn't Ormley realize he had several blatant invitations for trysts lying on his desk at home at this very minute? From beautiful Cyprians of the first water, married and unmarried? What need for amorous sport in a tavern, where the sheets weren't always clean, and neither were the whores?

But in less than the second it took to consider it, Justin dismissed all this, screwing himself to his purpose. After all, he hadn't pursued Ormley tonight for ordinary reasons; he'd attached himself to the fat dolt because Ormley's best friend, he'd learned, was none other than his sniveling, weak-livered cousin Wilbur Hart. And Justin intended to milk Ormley of all the information he could glean about his cousin—just in case he should ever need it to do battle, legal or otherwise—to save the dukedom from that impossible would-be heir.

So Justin forced himself to smile and nod ingratiatingly to the earl. "Why, Ormley, you amaze me!" he said. "Wouldn't you know you'd be suggesting just the thing!"

The earl's flaccid jowls hung in loose curves about a wide, lascivious smile, and he preened under the duke's approving scrutiny.

"To the Shakespeare's Head, then, Your Grace?"

"Indeed, m'lord," came the response, as Justin indicated

they should resume walking, "and, by the way, didn't I once hear that my cousin Wilbur frequents the Shakespeare's Head . . . ?"

Ned Bates stuffed the gold coins he'd just been tossed into a leather pouch he kept tied to a thong about his neck, hidden under his shirt. Two quid! It was more than he'd made last month, and he'd had to come up with more than a dozen doxies to do that!

The tavern waiter hurried down the stairs to the Shakespeare's common room, keeping an eye out for old Parker. He knew his employer was aware he and a couple of the others took a bit on the side to supplement their meager wages, though he pretended not to; but the tavernkeeper was in a foul mood tonight, what with the holiday crowds getting rowdy, and it wouldn't do to flaunt his little errand for that pair of toffs upstairs and earn Parker's displeasure.

Bates worked his way unobtrusively through the crowded common room, emerging at last into the crisp air and jostling crowds that thronged Covent Garden. His sharp eyes scanned the milling celebrants, knowing just what they sought. It shouldn't take too long, he thought, as his glance fell on one, and then another, painted face, before rejecting them as too coarse or grimy and moving on. "A pair of clean whores—and comely," the fat toff had whispered, "and if what you produce pleases me and my friend, here, there'll be another coin or two for you when we're finished."

Bates grinned to himself, remembering. Why, he might even come by another whole quid, if he was lucky. That lard bucket must be swelling his breeches with more than the coin he had in their pockets, he was so eager!

A brief frown puckered the waiter's brow as he recalled the man's tall companion. Now, he wondered, why would that one need to be spending such sums on some street doxy? With looks like his, you'd think the sluts would be offering it to him for *free*. And fancy pieces, too, not just—

Suddenly Bates's gaze stopped moving, fixing on a pair beneath one of the gaslights that had been introduced into the city a few years before. Eyes narrowed, he studied the two women, the tall one in the blue, and the slender little thing in the purple. Even at this distance he could see they were lookers, despite those half-masks. But it was their clothing that settled the waiter on this pair of streetwalkers. Quality, it was, or his name wasn't Ned Bates. And, from his years of experience at this business, he knew that a bird who took the blunt and the trouble to sport quality feathers was a tart who could probably satisfy the likes of those toffs upstairs.

He headed for the two women.

Several minutes later, Sabelle's heart was thumping so hard that she felt it was about to leap out of her chest as she followed the man from the tavern. Glancing about to make sure Jeannie was behind her, she almost quit and gave up the whole plot, then and there.

Jeannie looked terrified. And Sabelle *was* terrified. After all, as they'd stood across the street from the tavern and debated with Michael what to do after they'd seen Ormley and the duke enter, she'd never dreamed this man would approach and present them with the very opportunity they'd needed.

At least *she'd* seen it as their opportunity. Michael Kelly had been horrified at the thought of the women actually entering a common tavern, pretending to be streetwalkers. But that was what this man—this waiter—had been summoned to fetch. And that he'd been sent by Ormley, there'd been no doubt, for he'd described the fat earl, right down to the nonexistent chin!

She'd almost had to give up the idea in the wake of the big Irishman's incalcitrance. There'd been some fast and furious whispered exchanges between herself and the big man the waiter took for their procurer. The one from the Shakespeare's Head had stood off, impatiently, to one side during all this, pointedly murmuring, "Two foin toffs that look t' 'ave a right bit o' the blunt, me dearies!" and Michael had scowled and argued all the more.

But Sabelle had been nothing if not determined, and at

last poor Michael had agreed, pressing into Jeannie's hand a vial of laudanum he'd brought along, should they have needed help in subduing Ormley when he was waylaid. Michael passed it to her with the whispered instructions that she was to use it at the first opportunity to "spike me lords' drinks, and then relieve Ormley of his damned keys and return as quickly as ye may." He'd also added, his scowl blacker than they'd ever seen it, that he was giving the vial to the quavering Jeannie because it was becoming plain which of the two young women had greater common sense. "Here, lass," he'd whispered fiercely, "see that yer headstrong young mistress uses it t' render those two Sassenachs senseless!"

Now, as Sabelle hurried after the waiter leading them up the stairs from the noisy common room, she wondered if she oughtn't to have listened to Michael. Pretending to be something she had no knowledge of was bad enough—a far cry from the simple pretense of being a "climbing boy," as sweeps were often called. But pretending to be a streetwalker, a creature as alien to her as a Turk, and doing it before *the duke of Haverleigh*? It was madness! What had she gotten them into?

But a few moments later there was no more time to consider her folly; the waiter had tapped discreetly at one of several closed doors leading to chambers along the upstairs hallway, and at the command to enter, he had opened it and unceremoniously shoved the two women inside.

" 'Ere ye be, govs," Bates announced pertly from behind them, "a pair o' real lookers, an' clean, too, jest like ye tol' me. Ain't a bad smell or a smidge o' dirt betwixt 'em!"

Sabelle froze beside Jeannie, just inside the door. The chamber they'd entered was dark, despite the glow given off by a brass candelabrum on a rough oak table at its center and the light from the brightly burning fire. She tried to be calm and tell herself this was good, for the darker the chamber, the greater the chance their disguises wouldn't be seen through.

But, try as she might, she couldn't quell the pulse that was fluttering at her throat like one of Ormley's caged

birds; her eyes were drawn to the wide bunk at one end of
the room and the man who lounged carelessly across it, his
broad shoulders propped against the wall behind, his
booted feet crossed negligently before him as he sipped a
dark-colored liquid from a tumbler.

The duke of Haverleigh's eyes were hooded, his handsome features revealing nothing beyond, perhaps, a hint of
boredom as he allowed the earl to do all the talking. It was
Ormley who was ushering the women into the room, offering them each a glass of wine. Still, Sabelle had the distinct
impression that the duke missed not a jot of what was going on. Moreover, though she couldn't have proved it, she
was certain the chief object of his attention was herself.

Oh, but you're being silly, my girl! she scolded herself
silently as Ormley drew out a chair for her at the table and
then did the same for Jeannie. *Your disguise is excellent, so
it's certain he cannot recognize you. What other reason could
he have for singling you out? None! You're imagining things,
Sabelle Corstairs, because you're nervous, and you'd better
start mustering your courage, or you'll give the game away
altogether!*

But Sabelle was not imagining things when she thought
Justin Hart had been focusing on her. He was, though not
because he thought he recognized the petite, finely boned
figure of the young prostitute.

It was because, having braced himself to endure Ormley's distasteful notion of an evening's sport, he was utterly
unprepared for the delicate beauty of the smaller of the two
women the waiter had procured. That she was exquisite
was obvious, even beneath the demi-mask she wore. Her
finely contoured cheekbones and small, perfectly turned little nose were delightfully in evidence, as was a lush pair of
lips that seemed ripe for kissing, even if they did bear more
paint than was to his liking. And her hair, reddish gold in
the candlelight, was thick and luxuriant, a heavy mass of
shining curls that testified to the fact that the servingman
had been right: This was one whore who took pains to keep
herself clean.

Smiling to himself, Justin settled back against the cushions lining the bunk and decided the evening wasn't going to be such a bore after all.

"Ah, but you must allow me to take your cloaks, m'dears," Ormley was saying; a stiff and frightened Jeannie had thrust her hands to the clasp of her blue cape when the earl tried to relieve her of it. "It's far too warm in here for such apparel . . . and besides, you cannot expect my friend and me to take you on without having a good look now, can you?"

Jeannie had the presence of mind to divert her tenseness into a nervous giggle which caused the earl to smile and press her to drink more of the wine he'd poured.

"Come, come, don't be shy," said Ormley. Out of the corner of his eye he saw the duke stretch lazily and then rise to approach the girl in purple. So Hart had made his choice, had he? Well, no matter. The littler whore had the look of a real beauty about her, but this one wasn't half bad. And if he made a point of leaving Hart the tastier dish, who knew but that the duke wouldn't thank him for it later —and remember him fondly, should a favor ever be needed?

"And look there," Ormley added to Jeannie, "my friend has gotten *his* little companion to doff *her* cloak."

And, to Sabelle's utter dismay, so he had. And she hadn't even realized how he'd done it! One moment she'd been standing there, mesmerized at the sight of him and telling herself to be brave; and the next, she'd seen the duke approach with a lazy, half-formed smile, only to discover, a scarce second later, that her clasp had been undone, sending the purple cape sliding to the floor!

A soft gasp escaped her lips as she realized what had happened. Then, before she could raise her hands in an instinctive move to cover her daring décolletage, he had caught both of them in his own and held them gently, but firmly, to her sides while he gazed at her half-exposed breasts. And then, still with that lazy smile, he looked straight into her eyes behind the mask, murmuring, "Lovely . . . very lovely . . ."

Sabelle felt her face go hot with shame under his brief

but thorough perusal, and she stammered, saying the first thing to come into her head.

"I—I do not—do not wish to take a ch-chill, m'lord."

Justin's brows raised doubtfully at this, for it was warm in the room, what with the fire burning so well; but then a smug smile curved that handsome mouth, prompting Sabelle to grow more apprehensive as she wondered what it meant.

"Nervous, my dove?" he questioned in a voice that seemed huskier than she remembered. He released her hands and raised one of his to adjust an errant tendril of hair which curled above one of her delicate, shell shaped ears.

"Well, no matter," he went on as his glance moved, from the frightened eyes he'd been studying behind her mask, to the door. "I find I'm beginning to feel a bit, ah, uncomfortable with the air in this chamber myself."

And then, in a matter of minutes, and before Sabelle even realized what was happening, he had summoned the waiter and whisked her out of the chamber and into the one next door. Sabelle at last tried to voice a protest when she saw what he was about, but to no avail. Trying to deter Justin Hart from a purpose, she realized, was like trying to keep a runaway coach from charging down a steep hill!

The waiter left them with a knowing wink before he closed the door, and Sabelle was close to frantic. She was alone in a private chamber with the arrogant, perhaps dangerous, duke of Haverleigh. And more, Jeannie was still in that other room, and with her was the vial of laudanum!

❖Chapter 10❖

JUSTIN GAZED AT THE LOVELY APPARITION IN the lavender gown and felt his desire grow, despite his resolution to take things slowly. He'd at first been surprised by the fear in her eyes when he approached her in the other chamber, hardly expecting it in one of her profession. But then he'd quickly calculated, from the evidence presented, that she was fairly young and likely to be new to her craft. He'd surmised that she was probably encountering her first clients from the upper class, and assumed this added to her apprehensions; but then he had heard her speak—and was astounded to learn her accent was on a level with his and Ormley's!

Intrigued, he'd resolved to get her away from that ass Ormley, and put her at ease; and he thought, too, of perhaps getting to know her background a bit in the process, before availing himself of her considerable charms. And there, as well, he'd had some surprises. Who'd have thought that one so delicate and fragile-looking would possess such ripe, lush breasts? Or such a length of long, shapely thigh, evident beneath her gown's thin folds as she moved?

Hell! he thought as he watched her take a nervous sip of wine. *Even with that ridiculous little mask covering half her face, she's stunning!*

Smiling at this assessment, Justin loosened his cravat as he walked toward her, brandy in hand.

Sabelle took a quick step backward, almost spilling her wine. The duke laughed.

"Why so skittish, sweet? I don't bite, you know." Justin's cravat went the way of his coat, which he'd tossed on a chair flanking the oak table similar to the one in the other chamber.

"Tell me," he said when he'd come within an arm's length of her. He reached out with strong, sun-browned fingers to raise her chin. "What's your name, lovely?"

Sabelle felt a shiver course along her spine at the warmth of his fingers and almost blurted out the truth. "Sa—— Samantha," she managed to fabricate just in time.

"Samantha . . ." Justin murmured approvingly. "An exotic name for a very exotic-looking . . . lady . . ."

With each slowly intoned word, he took his hand and relieved her of one of the silly-looking purple plumes pinned to her coiffure, adding, "But I hardly credit these with creating that allure, m'dear, so let's be rid of them, shall we? Your hair is far too lovely to be hidden beneath such nonsense."

Nonsense? thought Sabelle in a sudden burst of panic. *He's stripping away my disguise!*

"My—my lord," she said, as she moved out of his reach when the last plume had fallen to the floor, "I—I seem to have f-finished my wine. May I—may I please have some more?"

Justin flashed her a grin, recognizing a stalling for time when he saw it, but then he shrugged and turned to the wine bottle the man had left. Why not humor her? he thought. He was, after all, in no particular hurry. And his vast experience with women told him that the longer he took with this seduction—was he really seducing a *whore?*— the greater the pleasure would be, for both of them.

Sabelle watched tensely as he finished his own drink, then poured a fresh one for each of them—hers from the wine bottle, his from a heavy glass decanter that had been left behind by the waiter. What on earth was she to do? What was *Jeannie* doing at this minute? Had she used the laudanum on Ormley yet? The only hope Sabelle had was for Jeannie to accomplish her task and then somehow come to this chamber and invent an excuse to rescue her before— before—

"Here you are, little one," said the duke, as he handed her the wine, "but sip it slowly this time, sweet. We wouldn't want the grape dulling our, ah, performance."

Performance? thought Sabelle. *Is that what he calls it when a man and woman—Good God! What am I thinking?*

"Ah, no, m'lord," she said to him. "It's just that I—*my lord!* What are you—?"

All her thoughts were arrested as Sabelle felt, rather than saw, him remove the glass from her hand. After she'd taken only a sip, he set it down on the table along with his own, and pulled her suddenly into his arms. Mesmerized, she made no move to resist as Justin Hart's dark, handsome head lowered and his mouth came down on hers in a demanding, utterly thorough kiss.

Totally unprepared for this, Sabelle was like a piece of putty in the strong arms that wrapped around her, molding her softness to his hard, muscular frame. With a strange sense of otherworldliness, almost as if she were standing outside herself, she noted that his lips were firm, but not really hard, as they moved over hers, forming them, making them into a shape that was right for his own. And then there was the sensation of his hands, expert hands she somehow realized, that knew just where to stroke, just how to move, along the soft curve of her shoulder, down along her spine. . . .

And then, just as she was wondering what he intended to do now that he'd gently forced her lips apart and his tongue was teasing their soft, inner recesses, now that she felt it grazing her teeth, he released her, though not completely. He still held her loosely within the circle of his arms, and she heard him let out his breath with a long, quivery sound that almost seemed a shudder.

"Samantha . . ." he whispered in a voice that had definitely grown hoarser, and then to her horror, she saw he was reaching up *to remove her mask!*

Knowing that she could not let that happen, Sabelle did

the only thing she could think of to stop him: She threw her arms about his neck and drew his face down to meet hers in what was to become their second thorough kiss in as many minutes.

Why, the little vixen! Justin thought with pleasure as Samantha surprised him yet again. *Just when she has me thinking she's new to the game, and that I must take special pains to coax her, she turns the tables on me! What an unexpected, delightful creature she is!*

This time, as his tongue probed and succeeded in gaining entrance to her mouth, as he breathed in the clean, sweet smell of her, Justin found himself wishing, oddly, that she were not a whore—or at least not a common streetwalker. Surely, he thought, with such luscious charms as these, with the looks and speech of a lady, though indeed she was something else, she could manage to find herself a better situation . . . for instance, a privately held set of discreet lodgings where only a single gentleman availed himself of her.

Tucking these thoughts away for future consideration, he turned his concentration to their embrace. He explored her mouth, and then her lips, with light little nibblings, while one hand moved unerringly to her breasts. And he smiled as he had the pleasure of feeling her shudder when his hand freed them from that barely existent bodice. And when he made bold with the delicate little peaks, he knew an instant satisfaction when he felt them hardening beneath his caresses.

Sabelle was regretting her impulsive method of forestalling the removal of her mask. She could hardly credit what was happening to her. Why was there a shiver running through her body when the room was almost too warm? And why did her head seem to spin and her stomach grow giddy when his teeth nibbled her lips that way? And why—

Oh, God! she thought, as she suddenly realized where his hand was straying. And then, all at once, there was no thought at all as mind gave way to sensation. She couldn't even collect in her brain the unthinkable thought that the odious duke of Haverleigh had pulled down her bodice to expose her bare breasts. That he was freely cupping them and stroking them, his thumbs brushing their nipples. All she knew was the pure rush of pleasure that sluiced through her body, coursing straight from the tingling tips of her breasts to that secret woman's place at the core of her.

Dimly, she heard an animal, moaning sound, and when the duke murmured husky approval, she realized that it had come from her own throat! Dimly, too, she realized that he had now picked her up and was depositing her on the wide, cushioned bunk near the fire.

And then his hands and mouth were everywhere—*everywhere!* Again and again, he pressed his lips to sensitive places, like her temples, like the tender spot beneath her ear and the hollow below her throat . . . and all the while his strong, sure fingers teased her breasts, found the curve of waist, buttock, and thigh through the thin fabric of her gown, making her breath come in quick, helpless little gasps. Oh, the pleasure! *Dear God, she had never known such pleasure!*

Sabelle was not alone in the sweet, pleasurable vortex that sucked with such intensity. Justin, too, found himself unaccountably shaken and drawn by it, reacting not only to the succulent young perfection of Sabelle's body, but to the wild abandon of her responses. He had heard that practiced whores were trained in faking such responses, of pretending rapture to gain a higher fee, but he found it impossible to relegate the incredibly convincing reactions of the woman in his arms to such an explanation.

On the other hand, he told himself with a secret smile, there were certain ways to find out. With a rapid, yet controlled movement, his fingers found the soft nest of curls at the apex of her thighs; he had his answer when he felt the hot, creamy wetness below; he exulted when he heard her cry out with pleasure.

"Does this please you, little Samantha?" he questioned in a husky whisper that was almost a rasp; his own passion was rising swiftly now, his control, especially in the light of his learning how ready she was, was nearly gone. He couldn't wait much longer; he gave the moist juncture between her thighs a final knowing stroke, captured her lips with a kiss that promised even more, then carefully withdrew and began to shed his clothes.

Whether it was his use of the false name or the sudden sense of loss when he disentangled his warmth from hers, something had broken through the sensual web that had held Sabelle. With a gasp, she sat up on the bunk and made a frantic effort to rearrange her skirts. She burned with shame as she went to pull up her bodice over her exposed breasts, but at that moment a pair of strong bronzed hands covered hers.

"Do not," said the duke in the husky rasp which had become too familiar. "They're beautiful, Samantha, as I'm sure I cannot be the first to have told you. I would look my fill of them, savor them as I take you."

As I take you . . . The words had a chilling, sobering effect on Sabelle, suddenly bringing home, as nothing else had, the stark danger of the game in which she'd gotten herself embroiled. *Dear God, while I've lain here like some panting beast, he almost . . . almost—*

"P-please, Your Grace," she nearly sobbed, "you must not! I'm not what you think! Oh, let me go, I beg you!"

Your Grace? The pleased smile on Justin's face suddenly vanished. So the little tart knew who he was. A frown crossed his handsome features as he pondered this; he found it disturbed him somehow, for it indicated the chit was not above playing games. She'd certainly given no indication initially that she knew he was a duke. Wondering about the nature of the game she played, he found it odd that he should find her duplicity so unsettling.

But in the next instant he cast these thoughts aside, finding the very sight of her sitting there on the bunk, hands crossed demurely over those lush breasts, too compelling to delay a moment longer. With a rapid movement, he was beside her amid the cushions on the bunk, drawing her into his arms, covering her slender body with his own.

"Come, sweet," he murmured thickly when he sensed her resistance, "the time for coyness is past."

His words rang in Sabelle's brain, and she began to

struggle as panic replaced passion. But she only heard him *laugh* as she fought him! With big, easy movements, he subdued her frantic attempts at escape as easily as if she were a weak, mewing kitten.

Hot tears coursed down her cheeks as she twisted from side to side to avoid his kisses; but he only lowered his head and, with an easy laugh, applied his efforts to her breasts instead. When she tried to push him away, he captured both her wrists and pinned them above her head with one hand, while with the other, and with his mouth, he had his way with her nipples, teasing them, nibbling, until she thought she would die of shame.

She heard herself cry out when he again raised her skirts. Knowing what he was about, she clamped her thighs together as tightly as she could, but again, he only laughed.

And then she knew why, because almost as easily as if she were a doll, a child's plaything, he forced her legs apart, wedging his knee between, until they both knew she was completely open to him. It was only a moment longer before she felt him lower himself over her twisting, struggling form, and she felt a sharp, tearing pain as he thrust home.

Sabelle's agonized scream was as much of a shock to Justin as the impossible reality of the barrier he'd felt—too late to avoid breaking, but there, nevertheless. Hardly able to credit this, he did the only thing possible in the situation: He smothered her cry with his mouth while the now unstoppable force of his passion played out the game below. Doing his best to keep his thrusts gentle, he rode her with several additional strokes until a shuddering spasm claimed him, and then it was over.

Several long minutes passed as Justin, dumbfounded and confused, held the sobbing girl in his arms. *A virgin! What in hell*—?

Questioning the conclusions he'd drawn, thinking them perhaps an illusion, he held her gently away from him. Her sobs had diminished to a series of soft, watery hiccoughs as he forced his gaze to her thighs—

And groaned.

There had been no illusion; the smears of blood that

appeared dark in the chamber's dim light were the final proof.

But a virgin whore? It didn't make sense! His gaze traveled to her face, and with a sudden sense of the absurd, he realized she still wore the mask. He almost laughed as he reached to take it off. But, seeing what he intended, the girl twisted away from him with a sob.

"Samantha . . ." he began, not really sure of what he meant to say, but then a movement again drew his attention.

Lowering his gaze, he caught sight of something he hadn't noticed before: High on the back of her right thigh, just below the buttock, was a curiously shaped birthmark of some kind. Fascinated by it, or perhaps as a means of delaying the moment when he would have to deal with the whole damnable situation, he touched his fingertips lightly to it, examining it more closely. Heart-shaped, it was, and no more than half an inch acr——

Justin felt an explosion of pain at the back of his head, then nothing at all as he slumped, senseless, over Sabelle's quietly sobbing form.

"Bluidy *Sassenach!*" hissed Jeannie as she lowered the candlestick she'd taken with her from the other chamber, where the earl of Larchmont lay peacefully sleeping under the effects of laudanum. "Sabelle, lass, are ye—God in heaven! What has he done t' ye?"

Shoving the insensate duke's body aside, the older girl, who'd succeeded in leaving the other chamber with her own virtue intact, took her trembling friend into her arms; then Jeannie listened with compassion as Sabelle sobbed out the wretched account of how she'd been forced to surrender.

"And to the duke of Haverleigh!" Sabelle spat as she finished her tale. "Oh, Jeannie! How *could* he—How could I—"

"Hush, now, hinny," said Jeannie, thrusting out to her the purple cloak. She'd brought it from the other chamber —along with Ormley's keys—when she heard Sabelle's cry of pain. Hurriedly, she began to help her friend straighten her clothes, going so far as to reattach the purple plumes, which she'd also had the foresight to grab before rushing to Sabelle's aid.

"Ach!" she exclaimed as she briefly recounted the success of her own encounter in the other chamber. "I only wish I'd been able t' come a mite sooner. Perhaps—"

"It doesn't matter," said Sabelle dully as she stared at Justin's still form.

"*Doesna matter?*" Jeannie queried incredulously. "Sabelle, hinny, certainly, it matters! That mon—"

"Will someday pay for what he's done," said Sabelle with a sudden look of resolution lighting her eyes. She met Jeannie's startled gaze—startled because there'd been nothing of such ferocity in Sabelle's demeanor a moment before.

"Oh, it's not that I'm not accepting some of the blame for what happened, you understand," Sabelle went on. "We knew there were risks. But *His Grace*"—she said this with a sneer—"the distinguished duke of Haverleigh, bears the greater fault, Jeannie. Because that arrogant bastard *forced himself on me!* And I don't care what he believed me to be, either! As far as I'm concerned, Justin Hart forced himself on a struggling, unwilling woman only half his size, and for that, I swear to you, there will be a *reckoning!* Do you hear me, Jeannie?" she added as the Scotswoman urged her toward the door. "A reckoning!"

❖Chapter 11❖

BEYOND HER RELIEF AT THEIR ESCAPE FROM the Shakespeare's Head and the subsequent release of the earl of Larchmont's birds, Sabelle allowed herself little time to reflect on the extraordinary events of Guy Fawkes Day. And if Jeannie noticed an unusually brittle and forced quality to her speech in the days immediately following, the young Scotswoman refrained from comment.

Of course, there were numerous pressing matters which came to interpose between Sabelle and her recollection of what happened to her on the fifth of November. Not only was her mother more concerned than ever that she be "kept from making a fool of herself—and indeed, of us all —upon her coming out," but that intrepid lady had actually prevailed upon Sir Jonathan to join her in such concerns.

Coming to the old man's town house tearfully on the morning of November 6, Marjorie Corstairs voiced her fears that despite all her hard work, Sabelle was still not ready. Managing to play on Sir Jonathan's belated doubts about his own responsibilities in the matter, she told him that she was particularly worried about her daughter's tendency to speak boldly and openly in polite company; instead of lowering her gaze and murmuring something safe and innocuous as a young lady should, she said, Sabelle, thanks to *his* influence, had the unpardonable habit of looking one straight in the eye and *actually voicing her opinions!* It would never suit, and what did he intend to do about it?

Sir Jonathan, now that he'd heard the specifics of her complaint, wasn't convinced that *anything* ought to be done about it. In his opinion there were entirely too many vapid, empty-headed young women being turned loose upon the world, thanks to the idiotic standards set forth by Marjorie and her set; and if Sabelle's being raised to have a mind of her own—a mind that could *think*—was able to make some small inroads on such a waste of human capabilities, why, then, so much the better!

But Sir Jonathan prudently said none of this to his daughter. Instead, he suggested that the next afternoon, on the day before Sabelle's coming out, he be allowed to take his granddaughter on a kind of "trial run." He had an invitation to tea that day, he explained, at the home of one of the *ton*'s foremost hostesses, a titled dowager of his own generation whose standards were at least as high as those of the patronesses of Almack's. He said he hadn't planned to attend, but that now he would, for he was sure he might arrange an invitation for Sabelle to accompany him. Then, once the tea was over, he would quietly ask their hostess, who was an old friend and could be prevailed upon to be discreet, exactly what she thought of Sabelle's demeanor.

"But what good will this do if she decides that Sabelle was horrid?" Marjorie cried. "It will be entirely too late to do anything about her!"

"True," said her father, "but I think it unlikely. You see, despite your fears about the child, my dear Marjorie, I suspect Sabelle is far more prepared than you give her credit for. You said yourself you've spent countless hours with her in recent weeks. Can you really think all that instruction has not taken hold?"

"But what about her habit of impertinent address?" queried Lady Corstairs, not the least bit reassured. "Surely your friend—and who *is* this *grande dame*, by the way? I cannot imagine, frankly, *your* having anything to do with someone who is so high *ton* in her standards."

Jonathan sighed. He'd been afraid Marjorie would question him on this; she might be dithered in her values, but she was no numbwit. But he knew, as soon as he mentioned the name of the old friend, there would be a barrage of questions, some of them quite personal in nature, and he wasn't sure he wished to share such information as they would elicit with his flighty offspring.

On the other hand, the more he thought about it, the more he was sure that the "trial run" he had in mind would be good for Sabelle. The poor child had been prodded and coached so mercilessly in these weeks since coming to London, he feared that her brave little spirit was in danger of being broken. Why, only last night, when she'd stopped by briefly to say their latest rescue had been accomplished, she'd had such a lack of sparkle in her eyes and such a weariness about her that he'd wondered if she was ill. She'd assured him she wasn't, however, attributing her appearance to worry about her coming out.

Very well, then, he thought as he looked his daughter in the eye, the child was tired and overworked with all those so-called lessons. She needed the afternoon off, in the company of a woman who, while having social standards as high as his daughter's, also had a great deal more humanity about her than Marjorie. This tea was the perfect thing.

"Her name," he said, "is Lady Millicent Strathmore, and she is the widow of the marquess of Win——"

"Lady Strathmore!" Marjorie squeaked. "Oh, Father, you cannot mean you actually *know* her!"

"Well, yes, of course I know her. I told you I——"

"But she is the most elusive, socially sought-after *grande dame* of them all! Why, even Castlereagh walks on tiptoes around *her*!"

"Really?" Jonathan looked bemused. He hadn't seen Millicent in decades, of course, not until they had met by chance in Hyde Park a few weeks ago. And having avoided London and the *ton* like the plague all those years himself, he supposed it was only natural that Millicent's current status might be a blank page to him. Still, the feeling made him slightly uncomfortable, considering that he was about to renew their old acquaintance for the sake of his granddaughter. He made a mental note to remedy this as soon as he found time.

". . . but you *must* tell me how you know her," Marjorie was saying, "and well enough for her to invite you to tea, too! Oh, this is splendid! And of course, Sabelle *must* go! Now tell me, Father. Out with it! How is it that you are acquainted with the marchioness of Wincanton?"

Jonathan gritted his teeth, for this was the difficult part, the question he had been expecting and dreading! How to handle it? If he told the truth, that he'd once been madly in love with Millicent Blair, as she'd been named at the time, he would never hear the end of it. Nor, as a gentleman, could he even obliquely allude to the fact that the lady had had a certain *tendre* for him. No, the truth was out of the question, but how was he to explain such an apparently coveted invitation to tea, from a woman he hadn't seen for more than fifty years, without admitting how close they had once been?

But Sir Jonathan was spared since, at that moment, his majordomo interrupted with the news that his employer had callers. Jonathan bade Marjorie a brisk farewell, promising to collect Sabelle for tea promptly at half past three the following afternoon.

Later on, Sir Jonathan was to regret his hasty dismissal of his daughter, however; for if he'd waited a few moments longer, he'd have gained some valuable information which Marjorie had been eager to impart: that the socially powerful Lady Strathmore had the additional distinction of being the maternal grandmother of none other than the duke of Haverleigh.

But on the afternoon of Lady Strathmore's tea, Sir Jonathan knew nothing of this as he proudly escorted Sabelle to her ladyship's home in Queen Street. Indeed, had he known, wild horses could not have dragged him there, and certainly not with his beloved granddaughter in tow.

Sabelle looked particularly fetching that afternoon, he thought. He gave her a sidelong glance in Lady Strathmore's vestibule while they waited for the majordomo to announce them. Her yellow velvet afternoon gown was "all the crack," as Marjorie had put it, which, he supposed, meant it was in fashion. High-waisted, it had long, tightly fitted sleeves and a high, rounded neckline; these were edged with bits of white lace, and her gloves, as well as the delicate slippers which peeped out from beneath her hemline, were of a kidskin dyed to match. Completing the outfit was a matching yellow bonnet whose demure brim framed her delicate heart-shaped face enchantingly. And the wide yellow satin ribbon that was tied to one side, beneath her chin, gave her a look, he thought, that was somewhere between that of angelic child and charming coquette.

He was also glad to see that some of the old sparkle had returned to those wide aquamarine eyes and decided that whatever the personal entanglements this visit might bring upon himself, it had been the right thing to do if it had restored the bloom to Sabelle's cheeks.

Of course, just as he was dismissing his own discomfort for the sake of his granddaughter's well-being, what Sir Jonathan couldn't know was that Sabelle was operating under the very same principle. Having questioned him quite carefully about the nature of his acquaintance with their hostess, Sabelle had been astounded to see her grandfather *blush* while murmuring something about having known the lady "too many years ago to bother about." And she had been so intrigued—and delighted—at the possibility of a resurrected romance between her beloved grandfather and this widow that she'd resolved, then and there, to cast aside her preoccupation with what she privately reffered to as the "tavern affair." She would concentrate on Sir Jonathan this afternoon!

And so, as the majordomo led them into the large, richly furnished drawing room in Queen Street, Sabelle found herself unwittingly freed of any self-consciousness which might have attended her first formal foray into one of the social rituals of the *ton*. Curious about the tall, white-haired dowager who had the power to raise the blood in her grandfather's cheeks, Sabelle curtsied and smiled, dimpled and nodded, and spoke in the softest tones imaginable.

"Tell me, my dear," Lady Strathmore was saying as she poured Sabelle a second cup of tea from a heavily chased silver teapot, "do you share Sir Jonathan's fondness for animals?"

"Oh, *yes,* m'lady! Unequivocally, if I may say so! And that, perhaps, is the chief reason why both Grandfather and I would prefer to spend our time in Surrey, rather than in the city. We've dozens of animals dependent on our care there, you see. And while they are well tended in our absence by excellent grooms and kennel men and the like, of course, it's still . . . Well, it isn't the same as it would be if we were there ourselves, laying hands on, so to speak."

Millicent watched the animation in Sabelle's face as she spoke, and the dowager smiled. So the child had spirit, as well as poise. And she was a beauty, though Millicent wondered whether Justin would see her as such, given his taste for the sophisticated appeal of women like Sarah Cavendish.

On the other hand, she decided it didn't matter much what her grandson thought of the girl's looks, so long as her lineage was impeccable—which, of course, Lady Isabelle's was. Moreover, there were some things more important than looks and lineage—things, she suspected, that she and her arrogant young pup of a grandson might even agree upon.

Sir Jonathan watched as the two women conversed, well satisfied with Sabelle's responses; but he wondered briefly at what seemed to be a calculating look in Millicent's eyes as she questioned his granddaughter. Was the old girl up to something? And, if so, what?

But in the next second he had no time to speculate further; the mantel clock chimed half past four, and Lady Strathmore subtly signaled that the tea was at an end. She rose to escort them toward the door.

"I am so glad you and Grandfather have decided to renew your former acquaintance," Sabelle offered as Lady Strathmore thanked them for coming.

"Humph!" said their hostess as her gray eyes sent

Jonathan a deprecating look. "We hardly knew he was here, for all he contributed to the conversation!"

Jonathan bristled. "As I recall, my dear, *you* always contributed enough for *both* of us!"

Millicent glared at him. "And what else, pray tell, was one to do when a certain *gentleman* appeared to have made the cat a gift of his tongue?"

"Better the cat than the gossips," Sabelle heard her grandfather mumble under his breath. But they were all saved from a continuation of this strange and sudden eruption of tempers by the arrival of the majordomo, bearing Sir Jonathan's hat and cane.

Flushing over their heated exchange, Sabelle made her thanks to Lady Strathmore. But she nearly groaned when Sir Jonathan told her to go ahead and wait for him in his carriage, as he wished a few words with their hostess in private.

Fortunately, her grandfather was all smiles when he joined her again. He settled himself contentedly against the squabs, signaling the driver to be off.

What Sabelle could not know was that Jonathan had learned that Sabelle passed Lady Strathmore's rigid standards with flying colors. "She is delightful, my dear Jonathan," Millicent had said to him. "And please tell that silly daughter of yours that I do *not* find her too bold and outspoken. Rather, she is like a breath of fresh air—a much-needed commodity in our stale London atmosphere, I dare say!"

And what Jonathan could not know was that Sabelle had decided there was, indeed, a romance to be fanned back into flame between the two older people; if they'd lost all feeling for each other, they would not have succumbed to such an exchange of sparks, she reasoned. All that remained was for her to find a way to encourage and feed that flame. What fun!

And, of course, what neither Sabelle nor Jonathan could know was that Lady Strathmore had her own plans as a result of their little meeting: Lady Isabelle Corstairs, she'd decided, would make a perfect duchess of Haverleigh!

⁂Chapter 12⁂

LADY CORSTAIRS WAS WELL PLEASED WITH herself tonight. Letting her gaze sweep over the well-dressed crowd of ladies and gentlemen who moved beneath the glittering chandeliers, she smiled. The spacious ballroom of her London town house was filled with the *crème de la crème* of society. Everyone who really mattered had accepted an invitation to see the daughter of the earl and countess of Rushton formally presented to the *ton*.

Marjorie's eyes darted toward the center of the ballroom, where the object being feted moved gracefully through the steps of a quadrille. The countess let out a sigh that signaled relief as well as pleasure.

Sabelle looked stunning in a high-waisted gown of blue-green silk to match the color of her eyes. No less than four layers of the diaphanous material had been used to create the graceful, swirling effect that enhanced her slender form as she moved to the music; but what Marjorie was remembering were the frantic last-minute corrections the dressmaker had been ordered to make only a week ago—when it was discovered that the gown's original *three* layers had left it too transparent to be decent.

And then, of course, there had been the problem of her hair. Whatever had possessed the girl to *henna* it? Marjorie still wasn't sure she ought to believe what seemed a Banbury tale about a Guy Fawkes Day costume. She only thanked her lucky stars that Mary, her ladies' maid, had recalled a concoction her former mistress, Lady Drum-thwackett, had once used to remove henna from the hair. Thank God it had worked!

But the final reason for the relief in Marjorie's sigh had nothing to do with Sabelle's physical appearance. The child was, after all, a beauty, and ball gowns and hairstyles could only enhance what was a natural, God-given gift. Her *behavior*, however, was quite another matter. Yet, try as she might, Lady Corstairs could find no fault with it tonight. Sabelle had been the model of comportment on this evening of her coming out, from her softly murmured responses in the reception line to the grace with which she'd been accepting a deluge of invitations to dance. Nowhere was there any hint of the little hoyden she'd been. Yes, all those exhausting lessons and lectures had paid off, and for this, above all, Marjorie gave a silent prayer of thanks.

But, as Lady Corstairs was congratulating herself on this promising start to her daughter's Season, there was another standing under those glittering chandeliers who cursed himself for it—or, to be more precise, for the part he'd played in it. Sir Jonathan Burke was, in fact, furious with himself as his gaze settled on a pair of tall, gray-eyed figures: the woman, elegant and white-haired; the man, dark and altogether too handsome for Sir Jonathan's comfort.

Damning himself thrice over for having handed Millicent Strathmore the invitation Marjorie had hastily penned when she'd learned he was acquainted with the dowager, Jonathan wondered how he could have been so stupid. Why hadn't he asked questions first? When Millicent had assured him she'd attend "especially to assure my grandson's going," why hadn't he thought to ask the identity of that grandson?

Of course, he thought, who'd ever have guessed that Millicent's grandson would turn out to be "Hart the Heartless"? He'd hardly believed his ears when Lord Ponsonly happened to drop this news in a bit of casual conversation a few minutes ago.

"Frederick," he'd said to the lord, "surely you jest!"

"Not at all, sir," Ponsonly had replied. "Haverleigh's

unfortunate mother, the last duchess, was the old girl's daughter."

Stunned, Jonathan had only been able to murmur, *"Unfortunate?"*

"Why, yes, didn't you know?" And he'd gone on to relate a shocking story involving adultery and rumors of an aborted child.

Jonathan's mouth tightened into a severe line as he thought of it now. Then his face went grim as he suddenly spied Millicent across the room. She was in the process of signaling to catch Sabelle's attention, and—*Dear God!* She was going to introduce her to Haverleigh!

Damn, he thought as he watched them over the heads of the crowd, *are the very fates conspiring to throw that man into the child's path?*

Sabelle forced herself to hang on to the smile that had lit her face when she saw Lady Strathmore beckoning. She rather liked the older woman and had been delighted to learn the tall, handsome dowager had accepted her mother's belated invitation to the ball. She had even told Lady Strathmore as much when they'd met in the reception line. And that had not been the easiest thing in the world because, standing beside the dowager in line had been that bastard, the duke of Haverleigh! Why had they invited *him*?

But just now, as she'd personally introduced them, Lady Strathmore had horrified her with the news that the bloody wretch was her *grandson!* It was all Sabelle could do to keep that smile pasted on her face as Justin Hart bowed graciously over her outstretched hand—*and clearly pretended they'd never met!*

But Sabelle was nothing if she wasn't quick-witted. Responding to an inner voice that told her to remain calm at all costs and to play along for the moment, she gritted her teeth and pretended to notice nothing untoward as Justin straightened and ran that cool silver gaze over her with a deliberate and uncalled-for thoroughness. And she made herself continue to smile at the blatant look of approval in his eyes and to ignore the slow, satisfied grin that was spreading across his handsome features. *Pray he doesn't rec-*

ognize something that mask did not cover, she entreated silently.

Ignoring the hammering of her heart while she kept her practiced smile in place—the very smile she silently thanked her mother for having had her perfect before a mirror for days on end—Sabelle studied his face. And she found herself drawing a couple of rapid conclusions—conclusions which she somehow knew, without knowing *how* she knew, were right on target.

First, she decided he'd deliberately chosen not to reveal to his grandmother that he recognized the little hoyden he'd encountered on a hunt one day; and second, but of infinitely greater importance, Justin Hart had no inkling he *ought* to be recognizing the young woman in front of him from a later, and far more intimate, encounter.

Her smile took on a secret hint of relief.

He doesn't know! Sabelle hugged that realization to herself with glee, and, at the same instant, she felt the tiniest germ of a plan begin to take root in her mind. Only half-formed at best, it was tucked carefully into a corner of her consciousness, and, with a look of satisfaction, she accepted Justin Hart's invitation to dance.

"Forgive me, Your Grace, but I am surprised you dance," said Sabelle, noticing his slight limp as he led her toward the center of the floor.

"Until recently, I have not," Justin replied with a smile, "but the leg is mending, and my physician suggests that mild exercise such as dancing might even be beneficial. I thank you for your concern, however, m'lady."

Sabelle nodded, remembering to smile.

Justin eyed the head of sun-kissed curls that barely met his chin, and he, too, smiled as he led Lady Corstairs's daughter onto the dance floor. So this was how the little chit had turned out! Who would have thought it? The stunningly beautiful creature whose coming-out ball his grandmother had dragged him to in no way resembled the cheeky little hoyden who'd irritated him so at that hunt, many weeks ago. Did a fashionable gown and this sophisticated, Grecian-styled hair make such a difference?

Of course, he decided as he heard the three-quarter time of a waltz the musicians had struck up, the polished effect could only run skin-deep; it was entirely possible that the little baggage had been transformed only on the surface.

He decided to probe a little.

"A waltz, Lady Isabelle?" Justin queried as he grasped her waist and began to whirl her gracefully around the floor. "I am surprised your mama would allow this shocking new dance on the, ah, tender occasion of your coming out."

Sabelle wanted to spit in his face. How *dare* he imply she was too young and callow to enjoy the dance that was sweeping London, as it had swept the Continent! "Mama would allow," indeed! Did he think her such an innocent that she—She almost laughed at the irony of *that! He* was responsible for her *loss of innocence,* the bastard!

But in the fleet second that all this ran through her mind, she also knew that she must allow him to suspect none of it. So Sabelle tilted her head in order to look up into the eyes of the man who'd stolen her virginity and concentrated on maintaining a pleasant expression on her face. *Be charming,* she said silently as she steeled herself for the role she'd decided to play. *Be absolutely charming and remember the reckoning you promised!*

"Indeed, Your Grace," she said to him, "my mother was not at all for it. But then we heard Lady Jersey and Princess Esterhazy were favoring it at Almack's and she was persuaded to, ah, come around. Mother cannot bear ignoring anything that has become all the crack, you see!"

Justin saw the tiniest glint of mischief in the sea-green eyes, and he laughed. She was not beyond admitting that she'd used the knowledge of a parent's weakness to manipulate that parent. There were shades of the imp there that could well belong to the little rebel on the hunt!

Yet, on the other hand, she'd failed to rise to the bait he'd offered when he characterized her more or less as a miss just out of the schoolroom. The green girl at the hunt, he felt sure, would have snapped at that bait.

"And what about you, m'lady?" Justin countered. "Are you also given to esteeming that which is 'all the crack'?"

It was Sabelle's turn to laugh. "Only when it pleases me to do so, Your Grace."

"And when does it not?" he prodded with a smile.

"Why, then, I merely 'crack' the rules a bit!"

Justin flashed her a grin. So the creature had wit as well as poise. Better and better. And he mustn't forget how smoothly she'd taken a cue from him and refrained from divulging to his grandmother that they'd met at the hunt—and not under the most agreeable circumstances!

"Tell me, m'lady," he said, deciding to test the waters a bit further, "are you still of the opinion that fox hunting ought to be banished?"

Sabelle's eyes narrowed, and she almost missed a step before she drew on every ounce of strength she had in an effort to remain calm.

"I have the exact same opinion of fox hunting, Your Grace," she said, "as the *fox!*"

Justin nearly threw his head back and laughed, but he managed to temper the urge; somehow, he had the notion that she didn't find this subject amusing, and he had no wish to push her too far.

He decided to change the subject, but not for the purpose of avoiding her ire. His grandmother had made no secret of her reason for insisting he attend Isabelle Corstairs's coming out; she had met the earl of Rushton's daughter and found her "highly suitable," as she'd put it, "to becoming a duchess."

He was here to look over the goods.

And so, for the remainder of the dance, Justin decided to ply Sabelle with questions designed to elicit information *he* deemed necessary before fulfilling the duty he'd recently accepted. The girl might be beautiful and satisfactorily polished, but for him that would not be enough. He needed to know that she had a *mind* to go with all that outward charm. Beauty and poise were all well and good, but they would not signify if she proved a bore over the breakfast table!

He therefore queried her on a host of things, from her tastes in art and music to her opinions on certain current events.

And to his astonishment, he found her extremely bright, and informed—educated, even—and well read! He thought hard, trying to remember the last time he'd met a female who gave evidence of having truly read the newspapers or who could flawlessly quote Shakespeare and Milton. The only woman who came close was Lady Melbourne, and she was twice Isabelle Corstairs's age!

Then, all too soon, Justin found himself thinking, the music came to an end, and he bowed politely over her hand and led her off the floor.

"I must tell you, Your Grace," said Sabelle, glancing up at him, "that your footwork was entirely up to snuff. How ever do you manage it? At one moment your incapacity is evident, and then at the next, it has vanished!"

Justin gave her a wicked grin. "That should not be so surprising, m'lady—to someone who made entire *foxes* vanish!"

Sabelle's eyebrows rose for a fraction of a second, and then she burst out laughing.

Justin's grin widened. *A sense of humor, too,* he thought approvingly.

A young officer from the Guards claimed her for the next dance, and he watched her move away from him with that well-remembered, graceful swaying of her hips. Justin shifted his gaze and met the inquiring eyes of the white-haired dowager standing a short distance away, and nodded.

His hand went briefly to his thigh, which was throbbing painfully, as if to mock him for the fiction he'd given about it. But what he'd wanted was the opportunity to question her, and nothing but the relative privacy of the dance floor would give it to him.

He sighed, wondering how much more his sense of duty would exact from him, wondering if his zealous friend Thomas hadn't had the right of it, after all.

A frown crossed his face as he recalled another unpleasant incident that had come out of his sense of duty toward the dukedom. If he hadn't been trying to ferret out information about that idiot cousin of his, he'd never have accompanied Ormley to that tavern and fallen prey to a treacherous little whore's tricks. His skull was still sore from the bashing it had taken. Odd thing, though—the motive of robbery, which he'd have assumed to be behind those sluts' actions, didn't wash: Not a single valuable, not a pound, not a shilling, had been taken from his person. Well, perhaps those trollops had heard someone coming and been forced to flee before completing their business. Bloody shame they hadn't been apprehended as well!

A familiar peal of musical laughter reached his ears over the gentle strains of the small orchestra, and his glance fell on a slender figure in an aquamarine gown moving under the glittering chandelier. Justin's mouth curved with a sardonic smile. Tomorrow he would go through the first bloody formality: He would ask the chit's father for permission to call on her.

⚜Chapter 13⚜

SABELLE SAT BOLT UPRIGHT IN BED AND RE-
alized she was drenched with sweat. Her breath came in
short gasps, and she could feel her heart pounding in her
chest. What had she—?

A dream, she told herself. *It was only a nightmare.*

But it had seemed so real!

Slowly, she looked about her London bedchamber, willing herself to be calm, making herself believe she was safe.
The pale gray light filtering through the curtained windows
told her it was early, perhaps just slightly after daybreak.
She leaned back against the pillows, and several minutes
passed before Sabelle felt her breathing slow to normal.
Only then did she dare try to recollect the details of the
nightmare that had frightened her so.

She had been at the ball again—had it been only last
night?—and once more she had been dancing with that
arrogant bastard, the duke of Haverleigh. She could feel
again the tremendous amount of energy it had taken to
pretend that nothing was amiss, to be charming, when all
the while the tension within was so palpable she'd have
sworn she could cut it with a knife. She had danced and
smiled—laughed, even!—and steeled herself to ignore that
raw sense of power the man exuded: the silvery gaze that at
times made her feel he could see right through her; the
flashing grin that always seemed to hold a hint of mockery;

the frightening, pantherlike smoothness of his movements, despite a wounded leg . . .

Suddenly Sabelle pushed her knuckles against her lips to stifle a sob, remembering how the dream had turned ugly. It had begun after he'd been asking her those questions about her interests. Yes, at one moment he was mentioning an article in the *Post* about a bill that would see to the hanging of Luddites, and then—*and then!* Ah, God, he had asked her if she knew about a bill he intended to introduce to the Lords tomorrow—*a bill to hang ladies who pretended to be harlots!* And at the same instant he had stopped dead in his tracks while, about them, the music halted and everyone in the ballroom stared at them. Then suddenly he had taken his hands and torn her gown asunder, and her undergarments as well, all the time screaming, "Harlot! Whore! Slut!" Until all the guests in the ballroom had taken up the chant as she stood there, shivering in shame: "Harlot!" they'd all cried. "Hang her! Hang her! Hang—"

Sabelle heard herself scream before she succumbed to a pitiful sobbing. The sound brought Jeannie, who slept in the adjoining chamber.

"Guid God, the Almighty!" exclaimed the young Scotswoman as she rushed toward the bed. "Lassie, wha' hae ye —Ach! Hinny, dinna weep!"

She climbed onto the high tester bed and took her sobbing friend into her arms.

"Hush, lass," she murmured soothingly. "I'm here and there's naught t' fear now . . . hush!"

Gradually the sobbing subsided as Jeannie stroked and soothed in a comforting tone. Sabelle continued to cling to her friend for several long minutes, until her distress diminished to a few halting hiccoughs and finally, a long, watery sigh.

"Ah, Jeannie, I'm sorry," she said at last. "I h-had a d-dream and—"

"Aye," said Jeannie, "a fearsome dream, yet dreams canna harm ye. But Sabelle, I've nae known ye t' gie yersel' up t' nightmares before! Wha' happened t' stir this one up, lass?"

Sabelle shuddered before raising her eyes to meet Jeannie's worried gaze. "Haverleigh," she said in a toneless whisper.

"Ach!" Jeannie exclaimed, and Sabelle heard her add something venomous in Gaelic.

Sabelle nodded as if she had understood, then heaved a tremulous sigh.

"D'ye wish t' tell me aboot it?" Jeannie's eyes were compassionate; Sabelle had made her privy to enough details about the disastrous turn of events at the Shakespeare's Head to give her nightmares of her own.

Nodding slowly, Sabelle began to outline the dream, hoping to defuse the terror it could hold for her by sharing it aloud with her friend. But as she went over its details and interwove them with a recounting of the ball—she'd been too exhausted to fill Jeannie in on it when she'd retired last night—she recalled, for the first time since she'd awakened, the dangerous plan which had formed in her head while she danced with Justin Hart.

My God, she thought as she examined her daring in the light of day, *could I really have been planning a means of getting even with that man? Justin Hart is no fool; everything about him cries "danger!" Would I really go through with such a thing? Do I have the courage? Or is it foolhardiness? But the scum deserves a reckoning! Oh, God, I wish I knew what to do!*

Jeannie noticed the distress on her lady's face. "Sabelle," she said, "are ye sure ye're all right? Ye maun tell me aboot—"

A sigh from Sabelle cut her off. "No, I'm not at all sure I'm all right," she said, "and I think I'd better tell you what's really worrying me . . ."

A couple of hours later, Sabelle was surprised to hear Jeannie tell her her grandfather was downstairs and wished to see her. She was mildly alarmed at this. It was still extremely early, and no one else was up yet, except for a few servants, for last night's fête had gone on quite late, and she had expected all those in attendance (who weren't troubled by nightmares) to sleep until noon. She hurried from her chambers. At Camelot Downs Grandfather had always been an early riser, but even he should have grown accustomed to the London habits of the *ton* by now. She hoped there wasn't something seriously amiss.

Jonathan greeted her with his familiar warm hug, but the moment she stepped back from the embrace, Sabelle noticed concern in his eyes.

"What is it, Grandfather? There's something wrong, I know it, else you wouldn't be calling at this early—"

"Nothing to fly up into the boughs about, as your mother would say," Jonathan told her. "I merely found it impossible to sleep late, and I thought—um, do you think it possible to send for a pot of breakfast tea, my dear? I rose so early, I hadn't the heart to awaken old Simmons, so—"

"So you thought you'd come over here to awaken us instead? Claptwaddle! You cannot fool me, sir! I saw the look in your—"

"Ahem! Sabelle, my dear . . ."

"Oh, of course, you shall have your dish of tea! Come, we shall repair to the breakfast room. Jeannie was mashing some tea for me when she came to tell me you were here."

"Fine girl, that Jeannie."

"Indeed," said Sabelle with a strong hint of irony. "But I warn you, sir, once you've sipped your brew, you'll have to explain yourself!"

As he followed her to the breakfast room, Jonathan's thoughts in no way matched the cheerful mien he'd shown Sabelle. In fact, they were absolutely gloomy.

He hadn't told her that in addition to rising early, he hadn't slept all night. That his mind had been preoccupied with her encounter with His Heartless Grace, the duke of Haverleigh, last night. That he'd been deeply troubled by the look in the duke's eyes as they'd followed her about the ballroom: the look of a wolf about to snap up a lamb!

And if he didn't sadly miss his guess, the wolf would be at her door before this day was over. He had to get Sabelle away from there before that happened—away from London and the damnable *ton*. And the thrice-damnable duke of Haverleigh!

In the breakfast room Jeannie served the tea, then left them alone.

Sabelle took a sip of the bracing brew, then looked directly at the old man sitting across the table from her. He was well groomed and carefully attired as usual, but the beloved lined face beneath the shock of thick white hair looked a bit ragged somehow. And she thought she detected the hint of a shadow in his eyes.

"What is it, Grandfather?" she queried softly. "Please tell me!"

Jonathan met her gaze and nodded. "As I left here in the wee hours of the morning, your mother was congratulating herself and the rest of the family on the huge success of your coming out."

Sabelle nodded, remembering Lady Corstairs's ecstatic exclamations over the success of the evening. People were calling Sabelle, she'd told them, "the belle of the Season!"

"Well," Jonathan said, "I suppose she was correct in that assessment. Judging by what I could see, you could well become the darling of the *ton* as soon as the word is spread."

Sabelle gave him a dismissive smile. "Oh, Grandfather, you know I've never cared—"

"Yes, exactly," Jonathan said, "but I wonder if you're prepared to *deal* with a huge success in that arena, now that it seems to have happened. Sabelle . . ." He leaned across the table to take her hand. "Up until this time I know you've been focused only on the ball, seeing it as a single hurdle that must be crossed, but, sweetheart, *think!* It may well be that as a result of last night's success, your life will be forever changed. Are you prepared for that?"

My life was already changed forever, Sabelle thought bitterly, *on the night of Guy Fawkes Day!*

"Think of it," Jonathan was saying, "cotillions, routs, balls, one heaped upon another, with not a moment, not a breath, left to run free in the woods or scamper through the fields as you used to do. It—it breaks my heart to think of what they'll turn you into!"

This was true enough, Jonathan assured himself, though he wasn't sure it was adequate reason for the unorthodox steps he was about to suggest. Only the threat of Haverleigh warranted those. But he also wished to avoid frightening Sabelle with his true reason, so he'd decided this would have to do. He hoped she would believe him.

Sabelle saw the honest distress in his eyes, but she wasn't sure what had dredged it up. They'd been over this ground before, even prior to her departure from Surrey, and she'd believed then that her grandfather had decided to capitulate to her parents' wishes. Why, he'd even joined her in railing against her mother's ambitions to form a match for her with the duke of—Good God! Was *that* it? Had he noticed Haverleigh's attentions to her (as indeed her mother had!)? Did he worry that she'd been charmed by him—as she'd pretended to be?

She decided to test her theory, but a bit obliquely.

"Grandfather," she began cautiously, "did you by any chance, ah, happen to hear, as I did last night, that your friend, Lady Strathmore, is—is the grandmother of the duke of Haverleigh?"

She saw alarm flare in his eyes when she mentioned the duke's name, and she knew she'd hit the mark.

"What is it, Grandfather? Is Haverleigh—Ah, surely you're not upset with yourself for having introduced me to Lady Strathmore? Why, I wouldn't have missed meeting her for anything, and I dare say His Grace would have attended the ball anyway. I learned Mother had topped her list with him weeks ago."

Jonathan made a gesture of disgust. "No, my dear, I'm afraid that is not entirely accurate. Lady Strathmore herself told me last night he'd definitely planned *not* to attend and that it was only by dint of her remarkable powers of persuasion that he at last consented to be present."

"I see," said Sabelle. She frowned at the concern in his eyes, then managed an insouciant air. "Nevertheless, sir, I will not have you wallowing in guilt over the matter! So

Justin Hart made an appearance. What of it? So did a number of other gentlemen."

"None of the other gentlemen looked *as if they wanted to swallow you up whole!*"

As soon as the words were out, Jonathan wanted to kick himself. He hadn't intended to let her see his concern. He hadn't intended to mention Haverleigh. And he certainly hadn't planned to indulge in such an uncharacteristic display of emotion. He decided to backtrack and perhaps repair some of the damage.

"Look, Sabelle," he said softly, "although the duke, as you can guess, is clearly not a favorite of mine, you must believe that I came here this morning for other reasons. I worry that you'll soon be trapped in London like—like one of those caged birds you freed. And I merely thought . . . well, if you must know, I was hoping you'd allow me to give you a respite. I—I'm suggesting you let me take you back to Somerset—now, before anyone's the wiser."

"You mean *now*, this very morning?" Sabelle breathed disbelievingly. It was almost too daring to contemplate: to leave London, with all its societal pressures, the thousand and one rules she must remember before she dared make a move, the *ton*, all of it—and, yes, this business of the plan she'd just shared with Jeannie, too . . . for a *reckoning*, as she'd come to call it . . . She'd be free from having to face Haverleigh—at least for a good while—and then perhaps she could reach a clearer decision on what she must do.

"You—you mean you're ready to travel immediately, Grandfather?"

Jonathan nodded, watching her face.

There was a moment of silence before he saw a corner of her mouth twitch.

"Mother will be furious," she said as she gave in to the grin.

Let her be! Jonathan wanted to shout. *So long as the child is removed, for whatever time I can manage, from the attentions of that rakehell duke!* "Then you'll come?" he asked.

Sabelle's grin was dazzling. "I'll come," she told him.

* * *

They managed, with Jeannie's help, to pack Sabelle's things and leave within the hour. A note was left for her parents by Jonathan. In it he stated simply that he'd felt the weeks of exhausting preparation for the ball had taken their toll on his granddaughter, and he was taking her back to the country for a rest. He also managed to suggest, quite wickedly, that if Sabelle collapsed from exhaustion, it would be on their heads.

Traveling due west out of the city, with Michael Kelley at the reins, they made excellent time, for her grandfather's team was strong, healthy, and well rested; also, they traveled light—Jonathan and Michael said they had all the clothes they required at Camelot Downs, and so did Sabelle: some rough castoffs of the stable lads would more than suit their purposes. They reached the lush, green, undulating landscape of Surrey some twelve hours after they had set out, and although it was dark, Sabelle could smell the familiar woodsmoke of autumn in the air and knew that she was home.

Her grandfather's staff greeted them with warmth and delight when they arrived. Mrs. Henderson, the housekeeper, vowed that the place hadn't been the same without the master and the young miss. There was a light supper of potato soup and fresh bread—Jonathan had long ago become a vegetarian on moral grounds—and then soft, comfortable beds with sheets deliciously toasted by warming pans.

Sabelle fell asleep almost the moment her head hit the pillow, and it was a deep, restful sleep, untroubled by dreams. When she awoke, refreshed and eager in the morning, it was to greet a day that was crisp and bright, with sunshine streaming through the mullioned windows of her chamber.

She found some freshly laundered boy's togs neatly folded on a chair in the bedchamber that was always kept ready for her in her grandfather's house; she washed, then donned them quickly, taking particular pleasure in being able to dress without the assistance her formal clothes had demanded in London.

Then, after some tea and toast with Jonathan, who grumbled that he needed to work on his estate books and therefore wouldn't be able to join her that day, she was off to enjoy the wonderful taste of freedom she'd been given.

Her first stop was at the stables, where she went directly to the big box stall where Jonathan had told her she would find Storm. The stallion they'd rescued from their neighbor's abusive son tossed his head and stomped on the floor for a brief moment when he saw her. But then, to Sabelle's utter delight, he came forward and accepted the hunk of sugar she offered on her outstretched palm.

Since her mare, Brandy, had been taken to London, Michael saddled Zeus, a young gray gelding he'd trained before they began their work with Storm; Sabelle would have loved to try the stallion, but she knew it would be a long time—filled with endless patience and tender care—before the mistreated animal could be ridden safely—if ever.

Then it was across the first pasture at an easy canter, until she got the feel of the gray—and of riding *astride* again! They took a low fence effortlessly, and then she urged Zeus into a gallop, letting him have his head. Her hair flying, she bent low over the gelding's withers, loving the feeling of speeding over the ground, reveling in it.

Only then, as she was racing across meadows and fields so familiar they made her ache, did Sabelle realize how much she'd missed the freedom she'd had before going to London. Suddenly all the long weeks of lessons and fittings and lectures became an oppressive weight that had to be shed. "Faster!" she cried to the galloping horse. "Oh, Zeus, faster!" And she laughed into the wind as the young horse seemed to know what she needed and answered her cry.

She spent the whole day outside, never thinking of a hairstyle or a gown or a waltz. Sometimes she rode, sometimes she went on foot, content to let the horse walk beside her as she felt the crackle of dry leaves underfoot; or, later, when she cast caution to the wind and shed her shoes, as she relished the squish of cold, sodden moss between her toes. She saw a small herd of deer near a stream and called softly to them, delighted when they didn't immediately bolt and disappear; rabbits, squirrels and chipmunks came within a few feet of her, accepting crumbs as she fed them from the bundle Cook had given her when she left; she spied a fox in a glade and, because she knew how to be very still and quiet, eventually the vixen's half-grown kits as well, when they came to drink with their mother at the pool nearby.

And when at last she realized it was growing dark, Sabelle made her way back to the house feeling pounds lighter than when she'd set out; the burden had been shed, and she marveled at how this had happened so readily.

"Oh, Grandfather," she said as the roofs and chimneys of the big Tudor house came into view, "what a wonderful gift you've given me!" She vowed that the next day she would pull Jonathan away from his books and ledgers and roam the fields and woods with him at her side.

But Sabelle's vow was to remain unfulfilled.

Later that evening, as she and Jonathan were completing a game of chess by the fire, a coach came rumbling up the drive. Before Jonathan's majordomo could hurry to the entry hall to see who might be arriving so late, and unannounced, the front door flew open, and an angry, red-faced earl of Rushton stormed in. Lady Corstairs trod in his wake, biting her lower lip against the tears which were obviously threatening.

"M—my lord," stammered the flabbergasted majordomo, unaccustomed to such unorthodox behavior, especially from his employer's prim, socially correct son-in-law. "Is—is there something—"

"Where are they?" roared the earl. "Where's that noodle-brained father-in-law of mine, *and where's my daughter?* I know they're here, so don't try to fob me off with some hare-brained tale. Take us to them at once!"

Even as he spoke, Cecil was shoving his hat and cape at the flustered servant and advancing into the hall, his eyes darting toward this doorway and that, looking for signs of his wayward daughter and her grandfather. Marjorie advanced a few steps as well, clutching her velvet pelisse with nervous fingers.

The majordomo took a deep breath and straightened, knowing the game was up. He'd been warned by his employer that the little miss's parents might turn up, but Sir Jonathan hadn't expected it to be for a few days yet. Now there was no help for it, but to show them up.

"They're in the library, my lord . . . ah, my lady?" He offered to take Marjorie's pelisse and had barely succeeded in doing so before he found himself hurrying after the earl, who was taking the carpeted stairs two at a time.

Congratulating himself on his nimbleness, the majordomo succeeded in reaching the library door before the outraged earl, but as he would have knocked, it opened.

Looking composed, if not resigned, Jonathan thanked the servant and quietly dismissed him before acknowledging his uninvited guests. "You made excellent time, m'lord," he told Cecil with a wry half-smile.

"Excellent time!" Cecil thundered. "I'll tell you about my time, you—you *kidnapper!*" His eyes swept the room, falling on Sabelle, who stood quietly by the fire, still wearing her stableboy's garb. "I've spent the last fourteen hours sitting in a damnably uncomfortable carriage, chasing after my daughter, when I could have been happily going about my business in London. Did you know I was scheduled to make a speech in the Lords today? *Did you?*"

Cecil's brows were drawn together in a straight, angry line as he addressed his father-in-law, and his face grew even redder as he spoke. Jonathan, however, remained silent and calm as he faced him.

"As if I have nothing better to do than go haring off about the countryside, fetching an errant offspring!" Cecil bellowed. "Sir," he said to Jonathan, "I demand an explanation—and an apology!"

"Won't you sit down first?" Jonathan inquired calmly. He'd never seen the earl in such a state, but he had no intention of giving in to his hysterics. He gestured courteously in the direction of a settee near the fire.

Cecil glanced in that direction and again noticed his daughter, but now, for the first time, he was taking in her attire.

"Ha! I might have known all those fancy gowns that threatened to beggar me hadn't made a lady of her! Isabelle, aren't you ashamed of yourself?"

As Sabelle opened her mouth to reply, her mother finally found her tongue. "Oh, Sabelle, how could you have run off like that?" She saw Jonathan move beside his granddaughter and take her hand and pat it.

"She needed a rest, Marjorie," Jonathan stated flatly. "The poor child was exhausted."

"Not too exhausted to go gallivanting about your estate on horseback!" countered Cecil, wrinkling his nose in distaste at the odor of the stables that emanated from his daughter.

"B-but I find riding relaxing," Sabelle ventured.

"Well, it certainly hasn't relaxed *us*," said her mother, beginning to find her stride now. "I've not been without my hartshorn since I read that dreadful note, and there we were, with the house filling up like a flower stall, and cards arriving in the dozens, and no daughter. It was all too, too depressing!"

"Flower stall? Cards?" Sabelle looked totally bemused.

"From your admirers, you little ninnyhammer!" Cecil roared. "Flowers and calling cards all over the place, and no 'belle of the Season' in sight! How do you expect to have someone offer for you if you are not there, daughter?"

"Oh . . . I see," Sabelle said in a tiny voice. "But—but I never thought—"

"That's just the trouble with you—with *all* women!" her father retorted. "You never *think*! Why, if I hadn't thought, and quickly, when the duke arrived, and told him that you were suddenly taken—"

"The duke?" Jonathan's eyes showed instant alertness. "What duke, and what about him?"

"Why, Haverleigh, of course!" Marjorie answered before Cecil could speak. "He actually arrived in person to ask if he might call on Sabelle. Ah, *think* of it! *A duchess!* My own daughter, a duchess!''

"Not if she doesn't return at once and let the man court her!" Cecil complained loudly.

Neither of them had noticed the reactions these last few exchanges had elicited from their daughter or her grandfather. Sabelle had grown very still, and she kept her eyes averted as she seemed to inspect a spot on the carpet; Jonathan's face had paled, and his mouth formed a grim line before he spoke. When he did, his voice trembled.

"You cannot allow that man to court her," he told them.

Astounded, Marjorie was the first to break the silence. "What! Not court her? Why, of course he must court her! And *wed* her—if the foolish girl doesn't ruin things, that is!" She glared at her daughter then, making no mistake as to what she thought her offspring was capable of. "Why, Haverleigh is the catch of the—"

"No."

"What was that?" Cecil looked at Jonathan as if he'd misheard him.

Jonathan sighed wearily. There was no hope for it now. He'd have to divulge the real reasons behind his behavior.

"I said, no," he told Sabelle's parents boldly. "You cannot allow Haverleigh to court the child because the duke is not—is unsuitable."

There was a chorus of protests, but Jonathan held up his hand and forced them to hear him out.

"I really have no choice but to tell you this, so tell you, I shall: His Grace, the duke of Haverleigh, is, for all intents and purposes we are here concerned with, a *rake,* unfit to propose courtship or anything else to an innocent child like Sabelle. He has an unsavory reputation with women, with a trail of broken hearts to his credit, which is, I assure you, a mile long. It is only his title and certain other accomplishments which allow him to move about in polite company, despite what a pack of foolish, avaricious mamas may be saying."

He looked straight at his son-in-law.

"If you'd taken the least bit of trouble to inquire, Cecil,

you would have learned as much. You have no business foisting the attentions of a man with Hart's character on such an innocent. And as for you, Marjorie, I'm surprised at you. Are you so bedazzled by thoughts of a dukedom that you would allow this child into the clutches of a man they dub *Hart the Heartless?*"

Both objects of his address began to bluster and sputter, but Jonathan's attention was now fixed on his granddaughter. She had been unusually silent through this, and he wondered what she was thinking. She looked quite pale, despite the wash of color the day spent outdoors had given her complexion, and her hands were clasped tensely in front of her. Surely she couldn't be too concerned; she'd never liked the rogue to begin with. What, then?

"Sabelle . . ." he said softly. "Have I upset you, child? I know such things are usually not spoken of in front of young innocents, but I felt I had to make them see. Do you understand?"

Sabelle winced. That was the third time he'd spoken of *innocence* in connection with her, and she wanted to scream "No, no, don't you see? I am *not* an innocent! Not anymore! Not since the night that arrogant wretch took the maidenhead of a foolish, but nevertheless *unwilling,* girl in a tavern." Oh, God, the *irony* of it!

But of course she could tell him none of this. She could merely pretend, playing along with his assumptions and hoping her parents could be brought to see—

Or could she? Was that not one of the *two* options open to her? What about the other one? Justin Hart deserved comeuppance for what he'd done to her. It was a daring, dangerous plan, as Jeannie had worriedly pointed out—was it just yesterday? Yet, the more she thought about that bastard, the more she wanted to serve him his just desserts. It would take great courage to get Justin Hart to propose marriage *and then leave him stranded at the altar!* But she felt she could do it, despite Jeannie's apprehensions.

Grandfather, of course, would be disappointed in her. He couldn't be expected to understand, and she didn't dare tell him. He'd never let her risk herself that way. But if she didn't take the risk, she might never have another chance.

She would plunge ahead.

"Grandfather," she said, swallowing the lump she felt forming in her throat as she began the lie, "I—I know you truly have . . . have my welfare at heart, b-but surely the duke cannot . . ."—she swallowed again—". . . cannot be *that* terrible! Perhaps . . . perhaps you've misunderstood. After all, he *is* Lady Strathmore's grandson, and *she* is a *nonpareil!*"

She avoided looking at her grandfather's face and turned quickly to her parents.

"Dearest Mother, I am so sorry to have caused you all this disquiet. Father, can you forgive me? And can you tell me what it was His Grace said when he came to call? La! Think of it! The duke of Haverleigh!"

Her parents were stunned, then delighted, by her response, having expected quite the contrary and been prepared to Do Battle and exert full parental pressure. Soon they were seated about their daughter on the settee, enthusiastically recounting the duke's visit and making plans to return to London in the morning.

No one saw Jonathan sadly shake his head and leave the room, looking suddenly old and very tired.

❖Chapter 14❖

IN THE WEEKS FOLLOWING HER RETURN TO London—with her parents, but without her grandfather —Sabelle did, indeed, become known as the belle of the Season. Calling cards arrived by the score, and with them came invitations to balls and routs, the opera, chaperoned strolls in Vauxhall Gardens, and Wednesday evenings at Almack's. Lady Isabelle Corstairs had become the darling of the hour, and no fashionable hostess could resist putting her name at the top of her list of invitations.

But whenever Sabelle's name appeared, so did the duke of Haverleigh's. If Sabelle was their darling, Hart was their man, and when the two were seen dancing together—he with his tall, dark male beauty, she with her fragile perfection—the rumor mills worked themselves into a frenzy. And on the sidelines, crestfallen beaus gritted their teeth while disappointed young misses went weeping to their mamas.

As the Christmas season drew near, the *ton* threw itself headlong into the holiday spirit. There were as many as three or four social functions every night, and Sabelle was determined to attend them all. She *would* be seen, she told Jeannie, with the man she intended to humiliate at the altar —as much as she possibly could; then, when the day of reckoning came, there would be not one left in the city who hadn't seen him at the height of his pride—and thus that much better comprehend his *fall!*

So it was not unusual for her to begin an evening at one ball, leave it to attend another, and wind up at a third or a fourth, with the duke somehow always showing up at the new place as well; she always attended these with her mother or another suitable chaperone, however, since neither His Grace nor any other eligible gentleman could be allowed to escort her alone—unless he was formally engaged to wed her.

As to the matter of His Grace's intentions, Sabelle bided her time, making every effort to appear the charming young innocent he and the world believed her to be. She knew they had to go through the formalities of courtship; the *ton* expected it. But she also knew he had already spoken to her father and that Lady Strathmore viewed her as an excellent prospect for her grandson. It was only a matter of time till he proposed. *And then she would have him.*

Of course, she realized there were risks for herself in this matter of revenge, as Jeannie, still her only confidante in the dangerous scheme, was never at a loss to point out.

"Ye ken ye'll nae be able t' show yer face t' the *ton* again, once 'tis finished, d' ye no'?" the young Scotswoman said to her as she was preparing for a cotillion at Almack's one evening in mid-December.

Sabelle peered into the looking glass above her dressing table. She saw Jeannie standing behind her, putting finishing touches on her coiffure. "Jeannie," she said, "when have you ever known me to give a fig about the *ton?*"

"Ach, lassie, I ken yer feelin's in the matter, but *think!* Wie the *ton* agin ye, there canna be other offers—from respectable gentlemen. D' ye no' wish t' wed *someone?* Is yer revenge worth windin' up a spinster all yer life?"

Sabelle shrugged. "I cannot say I am as frightened at the prospect of winding up on the shelf as some of the young ladies I've met since coming to London. Why, catching a suitable husband is all they *think* about!"

Jeannie nodded. " 'Tis a young woman's lot in life, I fear."

Sabelle watched her insert the final hairpin in the twist of curls and tendrils she'd fashioned into an elegant hairstyle in the Grecian mode, then turned to face her. "Well, it is not *this* young woman's lot in life!" She pointed to herself with a stab of her index finger. "And that's because I was raised to use the brain God gave me.

"Jeannie," she continued as she rose and walked toward the tall wardrobe where an exquisitely designed turquoise velvet gown hung in readiness, "there are dozens of things I'd love to be doing which do not require being wed! My work with animals, for instance, and reading books, and enjoying God's good green earth, with its flowers and trees and fields. Why, there wouldn't be hours enough in the day to do it all—and none of it needing a man beside me to say 'Tut-tut, Sabelle! Mustn't soil your gown!' "

"There are other things a man cuid gie ye," Jeannie said suggestively as she removed the gown from the wardrobe.

"Hmph! Children, I suppose you mean."

"Aye, but 'twas the pleasures o' gettin' 'em I was thinkin' aboot." Jeannie sported a mischievous grin as she helped Sabelle into the gown.

"Jeannie!" came Sabelle's muffled reply from under the folds of velvet.

Jeannie giggled, and Sabelle wondered whether her friend hadn't been keeping secrets from her with regard to her private affairs. The two young women were confidantes and had—she thought—shared everything of a private nature since they'd formed their friendship. Still, she wondered . . . She knew the Highlander spent a good part of her free time with Michael Kelly these days, and she'd noted the way the big Irish groom's eyes lit up whenever Jeannie came into sight. Did Jeannie know more about the things that went on between a man and a woman than she was telling?

It hurt a little to think that her friend hadn't confided in her if this were so. After all, she'd made Jeannie privy to the most devastating personal incident of her own life and—

Maybe that was it! The disaster at the Shakespeare's Head had left a nasty impression on Sabelle where intimacy with a man was concerned, and Jeannie knew this. Perhaps Jeannie was only being considerate in not bringing up such matters; maybe she realized a woman who'd been *forced* wouldn't find such discussions pleasant.

Unbidden, a memory of the pain she'd suffered at the loss of her virginity intruded, and Sabelle shivered. If that's what women had to endure in the marriage bed, she was well out of it!

Jeannie noticed Sabelle's distress and sighed as she gently turned her around and began fastening the row of tiny, velvet-covered buttons at the back of her high-waisted bodice. "Ach, Sabelle, fergie me. I hadna thought t' be bringin' *that* up! But, lassie, d' ye no' wish bairns aboot ye someday? They're a pleasure in themselves fer a woman." Jeannie had been a member of a large family before the illness had struck down her parents and siblings, and she remembered the little ones fondly.

Sabelle considered this quietly for a moment. It was true that she enjoyed children when she met them at other people's homes occasionally. They were such open, honest little creatures, and she thought there was nothing sweeter than a child's happy, untroubled laughter.

Also, as an only child growing up without seeing much of her parents, she had longed for brothers and sisters to play with; she had even sworn once, when she was very young, that she would someday have at least a good half-dozen or more. That way, she'd thought, they'd never be lonely or lacking someone to talk with.

Of course, she'd made do with an admirable substitute, she thought: The animals she'd always had about her and loved were much like her children. If she had to, she'd make do with them for the rest of her life as well, then, and she said as much to Jeannie.

The Scotswoman shook her head in disagreement. "I luv the dumb beasties, too, Sabelle, but I dinna see mysel' doin' wie nary a bairn because of it. Ye canna put Brendan in a cradle or hug Brandy t' yer breast on a cold winter's night! And a guid mon's arms aboot ye on sic a night wouldna hurt, either, na matter wha' ye maun think!"

A footman came to tell them that Lady Strathmore's carriage had arrived to collect Sabelle, for Justin's grand-

mother was to be her chaperone that evening; Lady
Marjorie had begged off, ironically complaining that her
daughter's mad dashes about the city's ballrooms had her
exhausted.

As Jeannie met the servant at the door, Sabelle considered her friend's words. A man's arms about her on a cold
winter's night? She remembered some warm sensations—as
well as some strongly exciting ones—when Justin Hart had
first taken her in his arms that night. But she also recalled
what it had all led to: fierce pain and bloodstained thighs!
No, *never*. On the shelf, she might be, but she would be
safe from such horrors on that shelf, and that was where she
would stay!

Thanking Jeannie for her help, Sabelle hurried toward
the stairs.

But when she descended those stairs, it was not some
footman or groom of the marchioness who waited to escort
her to her carriage. It was Justin Hart. Devastatingly handsome in his impeccably tailored evening attire, the duke
looked up at her, silver-gray eyes coursing over her slender
form. She stifled a gasp of surprise, then moved down the
stairs, entirely too conscious of those eyes that followed her
every step.

He was dressed all in black, except for the crisp white
folds of the cravat that showed at his neck, accentuating the
lean, bronzed contours of his face. And not for the first
time she was reminded of a large, sleek jungle cat—a pan-
ther, such as she'd once seen in a book in her grandfather's
library. Controlling an urge to turn around and run back to
her room, swearing off her entire scheme, she pasted a
smile on her face as she addressed him.

"What a surprise, Your Grace! But, I confess, a pleasant
one." She glanced about, certain her mother would be hurrying down the hall, wondering whether Lady Strathmore
was to be in attendance as well.

Justin's dimples framed a lazy grin like a pair of brackets
as he saw her darting glance. "Your mother is satisfied that
you'll be properly escorted and chaperoned, m'lady. We
spoke before she sent your footman up, and I explained to

her that my curricle threw a bolt this afternoon, so I decided to join my grandmother in her carriage. She awaits outside.''

Sabelle stiffened, then managed a nod she hoped appeared gracious. How had he *known* she'd been wondering about her mother? Quickly she reminded herself it was not the first time he'd seemed to read her very thoughts; and, also not for the first time, she cautioned herself to be extremely careful with Justin Hart. The man was no fool, and if her plan was to succeed, she'd need to keep her wits about her.

The footman who'd been hovering came forward with Sabelle's long evening cloak; of an aquamarine velvet that matched her gown, it was trimmed in ermine about its full, old-fashioned hood and at the hem. It had cost so much that her father bellowed mightily over the expense, complaining that he could have had a new carriage and the finest team in London for what it had set him back.

The duke stepped forward and took the cloak from the servant, setting it about Sabelle's shoulders himself. It was a personal gesture by the very manner in which he did it: aligning its shoulder seams along the sensitive flesh at the sides of her neck and shoulders; carefully raising the voluminous hood above her high coiffure before settling it gently in place; lightly touching his fingers to her throat as he fastened the single velvet frog to hold it in place.

When he had done all this, taking his time and completing the task expertly, he stepped back a pace and held her eyes with a gaze that bore a strange, silver-gray light.

''Beautiful,'' was all he said, but in a voice so low, Sabelle knew she was the only one to hear it, despite the footman's presence a few feet away.

Justin watched the uncertainty in her smile before it broadened and quickly became more confident. She was unaccustomed to compliments, this bright new little meteor of the Little Season, and he wondered why; she had, after all, been the recipient of praise from adoring young bucks for several weeks now. That alone ought to have accustomed her to such praise.

But then he recalled a sunny September day when she'd nearly tripped over her own feet to curtsy to him at that hunt. She'd been such a raw, unpolished little gem then, and he remembered, too, being taken aback by the changes he'd seen in her at her coming-out affair. All this glamour and finish were new to her, then, and he would swear the chit still didn't realize how beautiful she was. Accustomed as he was to women like Sarah Cavendish, who couldn't pass by a decorative wall mirror without admiring themselves, he found her refreshingly original.

Of course, he added to himself as he escorted her out to the carriage, he was beginning to find almost everything about her refreshing. For one thing, there was an open quality about her that cut across the artful posings of London's drawing rooms and ballrooms like a breath of fresh air. She'd never been taught to pretend or dissemble, and if this left her appearing a bit rough around the edges to sophisticates like Lady Sarah and her set, he couldn't care less. These were exactly the qualities he required in a wife. For once his grandmother had been right; she was an innocent, a *tabula rasa* which he could mold and finish according to his own preferences and needs. And her beauty was a definite bonus. She'd do.

"Good evening, my dear," said Lady Strathmore as Sabelle was handed up into the carriage.

"Good evening, my lady."

"I do hope you'll forgive this slight change of plans."

"Not at all, Lady Strathmore." Sabelle settled herself against the plush squabs of the carriage's richly upholstered interior and watched the duke swing himself gracefully up into the carriage—in a fluid motion that was characteristic of all his movements, despite an injured leg.

Like a cat, she thought as she watched him take the seat opposite her and the dowager, *a big, dangerous cat.* Then, realizing her face might be betraying the apprehension she felt, she dismissed these thoughts at once and offered him the practiced smile she'd begun to think of as her bait.

While his grandmother went on about the broken curricle and the absurdity of young men who insisted on taking the ribbons of such vehicles themselves—and in this frigid weather!—Justin studied Sabelle's face. There was another quality about her that drew him: Just when he began to think she was an open book, with her frank opinions on everything from fox hunts to Byron's poetry, he would catch the barest hint of some intrigue in a smile, such as the one she'd offered him just now. Of course, he knew he was no stranger to enigmatic smiles from women, just as he knew there was usually no enigma behind them at all. They were the stuff and substance of the coquette, the practiced flirt who often used her fan in conjunction with the unspoken messages.

But Isabelle Corstairs was no coquette. Yet he every so often sensed something mysterious brewing beneath the lovely surface, and the experienced soldier in him advised caution. In the next instant, however, he dismissed this as fanciful, if not unfair.

You've spent too much time in the campaign, old man, he told himself as he gave himself over to enjoying her exquisite profile while she conversed with his grandmother. *The wench is everything she appears to be, and you'll have her wedded and bedded by spring.*

The assembly rooms of Almack's were crowded with a glittering array of ladies and gentlemen in holiday mood. Lights from hundreds of chandeliers and sconces shown gaily on well-dressed heads, and festoons and swags of pine garland and holly marked the festive season. It was a place decked out for the *ton* at play, and the chosen few who were allowed within its exclusive walls were making the most of it.

"Good heavens!" exclaimed Lady Strathmore when her threesome entered the main ballroom. "The entire world is here tonight." She scanned the dance floor with a critical eye. "I wonder how they ever intend to get any dancing done."

"Indeed, my lady," said Sabelle, "it is exactly as my mother predicted. Everyone she knew, she said, would be in evidence and pretending they enjoyed being squashed, like herring in a barrel. It is the reason she decided on a case of the vapors and remained home."

Justin grinned down at her. "A convenient thing, sometimes, vapors and hartshorn for a lady. Do you follow your mother's example, m'lady, or are you more inventive?"

"I suppose one might say I am inventive by not inventing anything, Your Grace," Sabelle quipped. "I have always found that if I had no wish to do something, I had merely to say so."

Lady Strathmore raised an eyebrow. "Such an absence of strategy might have been useful in the country, perhaps, but I think you'll find that, here in London, one must occasionally . . . invent."

Justin gritted his teeth. It was so typical of the dowager to be frank about the practices of the *ton* and its use of artifice, but he wished she wouldn't preach it to Sabelle. The girl was guileless and forthright, dammit, and he wouldn't have such freshness spoiled by the bloody *ton* and its unwritten rules! Perhaps, once they were wed, he'd pack her off to Harthaven, his estate in Kent, and keep her there. He doubted she'd object too much; she was country-bred, after all. And, of course, that would leave him free to go about elsewhere, at his leisure, without a jealous duchess peeking over his shoulder at his comings and goings!

He picked out the brunette curls of Sarah Cavendish across the room, where she stood among a circle of admirers. Lady Sarah might not know it, but *her* jealousy had been showing lately. Oh, she tried to hide it, but Justin had caught some sullen glances when she thought he wasn't noticing, and they were always the result of his interest in Isabelle Corstairs. It was clear she disliked the competition, and this annoyed him. It wasn't as if he'd promised marriage, nor had she indicated she wanted that from him. Or had she?

Women, he thought, could definitely be tiresome. It seemed even the sophisticated Sarah wasn't immune. He made a mental note to send her some sort of trinket and a word or two, to signal the end of their affair. Then he smiled, putting these thoughts from his mind, and turned to Sabelle.

"May I request the honor of a dance, Lady Isabelle?" His leg had been acting up again in this damnably damp, cold weather they'd been having, and he'd have preferred not to take to the floor, but he was committed to his duty: Courtship had to have its embellishments, and the chit was a beauty, after all; he could think of worse things to endure.

Sabelle's eyes traveled to the overcrowded dance floor and her mouth formed a slight moue; then she tilted her head to one side and glanced up at him with a hint of mischief.

"Shall I be *inventive*, Your Grace? Or would you prefer an honest, out-and-out 'No'?"

He laughed, glancing to his other side to see his grandmother's reaction, but the dowager had been distracted by a pair of old friends who'd called a greeting.

"The latter, by all means, m'lady," he said with a grin as he took Sabelle's arm and began to lead her toward a corner of the room that appeared to be less crowded.

Lady Strathmore caught them out of the corner of her eye, and Sabelle saw her give an almost imperceptible nod of approval. It made Sabelle uncomfortable for a brief moment before she gave herself a mental shake, determined to dismiss it. She liked Lady Strathmore, and since she knew the dowager encouraged her grandson's attentions to Sabelle, she was not without some guilt over the fact that her plan would affect the marchioness as well as the duke. She dearly wished she could avoid this.

And, of course, there had been those brief thoughts she'd entertained of resurrecting a match between the dowager and her grandfather. That would be out of the question now, though.

Thinking of her grandfather brought her a spasm of even greater guilt. He'd looked so bewildered and defeated when she said she would go back to London with her parents. Dear God, how she wished she could have told him the truth! Of course, in the end he'd find out and perhaps even applaud her, but in the meantime it was difficult to think of the hurt she'd seen in his eyes when she left.

While they walked toward the less-crowded area, Justin fell into a mode of conversation which had become familiar to Sabelle during their courtship: He plied her with questions which were clearly designed to test her academic background and intellectual skills. She didn't know it, but more, even, than her ingenuous qualities and the suitability of her social background, the duke felt he had to be sure his future duchess had a discerning mind and the education to feed it. He was, as Thomas Long had known years before, always hungry for mental stimulation, and a wife who couldn't measure up in this capacity would be as much of an anathema to him as one who failed to pass the *ton*'s rigid social standards.

But what Sabelle did know was that she was beginning to find it irritating to be made to feel as if she had to pass a series of tests. And his questioning her seemed to indicate this. At first she had found the questions stimulating, but when they began to take on the form of a bombardment, she knew it wouldn't be long until she felt the need to counterattack.

Listening now to a question from him about Byron's opening cantos to the poem that had made him famous, Sabelle decided the time had come. "Indeed, Your Grace," she said, smiling sweetly up at him, "there can be no doubt the poet formed Childe Harold as a dream figure. But do you not think this enabled him to use his hero in a dramatic pose?"

"A dramatic pose?" Justin sounded intrigued.

"Yes, one which would free him—ah, the poet, that is—to speak to us all?"

"To us all? To whom, exactly?"

"All of us who've read the poem in such numbers, of course. It is not only the *ton* who have made Byron famous overnight, though I am sure we may begin with the aristocracy." She gestured toward the room and its glittering crowd. "These people have read the poem and, I am sure, loved identifying with Childe Harold's glamour and a certain sense of being above it all."

Justin was about to comment that his friend saw the aristocracy as a bored and jaded lot, and that if his hero had given any fresh meaning to their lives, it had been inadvertent on Byron's part. As he opened his mouth to speak, however, Sabelle asked her next question.

"But who else might have read the cantos?" she asked, and he thought he detected a humorous gleam in her eyes.

"Why, the common folk who can read, I suppose."

"Exactly so, Your Grace. The masses—everyone from the schoolmaster in his closet to the vicar in his country study. To them Byron's hero offers an exciting escape from their humdrum little lives, don't you agree?"

"I do, but—"

Her third question came barreling down atop the second. "And who else might be reading about the famous hero who, along with his creator, appears to have taken this country by storm?"

"Well, m'lady, let me—"

"Who would see the mysterious suggestions of evil in the hero's character as something to be vigorously reformed— if not vicariously"—here Sabelle added a sly little smile— "and secretly enjoyed?"

A slow grin began to form as Justin responded. "I suppose I must answer by saying the Puritans, with their reformist mentali——"

"Quite so, Your Grace, but tell me—"

An explosive laugh met her ears. It was dampened somewhat by the strains of the orchestra and the buzz of conversation in the room, but several nearby heads turned to glance at the duke.

As for Justin, he continued to laugh as he regarded Sabelle with pure delight. He'd begun to realize what she was about with the last question. The wench had turned the tables on him, by God, and quite neatly, too! Ah, she was an unexpected prize, this one, and he made a quick note not to prolong this much further: He would contrive a means of being in private with her and propose marriage at once!

"Forgive me, m'lady," he said, "but you see, it is not too often that I am caught in my own game. *Touché*, my dear Sabelle! I deserved that."

Then, without another word, he ushered her toward the dance floor, which had emptied somewhat, owing to the fact, she supposed, that the orchestra was playing a waltz. Not everyone at Almack's had yet learned—or perhaps accepted—this daring dance where gentlemen and ladies actually touched while they moved gracefully about the floor.

As she felt his hand clasp her waist, Sabelle forestalled a shiver that she knew had a great deal to do with his touch; it had a vaguely possessive quality to it, and his other hand, as it held hers, was firm and sure—and very warm.

But she was also aware of something else about him that was affecting her. She'd been oddly confused by his laughter of the moment before—discovering that Justin Hart, for all his arrogance, had the ability to *laugh at himself!* Through her grandfather's influence, she'd grown up valuing this ability, and, try as she might, she couldn't help being taken by it in the man she'd been certain she despised. In view of what she planned to do to him, the realization was unsettling; she made a mental note to double her guard.

They were halfway around the floor before the lilting effect of the music's three-quarter time relaxed her enough to look at her quarry. And as soon as she'd done so, she knew it was a mistake. Intense, silver-gray eyes locked with hers, their look unmistakable. She'd seen that look before, on starving cats and other animals she'd rescued, when she offered them their first meal. It left her wondering who, in this vengeful game she'd devised, was the true quarry—the duke, or herself!

Needing desperately to find some time alone to gather her thoughts and compose herself, Sabelle murmured a brief response to Justin and excused herself to find the ladies' retiring room.

As she entered the antechamber designed to afford additional privacy between the outdoor hallway and the retiring room itself, however, something happened which kept Sabelle from entering the secluded inner chamber: She heard a smoothly intoned female voice mentioning her own name, and then, to her astonishment, several feminine voices joined in laughter!

Sabelle froze, unsure what to do, when the original speaker went on. Where had she heard that voice before?

"Really, my dear Cecily," the woman was saying, "I cannot help but wonder what he sees in the chit. Why, she's a child, barely out of the schoolroom!"

"Nevertheless, my dear Sarah," said another voice, "my brother says that at Brooks's they're laying odds not on *whether* the duke will offer for her, but *when!*"

Sarah . . . Sabelle searched her memory frantically. *Sarah who?* And then she remembered. Her mother had told her that Haverleigh's name had been linked with a dark-haired woman they'd met at dinner at Carlton House . . . a very *beautiful* dark-haired woman, as she now recalled, named . . . *Lady Sarah Cavendish.*

The amused tinkle of Lady Sarah's laughter brought Sabelle's attention back to the hidden gossips.

"I do not wonder at that, Constance, dear. His Grace is not the only man of high *ton* who must take himself a virgin bride to ensure his inheritance. I fully expect him to do so. Then, while he settles her in the country somewhere and gets her with child every year or so, he will arrange to take his, ah, *better pleasures* elsewhere."

Titters of shocked amusement met Sarah's statement, and the one who hadn't yet spoken protested between giggles that Lady Sarah was being "too outrageous."

"Never say so," Sarah replied as Sabelle felt a rush of white-hot fury. "I know Justin. Do not be surprised," she went on snidely, "if he *weds* her, *beds* her, and, ah, *sheds* her, if you take my meaning."

Sarah laughed at her own wit, and titters from the others made Sabelle swallow the taste of bile in her throat. She managed to stagger back into the hallway.

Oh, God, she thought, *I've got to get away from here!*

Wishing for the first time that she carried some of the hartshorn her mother was never without, in her reticule, Sabelle took several deep breaths while looking wildly about for a place to hide.

The snide remarks of a woman who, with amazing clarity, she now realized must be Justin's mistress were all too terrible. But they weren't the main focus of her distress, though she thought she'd die if those women were to come out of the door right then and surmise that she'd overheard their vicious gossip.

She managed to straighten and make her way to a small alcove adjacent to one of the smaller assembly rooms. What truly rankled was the substance of Sarah Cavendish's remarks and, despite their cattiness, Sabelle's sudden conviction that they held more than a germ of *truth*. All the while she'd been playing at her little game to bring Justin Hart to his knees, *he'd* been playing a far more cruel game with *her!* After all, her plans involved the terrible humiliation of someone who, in her mind, had earned it; but it wasn't as if it would go on forever, affecting him for a lifetime. Sooner or later the gossip over his embarrassment would die down and he could resume a normal life, couldn't he?

But what he had planned for *her* was far, far worse: While his duchess was tucked away somewhere, bearing his heirs, he would humiliate her again and again by pursuing his dalliances—*throughout the whole of their married lives!* The pain she'd be forced to bear—trying to hold her head up in public while tongues wagged behind her back and people looked pityingly at her—was too much to even think about!

That she had never, from the beginning, intended to *be* that duchess didn't signify. Someone would have to go to the altar with the duke of Haverleigh someday—some poor, unsuspecting creature who had no idea her life was about to be made a misery.

Oh, the bastard! Sabelle thought to herself as her spinning brain began to settle into a new phase of reaction, and this one as clearly calculating and cold as polar ice. *Do that*

to some unsuspecting innocent, would he? Not if I have any-
thing to say about it!

And with a look of grim determination, she set about
relocating her quarry.

❖Chapter 15❖

AFTER LEAVING ALMACK'S, LADY STRATH-
more's small party traveled to St. James Square, where
a crushing rout was in progress. Sabelle remarked that perhaps, instead, they ought to have gone directly to their
third destination, a ball given by the duke and duchess of
Devonshire. The marchioness grumbled to her grandson
that she was becoming too advanced in years to endure
such a marathon.

It was then Justin delighted her, informing the dowager
that he intended to propose marriage to Lady Isabelle that
night. And if she were to shut her eyes to the slight irregularity he wished to impose upon her duty as chaperone, he
further informed her, she might have her wish to retire
earlier than the pre-dawn hours most of the *ton* were accustomed to—and the pleasure of greeting Isabelle Corstairs as
her future granddaughter-in-law the next day: She need
only agree to being taken home immediately from this
rout, allowing him time alone with his intended to pop the
age-old question.

"My dear Justin," said the marchioness in the moment
they had for this exchange, for Sabelle, greeted by a pair of
distant cousins of her mother's, had turned aside for a few
words with them, "if anyone were to learn of your being
alone with the young lady in a closed carriage—"

"Yes, yes," Justin cut in impatiently, "but how the devil
am I to propose if I'm not alone with her?"

"Nevertheless, a privacy of the sort you've set forth is quite improper."

Justin was losing his patience by the second. His behavior had been exemplary for weeks—never touching the chit, except in ridiculously circumscribed ways, always seeing her in the presence of acceptable companions, adhering to every convention and rule, written or unwritten. But his appetite had been whetted, particularly in those moments when he'd danced with her following her endearing little set-down at Almack's. Moreover, he was beginning to be more and more aware of an underlying passion in Sabelle, something he'd almost forgotten glimpsing long ago, during a brief, but heated, exchange at that hunt. She had a natural sensuality about her, a quality that he was certain she wasn't aware of herself, but which, perhaps, he was beginning to draw to the surface: He'd felt her tremble when he took her in his arms for that waltz!

He sent the dowager a look that would have had the men under his command shaking in their boots. "What, madam, do you expect me to do? Sweep her off her feet and propose under the refreshment table?"

Undaunted by the look she knew had cowed less stalwart creatures, Lady Strathmore gave him a quelling one in return. "Impertinence does not become you, Your Grace!" But a glance to the sidelines told her the object of their discussion would be returning in a moment; so she heaved a sigh, deciding to relent. This engagement had, after all, been her idea to begin with, and she was growing weary, with all these late-night functions the courtship necessitated.

"Very well, Justin, you've made your point. So long as I have your word that you will carry this out with an eye to the utmost discretion and—"

"You have it."

The dowager accepted this with a regal nod. "Now," she said, as she saw Sabelle coming toward them, "for a little *invention* of my own."

Justin caught the barest glint of amusement in her eyes before it was gone and she addressed Sabelle.

"My dear, I'm terribly sorry, but it seems I've been taken with the fiercest of megrims . . ."

Half an hour later Lady Strathmore was comfortably ensconced in her bedchamber while the duke retained use of her carriage to escort Sabelle home.

"So good of you to allow this little deviation to accommodate the marchioness," said Justin after directing the driver to proceed to the Corstairses' address by the longest route possible.

Sabelle eyed with trepidation the leather window shades that were now drawn closed—shut at the direction of the dowager herself when she explained that the duke would be seeing Sabelle home after dropping her off. Lady Strathmore further explained that, "for the sake of propriety, my dear, it would be wisest not to allow passers-by to see who is—and is not!—in the carriage."

The dowager had assured Sabelle she was not to trouble herself about the irregularity, saying her grandson was "the very soul of honor."

Sabelle had felt herself stiffen at this. The marchioness, of course, did not have the benefit of Sabelle's experience with her grandson, Sabelle found herself thinking bitterly, or she'd not have used the man's name in connection with the word *honor!*

Now Justin was seating himself on the seat just vacated by his grandmother—*beside* her, and not across from her, as before—and Sabelle felt the walls of panic close in on her.

Don't be a ninny! she reprimanded herself. *He hardly takes you for a defenseless girl in a tavern. You're a lady, a respected member of the* ton, *and for that reason you're safe. He'll respect the title,* she couldn't refrain from thinking cynically, *if not the woman.*

With a determination born of sheer will, Sabelle put an end to the trembling which had begun to invade her body and managed to look up at him with a smile.

But not much escaped Justin's notice. "You're cold," he said as he noticed her shiver. He reached for the gloved hands she held in her lap.

A new tremor ran through her, and cold had little to do

with it. His hands, long-fingered, strong, and masculine, were nevertheless gentle as they covered hers. She could feel their warmth right through the satin of her gloves, and this had an unsettling effect she was at a loss to explain.

"It—it was just that gust of wind as the door opened," she prevaricated, then grew silent. Justin was looking down at her now, and the glow from the small lantern inside the carriage had turned his eyes a warm, burnished color that in no way resembled the steely hue she remembered. They were a man's eyes, she found herself thinking, despite the thick, beautiful black lashes some women would die for . . . deepset . . . intelligent . . . riveting, when he wanted them to be—as now—when she was finding it impossible to turn away . . .

"Then we shall have to take care that no 'rough winds do shake the darling buds of May,' " he murmured with a small half-smile.

Sabelle sent him an answering smile, recognizing the lines from one of her favorite Shakespearean sonnets. " 'For summer's lease hath all too short a date,' " she responded in a whisper, still held by the magic of his gaze.

She could tell he was pleased by the way she'd picked up the quotation; his smile broadened, and the light in his eyes danced as he answered her.

"For my part, m'lady, it is this *autumn's* lease which hath all too *long* a date!"

She was intrigued. "How so?"

One of his hands left hers and moved to an errant curl which had escaped the confines of her coiffure; gently, he tucked it behind her ear, then carefully, with both hands now, he raised the wide hood of her cape until it covered her head and framed the contours of her face. Sabelle was instantly reminded of those moments when he'd helped her on with it in her entry hall at home: It was again an intensely personal gesture.

"Too many weeks have gone by, Sabelle," he told her in a voice that was both low and vibrant, "since I met you in the early autumn. And now it is nearly winter. The season has been long and seemed even longer. But I have curbed my impatience, though at the outset, I knew what I wanted."

Sabelle had grown so still, she hardly seemed to breathe. *Here it comes*, she thought, *after all these weeks and days. Yes, Your Grace, it has been long, for I have waited, too, but now I'll have you, exactly where I want you—trapped!*

Justin curled his forefinger under her chin, tilting it up for a better view of her face in the lanternlight. "And what I want is *you*, lovely creature," he continued softly. "Marry me, Sabelle."

Sabelle felt a momentary urge to laugh, but instantly quelled it. *How very like him, this arrogant man who thinks he can snap his fingers and the world will come running! Not, "Will you marry me, Sabelle?" Or: "Please, will you do me the honor of wedding me, Sabelle?" Oh, no! For the great duke of Haverleigh, an imperative is sufficient. "Marry me, Sabelle," as if I were too unworldly, too . . . innocent to know my own mind and must be told.*

Very well, then, Your Grace, you have said it.

"Yes, Your Grace," she told him aloud in a voice clear and steady, "I'll marry you."

Justin's smile was slow and sure as he heard her response. "Never so formal then, Sabelle. The name . . ."—he slowly lowered his head to claim her lips with a soft kiss that lingered just a moment too long to be entirely chaste— ". . . the name is Justin," he whispered as his mouth hovered above hers.

"Jus—Justin . . ." Sabelle whispered, wondering why everything she thought had suddenly flown out of her head and she was shivering again, though the air in the carriage had grown quite warm.

Justin smiled at the wondering look on her face and guessed she hadn't been kissed before, not that that was any surprise: The *ton* guarded its virgin daughters like prized fillies. But her trembling told him she was delectably responsive. Ah, but he was going to enjoy breaking this little filly to saddle!

With a quick and easy movement, he reached beneath her cape and caught her about the waist with one hand, while, with the other, he slipped his fingers inside her hood and around the soft nape of her neck. Then, holding her thus, he again covered her mouth with his.

It was a much longer kiss than the first. Beginning slowly, with a light pressure that accustomed her to the feel of his lips as they moved over hers, it began to build as he sensed her untutored response. For Sabelle *was* responding.

Without realizing it, she had moved her hands from where they'd been, braced lightly against the brocade of his waistcoat, steadily upward as the movement of his mouth on hers began to play havoc with her senses. Soon, without her knowing how they got there, her arms were wound about his neck and her lips parted to admit his tongue, which slipped, ever so gently, between.

Then, as his questing tongue grazed her teeth and the sensitive skin of her inner lips, she thought she heard a soft groan and felt his hand slide to her throat, felt the velvet frog give way, releasing the folds of her cape, and then— *Oh, God!*

Justin's hand found the ripe, lush contours of her breast and stroked it, while a thumb went unerringly to the soft peak. Through the velvet, he felt it harden beneath his touch. The response seemed to inflame him, and he increased the pressure of his mouth, expertly urging her lips farther apart to allow him access. But when he felt her draw back with a start, he forced himself to remember her newness at this game. Reluctantly, recalling his promise to the dowager, he released her mouth, and then her sweetly yielding body.

"Ah, m'lady," he breathed in a voice that was none too steady, "you tempt me, truly you do."

Sabelle felt the spinning world of the carriage interior tilt yet a moment before it was set aright. What had *happened* to her? One moment she was steeling herself to accept the kiss she'd expected as a sealing of the bargain his words to her father would render official tomorrow; then the next thing she knew, she was losing herself in the sensations aroused by this man she despised! When had her arms learned to cling to him with a will of their own? How had her own body become a traitor that sent a liquid heat pulsing between her thighs when he'd dared that intimate contact? When had she become capable of losing all reason in Justin Hart's arms?

Troubled more deeply than she wished to admit by these questions, and even more by the answers she might find, she stared numbly at her hands, which were again folded demurely in her lap. She did not dare look at the man who held the key.

Dimly, she felt the carriage slow and draw to a stop, and she was only half aware of capable masculine hands rearranging the folds of her outer garment.

Then, to her amazement, she heard him chuckle.

"Ah, Sabelle, what a little innocent you are! But no, don't pull away, for you must know it pleases me . . . I'd have you no other way. You can look at me, sweet . . . I won't bite, you know."

At his words Sabelle raised her eyes. She hoped he wouldn't see in them the sudden fury he'd rekindled.

There it was, that word again. *Innocent.* Dear God, how she'd like to spit the truth in his face! Just as she'd like to have told those women and his mistress how—But, no, it would all have to wait—wait for the new resolution which had begun to form in her mind in that alcove at Almack's. For Sabelle would no longer merely leave Justin at the altar; she'd make his punishment far more enduring, just as *his* cruelty would have endured, had he captured a true innocent: She would *wed* Justin Hart and have the pleasure of laughing in his face on their wedding night, at the moment he learned he'd tied himself to a sullied bride!

"That's better," Justin was murmuring as he bent to kiss a dampened tendril that clung to her brow.

The kiss was so feather-light, so tender and full of gentle promise, it nearly proved her undoing. Oh, why did she allow these displays of tender caring to affect her so? It wasn't as if she didn't know they were all a sham designed to lure her into a lifetime of misery. While he took his "better pleasures" elsewhere!

And then, as he handed her down from the carriage and led her to her parents' door, a tiny warning insinuated itself in the depths of her brain. Unbidden, her silent words of moments before—*a lifetime of misery*—began to penetrate her consciousness. And for the first time Sabelle wondered if she had bitten off more than she could safely chew.

Late the following morning Justin sat at a table near the fire, in the front room of White's, with a copy of the *Morning Post* before him. His mind was not on the news, however. Instead, he focused on an inner image, a pair of sea-green eyes making mischief in a heart-shaped face, and their owner smiling impishly back at him while throwing out questions like a schoolmaster with his pupil.

A sharp gust of wind from the door cut across his reverie, and he raised his head and spied three familiar faces; Shelley and Byron came in at once and were followed by Thomas Long, who shut the door in their wake.

"I say, George, look who's about even earlier than we on such a dastardly cold morning! And after dancing the night away, too, from what I hear!" said Shelley jovially.

"Hmm," murmured Byron as he joined his fellow poet by the fire and began to warm his hands, "but you see, my dear Shelley, dukes possess blood which is not only bluer, but richer, than the rest of ours, fitting them to withstand all manner of rigors."

"Egad!" exclaimed Shelley as he pretended to eye Justin with alarm. "Never say so!"

"I have seen evidence of it at least a dozen times," Byron went on with mock seriousness. "One may meet His Grace in the morning for a ride in the park, dine with him, sup, wench, and imbibe with him until all hours, and then, when one is himself well into his cups—and under the table —watch the bloody sod ride off to enjoy his mistress, not the least bit tired or foxed! I tell you, Percy, they are a hardy lot, these paradigms of the peerage!"

" 'Paradigms of the peerage . . . a pretty piece of alliteration, m'lord, but do you not think it a bit, ah, base, used to describe such a—"

"Thomas," Justin cut in with a grin he wasn't able to stifle, "send the waiter after three more coffees while I consider a means of gagging these two with their own cravats, will you?"

The two standing by the fire grinned and drew a pair of chairs up to their friend's table, followed a moment later by Long.

"I say, Justin," said Shelley, "you are looking rather pleased with yourself this morning. Any reason in particular, or oughtn't I ask?"

"You may ask," Justin replied, "but I'm not certain I'll answer . . . at least not until I've spoken to the lady's father."

"Good Lord, man, you've done it!" Shelley seemed genuinely astounded.

"Who is she?" queried Byron, who'd been out of the city for several weeks.

Long said nothing at all, but accepted the coffee the waiter brought him.

"That is precisely the sort of particular I cannot give out yet," the duke said to Byron.

"Ah, but he really needn't," said Shelley. "The entire *ton*'s atwattle, or so I'm told, over the duke's attentions to a certain honey-haired earl's daughter who's set them on their collective ear with her beauty."

"I say, old boy," said Byron, shaking his head in surprise as he reached for his coffee, "you've beaten me at my own brand of insanity."

"He means the Milbank heiress has continued to prove elusive," Shelley chimed in, then paused to study Justin's face.

"Well," he said after a moment, "you certainly look like the cat who's gotten the proverbial canary. Therefore, I suppose there's no help for it but to offer congratulations, eh, gentlemen?"

"Congratulations, Your Grace," Byron murmured . . . *"I think!"*

Justin cocked an eyebrow at this cynical amendment, noting at the same time that his former tutor hadn't yet said a word. Knowing Thomas's views on marriage, he guessed the reason, but he found the man's sullen silence irritating nonetheless.

Shelley gave Justin a wry smile. "My friend," he said, "on that note I believe I'll offer my own bit of advice, if you'll allow me. A bit of verse that's been floating about in my brain of late."

All, even Long, looked up expectantly.

Leaning back on his chair, Shelley began to recite:

> I never was attached to that great sect,
> Whose doctrine is, that each one should select
> Out of the crowd a mistress or a friend,
> And all the rest, though fair and wise, commend
> To cold oblivion, though it is in the code
> Of modern morals . . .

His words trailed off, and he looked at Justin, who was smiling sardonically.

Shelley shrugged, throwing him a boyish grin. "I never said anything different when we spoke of marriage before, if you'll recall, so I do hope I haven't trodden on your ducal toes, old boy. If I have, I—"

"Excuse me, gentlemen," Long said abruptly as he rose from the table, "but I've something I must attend to. Good day." He grabbed his greatcoat and left without another word. The remaining three stared after him in awkward silence.

"Well," said Shelley after a moment, "I don't suppose there's any need to analyze *his* reaction to your news, Justin, but I do feel he could have been less dour about it."

Byron shrugged. "Odd duck, that Long . . . never could feel all that comfortable around him. Excellent scholar, though . . ."

Justin nodded, but his eyes continued to gaze absently at the door through which his old friend had vanished. Had he imagined it, or had Thomas actually been in pain, somehow, when he'd left? Could his news really have affected Thomas so severely? He knew idealists like Long often suffered over things the rest of the world accepted quite naturally. But Thomas's moroseness had begun to grate in recent times, and he knew they weren't as close as they'd once been.

Still, the·man had been a friend for years, and perhaps he deserved some extra consideration . . .

That evening, after he'd called upon the earl and countess of Rushton to formalize what he and their daughter had set into motion the night before, Justin sat in his library and penned a letter. It began:

Dear Thomas,

Having observed your reaction to my news at White's this morning, I cannot help but be disturbed to see how distressed . . .

❧Chapter 16❧

THE DUKE OF HAVERLEIGH'S OFFER FOR LADY Isabelle Corstairs spurred a variety of reactions amongst the *ton*, some of them favorable, some less so, all marked with a great deal of interest and talk. Most of society greeted the announcement with delight: Now there was even more reason to fête this glamorous pair who'd been the object of their speculation for weeks. Men who'd wagered small fortunes on the event and its timing either collected their winnings with smiles, or cursed their luck and the affianced couple, as well. And, of course, though hardly surprised by it, none met Haverleigh's offer with greater joy than the earl and countess of Rushton—except, perhaps, the woman who'd engineered it all, the marchioness of Wincanton.

Lady Corstairs made immediate plans to hold yet another elaborate ball to honor the occasion and was thrilled beyond measure when Lady Strathmore asked to be co-hostess. And so, on the twenty-third of December, in a ballroom decked with holly and mistletoe, Sabelle again found herself standing in a reception line, wearing the practiced smile she'd lately come to think of as her armor. And if the smile wasn't reflected in her lovely aquamarine eyes as well-wishers came to *ooh!* and *ah!* over the priceless emerald-and-diamond betrothal ring Justin had given her, no one seemed to notice.

The wedding was set for the third of May, when it was

expected the weather had a hope of being fair, with the
ceremony to be held in St. Paul's, followed by a grand
reception at the home of the bride's parents. Anyone who
was anyone was invited, including Lady Sarah Cavendish,
who, when she received the invitation, it was rumored,
boxed her maid's ears and then proceeded to decorate the
carpet in her bedchamber with the remains of every break-
able object in sight.

But there were two others whose feelings about the
"wedding of the year" were similar to Lady Sarah's, if not
as demonstrative. In fact, they shared the singularly unique
feature of responding with utter silence: Thomas Long
spent the dreary weeks of winter holed up in his rented
quarters near Fleet Street and was seen by no one, not even
the proprietors of the nearby bookstalls he'd long been
known to frequent with a near-religious fervor; and Sir Jonathan Burke, citing a reluctance to brave the winter's cold
as his only reason for not accepting the scolding invitations
of his daughter to come to London, immersed himself in
the quiet solitude of his beloved Camelot Downs, reading
tales of the ill-fated marriage of King Arthur and Queen
Guinevere.

Eventually, the cold, rainy months of the English winter
gave way to the lengthening days of spring, though the
weather remained for the most part wet and overcast. And
for Sabelle, whose life again revolved around teas and parties and balls, not to mention appointments with the dressmaker and trips to the milliner and glover, the weather
seemed to underscore her mood. She spoke to no one
about her upcoming marriage, and for the longest time she
shared not even with Jeannie the abrupt change of plans
brought on by her anger that night at Almack's, and later
by the duke himself when he proposed.

But her friend had not grown up in a large family without learning to discern nuances in the behavior and moods
of those around her. The Scotswoman began to notice the
faint shadows beneath Sabelle's eyes and that her appetite
had diminished considerably since the engagement was an-

nounced, and she decided it was time to ask some questions. But when she at last dragged the answers out of a reluctant Sabelle, she almost wished she hadn't.

"Ha' ye lost yer wits, lassie?" Jeannie queried in a tone that left no doubt as to what she thought the answer to *that* question should be. Aghast, she pressed forward, despite Sabelle's refusal to meet her eyes. "Wed yersel' t' this mon ye despise—*fer life*? 'Tis daft, and ye *know* it!"

Sabelle sighed and dragged her gaze away from the shortbread Jeannie had baked to whet her flagging appetite; her eyes seemed listless and pale as she looked up at her friend. "Perhaps it is, Jeannie, but I must do it . . . I— I'm committed now."

"Committed? I dinna understand. Surely ye maun at least change back t' yer plans t' leave the rotter hangin' about the kirk!"

Sabelle almost smiled. Jeannie had picked up some colorful East End language during their forays into the back alleys, and they meshed amusingly with the bits of native Scots dialect that had always peppered her speech. But her face was somber as she responded to the suggestion she'd known was coming.

"No, Jeannie, I won't."

She pushed aside the tray bearing the shortbread and an untouched cup of tea, and signaled Jeannie to join her on the settee where she'd been sitting.

"You see, Jeannie, I began to have the idea that there must be more to it than a single blow. That man is planning to marry a helpless young woman—someone he thinks a total innocent—in order to use her as a *broodmare* for his heirs, nothing more. He plans to bury her alive in one of his houses somewhere—probably deep in the country, from what I've been able to ferret out—and keep her there with a—a big belly, while he goes about enjoying his trollops and mistresses, just as he's always done. Do you see?"

Jeannie nodded sadly. "Aye, and ye've decided t' *be* that broodmare."

"No! I mean, yes, I suppose I shall have to eventually

bear his children. But I would have done this anyway, no matter whom I wed.

"But what I *won't* be, Jeannie, is a duped innocent he's led to the slaughter. I'm going into this marriage to teach Justin Hart a lesson he'll spend a lifetime trying to forget. Don't you see? If I merely humiliate him on the third of May, he'll simply be free to find some other victim eventually.

"Oh, he'd be humbled well enough if I jilted him, but, as you once pointed out, that could also prove costly to me —and to my family, by the way. And it would be only a single blow to his pride. *It's not enough!*

"Jeannie, the bastard is so caught up in this need to have an unsullied virgin bride, you would not believe it!"

"So is almost every mon," Jeannie interjected, "though wie the high and mighty, 'tis more than their masculine pride they wish t' preserve—'tis their bluidlines."

"Indeed," agreed Sabelle with a wicked smile. "And I'm about to deal the duke of Haverleigh a blow to his pride *and* make him worry about his precious bloodlines! Oh, Jeannie, can't you just picture him when he thinks someone else has ruined the sacred purity of his bride . . . his *broodmare?*"

The Scotswoman took Sabelle's hand and patted it, but her look was worried. "Aye," she said, "but wha' has me sae afraid is tha' *ye'll* be havin' t' do more than *picture* him. Ye'll have t' *face* him—in the flesh!"

The thought of facing Justin's anger was something Sabelle didn't allow herself to dwell on. The more time she'd spent with him, the more she'd become aware that Justin was a formidable foe. This was no foppish dandy to be led about by the nose. He was a hardened military man, accustomed to giving orders and seeing them obeyed. And he was possessed of a keen native intelligence, augmented by an impressive formal education. Indeed, it was hard to tell which had influenced him more—the rigors of military discipline which shaped him as a man of action, or the strenuous academic discipline that had honed his intellect.

And finally, there was something else to make her wary:

his undeniable physical attraction and a raw animal magnetism which lurked just beneath the surface of his civilized façade. After that one indiscreet moment in his grandmother's carriage, he'd been the model of gentlemanly comportment during the weeks following the engagement; but she was continually aware of this masculine power he exuded, even when he kept it leashed. She would catch a look, a glance, a subtle movement, until there was no way she could deny what she saw—*Justin Hart wanted her physically!* Coupled with her memories of the Shakespeare's Head, this had kept her lying fearfully awake on more nights than she would ever confess to Jeannie.

And so Sabelle did the only thing she could to keep herself focused: She concentrated on her anger and the burning need for revenge. As March flew by, Sabelle allowed herself to be thrown headlong into the prenuptial rituals which were expected of her. April, too, saw her partying and dancing the night away, until, just a few days before the wedding, she was forced to slow her pace and take a rest; she had fainted during a fitting of her bridal gown, and the physician Lady Corstairs had summoned pronounced her on the verge of total exhaustion. She had to cancel all engagements and rest at home until the wedding.

It was on the thirtieth of April, three days before the wedding, then, that an unexpected visitor found her at home, even though the rest of the high *ton,* including her parents, were attending a reception at Clarence House, the home of the Regent's brother. Unheeding of Jeannie's admonition to move slowly, Sabelle flew down the stairs and into the drawing room, where her grandfather waited, then flung herself into his outstretched arms.

"Grandfather! Oh, Grandfather, I've missed you so!" Tears coursed freely down Sabelle's cheeks, but there was a radiant smile on her face. Had her fiancé seen it, he would have known in an instant that what she'd been showing him for months was far from the genuine article.

"Dearest Sabelle . . ." Jonathan's own eyes were moist as he held her close. "Ah, child, you cannot imagine how difficult it's been to keep away!"

"Then why did you?" She pulled back to look at him. "I never meant to—" *I never meant to hurt you when I decided on this dangerous game,* she wanted to tell him, but she knew she couldn't—not now, not yet. "I never meant to appear to be taking sides."

Jonathan shook his head sadly as he patted her hand and led her to the settee by the fire. "Darling girl, don't you know it is *I* who is at fault? I ought never to have put *you* in a position where *you had to take sides.*"

"Oh, but—"

"No, child, hear me out," he said as they sat. "I was aware of your fiancé's nature from the very first. But because I saw your antipathy toward the man, a match between the duke and yourself seemed as farfetched as the moon and the stars.

"But circumstances threw you together and it was a mistake to try to stuff the man's unsavory aspects down your throat in a last-minute appeal to your reason. Given what your mother and father wanted, it put you in an untenable position. I am sorry for it, Sabelle, more than I can tell you."

Sabelle nodded, but tears were again spilling onto her cheeks. *It was I who put* him *in an untenable position! Oh, Grandfather, forgive me!*

She managed to find her voice. "And—and now?"

The old man sighed, taking her hands in his. "Now I have come to London—first of all, to see if you are well. I received the disturbing news that you'd fainted and—" He searched her face anxiously. "Tell me the truth, child, are you—are you ill?"

A warmth suffused her face as she wondered if he could be implying more. He was the one who'd called Justin a rake, and might that not mean he feared the duke had taken advantage of her and gotten her—

Fiercely, she stifled a hysterical giggle. Did the ironies never end? She thought of the long days she and Jeannie had anxiously watched the calendar after the Shakespeare's Head—and the relief with which she'd greeted her monthly flux. Yet her grandfather could only be worried about the current period of courtship and engagement, when Justin Hart had been the soul of courtesy, and never once tried to force her to surrender her supposed virginity!

She made herself maintain an even voice. "No, Grandfather, I had merely overdone things a bit. You needn't worry—truly."

Jonathan searched her face, then slowly nodded. "On to my second reason for coming," he said. "Are you as determined as you were before to wed this man, Sabelle? Answer me truly, because if you've changed your mind, I'll help you extricate yourself. Never fear that it's too late simply because of all the planning and months of—"

"I am, Grandfather." There, she'd done it. Despite the reprieve he'd offered her. She'd thought for a split-second how wonderful it would be if she could flee into his warm care, as she had when she was a child, and let this wonderful man make the world right for her again. *But I am no longer a child, Grandfather, and Justin Hart must pay!*

"Very well, my dear," Jonathan told her, his smile tinged with regret. "Then I should like to attend your wedding . . . if you'll still have me?"

Sabelle gave him a tremulous smile and threw her arms about his shoulders. "Oh, Grandfather, I love you so!"

People said for days afterward that St. Paul's had never seen such a wedding. Dozens upon dozens of the finest coaches and carriages thronged the streets leading to the London cathedral of the Church of England, during a steady drizzle that did nothing to keep the crowds away. Hundreds of common folk crowded the cathedral and churchyard themselves, while thousands more packed every lane from Ludgate Street to Paternoster Row. Child's Coffee House, which stood nearby, was said to have done a sellout business trying to accommodate sodden onlookers who'd waited hours in the soaking rain merely to catch a glimpse of the carriages bearing the duke and the beautiful earl's daughter. And all who attended the ceremony said it was a fitting setting for such an auspicious joining of two important families.

Constructed of Portland stone between 1675 and 1710, St. Paul's had been designed in a restrained, classical Baroque style by the great architect Sir Christopher Wren. Imposing in size, the very immensity of the structure made the people inside feel small and insignificant in the face of the Almighty. Not least among these was Sabelle, who stood beside the powerful man she'd chosen to defy and spoke, in a tremulous voice, holy vows she only then realized were a defiance of God Himself. As she promised to love, honor, and obey Justin Derek Andrew Hart, she almost flinched, expecting the hand of God Himself to smite her where she stood.

But the floor failed to open up and swallow her, and no earthquakes threatened as she accepted her new husband's kiss and turned with him to proceed back down the long aisle. More to her surprise, when they reached the huge arched doors and stepped outside, the sun had broken through a cloud and all was washed in a brilliant burst of late-afternoon sunshine.

"Do you believe in portents, Lady Strathmore?" Sabelle heard her mother ask with this belated brilliance.

"Nonsense, Marjorie," she heard her grandfather remark. "The sun simply realized it didn't dare hide its face any longer, for an occasion encouraged by the marchioness!"

They made their way slowly, because of the crowds, back to the Corstairses' home, and by then it had begun to grow dark. The gas lamps were lit, and hundreds of small flaming points led the families and their guests to the Georgian brick house that, itself, was ablaze with light.

Inside, dozens of footmen moved under the watchful eyes of the majordomo, bearing huge silver trays of a mouth-watering assortment of appetizing foods: Smoked Scottish salmon rested on wafer-thin slivers of bread; *pâté de fois gras*, patriotically referred to as goose-liver paste because of the war which was never very far from everyone's mind, tempted the palate; crisp bits of pork grilled with apple vied with succulent shrimp dipped in ginger sauce.

And alternating with the morsels were trays laden with goblets of the finest Champagne.

Virtually every formal chamber in the house had been prepared to receive guests; dressed in the finest silks and satins, the bejeweled figures of ladies in high-waisted gowns chatted animatedly with gentlemen in perfectly tied cravats and well-tailored frock coats.

Sabelle entered her parents' home on Justin's arm and became truly aware that she was a duchess, when the servants in the entry greeted her as "Your Grace." She blushed and offered them a weak, tentative smile as they wished the bridal couple happiness and a long life together. When a few even ventured to add, "And many healthy children," she felt the blush deepen. Unable to find her tongue, she nodded hesitantly and peered at the toes of her ivory satin slippers; she didn't dare meet the eyes of the tall figure beside her whose hand tightened pointedly over the satin-gloved fingers she rested on his arm.

She heard Justin thank them in the deep voice whose resonant tones had, by now, grown all too familiar, and she tried to think of something to still the frantic beating of her heart. Children . . . yes, he would in all likelihood beget children on her, as she'd admitted to Jeannie that time, unless—unless, what he was about to discover later on this very night enraged him so, he discarded her and never— *Dear God, you must stop this!* she chastised. *Or are you such a weak-kneed fool that you cannot see your own daring to its fruition? Next thing you'll be crying for Mother's hartshorn and water!*

She forced herself to raise her head, and what she saw nearly made her duck it again. The duke's silvery gaze was bent on her face, its unmistakable message one of fiercely possessive pride. *You are mine now,* it said, *to do with as I wish, and that possession begins now—tonight!*

As if to reinforce his look, he bent his head and murmured so only she could hear, "I realize we're required to go inside, that I must share you with a few hundred more well-wishers. But I warn you, sweet, my hunger grows, and I don't intend to prolong this phase of the evening!"

Sabelle murmured what she hoped was an appropriate response, though if someone had asked her, she couldn't have repeated a word she said. The hour of reckoning was at hand, and she was terrified.

What a fool I've been to think I could manage this man with impunity! she thought wildly as she allowed the iron-eyed man beside her to escort her inside. *I cannot begin to imagine anyone—least of all me—bringing Justin Hart to heel!*

She recalled an incident that had occurred outside the Drury Lane one night, just as they'd been about to enter their carriage after the theater. A pair of rather large, rough-looking men, two of the standing crowd who'd been heckling the actors from the pit, had eyed her lasciviously, and one of them made a lewd comment to his friend. Before she or either of them knew what was happening, Justin had set her safely aside and taken them bodily, each by the scruff of the neck, slamming their heads together and knocking them senseless in a single movement.

And there was the time, just a few weeks ago, at a party at Holland House, when she'd stumbled upon him talking to an older man she later found out was a powerful ally of the prime minister. She'd caught only the tail end of what must have been a lengthy exchange, but Justin's parting words to his peer had chilled her to the bone: "Never lie to me again, m'lord," he'd murmured in a voice deceptively soft for the threat it implied. "Your opposition to me on the floor of the Lords . . . that I can accept without rancor. It's part of the game, after all. But if you ever dare to extend your support to me with one hand while conspiring to undermine it with the other, I'll destroy you . . . utterly."

She had retreated hastily, but not before she'd noticed the lord's face turn ashen at the duke's words, and, in Justin's eyes she'd seen a look that froze her to the marrow.

Now, here she was, a mere slip of a woman, planning to avenge herself on him, to demean one of the major steps in his life and—*No,* she told herself ruthlessly as she accepted a glass of Champagne Justin handed her from a passing footman's tray, *don't think of it! Don't think of anything but the immediate moment, and somehow you'll get through it. You* must, *God help you. Somehow, you must!*

As they made their way among the guests, smiling, accepting congratulations and the like, Sabelle concentrated on the voice in her head and retreated behind the smile which hid her burgeoning fears. At some point she became separated from her groom and made her way toward a corner of the ballroom with her second glass of Champagne, nodding to well-wishers as she passed.

Once there, she moved behind a pair of stout matrons engaged in a juicy bit of gossip; there she was able to feel safe and secluded while she sipped the Champagne and gazed over the crowd of guests. She saw her mother and father dancing together and was able to smile: At least *some* in the family were enjoying themselves.

She wasn't so sure about her grandfather, who looked somber as he stood deep in conversation with a man she'd only met tonight for the first time, although Justin had characterized him as his oldest friend. What was his name? Thomas . . . Thomas Long. She remembered, because at the time they'd been introduced, she'd made a mental notation: Long, for his long face.

Then she spied Justin in conversation with a brunette beauty she recognized instantly. Lady Sarah Cavendish. Coming from an important family, Lady Sarah had had to be invited, but Sabelle found herself wishing she hadn't accepted. Sabelle had enough to concentrate on tonight without worrying about her husband's mistresses!

She hurriedly tossed down the remainder of her Champagne when she saw Sarah pout coyly at something Justin said to her, but in the next moment he was introducing her to Thomas Long. Then she saw him look about the room as if in search of someone.

Herself, no doubt.

Swallowing to dislodge a tiny lump of fear, Sabelle hastily grabbed another glass of Champagne from a passing tray. She'd retreated again behind the plump figures of the gossiping matrons and was about to gulp its contents, when a strong hand forestalled her.

"Sorry, pet," said Justin as he set the Champagne glass on the windowsill behind her, "but I've no wish to bed an insensate bride." A smile played about the corners of his handsome mouth, but the amused light in his silvery eyes dared her to demur.

Sabelle felt her face go scarlet, prompting low laughter from her husband. She tried to avert her eyes, hoping he hadn't read the truth in them: She *had* been trying to numb her senses with the bubbly liquid, but not out of maidenly fear. Then she felt him take her chin with fingers that were surprisingly gentle and tilt it upward, forcing her to look at him.

"You've no cause to be afraid, Sabelle," he told her. "I've been told I'm a considerate lover, and I've every intention of being gentle with you when I . . . when we reach the marital bedchamber."

His eyes held hers a moment longer before he released his hold. Then he caught her hand and raised it to his lips in a courtly gesture that was somehow highly sensual.

"Come," he said in a low voice that barely carried above the strains of the small orchestra, "I've sent for our carriage."

As Sabelle allowed him to lead her through the throng in the ballroom, she was only dimly aware of the people and sights around her: two poets she'd just met conversing earnestly in a corner; the slender, still-straight form of her grandfather waltzing with Lady Strathmore; Lady Sarah Cavendish deep in conversation with Thomas Long . . . All these, and more, passed as if in a dream, while the brand-new duchess of Haverleigh approached her wedding night with the enthusiasm of a condemned prisoner facing the axe.

❧Chapter 17❧

JUSTIN GAZED DOWN AT THE TENSE FIGURE of his bride as they entered his town house. It was there they planned to spend the night, prior to a wedding trip to the Hebrides. He noted the pallor of Sabelle's face, the lips she compressed in a tightly drawn line, and sighed. Perhaps he should have let her drink the third glass of Champagne after all. But, dammit, he meant to show her the pleasures of the marriage bed, not let her suffer through it in an alcohol-induced haze!

"Sabelle . . ." he said softly after he'd handed a footman their wraps and watched the servant discreetly disappear.

A small dart of irritation pricked him as he felt her start; then, when she raised huge, fear-filled eyes to him, he relented. *She really is afraid!* He searched his memory, trying to think of something, anything, he might have done to incite such fear, but could recall nothing. Quite the opposite, in fact, for he remembered with vivid clarity her ready response to his intimate exploratory touch the night he'd proposed. He knew he'd struck a pleasurable chord in her, just as he knew she'd respond even more deeply to all he intended to initiate her into when he took her upstairs tonight. So why in hell—

Suddenly Justin saw her shiver and manage what seemed an embarrassed smile. Just normal prenuptial jitters, then, he quickly decided, and with a gentle touch, he took her by the shoulders.

"To prove I'm not the insensitive ogre you seem to be imagining, sweet, I've decided to leave you some time by yourself to . . . compose yourself." He gestured toward the carpeted stairway rising from the end of the entry hall. "Why don't you find my—the master suite on your own— first door to the right—while I tend to a few last-minute traveling details with my man downstairs, here, hmm?"

Sabelle wanted to ignore the look she saw in his eyes, finding it unsettling. Was that compassion she read there? Then a small, sharp jolt of the old anger had her ruthlessly dismissing this as a fanciful notion. It was, more likely, a smooth ploy to gain a virgin's compliance in bed! Raising her chin a notch, she murmured a curt "Thank you, Your Grace," then headed toward the stairs.

Justin watched her go with a smile that hovered on the edge of satisfaction. He wasn't at all sure what he'd said to prompt that spark of animation he'd glimpsed in her eyes, but it *had* been there, and that was what signified: His new duchess was a lively, passionate little creature, and he had no doubt he could turn that passion to an advantage—for both of them!

Sabelle entered the bedchamber to which she'd been directed with trepidation, the last vestiges of anger overtaken again by fear. As she gazed about the huge masculine-looking chamber with its claret-colored velvet draperies, heavy mahogany furniture, and jewel-toned carpet underfoot, a terrible sense of the enormity of her scheme overwhelmed her. *What had she done?*

Frantically, her eyes darted about the room as if seeking an escape route, but all she could see was the large, velvet-canopied Chippendale bed in its center. She tried to tell herself this was because the only source of light in the room was the illumination from a tiered candelabrum on a stand beside it, but she knew it was more than that. The bed's crewel-embroidered coverlet had been turned down invitingly, and at the foot she spied the diaphanous folds of a semi-transparent negligée her mother had had made for her. Someone had apparently withdrawn it from her portmanteau, which rested on the carpet below.

She imagined herself, in just a few moments, being pushed down onto the mattress of that bed, her thighs forced apart with the same ruthless disregard for her struggles she recalled from that night on the fifth of November, which was etched indelibly on her memory.

She sobbed and whirled toward the door—the door which any minute would open and—

She halted, her eyes riveted on an ornate brass key inserted in the keyhole. Fighting the hysteria that threatened, she moved slowly toward it . . .

Justin gave the walnut tall-case clock in the corner of the hallway a final glance, then hurried up the stairs. He knew he'd given her more than enough time. And his hunger for the prize that awaited him after all those weeks and months of acting the perfect gentleman demanded fulfillment.

Smiling to himself with anticipation, he quickly reached the door to his chambers, turned the handle—

Locked.

Disbelief warred with a swiftly rising anger as he tried it again, trying to convince himself it had been his imagination. But, no, the bloody door to his own chambers was *locked shut!*

The little fool had actually dared to lock him out!

Biting back his rage, he forced himself to keep from shouting an obscenity, and rapped sharply on one of the door's raised panels.

Silence.

"Sabelle!" This time there was no restraint. His voice rose with each syllable: "Open the door, Sabelle—*now!*"

On the other side of the door, Sabelle remained frozen where she'd stood since turning the key. She'd heard him, of course. Yet as she continued to stare at the door he was now pounding furiously with his fists, she simply couldn't think.

And so she stood there, listening to the equally furious pounding of her heart, unable to move a muscle until—

She screamed when a devastating crack resounded and the door crashed in. It had been torn loose from its hinges. She took another step backward, and another, watching Justin stalk toward her, his face rigid with anger.

"S-stay away . . . from me, Justin," she stammered as she somehow found her tongue. "I'll not—"

"No one locks me out of my own chambers, Sabelle," he gritted between clenched jaws. "Do you understand? *No one!*"

"I—I . . ." Her heart pounded as she met his eyes. They were a dark, stormy gray with silvery glints that telegraphed his anger. Sabelle's words died in her throat.

"You little fool! Exactly what did you hope to accomplish by such insanity? And what, in the name of hell, have I ever done to warrant this—this—" He gestured with restrained fury at the door hanging crazily off its hinges; then, with a rapid movement, he whirled on it and levied it back in place, securing it with a furious kick that hammered it shut.

But in the next instant he was stalking her again, his words coming out in clipped, measured syllables as he closed the gap between them. "I asked you a question, Sabelle. Have I ever done anything to cause such irrational behavior—*have I?* What reason could you possibly have *to lock me out on our wedding night?*"

Every reason in the world! she wanted to shout. *I am the woman you dishonored in a tawdry tavern, and I hate you for it, hate—*

But this and anything else she wished to shout at him died an instant death as she felt the back of her thighs meet the hard, resisting contours of the bed. There came to her mind a sense of being physically trapped—of Justin the predator, the big jungle cat she always likened him to, and her, his helpless prey. It was all suddenly more than she could bear, and, to her utter chagrin, she burst into tears.

Justin heard only the first sob before he felt the anger drain out of him. Her tears, more than anything she could have told him, reinforced in his mind his earlier conviction that she was suffering from nothing worse than maidenly fears . . . an extreme case of them, to be sure, but nothing more. *This was something he could handle!*

With a small half-smile he reached for her and pulled her into his arms. She resisted for an instant, but then he felt her acquiesce. A second later he was cradling her against him, murmuring soothing words to her, while the sobbing gradually subsided, diminishing to a few watery hiccoughs, and finally silence.

"Sabelle . . . ?" Justin's voice was a hushed whisper in the still chamber. He breathed her name against her hair, which had come loose from its pins and tumbled down her back, along with her bridal veil, the gossamer folds of which were caught on the foot of his bed.

Slowly, she raised her head and pulled slightly away to look up at him. He saw eyes that were a deep aquamarine now, more green than blue, and surrounding them, thick, wet lashes gone spikey from her tears. They were huge in her face, those eyes, and lovely beyond anything he'd ever imagined. Looking up at him from that exquisite, heart-shaped face, they aroused in him a protective instinct he couldn't remember feeling before. Suddenly he was willing to forgive her anything, anything at all, and his smile said as much before he pressed a tender kiss to her brow.

"Better?" he questioned as he tilted her chin up to capture her eyes again.

"B-better," Sabelle murmured, and the fact of it was, she *did* feel better. Her brow puckered with a puzzled frown. What was wrong with her? She'd gone into his arms like a hurt child—indeed, just like the child her grandfather used to hold and comfort—and she'd actually *felt* comforted in Justin Hart's arms. How was that possible, when—

Her thoughts skittered crazily as she felt him pull her close again. There was nothing alarming in the movement itself, for his arms were warm and enveloping as they drew her against the lean length of him; but there was something about this embrace that told her it had little to do with comfort . . . little or nothing at all . . .

His next act confirmed this. She felt his warm breath on her ear, followed by a nuzzling kiss which sent a strange thrill of pleasure rippling along her spine. All at once she recognized his intent, but when she would have pulled away, he drew her even closer.

"Relax," she heard him say. It was a throaty whisper, and in spite of herself, she felt the tenseness leave her limbs. With the butterfly touch of his tongue at her ear, another shiver of pleasure claimed her.

Justin felt the tremor and smiled against the tender spot beneath her jaw.

"That's better," he whispered, and had the satisfaction of feeling her tremble anew. She was his now, despite her virgin fears. It only required patience . . . and expertise, of course, and he had no doubts about his capacities with regard to either. His experience with women was vast, and he'd long ago made it his business to know exactly how to arouse them and then satisfy them. And, surprisingly enough, he'd found two essential elements—patience and technique—to be the key to any woman's pleasure, be she a practiced courtesan or virgin.

Not that I've had all that much contact with virgins, though, he thought as he continued to keep his mind deliberately at a distance and pressed sensual kisses along his bride's throat. *In fact, the only virgin I've ever had was that little whore in the—*

Now, why had he brought *that* up? It wasn't even a pleasant memory, he realized angrily, as an image of a heart-shaped birthmark high on the back of a shapely thigh intruded. *Concentrate a bit more closely on objects at hand, old boy!*

The immediate object at hand was his wife's face, and he took his hands and cupped it, letting his eyes roam over her delicate features. When he saw her eyes flutter open and lock with his, he felt his breath catch in his throat.

Sweet Christ, she's lovely! he thought as he drank in their sea-green depths. He felt the silken mass of her hair wound about his fingers, caught the faint floral fragrance of it, and felt a tightening in his loins, prompting him to lower his gaze to her mouth. Slowly, ever so slowly, he brought his own down to cover it in a kiss that was sensual even before it began.

Sabelle closed her eyes and gave herself up to the touch of his mouth on hers. His lips were warm and pliant as they moved over her own, molding their contours until it seemed the most natural thing in the world to be joined to him this way. Languidly, she accepted the subtle gliding of his tongue along the seam of her lips; then she found them parting to accept its gentle thrust against the tip of hers, and she shuddered.

When his hands slid along the sides of her neck, she was scarcely aware of it, nor of their downward course, until they cupped the fullness of her breasts. But this brought instant awareness, and she drew sharply back, only to find the bed blocking her retreat. Her startled gasp echoed in the silent chamber as their lips broke apart. But before she could utter another sound, his hands had resumed their work, thumbs deftly grazing her nipples until, all at once, Sabelle felt a jolt of pure pleasure sluice through her and settle in the woman's place at the juncture of her thighs.

Remembering another night when his knowing fingers had had such an effect on her, she felt herself caught midway between alarm and the deep, pleasurable sensations at her core. She tried to force herself to remember that, whatever he did to her, she had to endure it; it was all part of her plan. But then he was kissing her again, his tongue playing havoc with the sensitive insides of her lips, while, below, those teasing thumbs never ceased their devastating assault. Helpless to stop it, she found herself riding on a vast tidal wave of passion.

Conscious of nothing beyond his mouth and hands on her, and the sweet liquid heat gathering between her thighs, she never knew exactly when the costly bridal gown of ivory silk fell in a puddle about her feet—or how. Lost in a world of sensation, she was oblivious to the downward course of her shift as it followed the gown. It was only when Justin's lips trailed a path of fire across her shoulders and suddenly found the taut peaks of her bared breasts that she knew—*oh, yes, she knew!*

Then he was gathering her into his arms, his face a study in controlled passion as he whispered her name. "Sabelle . . . look at me, Sabelle . . ."

She raised heavy-lidded eyes to his, trying to remember something . . . something that seemed important, but all she could focus on was the heat of his gaze, the strength of his arms as they held her and the liquid fire in her veins.

"You've nothing to fear from me, little one," she heard him continue as he lowered her to the bed. "I'm aware of your"—he offered a tender smile—"maidenly modesty, sweet, and just to prove it—here, let me show you . . ."

And he turned aside after setting her down and snuffed out all the candles in the brightly burning bedside candelabrum, save one, plunging the room into semi-darkness.

"There," he said soothingly, and in the next moment she was aware of him shedding his clothes, the whisper of fabric against corded muscle and sinewed limb telling her more of this than his pantherlike movements, which were half-shrouded in darkness.

Then he was joining her on the bed, taking her in his arms, pressing lazy kisses to her eyes, her brow, the sensitive skin along the slender column of her neck and throat. She felt his hands again at her breasts, teasing their straining peaks, renewing the searing shaft of pleasure that went directly to the hot, moist place below.

Soon her need grew so intense, she cried out with it. And she heard him answer with a groan before his mouth claimed hers in a kiss that was suddenly demanding and hot, beyond anything he'd yet shown her. She felt his hand sweep her thighs with a sudden urgency, then nestle in the soft curls at their apex. Before she could pull away in alarm, his finger grazed the tiny nub below, and Sabelle's world exploded into shards of crystal fire.

Justin felt her shudder in response to this latest touch, and his own arousal reached a fevered pitch. *He'd never known a woman to respond so readily!* Desperate to slow his pace, he tried to summon some of the distancing maneuvers that had served him in the past, but at that instant Sabelle arched up against his touch and he found his fingers slipping inside her; the creamy wetness of her arousal, telling him as nothing else could, how ready she was, nearly drove him over the edge.

With a groan, he tore his lips away from hers and buried them in her hair, even as he felt her climax again, her tight little sheath pulsing around his fingers as he stroked.

"Sabelle," he whispered, his voice a rasping sound against her ear, "open to me, sweet . . . open your thighs to me . . ."

Sabelle heard the hoarse command and obeyed without thought. She was a collection of pure feelings now, her rational self suspended somewhere far away, her only reality the man beside her and the erotic sensations he aroused in her body.

She felt, rather than saw, him rise up above her, felt the swollen, probing shaft of his manhood press against the sensitive nub he'd touched before. She cried out as another explosion rocked her. Wildly, she arched upward, then felt him enter and drive home. Again, she came, and again, as he plunged and plunged anew, until she heard him cry out and felt his body convulse with hers in a blinding climax of mutual heat.

Minutes must have passed, or hours . . . Sabelle hardly knew. After a time, when her mind came back to claim her body, she gradually became aware of her slowed breathing, of the room, and the weight of the man pressing against her.

Dear God in heaven, what had *happened* to her? How on earth had—All at once the memory of her determination to thwart this man came tumbling down on her, and she bit her lip to keep from crying out in despair. *How could I have succumbed so readily? I didn't really even fight him! I just let him—*

Pausing in this self-condemnation, she found herself reflecting for a moment on what had transpired between them. And she was just beginning to wonder at the difference between the considerate lover he'd been this night—speaking softly, reassuring her, even dimming the lights—

and the man who'd taken her so ruthlessly in the tavern. Then, suddenly, she felt Justin stir beside her.

Surprised, for she'd thought him asleep, she felt herself blushing at having to face him after those intimacies; moreover, she knew she still hadn't cleared her head yet, in the aftermath of—

Oh, God!

Justin had risen to a sitting position on the bed, and even in the dim light she could see the rigid, stony contours of his face. The hazy aftermath of passion vanished, and she was brought sharply back to the reality of what she'd done.

"You deceiving little whore." His voice was dangerously soft, yet the single candle's glow revealed enough of the contempt in his eyes to make her absolutely certain of what must be going through his mind.

As for Justin, he'd felt the ease of entry—no barrier at all —and now no virgin's blood. And now, too, her hot responses made all too much sense: They'd never been the reactions of a virgin, damn her sluttish hide! She'd made an utter fool of him!

Sabelle pulled a tangled sheet up to cover her, then held herself completely still. This was the moment she had waited for, and yet, where she had often pictured herself smiling, not even a muscle moved. For some odd reason, the anticipated glow of triumph didn't come, and all she could focus on was a terrible need to show no emotion whatsoever in the face of the rage she saw building in the man before her.

"What, no words to defend yourself?" Justin continued with growing heat. "No maidenly pleas that I must be mistaken? *Say* something, you conniving little slut!"

Sabelle remained as she was, staring wordlessly at the hands she held folded over the sheet, and this seemed to fuel his ire.

"Bitch!" he raged, grabbing her chin, forcing her to look at him. "How far did you think you'd go, playing the unsullied innocent before I'd—" He gave a sudden, mirthless laugh. "Far enough, I suppose," he said, his mouth twisted in disgust.

He dropped her chin and grabbed her hand to study the third finger, where she wore his wedding and betrothal rings.

"More the fool, I!" he spat, dropping her hand as if it were a live snake.

He heaved himself off the bed.

"Well, my clever little *duchess,* you've gotten what you wanted—the title, the status—all of it." He began jerking on his clothes. "But I'll tell you one thing: You'd better get on your knees and pray that there's no life growing in your belly right now. Because if there is, if I learn you're breeding, I swear to you, I'll never recognize the child as mine! I'll move to divorce you faster than you can say the word, and you can go to your bastard's sire for succor—that is, if you can remember *who he is!*"

Sabelle winced as if she'd been struck a blow, prompting a bitter gust of laughter from her husband.

"Hit home, have I? Well, that shouldn't trouble you too greatly." He shoved himself into his boots, then paused to glare at her. "Just fasten your mind on the things your avaricious little soul has bartered for a conscience: the wealth and position that attach to being a duchess. Enjoy them, *Your Grace*—while you can!"

He headed for the door, then turned for a parting shot.

"Christ! I'm heartily sick of the sight of you!"

He stormed out of the chamber, and Sabelle looked up to see the damaged door tilted crazily against the wall. A few moments later she heard the front door slam and knew he'd left the house.

It's done, she thought as she digested all this, and wondered why she felt like weeping.

❖Chapter 18❖

S ABELLE SPENT THE REMAINDER OF HER wedding night unable to sleep, though it wasn't for lack of trying. She knew the morning would bring a host of decisions to be made and that she ought to be well rested if she wished to make them wisely. But as she tossed and turned in the large bed, sleep wouldn't come. Instead, she was beset by myriad images of what had transpired between her and Justin in that bed and worries about the future.

She knew, too, she was listening for Justin's return. Although she thought she'd do very well if she never saw him again, a part of her wanted him back—to watch him suffer, she told herself. She also realized a good portion of those sleepless hours were spent trying to come to terms with what she'd done, and this disturbed her. Indeed, the conscience he'd accused her of lacking was being inordinately troublesome!

Why am I trying to justify my own behavior when it was his that precipitated it? she asked herself as the first pale streaks of dawn began to filter through the windows. *I suppose I'm simply not accustomed to dealing with retribution,* she reasoned as she dragged herself wearily from the bed.

Then the sight of the broken door leaning clumsily against the aperture—it was the best she could do with it on her own after Justin's departure—brought her back to practical matters. Somehow, she would have to see to its repair. She only hoped she could achieve this before the servants' grapevine sent the news avalanching through the *ton*. There were some risks she was prepared to take, but the chance of a scandal having to do with the intimate details of the bridal bedchamber was not one of them!

As luck would have it, the broken door wasn't a problem. She located a young footman whose job it was to stoke the fire in the kitchen hearth before the rest of the staff awoke and the hinges were repaired before anyone else had arisen.

But if the repair of the door posed no problem, the unexpected stream of callers who began to arrive later that morning did; there was still no sign of her husband, and she was forced to make up excuses for his absence.

Lady Corstairs was the first to arrive, scolding her daughter for "haring off in the midst of your own reception with no word of good-bye and without even your ladies' maid."

She'd brought Jeannie with her and announced their intention of helping Sabelle with her last-minute packing for the wedding trip.

The young Scotswoman's concerned, but smiling, countenance gave Sabelle the courage to invent a credible story for Justin's absence: The duke, she told her mother, had gone to consult with a friend who'd just returned from the Hebrides, to learn what might be useful on their journey.

Once the packing was done, she succeeded in getting rid of her mother by feigning a headache. But just as she was about to fill Jeannie in on the previous night's events, Justin's majordomo announced the arrival of new callers below. The two couples clearly had anticipated being greeted by Justin, or at best by both the duke and his new wife, but hardly by Sabelle alone.

Percy Shelley introduced an attractive young woman named Mary Godwin. Both quickly covered their surprise at finding Sabelle alone and were laughing and in good spirits as they announced they'd come to persuade the newlyweds to forgo the "wild and chilly Hebrides and travel to sunny Italy instead."

Appearing like a dark and somber counterpoint to the buoyant poet and his lady friend were Thomas Long and Lady Sarah Cavendish. Justin's longtime friend regarded

Sabelle with pale, brooding eyes, and Sarah looked sullen,
despite a polite façade. Sabelle again pretended all was well
with her marriage and offered her invented excuse for Justin's absence. That she had once boasted proudly of es-
chewing "inventions" such as the one she was now reduced
to using had Sabelle smiling bitterly to herself. Moreover, it
was all she could do to remain polite to Justin's spiteful
mistress.

"Do tell Justin we were sorely aggrieved to have missed
him," the brunette beauty purred as Sabelle saw the four-
some out. "And tell him from me, my dear, what a naughty
boy I think he was to leave his bride to, ah, her own devices
this soon."

The catty innuendo and the entire strain of putting up a
false front had Sabelle on the verge of tears after they'd
gone. She was just about to run upstairs to borrow Jeannie's shoulder for a welcome release when her grandfather
arrived. Sir Jonathan, much to her relief, never asked where
her husband was, but he was profoundly apologetic for disturbing her, prompting Sabelle's immediate protest.

"Nonsense, Grandfather!" she said, giving him a warm
hug. But as she clasped his thin shoulders and breathed the
dearly familiar scent of him—woodsy and redolent of
horses, even there in the city—it was all she could do not to
release those tears she'd been saving for Jeannie's shoulder.

"Nevertheless, I shan't stay more than a moment," said
Jonathan as he took her hands and gave them a squeeze.
"I . . . only came to say good-bye, child . . . and wish
you a safe journey."

Jonathan continued to hold her hands while he searched
her face. He felt there was something terribly amiss with
her decision to wed Haverleigh—indeed, with the marriage
itself; he'd thought about it long and hard, and Sabelle's
behavior simply didn't convince him she was happy.

"Thank you, Grandfather." Sabelle watched the subtle
play of emotions cross his features and knew he was worried
about her. She'd known that beloved face too long and too
well to be fooled by the nonchalance he tried to affect.

What to do? Should she confess all to him now, this very minute, and be done with it? Let him take her in his arms and comfort her as he'd done when she was a child?

But I'm not a child anymore, and grandfather's getting on in years. What right have I to inflict this sorry business on him?

So, though yearning to unburden herself, Sabelle held her tongue and allowed her grandfather to take his leave.

With his departure, Sabelle suddenly found herself in no hurry to go back upstairs. Amid the coming and going of the morning's callers, she'd caught glimpses of the perplexed or embarrassed faces of various servants, had seen them tiptoeing about as if to underscore what she couldn't help knowing they were aware of: the unexplained absence of the duke on the morning after his wedding.

Now, as she drifted through the elegant rooms of the town house, that absence was more apparent to Sabelle than in all the silent hours of the night. As her footsteps echoed in the empty chambers, she fancied she was hearing the footsteps of her life, through the long, empty years of the future, consigned there by this loveless travesty of a marriage.

She recalled resigning herself to bearing Justin's heirs and realized now that she'd even regarded that duty as something she might look forward to, that the children she bore might be a lovely consolation for the emptiness of her relationship with her husband. Only now the parting words of that husband came ringing back—*pray there's no life growing*—and she wondered if her thirst for revenge had robbed her of both of the joys it was said a woman looked forward to—a happy marriage, and the children that came of it.

Growing fanciful as she wandered about the town house's quiet chambers, she tried to imagine what they would be like, lived in by a husband she loved—and who loved her—and filled with the laughter of children they both adored. She passed through the dining room, picturing herself seated at the foot of the long, mahogany table, her husband at its head, with a large and lively group of youngsters gathered about . . . She imagined herself moving up the stairs with a babe in her arms, her husband beside her as they went to tuck it into its cradle for the night . . .

Soon, not quite knowing how she got there, she found herself in a large chamber whose walls were lined with books, and she knew she'd stumbled across Justin's library. The large oak desk near a window at one end reminded her of its owner; the grace and proportion of its lines in no way detracted from a sense of strength and substance created by its solid construction. She could almost feel the power of the man who used it as she drew near, and yet her fancy continued. There she might greet her husband at the end of a day, perhaps joining him in drinking a glass of sherry, she thought, as she noted a tray with a decanter of the golden liquid and some sherry glasses nearby. And maybe he'd tell her about some correspondence he'd—

Suddenly Sabelle's glance caught sight of just such a piece of correspondence—a letter, oddly creased and lined, as if it had been folded and then smoothed flat again—lying on the desk. Recognizing the duke's unmistakably bold script even from her upside-down perspective, she felt a surge of curiosity so strong that it drew her at once around the desk. Prompted by some unknown force which made her violate one of the basic tenets by which she'd been raised—never to peruse correspondence not intended for her—she began to read:

Dear Thomas,

Having observed your reaction to my news at White's this morning, I cannot help but be disturbed to see it distressed you. But surely you haven't forgotten the reasons I must wed. Need I remind you that any highly placed peer of the realm has a duty to produce an heir? Unlike our friend Shelley, you see, I do have obligations which involve "the code of modern morals": The dukedom must have legitimate progeny, and for that I require a wife.

As for that ephemeral thing men like Byron and Shelley call love, let me simply say that perhaps that is best left to the poets—and dreamers. You may ascribe it to my long-held cynicism, but I truly believe that idealized emotion to be beyond me—or any thinking, rational man.

As for my wedding this child, what do I surrender? I assure you, my friend, nothing—and, least of all, my sexual freedom!

I remain

Your friend,
Justin H

Sabelle found herself trembling with the kind of fury she hadn't experienced in weeks. All the rage and humiliation she'd felt the night she overheard Sarah Cavendish's mocking words at Almack's came rushing in on her. White-lipped, she staggered from the room, the damning letter crushed in her fist.

It took her only moments to locate Jeannie and the bags they'd packed, but she found it slower going when she tried to tell the Highlander what was wrong. Finally she thrust the crumpled letter into Jeannie's hand, at a loss to explain the dull pain that clogged her throat and wouldn't let her speak.

It took Jeannie several minutes to make out the words on the paper; she'd left Scotland an illiterate and had only begun to learn to read under Sabelle's tutelage. Finally her eyes reached the duke's bold signature, and she raised her head and slowly nodded.

It was worse than she'd suspected. She'd known, of course, of the difficult circumstances under which Sabelle's marriage had been launched, but Jeannie was, at heart, an optimist. She'd secretly hoped, despite everything, that there might be a chance for this union, however slight: that Sabelle and the proud duke could somehow get beyond the wrong reasons that had brought them together in this misbegotten alliance, that they might yet learn to love and value each other. But now the duke's hard words told her how foolish her hope had been.

And Sabelle's pale face told her that perhaps she hadn't been the only one harboring such a hope.

Jeannie's heart went out to her friend, and she sought words to express the sympathy she felt. But when she would have spoken, Sabelle turned away and reached for one of the bags on the floor.

Jeannie's eyes widened as she saw her pick it up and head for the door. "Ach, lassie, where are ye—"

"I'm not sure, Jeannie," Sabelle said as she turned back toward the Scotswoman, "but I'll not spend another minute in this house!"

Suddenly a look of pleading entered the aquamarine eyes. "Will you come?" she added in a whisper.

"Aye," came the unwavering response.

Pausing only long enough for Jeannie to grab a second piece of baggage, the two women left the house.

⚜ Chapter 19 ⚜

JUSTIN SWUNG DOWN FROM THE SEAT OF HIS curricle and called to the groom who came running out from the stables behind the town house.

"See they get a good rubdown, Hawkins." He indicated the fine pair of matched grays hitched to the open carriage. "I'm afraid I drove them a bit hard, trying to make it home before this bloody rain started."

Hawkins cocked an eye at the lowering sky. "Been a wet spring, it 'as, Yer Grace."

Justin nodded absently and watched the servant lead the team away, his thoughts not really on the present. Instead, he stood in the soft drizzle puddling the drive, his mind beset by images of the night just past. Of his bride of less than twenty-four hours, whose perfidy had tied him up in knots of rage for the better part of that time.

He would have sworn she'd been an innocent! Even her foolish act of locking him out of his chamber had convinced him of that—though he'd had no reason to doubt it beforehand. Only now he saw that act for what it had been —a patent case of dread at the moment she must face the bridegroom as used goods!

Justin ran a hand through his dampening curls and swore softly to himself. No wonder she'd warmed that bed with so much heat! She was no neophyte, but a practiced—

Abruptly, an image seized him, of shy, trembling responses and untutored kisses that grew warm only when he'd plied her with the expertise of his own practiced skills. Never once during their lovemaking had *she* really initiated any of what passed between them.

He felt a searing heat grip his loins even now, standing before his house in the rain, recalling those heated moments. The impossible certainty that Sabelle had given him the most satisfying bedding of his life! Yet he felt sure it had all been because of her *responses*—not her knowledge of the game. No, he'd reacted to a delicious combination he couldn't even now deny experiencing: untutored innocence coupled with an underlying natural passion that came of what she *was*, and not what she'd been *taught*.

But she'd been no innocent virgin, dammit! Someone had had her before!

Feeling the rage building all over again, Justin began to pace the drive, not yet ready to go inside. If he faced his wife right now, he thought he might kill her.

Not for the first time since he'd stormed out of the house last night, his thoughts turned to who it might have been. *Who'd had her before him?* There had been dozens of young men flocking about her during the Season, but he immediately rejected the notion of one of those young puppies daring what had been done. And he knew from her parents that all other suits had been rejected. Who, then? Someone not directly of the *ton*? From the country, perhaps? She'd spent almost all of her years in Surrey . . . *Had there been more than one?*

"Ah, hell!" he swore aloud. This sort of thinking was driving him to Bedlam! And wasn't that just what Thomas had said when he'd arrived at the tutor's quarters last night, needing a place to stay and sort this thing out?

His mind tripped on the memory of his friend, smiling thinly, all sympathetic concern for this damnable coil his marriage had brought. Thomas . . . who never said a word in reproof, but whose pale eyes communicated with every glance "I told you so."

Well, he'd finally had enough of those brooding, sanctimonious looks. As soon as his head had cleared somewhat —God, the untold brandies they'd consumed in the small hours of the morning!—he'd made up his mind: He would return home and face the little bitch—put her in her proper place! Then he'd get on with his life as best he could.

Thomas wouldn't love him for this, he thought. But Thomas had left his quarters well ahead of Justin, for what reasons he neither knew nor cared. The tutor was hardly his concern right now. His concern was his new bitch wife!

He'd never forgive her for deceiving him, of course. That was inconceivable. And then there was the matter of the obvious reasons she'd trapped him into marriage: his wealth, his position—*her greed!* Odd, though, that she'd never appeared to set much store by those things. Why, when he'd met her in Surrey, she'd seemed the last female on earth who'd—

Enough! He turned toward his front door. His new duchess was a conniving little slut, but he would put an end to her scheming—and her whoredom! The wedding trip to the Hebrides was now out of the question, of course. He would send the little cheat to Kent instead—to Harthaven, his country estate. He had a host of loyal servants there—a staff that would watch her night and day. They'd help keep her obedient—and *chaste!* Even if he had to have them tie her up to do so! Then, when he could be sure she wasn't carrying someone else's bastard—

"Good day, Your Grace." His majordomo greeted him as the door swung open, the man's voice betraying not a hint that there could be anything untoward in the duke's sudden appearance at his door, soaking wet—following his wedding night. But in old Stewart's eyes Justin thought he detected a small flicker of uncertainty, and he was in no mood to deal with it. Fortunately, he knew the well-trained servant wouldn't expect him to.

"Tell my wife I wish to see her in the drawing room, Stewart—in exactly ten minutes!"

The majordomo faced him squarely, but his face seemed to have paled slightly. "Her Grace is not here, Your—"

"*Not here?* What in hell are you talking about?"

"Ah, exactly what I have said, Your Grace. Her Grace has been gone approximately—"

"Gone! Where, for God's sake?"

"Ahem, that I cannot say, Your Grace. She left without informing anyone of where she—"

"Christ! When?"

"Approximately an hour ago, Your Grace." The servant looked apprehensive. "Ah, she appears to have taken her ladies' maid and some of her baggage with her."

"But she had no ladies' maid here! I was going to send for the girl today."

"Indeed, Your Grace, but Lady Corstairs arrived this morning with the young woman and—"

"The countess! Did she go with her mother, then?"

"I do not think so, Your Grace. The countess of Rushton left well before—"

The majordomo left off as his employer whirled and headed for the stairs.

"Ah, will there be anything else, Your Grace?" Stewart called after him.

Justin paused on the stairs for a moment, then barked at the man over his shoulder. "Get Weeks up to my chambers to help me into dry clothes. And tell Hawkins to saddle my mount at once!"

While the majordomo went to comply, Justin tore up the rest of the stairs and charged into his chambers. A wry, bitter smile twisted his mouth as he noted in passing that the door had been repaired.

Run off, would she? Well, he'd see about that! How dare she, the little bitch! It was hellish enough to think she'd made a fool of him, deceived him into this marriage; but if she thought to get away with running out and making a fool of him before the entire world, she was sadly—*sadly* mistaken! He'd find her. He swore he would! And when he did, he'd haul her back there and give her a taste of what *real* humiliation was!

Sabelle sipped gratefully from the tea Sir Jonathan's housekeeper had sent up. Her throat was raw from weeping, and she savored the soothing liquid as it went down. Taking yet

another swallow, she raised red-rimmed eyes to her grandfather and braved a smile.

"So now you have it all, Grandfather—the entire sorry
tale of my marriage to 'Hart the Heartless.'"

The old man gave her a warm smile, despite the sadness
in his eyes, and reached out to take her hand. They were in
an upstairs sitting room in his town house, Sabelle beside
him on an upholstered settee and Jeannie across from them
in an old-fashioned wing chair. The two young women had
arrived less than a half-hour before, the Highlander grim-
faced, his granddaughter bursting into tears. And after he'd
comforted Sabelle as best he could without knowing the
cause of her distress, he'd led them upstairs, where at last
he got her to pour out all her misery to him.

Of course, it couldn't be said that he was entirely
shocked by her story. Upset, yes, that she could have en-
dangered her happiness this way. And dreadfully, dreadfully
sorry that he hadn't been able to prevent what she'd endured at the hands of Haverleigh.

"Ah, my poor, poor Sabelle," he murmured as he felt
her hand tremble. "Come now, my darling, no more tears.
There's nothing so terrible that it cannot be mended."

Sabelle dashed at her tears with an angry swipe of her
hand. "Oh, Grandfather, you must think I've been so
f-foolish!"

"Nonsense, child!" Jonathan's tone was compassionate
and loving. "What you have done involves a mistake or
two, and perhaps some errors in judgment, but these do
not signify the end of the world. Nor do they mark you as
foolish," he went on. "Ingenuous, perhaps, yes, but to say
you've been foolish is to say that anyone who was ever
young was a fool. Now dry your eyes and promise me
you'll stop blaming yourself."

Sabelle gave him a grateful smile, but it faded quickly.
"But what am I to do now, Grandfather? It—it is all well
and good to say I am not to blame, but how do I manage
from here? I—I am still wed to Justin Hart."

Jonathan paused reflectively. "Hmm," he murmured after a moment, and glanced up to see both young women gazing intently at him.

Several minutes passed, and the ticking of the mantel clock seemed loud in the quiet room, but at last Jonathan told them he had a plan. It was a tenuous one, at best, but for the moment, he told them, it would have to do.

Since Sabelle was unsure of what she herself wished to do about this disastrous marriage, Jonathan felt the least they ought to do was give her time—and a safe haven—to make some decisions in the matter. So he would hide both women, right there in town, by dressing them as a pair of young footmen by day—*and chimney sweeps at night!*

Sabelle and Jeannie smiled at this, but their smiles turned to grins when he told them of an opportunity to rescue some pit dogs . . .

❖Chapter 20❖

JUSTIN HART WAS NOT ALWAYS A PATIENT man, but what he lacked in patience, he made up for in determination. Set on finding his errant wife, and convinced he *would* find her, he embarked upon a search which was avid but also infuriating—for it lacked the immediate results his nature demanded.

The first place he went to was the Corstairses' town house, but all he encountered was a bewildered countess of Rushton, who was soon calling for her hartshorn and water. The earl was sent for at his club, but aside from blustering about dukes who misplaced their brides, he could offer only one suggestion: They must question Sir Jonathan Burke.

All three went to the home of Sabelle's grandfather. But the open-faced, obviously sincere response they received from the old man was this: The only people to arrive at his house all day were a pair of youngsters his majordomo would be training as footmen. And, no, he had received no note or letter from his granddaughter telling him where she'd gone.

A letter did arrive for Marjorie that night, however. It was from Jonathan. Delivered by private messenger, it explained that Sabelle was well, and under his protection, but that if his daughter and the earl wished to avoid a scandal that would titillate the *ton*, they would say nothing of this to anyone until further word came from him or their daughter. The earl promptly sent a footman out to replenish his wife's supply of hartshorn.

In the meantime, Justin intensified his search. One of the most aggravating difficulties he encountered in the whole infuriating process was being confronted by his grandmother when she caught wind of what had happened. Glaring at him, she said in no uncertain terms that "proper ducal marriages cannot survive missing duchesses!" He must find her at once—and then remedy whatever it was he'd said or done to cause her to depart!

The marchioness did, however, promise to aid him as best she might. First, she called a conference with Sabelle's parents to concoct a plausible explanation for the conspicuous absence of their daughter: The word to the *ton* would be, she told them, that the duchess of Haverleigh had taken ill suddenly, and repaired to the country to recuperate. Beyond this, she also advised the duke to "quell the anger I've noted brewing beneath that handsome exterior and ride to the country to look for the clever little baggage."

"Clever?" came the outraged retort. "How can you call her clever?"

"Because you are no dimwit, my boy, and she's managed to elude *you* for days. I'd call that clever . . . or would you rather I said *ingenious?"*

Justin's response was less than gentlemanly, and the marchioness told him so. Nevertheless, she had the satisfaction of seeing him take her advice. He spent three days searching about the Surrey estates of his wife's parents and grandfather, but with no success. And the temper he was in when he returned had even his grandmother avoiding his company.

And so the weeks passed with no sign of Sabelle. May gave way to the warmer days of June, and the *ton* of London began to think of leaving the city in favor of resorts like Bath and, especially, Brighton, where the Regent was furnishing his famous Marine Pavilion. Justin's mood as he hunted for his wife was largely marked by a simmering fury, but as the weeks dragged on without a clue as to her whereabouts, he began to experience an occasional twinge of something new in his attitude toward her disappearance.

It usually happened late at night, when he was alone with his thoughts, or trying to find sleep, which frequently eluded him now when he lay in the large bed where he'd last seen Sabelle. It was then, during these silent moments, that his mind began to form disturbing questions: What if something had happened to her? What if she was not hiding at all, but, in her careless attempt at flight—with no one but an equally defenseless maid to accompany her—she had fallen prey to the countless dangers of the London streets? What if her body was lying in an alley somewhere, horribly broken, because he'd been too obsessed by fury to search properly? What if—

And then he would curse the moment, and his own damnable imagination, and promise himself to redouble his efforts on the morrow.

Sometimes he would ride through the city alone, stopping at places they'd gone together during the courtship: Vauxhall Gardens, where he further infuriated himself by imagining her hidden along the Dark Walk with her lover; Hyde Park, where he fancied she might be brazen enough to ride and take the air with that lover; even among the booksellers of Fleet Street, where he'd accompanied her to purchase some of the books they both enjoyed, books he now pictured being bought for her by that same unknown man who'd tasted the pleasures of her body before him.

He also took his grandmother's advice to enlist the aid of the former Bow Street runners who were still seeking the person responsible for his mother's death. These men were less than optimistic, however, when he made it clear that any out-and-out questioning of the *ton* was not to be risked for fear of stirring up rumors.

The rumormongers had not been entirely pacified by his grandmother's Banbury tale as it was. And while Justin had never been particularly bothered by the gossips before, having had his casual affairs relished by them from one end of London to the other, he was nearly as reluctant as his grandmother to suffer the impugning of a Haverleigh duchess—no matter how guilty she was!

There was one other person outside the family who'd been made privy to the duke's plight, yet Justin was surprised when Thomas Long offered to help him search for Sabelle. Suspecting the tutor's motives to be based on the premise that one could not divorce a wife until one had located her, he did not scruple to disabuse Thomas of such a notion—divorce for a man in Justin's position, despite what he'd once told Sabelle, was out of the question. Justin gratefully accepted Thomas's help.

It so happened, then, that Thomas was at his side one night as he was leaving a public house near Covent Garden, when a most unusual incident drew their attention. They were heading for their carriage, just turning the corner into Bow Street, when suddenly, out of the darkness near Russel Street, a block away, they heard a commotion. It seemed to be comprised of frantic, high-pitched yells and several dogs barking.

"Good heavens!" said Thomas. "What d'you suppose—"

"Somebody chasing something or—"

Justin broke off as he spied two slight figures running toward them, and at their heels was a small pack of dogs. They were coming very fast, and he could see the dogs more clearly now; there were five of them, and they were attached to the fleeing humans by leashes, or perhaps ropes.

"It's a pair of climbing boys!" shouted Thomas. "But what are they doing with those—"

"Come back 'ere, ye bufe-nabbin' little coves!" sounded a new voice.

Justin looked to see a huge, burly man about ten yards behind the sweeps. Roughly dressed and brutish-looking, he brandished a horsewhip and was moving faster than might be assumed for a man his size.

The boys with the dogs were drawing closer now, and Justin could see that one was rather tall for a climbing boy. This one darted occasional quick glances over his thin shoulders as he ran, while the smaller lad kept his head down and raced pell-mell toward him and Thomas.

"That ruffian's gaining on them," said the tutor. "What d'you suppose they've done to—"

"I don't know," said Justin as he watched the man's whip snake out, barely missing the dog in the rear. "But I don't like his methods—and I don't like the *odds!* Hold my coat, Thomas!"

Justin had removed the coat he handed him so quickly, Thomas hadn't even noticed him do it. He watched in amazement as the duke went tearing off in the direction of the man with the whip, agilely skirting sweeps and dogs, his limp hardly in evidence as his long strides led him to their pursuer.

The dogs were lunging about wildly now, their ropes tangled, making it hard for the boys to hang on to them. The smaller lad shouted something to the other, but Thomas couldn't make it out because of the noise. "Just run!" he heard the taller one shout, and in the din he couldn't be sure, but had that been a Scots accent?

A huge bellow had Thomas's head whipping about to see Justin yanking the whip out of the coarse one's hand. As he flung it into the street, the brute lunged at him, but the duke stopped him with a powerful fist to his midsection. Then, when the man began to double over, he delivered a clean left to the jaw.

The lout staggered, but then seemed to recover himself and came at the duke with a mighty roar, his hands poised for his opponent's throat. But Justin deftly sidestepped him and thrust out his leg in a tripping maneuver. The brute began to topple and Justin finished him off with a blow to the back of the head.

As he saw the duke turn and come toward him, Thomas noticed the sweeps had untangled the dogs, and were eyeing Thomas apprehensively. He thought he heard the taller one yelp as he noticed the duke, but with all the barking, it was hard to be certain.

Then all at once, in the near distance, there was the thudding of heavy feet and several male voices shouting.

"It's the other pit masters!" shouted the smaller sweep. *"Run!"*

Justin's head jerked in the direction of the sound, and he eyed the sweep peculiarly, even as the boy began to take off again with his companion.

"No, wait!" the duke shouted as Thomas saw four men running toward them from Russell Street.

The climbing boys paid him no heed, but Justin ran after them, shouting over his shoulder, "Thomas—the carriage! Fetch it and tell my driver to go to the square. *Hurry!"*

Justin pursued the fleeing pack slowly, not trying to catch up—not yet. He knew he could force them toward the square with a little maneuvering, and once there, he would rescue them from their new pursuers by herding them into his carriage.

Evidently, they'd stolen the dogs from those pit masters. Well, he had no problem with that. Pitting dogs one against the other was an ugly business.

But what was uppermost in his mind right now was the identity of the dogs' *new* masters—or should he say *mistress? He'd recognize that voice anywhere!* It had obsessed and haunted him for weeks.

Justin smiled as he kept up the chase: He doubted his wife would thank him for her rescue!

Sabelle sat in her husband's carriage and stewed. She knew he'd recognized her. If it hadn't been apparent from his pursuit after he dispatched that bully, it had certainly come home to her when he forced them into his barouche: There was no way she would believe the duke of Haverleigh would pinch a climbing boy's bottom as he ushered him into a carriage!

Across from her on the carriage seat, Jeannie sat rigidly against the squabs, a muzzled terrier on either side of her. The poor things had been frightened, and had snapped and growled at the men when they tried to put them in the barouche; so her husband had had the driver muzzle them with strips torn from the duke's pocket handkerchief. The dogs were sleeping now, so she supposed they couldn't be too uncomfortable; but she hated the sight of muzzled animals, nevertheless.

On the floor another terrier and two bulldoglike mongrels slept without those confinements. They, too, had seemed frightened, but proved biddable enough when she and Jeannie had been ordered by Justin to settle them down.

Justin . . . After eluding him successfully for weeks, the very thought of how she'd stumbled into him made her want to cry. *Damn the rotten luck!* And now, there she was, sandwiched between him and that odious dropface, Thomas Long, being taken in a carriage to God-knew-where. It didn't bear thinking on!

From beneath lowered lashes, she chanced a sidelong glance at him. He sat tall and erect, his impeccably tailored evening clothes molded to his muscular frame as if he'd been born into them. Not a stitch out of place; the only evidence of the scuffle with the pit master was a fall of midnight curls that hung loose over his forehead. As handsome as ever, his heart-stopping masculine profile etched in relief by the moonlight slanting through the window, he seemed distant as the moors . . . and utterly, utterly sure of himself. Here was the man she'd wed for revenge, the man who'd ravished her and courted her even while he dangled his mistress on a string . . . the man who'd made sweet, unholy love to her on their wedding night, arousing fires that even now, as she remembered, made her burn.

The shame of her capitulation that night—and how he'd accomplished it—had tormented her for weeks. Dear God, how she hated him!

Well, the fat was in the fire now.

Justin caught her faint, bitter smile and wondered what she was thinking. He hadn't divulged a word about their destination.

Let her squirm.

He could hardly believe how grubby and shabbily dressed she was: an effective disguise. Even Thomas still believed the pair to be chimney sweeps. Justin wasn't sure why he hadn't yet disabused him of that notion. Thomas was such an enigma sometimes, Justin often wondered if he really knew the man; but he did know that anything dealing with his marriage was best handled gingerly around the tutor.

Sabelle stirred and turned her head to gaze into the darkness outside, and Justin took the opportunity to study her without her being aware of it. She was clothed all in black, a pair of torn and dusty knee breeches meeting coarse cotton hose spattered with mud, the hose meeting scuffed black shoes that looked ready for the dustbin. Covering her upper torso was an ill-fitting coat that was out at the elbows, and she wore a battered hat, of the type frequently seen on sweeps all over London, which had been pulled down over her ears, effectively hiding her hair.

No wonder Thomas hadn't recognized her! With her smudged face and hands, she looked for all the world like a dirty little urchin. If he hadn't heard her voice—and later seen her unmistakable aquamarine eyes—he'd likely have been fooled as well.

His gaze slid to the Scots maid . . . Jeannie, he recalled her name was. She was dressed exactly like his wife, but he wondered why he hadn't spotted something amiss when he first noticed them; she was too big for a climbing boy.

The poor girl looked frightened out of her wits. He wondered what Sabelle had told her about him—or even if she now realized who he was. After all, she'd seen him only once or twice in the past, and just in passing. Did she think they were being abducted by strangers? He knew he'd given them no opportunity to talk, and he'd purposely been maintaining silence in the carriage—he thought it an admirable tactic for intimidating his wife.

Ah, well, he thought as he settled himself more comfortably against the squabs, *there's no help for it;* he'd simply have to put the lassie in the motherly hands of Mrs. Small when they reached Harthaven. She'd soothe the chit. No sense making the maid suffer for the mistress's sins!

It was after midnight when they arrived at their destination. Sabelle had endured the silent journey without sleep, although Jeannie had been dozing for the final two hours or so.

Because there was a moon, she saw clearly the immense, yet graceful, dwelling before the wide circular drive as they came upon it. Ivy-covered brick shone silver in the moonlight, and well-clipped lawns stretched to either side, giving it a well-tended, civilized aspect. It was the enormous estate house of someone important—and wealthy—and she found herself throwing a questioning glance at Justin, despite her resolve to ignore him.

It was Justin who ignored *her*, however, but she had the answer to her unspoken query, nevertheless, when, a moment after the carriage halted, he addressed Long.

"I collect you've not been at Harthaven since I was a lad, Thomas, but I'm sure Mrs. Small can have your old quarters ready for you in a trice. Will that suit?"

"Admirably," said the tutor, as a young footman with a torch came running down the steps to open the door for them. "But what about . . . er . . ." He gestured toward the other occupants of the carriage.

"Leave them to me," said the duke, as they alighted from the vehicle. "I'll have the driver take the dogs down to the stables, where there's a groom who does wonders with canines. And as to these"—he indicated Jeannie, who regarded him with solemn brown eyes, and Sabelle, who stood studying her toes on the gravel—"leave them, *especially*, to me!"

Justin gave instructions to the driver, then took each "boy" by the shoulder and ushered "him" up the steps.

Lights were appearing in a few windows as the door opened. A tall, exceedingly thin man bowed politely, as if it were nothing at all to be roused to welcome the master in the middle of the night.

"Your Grace," the man intoned. He was in his dressing gown, but he spoke as if he were addressing him in the most presentable attire.

"Sorry for the hour, Haskins, but we'll need some rooms prepared, and water for bathing, too, I imagine." This last was said with a distasteful glance at Sabelle and Jeannie. "Is Mrs.—uh, there you are, Mrs. Small!"

The largest woman Sabelle had ever seen came hurrying from the end of the hallway. She was easily as tall as the duke, and a good three or four stone heavier, though little of this poundage was given to fat. Her homely face bore a kindly look. Sabelle eyed her curiously as she approached. She noted the woman had obviously dressed in haste; she was stocking-footed, her long braid of gray hair flew behind her, and she tied on an apron as she ran.

"Welcome back, Your Grace!" she said, catching her breath. "And Mr. Long! It's been years since we've seen your face at Harthaven."

"Indeed, dear lady," replied the tutor, "but I can still remember the excellent chocolate and biscuits you sent up to our lessons."

"Well, well, and what have we here?" asked the house-keeper as she scrutinized the two figures between her employer and the tutor. "A pair of sweeps, is it? And looking well in need of some food and a bath, too."

Justin blessed the unflappable nature of this large woman, who'd been housekeeper there since he was a boy. She'd been motherly then, and it was certain she hadn't changed: no curious questions for a pair of little beggars produced in the middle of the night—just food and a bath.

"Indeed, Mrs. Small," he said, "and if you would be so kind as to take them in hand, I'll have Haskins, here, see to Mr. Long's comfort."

The majordomo took his cue and nodded deferentially to the tutor.

Thomas said good-night to Justin and followed the servant, while the duke murmured quietly to the housekeeper, "I shall find my own way up to my rooms, Mrs. Small, and I'll require a bath myself. But as to these two"—he indicated her grubby charges—"I think there is something you should know before you proceed with their baths . . ."

Sabelle stood staring at a huge, old-fashioned brass tub, in a dressing alcove of some sort, on the second floor. She wasn't sure whose dressing alcove, or, indeed, whose tub this was; the rooms through which she'd been led by the housekeeper were dark. But there were a number of decidedly feminine touches about the small enclosure, not the least of these being the perfumed bath salts a sleepy-eyed chambermaid was pouring into the steaming tub.

The young, freckle-faced woman said not a word as she made the bath ready. But it was clear, from the peculiar looks she threw Sabelle, that she'd not been made privy by Mrs. Small to the fact that Sabelle was female.

She placed a stack of scented towels on a stool beside the tub, threw Sabelle an odd glance, shrugged, and withdrew from the chamber.

Sabelle stared at the fragrant, steaming water and the pair of huge buckets of cooler water left on a nearby stand. She would have dearly loved to strip off her sooty garments and sink into that inviting tub, but she couldn't bring herself to do it. Not as long as she didn't know what Justin's plans were—what he intended to do with her.

Or *to* her.

Moreover, she realized only too well where she was: far down in the country, in Justin's ancestral home, where he had total power. She refused to make herself more vulnerable by disrobing, even if it meant forgoing the bath she longed for.

And where was her husband at this moment? After he'd left them in the hands of the housekeeper, along with an explanation as to who they were, he'd trotted off upstairs with nary another glance for his wife and her maid.

Mrs. Small had been warm and cheerful as she fed them tea and sandwiches in the kitchen, and Jeannie was being bathed belowstairs this very moment, with a warm assurance from the housekeeper that she'd share comfortable quarters with Betty, her niece.

But Sabelle had been led upstairs. And she had no idea where her husband was. She did not have long to wait.

A door beyond the alcove opened, then slammed shut, and a second later, Justin appeared.

"What the—*Why the devil haven't you bathed?*"

It was not a question, but a demand, and Sabelle raised defiant eyes. "I do not wish a bath."

Silence. Justin stepped into the alcove, his silver eyes never leaving her face. A muscle contracted ominously along the harsh plane of his jaw.

"You will take it," he said in a voice that was entirely too soft.

Sabelle held her ground, much as she was inclined to step back from the menace she sensed in his stance. He loomed tall and muscular, only a few feet from her, and she'd never felt smaller or more vulnerable in his presence. Dressed casually in tight, buff-colored breeches and a soft muslin shirt he wore open to the waist, he stood with booted feet planted apart, his hands on his lean hips, clenched into fists.

She noted he himself had bathed, for his hair was damply curling and fell negligently over his forehead. It gave him almost a boyish look, which was at odds with his threatening posture.

Ignoring the fury she saw smoldering in his eyes, Sabelle raised her chin a notch, never so conscious of this as an act of bravado. Then, when she found herself opening her mouth to speak, she realized too late where the *real* bravado lay.

"You cannot force me, Your Grace."

Had she really said that? Justin seemed to question this, too. He blinked, and the tic in his jaw worked furiously.

"Can't I?" The words were again spoken softly, totally at odds with the message in his eyes . . .

Then, in a single lightning move, he was upon her, an arm snaking about her waist, yanking her against the lean, hard side of him. With the other hand he reached up to tear the sweep's hat off her head.

Sabelle shrieked, half in fear, half in anger, as she felt her heavy mane of hair come tumbling loose from its pins. Justin paid no heed.

"Defy me, would you?" he bit off between clenched jaws as he stripped off her ragged coat. "First deceit . . ."

Her coat landed on the floor beside her hat.

"And then flight . . ."

The shirt went the way of the coat.

"And now *defiance!*"

He began to peel off her filthy breeches.

"I tell you, madam, I'll have no more of it, d'you hear? Your days of treachery and disobedience are done—finished!"

Sabelle was thrashing about and yelling like a wild thing now, but Justin wrestled her out of her garb as easily as if she were a doll, a child's plaything. His movements were abrupt, but sure, fed by the anger that had been building for weeks, and he was giving no quarter. She had tricked him, tried to humiliate him, and now she would pay!

In moments he had stripped her down to her plain cotton shift. It was old and patched, a remnant from her days at Camelot Downs. Setting her down and holding her thrashing arms still for a moment, he eyed it contemptuously, and a sneer shaped his words.

"Look at you! You have what you wanted from me—*I made you a duchess!*—and how do you repay that unmerited act? By dressing in *rags!* By God, woman, you tempt much!"

Sabelle stared up at him, a mutinous look in her eyes. She was breathing hard from her exertions, and she could feel the tight fabric of her shift—an old one, purchased in the days when she had been as flat as the boys whose clothes she borrowed—stretching tautly across her breasts.

Justin noticed it, too. His gaze dropped, and a nasty smile began to curve his mouth as he raised his eyes to hers again. Then, before she had time to guess his intent, his hands moved from their grip on her arms to her neckline, and with a sharp tear, he rent the shift apart.

Sabelle gasped, her hands jerking to the severed pieces of the bodice in a desperate attempt to cover herself. But it was futile. Low, jeering laughter met her ears as her husband tore the useless garment from her fingers and flung it aside.

At last Sabelle found her voice. "What sort of a man are you?" she shrieked. "What, *so noble*, Your Grace? That you must prove your superiority by overpowering a small, defenseless woman and—*No!*"

Justin had had enough. With renewed fury, he lunged at her, bent to scoop an arm beneath her thighs, and heaved her bodily into the steaming tub.

Sabelle screamed as she hit the water.

"How dare you?" she shouted at the top of her lungs when she'd caught her breath. *"How dare you?"*

"I dare—" said Justin in a quiet fury, "because I am your husband, Sabelle . . ."—he leaned over the tub, his hands braced on its rim—". . . and that, in case you hadn't realized it, means *you belong to me*. I *own* you, my unbeloved wife, and don't ever forget it!"

As she shrank back in the tub from the force of his rage, he grabbed a sponge from the stand nearby, then the bar of perfumed soap the maid had left; and after dipping them in the water, he began to scrub at the sooty streaks running down the sides of her neck and shoulders.

Infuriated, quivering with anger, Sabelle squirmed and twisted, twisted and squirmed, but to no avail. Justin had many times her strength, and he was, by far, in the superior position. Amid her shrieks and shouts, water sloshed and suds went flying. At one point she tried to stand up, only to find herself shoved entirely underwater in the deep tub.

She came up coughing and sputtering to hear Justin mock her with rude laughter and, as he pulled aside the curtain of wet hair that hung over her face, ask if she'd learned her lesson yet.

"You bastard!" she cried, then yelped as a bucketful of cold water coursed over her head. And before she could tell him what else she thought of him, strong hands grasped her about the waist and she was hauled, sputtering and fuming, out of the tub.

Water was everywhere. It was sluicing down her body, sloshing over the floor, and she had an instant to realize her tormenter was nearly as wet as she was before she found herself enveloped in a huge towel.

Her hands and arms were helpless now, for he'd wrapped her in the thick fabric like a cocoon, but as he would have wrapped a second towel about her hair she jerked her head about and bit his hand—hard.

"You bitch!" he shouted, pulling his hand away to suck at the blood she'd drawn.

"Bitch, am I? You—"

She was cut off by a murderous snarl, then yanked upward until she found herself slung over his shoulder like a sack of flour.

Sabelle tried to scream but found the wind had been knocked out of her. Then he was carrying her out of the alcove and through the darkened room beyond. A doorway appeared. The door had been left open, and she could see light beyond it as he stalked through with her on his shoulder.

She saw a booted foot lash out to kick the door closed, then found herself being set down, none too gently, on the floor beside an enormous tester bed.

Endeavoring to catch her breath, Sabelle stared at the beautiful Aubusson carpet beneath her feet for several seconds, then slowly raised her eyes to meet his gaze. And flinched.

Hard and flinty in his face, Justin's eyes burned with unspeakable fury. She was reminded instantly of all the countless warnings she'd issued herself in the months and weeks of waiting to put her revenge plan into action, and she wished to God she'd heeded them. Here was a man nobody could toy with—and come away unscathed. Here was a man who'd killed on the fields of battle, who'd set ministers and their minions quaking in their boots, a man thoroughly capable of hunting down an enemy and making him—or her—wish he'd never been born.

Their eyes remained locked for several long seconds. A log fell in the fireplace across the room, sending up a shower of sparks. It broke the taut thread that held them.

Justin ground out an unintelligible oath and roughly unwound the swath of toweling which bound her. Sabelle clutched at it with a small cry as it would have fallen to the floor, but Justin was quicker. With total disregard for whatever she meant to salvage by keeping this thin barrier to her nakedness, he tore the cloth from her fingers. Then, ignoring her futile whimper and her reddening face, he applied it roughly to her hair, completing the toweling he would have done earlier.

His rough movements tangled her long hair, pulling it at the scalp until she felt genuine pain. The effect was to accomplish what all his bullying had not. She felt hot tears sting her eyes and her voice cracked on a sob.

"B-brute! Justin, *stop*—you're *hurting* me!"

Justin paused in the act of using the other end of the towel to wipe his sodden shirt. Then he whipped it away from both of them and flung it aside. There was silence while he examined her face, as if to gauge the truth of her words.

Sabelle's eyes were huge in her small, heart-shaped face as she looked up at him. The brilliance of unshed tears studded their luminous aquamarine depths as they caught the firelight, and Justin felt his breath catch in his throat.

Whatever she'd done, whatever she was, she was also the most singularly lovely creature he'd ever seen. He watched the play of firelight over her taut, sculpted features, drank in the exquisite proportions of nose, mouth, curve of neck . . . Then he found his gaze dropping to the lush ripeness below, and the heat rose in his loins.

Sabelle followed his glance and, with a sharp intake of breath, guessed his mind.

"No . . ." she whispered, but even as she breathed the word, she heard him groan, felt him reach for her and pull her into his arms.

Justin's mouth descended with hungry force. Demanding, caught fierce in a blinding need that had him helplessly recalling that other night of passion that had tormented him for weeks, he crushed her to him in a maelstrom of desire and white-hot passion.

Sabelle struggled fervently against the onslaught, but he was big and overpowering. She tried to twist her head aside to escape the force of the kiss, acutely aware of how it was meant to punish and subdue. But she succeeded only in parting her lips to give him the access he sought. She braced herself for the rape by his tongue, trying to deny the leap of panic she felt as she became aware of his hard shaft pressing against her belly through the dampness of his breeches.

But as she steeled herself for the invasion of his tongue, a curious thing happened. The touch when it came, was suddenly gentle. Slowly, almost tentatively, he probed the soft inner recesses of her mouth, touching here, gliding there, willing her still with a seductive subtlety.

She felt his arms release their crushing hold, felt his hands slide along the naked curves of her back and shoulders, gentling her, bringing her with him in this strange new game. And stranger still to her, she let him, ceasing her struggle like a pacified child.

A coiling sensation deep in her belly wound its way with tingling heat to the place beneath, as his mouth released hers and he breathed her name on a ragged sigh.

"Sabelle . . . *Sweet Christ, how lovely you are!*"

His mouth slid to the damp hair at her ear. Then, softly, he repeated her name against it, and he felt her shudder. Her unmistakable response had him recalling at once the answering passion she'd shown on their wedding night. He sucked in his breath at the force of the memory.

"God help me, Sabelle," he whispered hoarsely as he again pressed her close, "but I haven't been able to get you out of my mind!"

Dimly, Sabelle was aware that she ought to be feeling triumphant. If what he said were true . . .

But the thought fled her mind as Justin's mouth trailed a line of fire along her throat; and when his hands cupped her breasts and she felt his thumbs graze their taut, outthrust peaks, she moaned, conscious only of the tight, coiling heat below her belly.

And then, when he bent and his mouth closed over one aching crest, she cried his name, reaching for his shoulders with trembling hands as her knees threatened to buckle and give way.

"Easy, sweetheart," he murmured as he raised his head and moved his hands about her tiny waist to steady her. But the florals of the bath, mixed with the musky scent of her arousal, drifted through his senses, and he was none too steady himself when Sabelle threw her arms about him and arched against him with a small cry.

Greedily, he covered her mouth with his, astonished by the sweet, open wetness of it when they met in a heady thrusting of tongues. Seconds passed while they fenced this way, until the passion of the kiss left them both gasping for breath.

Justin's hands were everywhere, roaming her bath-damp flesh, learning her, finding just where to touch, and how, to bring the soft little gasps of pleasure he wrought.

And then he was sweeping her into his arms and taking her to the big tester bed in the center of the room. The jewel-toned hues of the embroidered canopy seemed to spin overhead as he laid her gently down. Then her senses gathered enough to let her know she no longer felt his warmth, and she uttered a soft cry, feeling bereft.

But now he was beside her again, the firm touch of his warm flesh telling her he'd paused only to shed his clothes. And when he reached to take her into his arms, she welcomed him with a quavering groan that was pure longing.

Justin laughed softly as he held her against him. "So eager, my sweet?" he murmured against her ear. But Sabelle was in motion now, moving restlessly against him, pressing soft kisses where she might, and when he felt her lips brush hesitantly across the flesh of an erect male nipple, he shuddered, all thoughts of gentle teasing gone.

With a low growl, he moved until he had her under him, then stopped, his breath caught in his throat. She lay on the counterpane beneath him, her eyes wide and searching, as if to ask what she'd done to elicit this response. Light from a bedside lamp spilled over her hair, which was damp and curling, a silken amalgam of silver and gold as it framed her flawless face. Dimly, he was aware that her lips trembled as she tried to speak, but no sound emerged. Only the soundless forming of his name as the deep sea-green of her eyes held him.

She was all things female to him now, softness, and

beauty, and light, yet with an underlying strength about it all—the quintessence of that mystery called woman.

Gently, half afraid she would vanish if he mistook the moment, he threaded his fingers through the hair on either side of her head and cupped her face.

And when he slowly lowered his head to capture her lips, the kiss plied the honey from her core. Sabelle pressed her hands against his chest as she gave herself up to him entirely, to this hot, aching melding of their lips that had an echo in the piercing sweetness curling through her woman's place.

Justin sensed her surrender, and the blood sang in his veins. Again and again he kissed her, and the fire between them burned. Kiss upon kiss, openmouthed, wet, clinging, and his hands began to work the ancient magic . . . on breasts, tip-tilted and ripe, on the velvet sweep of hip and thigh, on softly rounded buttocks that tempted beyond reason—

His hand caressed the lush curve of her tight little derriere when he whispered something into her ear, his voice thick with passion.

Sabelle murmured something questioning in return—a breathless whisper, her voice colored by the heat building inside her. Then she heard him coax again and felt the tip of his tongue in her ear, while at the same time his finger stroked the cleft between her buttocks.

With a moan, she did as he bade her, twisting until she lay on her belly. She had a moment to wonder what he was about when she felt him raise her hips, cupping his hand under the mound covered by soft golden curls.

"Justin . . . ?" she questioned softly when she felt his warmth cover her from behind. But then she gasped as a strong finger in front stroked the slit which had gone slippery and hot; and then she had no time to question anything as his finger found the tiny bud above and made her moan his name.

"Yes, sweetheart, yes!" he rasped in her ear as she began to squirm and push against him. His other hand came around to cup and tease her breasts, while below, a finger entered her wet warmth, testing it for entry. "Yes, ah, yes," Justin coaxed anew. "Ah, Sabelle, how tight you are! God, but I love the tight, wet heat of you!"

And Sabelle was lost—lost to the rhythm of the multiple sensations he worked on her body. She barely knew when his finger left that encasing warmth, barely knew when he drew her hips and buttocks even higher, forcing her up on knees and elbows. But then, when she felt him at the entrance where his fingers had prepared the way, then she knew. And she screamed his name when he drove into her, hot and hard.

"Sabelle," he rasped when he felt her push against him, eagerly receiving his thrust. "Sabelle, move with me now, sweet . . . *Yes!*"

And she found his rhythm, caught up hotly in this wild, sweet novel pleasure of the age-old dance. Soon they were moving at a fever pitch, and when Justin began to feel her convulse beneath him, he buried his face in her hair and let the shudders rock him. Again he felt her climax, and again, while his seed spewed hotly into her core, until the last shudder claimed him and they lay spent in the quiet of the night.

The fire in the hearth burned low when Justin felt at last he could move.

"Sabelle . . . ?" he whispered as he slowly disengaged and rose above her. Then he smiled, seeing she dozed and knowing full well the cause.

A frown of consternation suddenly knotted his brow. He'd sworn not to touch her. Not until enough time had passed that he could be sure any child she carried was *his*. But, somehow, things had gotten out of control the moment he'd laid hands on that sweet flesh. Somehow, his normally well-ordered mind lost all sense of the rational when Sabelle was near him.

Again Justin smiled as he gazed at her.

When had he ever had a woman bring such passion to his bed? Small wonder she'd exhausted herself: Look what she'd given! His eyes traveled the length of her prone form, and he took renewed pleasure in what he saw. Her hair, tousled and silver-gold in the lamplight, tangled wildly over the perfect curves of her shoulders and back . . . her long, beautifully shaped legs stretched gracefully away from that sweet little derriere which—

Justin paused. Blinked. And stared.

Then he leaned forward carefully, not able to credit what he thought he saw . . .

What in hell . . . ?

But it was there. Riding high on her left thigh, just below the buttock, was the tiny heart-shaped birthmark he'd never forget; he'd seen it before—*on the virgin whore in the tavern!*

Justin shook his head as if to clear it, his brain reeling with the impact of what this implied. At once, his glance darted to the still profile of his wife as she slept.

Sabelle? How in the name of—?

He sucked in his breath, passing unsteady fingers softly across the birthmark, not yet ready to trust his senses.

It was real.

At the same moment he felt her stir, and his eyes flew to her face. Justin's jaw clenched. He'd have some answers—*now!*

✢Chapter 21✢

S ABELLE TRIED TO SNUGGLE MORE DEEPLY into the bedclothes, but an insistent hand on her shoulder was making it difficult.

"Jeannie, you tyrant," she muttered sleepily, "go 'way!"

She fancied she heard an exasperated grunt, which did not sound at all like Jeannie. But she began, nevertheless, to burrow again into the pillows.

Until a rude slap on the buttocks made her yelp and come instantly awake.

"Who—?" Her eyes took in the muscular form of her husband looming above the bed. Then it all came back to her. Feeling the heat rise to her face, she quickly twisted into a sitting position and yanked up the counterpane to cover her nakedness.

Justin smiled sardonically. "A little late for that, wouldn't you say . . . *Samantha?*"

Her eyes flew to his face. *Dear heaven! He knows! But how could he?*

Justin seemed to read her thoughts. "You have a very unique birthmark on the back of your thigh, my dear. Didn't you know?"

That heart-shaped mark she'd been born with! She'd forgotten it entirely. It had been the subject of a brief discussion with her nursemaid when she was very small, and they never mentioned it again. Small wonder it had slipped her mind. It wasn't as if it were somewhere she might see it regularly, even in a mirror!

But it was something a lover might notice, especially if it weren't too dark in the bedchamber, and with the position they'd assumed when—

She felt herself going beet-red.

"I see you recall *something*," said Justin with a mocking half smile as he slung a lean hip alongside her on the bed.

"Now, Your Grace," he continued as he held her eyes with that piercing silvery gaze, *"we talk!"*

He was still unclothed, of course, and if that wasn't disconcerting enough, his nearness and the intensity of his look were. She squirmed and tried to look away, but couldn't.

"Well, madam?" he asked, each syllable short and clipped. "It *was* you in the Shakespeare's Head on Guy Fawkes Day, was it not?"

Mutely, unable to tear her eyes away, Sabelle nodded.

"Excellent," came the sarcastic reply. "We're making progress." He shifted the leg which was on the bed and leaned forward, bracing an elbow on his bent knee. "Now, suppose you explain just how and why you came to be there, hmm?"

Sabelle swallowed hard and somehow found her voice. "It—it was an accident, I'm afraid. I—I did not intend to be there."

"I am gratified to hear it."

The irony in his voice was unnerving, but she made herself continue. "It was—it was all because of Ormley and his—"

"Ormley? How the devil is Ormley involved? I wasn't aware you even knew him."

"I do not—*did not.* I—"

"Sabelle, I warn you, I'm not a man of excessive patience! Kindly explain—"

"I am trying to, Your Grace!" She hadn't meant to snap at him; indeed, she wondered how she had the temerity when he sat there facing her so formidably. And now the scowl which darkened his face. . . . She made herself continue, stumbling over the words at first, then finding it easier to explain as she went on. A quiet kind of relief settled in with the knowledge she could at last unburden herself.

Many long minutes later, Sabelle came to the end of the story of her rescue work. She omitted nothing, not its beginnings at Camelot Downs with her grandfather; not the details behind what Justin had seen her doing with the fox at the hunt that day; and, of course, none of what had transpired to bring her haplessly to the Shakespeare's Head the night he took her for a young, inexperienced whore.

Justin sat unmoving through the entire tale. The only indication of emotion was the silent working of his jaw when she touched on incidents involving her forays into East End quarters, of her need to mingle with the denizens of that unsavory part of London, disguised as a chimney sweep.

". . . and so you see, Justin, how we never intended that we should follow Ormley *inside* that place. All the risk of the venture was to have been taken by Mr. Kelly," she finished at last.

Justin ran a hand through his hair and swore softly to himself, then looked at her severely. "*All* the risk? Sabelle, didn't it ever occur to you—or your grandfather—that there is risk for a woman on the streets of London *whenever* she goes out unprotected?"

"But we had Michael to protect us! And Brendan!"

"Really?" he questioned softly. "Then would you care to explain to me how it was that their *protection* brought about *the loss of your maidenhead?*"

Sabelle flushed at the harsh reminder, but Justin was secretly pleased. While it was unnerving to learn *she* had been that mysteriously virginal "trollop" he'd tumbled, he now knew that he'd been the first. *He* was the unknown lover he'd been taunting himself with all these weeks. He was the object of his own jealousy!

It almost made him laugh—until the thought of the past weeks brought him up short. *She'd let him think—*

Roughly, his hand shot out and captured her chin, forcing her to look at him.

"*Why,* Sabelle? *Why did you marry me?*"

Sabelle trembled at the familiar anger burning in his gaze. But it was too late to stop now. He knew too much not to be told the rest of it. And perhaps he had a right to know . . .

With honest chagrin, Sabelle began the story of her plans to avenge the loss of her honor. She realized as she spoke that she'd been wading in remorse for weeks—over the foolishness of her actions. The chance to unburden herself of the guilt was something she welcomed.

She admitted it all to him: her anger at being *forced*, no matter that she appeared to him in disguise; her plan to strand him at the church; her humiliation and fury upon overhearing the cruel, but revealing, words of his mistress; her resolve to make him pay for the whole of their married lives.

Tears were coursing down her cheeks as she finished. Remorse and contrition filled her brimming eyes as she looked up at him, and her final words, when she spoke, came out brokenly.

"If—if it is any consolation to you, Justin, I've recognized that revenge can be a double-edged sword: It can wound the wielder as well as the victim . . . I—I see I've made a mockery of this—this marriage I've cursed us with for the—Oh, God!—for the rest of our lives!"

She buried her face in her hands and sobbed, but wrenched her hands away when she felt him stir and looked bleakly up at him. "I want you to know I'm heartily ashamed of what I've done, Justin—to both of us—and I cannot—cannot think but that you should truly hate me now."

Justin sat frozen as he considered all she'd confessed. Sweet Christ, what a coil she'd wrapped them in! This fragile-looking little creature looking up at him now with huge, tear-filled eyes. He found himself oddly moved by her, by her honesty, and an inexplicable warmth began to replace his anger.

Of course, he was not so moved as to be free of astonishment. Incredible to think that she, this little slip of a thing —an innocent after all—had borne so much enmity, been capable of so much irate, passionate—

Ah, but was it truly so surprising? Sabelle Corstairs— Sabelle *Hart,* he amended—had been nothing, if she wasn't passionate. Why, then, wonder that she'd displayed similar heat with her negative emotions? He had her full measure now: His wife was a passionate little firebrand who embraced life fiercely. She might be an innocent, but she would never be accused of being fainthearted, and, strangely enough, he welcomed this insight.

Reaching out to wipe the tears from her cheeks with gentle fingers, he offered a smile. "Hate you? No, little one, I cannot say I hate you. But I—Oh, you foolish little minx, come here!"

Reaching for her as her tears began anew, he pulled her toward him and wrapped her protectively in his arms.

"I thought I hated you when I believed you'd played me false," he murmured into her hair. "And you were the devil's own imp to do what you did. But now that I know—"

Suddenly he clutched her far too tightly, bending fiercely over her. "There have been no others since?" he growled.

Sabelle went utterly still. She knew she ought to resent this insulting probe, but, oddly enough, she did not. She even felt unpredictably warmed by such high-handed possessiveness, though she couldn't say why.

Quietly, she pulled apart to look at him. "No, Justin," she said in a clear, honest voice, "there's been no one. I swear it."

Justin read the unquestionable sincerity in her eyes and nodded; then he let his gaze drop, his eyes running over her unclothed form, before returning to settle on her mouth. A sudden heat seized his loins, and he groaned, pulling her into his arms.

They made love slowly this time, with none of the hectic passion that had marked the earlier union. Yet, when at last their bodies joined in the primal rhythm, they again reached a soaring mutual climax that left them spent and weak amid the crumpled covers.

In the aftermath they slept, tangled in each other's arms. The pale flush of dawn blossomed and became the golden light of a June morning before either of them stirred, and then it was to make love again, with a heat that left them breathless and replete.

Sabelle was the first to stir in the aftermath of their passion. A languid glow suffused her entire body, and she smiled as she wondered at this. She was remembering her resolve that time, to remain blissfully on the shelf, rather than submit again to that painful and bestial act. How ignorant she'd been! And how ironic that the very man who'd engendered those feelings should be the cause of this sweet lassitude pervading her body and mind.

"A penny for the thoughts that bring that smile to your face, sweet."

Her eyes opened to behold the face of her husband. He was smiling lazily, but his eyes held a curious glint.

The truth was that Justin would have given a great deal more than a penny as he beheld that smile. It was so vastly different from anything she'd ever displayed during the long months of their courtship. Indeed, he wondered if he'd ever really seen her smile before.

Sabelle flushed and tried to bury her face in the curve of his shoulder. *Feeling* the powerful effects their lovemaking had on her was one thing, but *discussing* it with him was quite another! It was too intimate, too—

"Come now." He smiled, tilting her chin up gently. "You are my wife, Sabelle, and there can be no more secrets between us."

Shyly, hesitantly, she met his gaze. His eyes were a beautiful translucent gray now, open and compelling in the handsome face. The intimacies they'd shared were reflected there, an almost palpable thing between them, and she wondered if she would ever be the same.

Uneasily, she felt those disturbing words of Sarah Cavendish trip something deep in her consciousness: *Do not be surprised if he weds her, beds her, and sheds her . . .*

And yet he was saying there could be no secrets between them. Did that mean no secrets for either of them, or was it all one-sided, as things often were in this man's world they lived in? What about his letter to his friend Long? Didn't it proclaim his belief in a husbandly prerogative to seek his "better pleasures" outside the marriage?

Tempted to brood on this, if not to confront him outright, she stilled the urge. Things were too newly mended between them. And at least, at the moment, she was not facing a marriage that loomed before her as years of unmitigated enmity—an out-and-out battleground. They were not true lovers, but they were not open enemies, either. Somehow, she felt her best hope for the future would lie in trying to keep it that way, even though a warning buzzed in the back of her brain that, in doing so, she herself was keeping a secret between them.

"I—I was just thinking," she said to Justin by way of a reply to his question, "of how—how different I feel now, from . . ."

"Go on," he urged gently, his eyes steady on hers.

"From the first time, Your Grace."

"The first—"

"Yes," she broke in quickly, determined to get on with it before her embarrassment had her stumbling over her words. "The first time you—that is, the night at—at the Shakespeare's Head. You . . . hurt me, Justin. Hurt me and frightened me, so much that I was determined never to allow such—such things between myself and a man again. In fact, I was looking forward to a lifetime happily on the shelf! And if, later, my anger at what you'd done hadn't got the best of me, I should have been there at this moment."

Justin digested this soberly, struck at once by the degree of courage—and fury—it must have taken for her to go through with the marriage. Had she really feared and hated him that much? He knew something of rape from the war. In one of the worst recollections he had of the Peninsular campaign, he remembered having three of his men flogged for disobeying his orders and raping a peasant farmer's wife. Despite what Sabelle implied, what he had done that night in the tavern bore little resemblance to rape as he knew it. Still, he vaguely recalled the unexpected struggles of the young "whore," and that he'd ignored them, thinking it a part of some game she played. And of course, he'd had no inkling he was deflowering a virgin, so he wasn't as gentle as he might have been . . . Good God, he supposed he was lucky she hadn't turned frigid for life!

Sighing, he pulled her tightly against him. "God knows I'd not have hurt you intentionally, Sabelle," he told her. "Among other things, I'd been drinking—though I realize that is a poor excuse. But had I known you were a virgin, let alone your identity—

"Christ!" he swore as he rolled her beneath him and stared intently into her eyes.

"The *danger* you put yourself in! Suppose it had been Ormley, or some other randy fop who'd had you at his mercy! Sweet God in heaven, it does not bear thinking on!"

Abruptly, he took his hands and captured her face. "Never think to place yourself in such danger again. You are *mine*, Sabelle, and I'd kill any man who dared to touch you!"

Still holding her thus, he caught her mouth in a demanding kiss that asserted the possessive stamp of his words.

Sabelle succumbed to the kiss without resistance, the fragile link formed by the intimacies they'd shared, something she was not ready to sunder. But that strange acceptance of his high-handedness began to teeter. What if he began asserting his power over her in other ways? What other forms might his possessiveness take?

She did not have to wait long for her answer.

"You will, of course, cease these dangerous 'rescues,' as you call them," he told her as he began reaching for his clothes. "Your compassion for mistreated animals is admirable, but not to the point of risking your life or—"

"Risking my life?" Sabelle jerked upward on the bed. "I risk no such thing! Our rescues are always very well planned and—"

"As well planned as on Guy Fawkes Day?" he shot back as he thrust his arms into the sleeves of his shirt.

Sabelle flung herself off the bed, grinding her teeth in an effort to keep from shouting. "My rescue work is very important to me, Justin! Grandfather and I have been involved in it for years, and—"

"Then let your grandfather continue with it if he's foolish enough not to realize the dangers—but without *you!*"

He finished stuffing his shirt into his breeches, then paused to catch her hand and bring it toward him. Prying open her clenched fingers, he grazed them with his lips, then drew her into an embrace.

"I cannot bear to think of seeing you hurt, Sabelle," he murmured against her hair. "You are too important to me, not to mention the children we might have. Why, right now you could be carrying our child. Would you expose the two of you to such risks? I'll not have it, I tell you."

Sabelle wavered, warmed by the concern in his voice. Could it be that he might be coming to care for her after all? Or was it the child he mentioned—his heir—that loomed uppermost?

Justin released her as she pondered this; he bent to retrieve his boots and casually changed the subject, asking what she would like for breakfast.

Clearly, he was declaring the subject closed, as if his words on the matter had settled it. Sabelle fumed, recalling he'd extracted no promises from her. To his arrogant way of thinking, none was necessary: She would follow like a good, obedient little mouse and never question him further.

Well, Your Grace, Sabelle said to herself while she watched his graceful, pantherlike movements as he finished dressing, *as all the clever mice know, there is more than one way to evade the cat!*

Later that morning, two things happened: Thomas Long left, and Brendan arrived. The tutor's departure was predictable. It came hot on the heels of his discovery that one of the climbing boys they'd rescued was the duke's bride and that, instead of making plans to set her aside after her "desertion," her husband had actually invited her to stay on there! Brendan's bedraggled appearance—it was clear the great hound had run all night—was the surprise. He came limping into the stableyard just as Justin and Sabelle were mounting up for a tour of the estate, to familiarize Sabelle with Justin's ancestral home.

And Sabelle was no sooner exclaiming over the poor hound's shocking condition than Michael Kelly came galloping in.

"Ach! The poor lad!" exclaimed the big Irishman as he hurriedly dismounted and bent to examine the hound. "He picked up yer trail in London, and there was no stoppin' him, though I tried t' hold him to a sensible pace, Miss Sa—er, Your Grace. Then me horse threw a shoe near an inn a short way back. I tried t' keep the lad with me whilst I went t' change horses, but Brendan was fierce after findin' ye, weren't ye, lad?"

The hound whined and licked Sabelle's face, his gracefully curved tail thumping against Kelly's leg.

"Poor Brendan," Sabelle crooned. "I was worried about what you'd do when I—that is—"

"My wife and I came here to Kent somewhat, ah, unexpectedly, Mr.—Kelly, is it?"

"It is," said the Irishman, not the least bit shy about shaking the hand the duke proffered.

"And if ye'll fergive me fer sayin' so, Yer Grace, I was well aware o' who it was the lass went off with. I'd seen yer carriage with yer crest on the door. 'Twas also how I was able t' find ye after I lost sight o' the lad, here. Several villagers knew yer crest when I described it t' them and directed me t' yer place.

"Brendan, lad," he said affectionately to the dog, "I don't know how ye did it! Ye're a *sight* hound, not a *scent* hound, yet ye found the lass all the same. 'Tis glad I am, ye're so clever, but I wish ye hadn't set yerself such a punishin' pace."

"How is he?" There was concern in Justin's voice as he ran a worried glance over the exhausted hound, and Sabelle found herself instantly warmed, despite her concern for the dog.

"Just a wee bit tired, I'm thinkin'," answered the groom as he patted the big dog's head.

"But he was limping!" cried Sabelle.

Michael nodded. "The pads o' his feet are raw, but 'tis a minor thing." He reached for a saddle pack on the horse he'd ridden. "A few days' treatment with this salve I have, and some rest, and he'll be as good as new, won't ye, lad?"

In answer, Brendan licked his face, and Justin marveled at this; Kelly, for all his height, had to bend very little for the huge beast to reach his cheek. He was easily the largest canine he'd ever laid eyes on, and although he'd seen Brendan before, it had not been brought home to him then as when they were up close. *He must be a good three feet at the withers!* he realized, at the same time noting his petite wife had merely to reach an arm out at chest level to hug the shaggy neck.

Kelly was introduced to the duke's head groom after being assured that a footman had been sent to carry word to Sir Jonathan and Sabelle's parents that she was well and staying at Harthaven with her husband. Justin's groom took Kelly and Brendan to a place in the stables where the Irishman could comfortably tend the dog, and another messenger was sent to Sir Jonathan to explain that Brendan and Kelly had arrived safely in Kent as well.

Sabelle would have stayed to help tend her beloved hound, but Justin persuaded her to continue with their plans by appealing to her faith in Kelly's skills. They cantered off in the direction of the small village that was near the estate.

Sabelle rode sidesaddle, although she would have preferred to ride astride in the borrowed breeches she'd come in; but Justin had ordered the entire outfit burned. He'd presented her with an old-fashioned riding habit which Mrs. Small had located in a trunk in the attic and shortened for her; it had belonged to Justin's mother, who'd been slender, but taller than Sabelle. Deep blue in color, it came with a jaunty little hat which perched on one side of her head, and Justin had nodded when he saw her dressed, apparently satisfied with how she looked.

"We'll send to London for your own clothes," he'd told her, "but for now these remnants from the attic will have to do. The folk hereabouts are country people and not much acquainted with the fashions of the *ton,* so I hardly think you need worry you'll appear outmoded."

Sabelle wondered who it was he'd been trying to reassure. *She'd* have been most comfortable in cast-off breeches, and *he'd* been the one to order hers burned! Still, she clung to the newfound peace between them and refrained from commenting.

They visited a few tenant farms on their way to the village, where they planned to take a meal at a small inn. Each time they stopped, Sabelle noticed how the tenants smiled at their master's approach and seemed eager to talk with him. She noted, too, that the questions he asked them were knowledgeable and that he knew each member of each family by name: How was Mary faring after the birth of the twins? he'd inquire. Or: Was that new heiffer Will bought last spring in calf yet? Moreover, he seemed genuinely concerned with their problems, taking time with them, answering their questions patiently, giving considerable thought to their replies.

As they made their way toward the village, with these humble men and their wives smiling and bowing deferentially to the new duchess when Justin introduced her, Sabelle began to see a whole new person emerging from the picture she'd long held in her mind. There in the country Justin was solidly on his own turf and Hart the Heartless did not seem to exist; there he was merely the just and caring overlord, happily keeping in touch with the people who depended on him. It was a sobering reminder that she hardly knew the man to whom she was married.

Word of their coming had apparently preceded them; several shopkeepers and other tradesmen greeted their approach with smiles and cheers; and a number of humbly dressed women stood about the little green at the village center, waving coarse cotton handkerchiefs, with a handful of children peeking shyly from behind their homespun skirts.

Sabelle knew these were hard times for many of the common folk in England, what with the war abroad and civil unrest sparked by the introduction of mechanical looms in the weaving industry; yet none of these people gave evidence of deprivation. To the last child, they appeared well nourished and cared for, and the smiles on their plain, simple faces seemed to indicate they were happy with their lot.

Justin had given her some money before they left, urging her to spend it where she might when they arrived in the village. The tradesmen, like everyone else there, depended on the economy generated by his management of the estate, and he thought it wouldn't hurt for their new duchess to be seen enhancing their incomes even more directly. So Sabelle purchased some yard goods at the draper's and an assortment of creams and cosmetic ointments at the apothecary. She ordered three new pairs of half-boots from the cobbler and was measured for riding boots as well, since those on her feet were too large and had had to be worn with double hose and stuffed with cotton flannel to fit well enough for her to ride or walk at all.

At each of these stops the humble proprietors regarded her with awe; but Sabelle had been well used to setting such folk at ease in her own family's village in Surrey, so she set about doing what she could to help them relax in her presence.

She complimented the draper on the quality of his goods and even went so far as to ask his opinion on color; by the time they left, the nervous little man's face beamed with pleasure, and he told Justin, with just a hint of shyness, what a fine lady His Grace had wed.

At the apothecary shop it became quickly obvious that it was the man's wife who ran things, and Sabelle made her entire selection only after conferring with the woman and asking her to recommend a certain cream or salve. When she departed, the woman, who'd greeted her with a stiff-necked reserve, was grinning from ear to ear and promising to send up to the manor house soon some of her own private blend of floral-scented foot balm (she'd noticed Sabelle's difficulties with the overly large boots) as a gift.

Justin eyed Sabelle curiously as they headed for the cobbler's. "What ever did you say to that old crone?"

"Say to her?" She knew he'd been busy with the husband while she dealt with the wife, but Sabelle couldn't imagine why Justin might be interested in what had been said.

"To bring about that transformation. I don't believe I've ever seen her smile in all the years I've known her, and her husband complains she's as tightfisted as they come. I thought he'd sink into the ground when she promised you a *gift!*"

Sabelle's eyes twinkled, and a small smile curved her mouth as she appeared to think.

"It was clear the woman's a scold," she said after a moment. "You can see it from the sour lines in her face. But I've met scolds before, and it occurred to me that they are frequently people who feel unappreciated. I . . . merely went a bit out of my way to assure her she is very much appreciated. It was nothing more than that."

Nothing more than that, Justin mused, and yet she'd had the old sourpuss eating out of her hand! As they walked, he covertly studied his wife. To look at her, one would think her nothing more than a child—a very beautiful child, of course, but still a child . . . delicate and fragile-looking. Yet now he saw her acting with a wisdom rarely found in those twice her age. What a constant surprise she was, this small package he'd married!

Moreover, though he hadn't voiced it, he'd been ruminating this morning on last night's astounding revelations —in particular, over what manner of female she might be, to have hatched such a devastating revenge, no matter how severe the cause. And it hadn't rested entirely easy with him to see her in such a light. Who wanted a calculating woman for a wife? Yet now he saw her putting such calculating to beneficent use, and who might quarrel with that?

As they entered the cobbler's, Justin swore to himself to

use the time in Kent to get to know Sabelle better and find out just exactly what sort of female he'd married.

Inventing a tale about the duchess's baggage having been lost, Justin set about ordering her new boots; he smiled, however, when, in an aside, his wife whispered with some asperity that she hoped this would be the last "invention" required of her.

Sabelle saw, by the way the man traced her foot patterns so stiffly, that the cobbler was no less apprehensive about the new duchess than others they'd met. But she'd also glimpsed a lively intelligence in the man's eyes when he'd called to his apprentice with a homely pun designed to get the sluggard moving. Wit was the key to this one's ease, she decided, and she soon had him laughing with a play on the word *boots*, and the *boats* she'd tromped in with. Even Justin chuckled, and he was laughing outright when they left the shop in the aftermath of three additional, lightning-quick exchanges of wit between the cobbler and his duchess.

"You deal uncommonly well with these simple folk," the duke told her as they sat to take their meal at the inn.

Sabelle shrugged. "It comes of practice, I suppose. The folk about our estates in Surrey were long in awe of me for reasons which had little to do with being a highborn lady. I learned to do what I could to offset their unease when I found it necessary to get on with them from time to time."

"Unease?"

She nodded, pausing to praise the innkeeper for the quality of the fare he'd served. They watched him flush and go off smiling before she continued. "These simple folk, as I'm sure you know, can be very . . . superstitious, despite their Christian beliefs. They were convinced I was some sort of, oh, wood sprite, I suppose."

Justin abruptly set down the tankard of ale he'd been about to sip. *"Wood sprite?"*

Sabelle smiled, the impish look on her elfin face at once hinting at what may have inspired this attribution, even before she explained.

"A wild thing who ran in the woods with the deer and was known to discourse with horses."

Justin smiled, remembering the little hoyden who'd set an entire hunt party on its ears by absconding with its quarry. "And did you?" he queried with a glint of amusement in his eyes.

"Did I what?"

"Run with the deer and talk to horses."

The aquamarine eyes twinkled. "When I was quite young, about nine or ten, I collect, Grandfather had an interesting man come to stay for a few days as his guest. Sheikh ibn Ari Sharaz was an old friend whose life Grandfather had saved once when they were both young. Although I never learned the particulars—Grandfather was far too modest to mention the incident at all—it was the sheikh who told of it."

She paused to take a sip of the fine wine the innkeeper had poured, noting she had Justin's complete attention.

"At any rate," she went on, "the sheikh was not only a prince of sorts in his desert country in the East; he was also a master with horses—a *master!* Grandfather said he owned a herd of the finest Arabians and lived among them in a manner no Englishman would. He called them his children —slept with them, ate with them, and . . . *spoke* to them . . ."

Justin hadn't moved since she'd begun her tale; but when she paused to take a bite of the excellent poached turbot they'd been served, he did the same, though it was clear his attention was on what she would say next.

"Oh, it was not a speech in language as we know it," Sabelle continued, "though he made sounds when he approached an animal, and these were always low and soothing. But, more than that, it was what he did when he got up close. He began with what we often see horses doing with one another . . . exchanging scents, nose to nose, nostrils softly inhaling and exhaling . . .

"He said you had to begin by acting like one of them, and then, if you were blessed by God—Allah, he called Him—with a certain . . . sensitivity, I suppose you might call it, once you could *act* like a horse, it might become possible to *think* like a horse, and—"

"He taught you these things, in a few days' time?"

She shrugged, reaching for her wineglass. "It was not so difficult. There was a half-grown foal who'd lost its dam and grown quite skittish by the time Grandfather had rescued it. He—*we*—were in the rescue business even then, I suppose. At any rate, with our guest beside me, I . . . Well, I surprised even the sheikh. The little fellow was eating out of my hand and following me around like a puppy before the afternoon was over."

Justin's face grew stern. "A half-grown foal is no lightweight, and certainly not a puppy! How the devil could your grandfather allow a child of nine or ten—"

"Oh, he wasn't at all keen on it at first," Sabelle interjected quickly when she saw the direction his thoughts were taking. "You must believe we took every precaution, and I wouldn't have been allowed to attempt it without his friend in attendance.

"But you see, Justin," she went on, "the sheikh determined, after only a few minutes, that I had this . . . gift of Allah, and—"

"And that made everything all right, I suppose."

Again, she shrugged. "It did to the sheikh, and it did to Grandfather. And, after that, I began to test what I'd learned—carefully . . . sparingly. The deer were easy. I'd been playing among them for years, and—"

"You employed this—this techni——"

"Gift, you mean?"

"Whatever! You used it on *wild deer?*"

"Only when they needed me."

"Needed you?"

"Well, there was a poacher on the loose on my parents' estate once, and until they caught the man, I had to tell the deer how to avoid him, didn't I?"

"You told the wild deer on your parents' estate how to avoid a poacher." The slow enunciation of each word underscored his disbelief, but Sabelle proceeded as if she hadn't noticed.

"The rabbits and foxes, too, although foxes are a bit harder. They have to be located first, and are very clever. In fact, that was my problem with the one targeted for quarry at my parents' hunt that day; so we had no choice but to use more drastic measures."

"So I noticed."

Sabelle flushed, though not so much from the irony dripping from his syllables as from her memory of that discomforting encounter. Raising her small chin defiantly, she made herself look him straight in the eyes.

"I am not in the least sorry for what we accomplished that day, Your Grace!"

She was saved from anything else he might have said by the arrival of the innkeeper with a bowl of strawberries with clotted cream on the side. Knowing her best hope of diverting her husband from a topic that threatened their truce, she kept their host at the table for several minutes with words of praise for their excellent meal.

It worked. When the man left, wearing a face wreathed in smiles, Justin winked at her, "Round four to the duchess. A perfect score, Your Grace!"

They returned to Harthaven with each of them privately committed to getting to know the other better. Sabelle was installed in the lovely blue-and-cream bedchamber adjoining the bathing alcove she'd used the night she arrived. She learned it had belonged to Justin's mother and had remained unoccupied since her death, but this information came from Mrs. Small; Justin offered not a word about it. Indeed, he seemed quite closemouthed whenever the subject of his parents arose, as it did several times during the afternoon, and again during a particular conversation at dinner.

Sabelle noted, when he arrived to escort her down to the dining hall, that he became suddenly silent and withdrawn. He ran his eyes over the elegant tight-waisted and panniered gown the housekeeper had also found in the attic and altered, and his features grew rigid, his eyes at once shuttered and unrevealing.

"Don't—don't you like it?" she queried. "I own it is a bit old-fash——"

"It is quite lovely," he interrupted curtly, then changed the subject as he ushered her downstairs.

When they sat to have their supper, however, he seemed himself again, and Sabelle soon forgot the incident. Later, she was to wish she'd remembered and been more careful of her tongue.

It happened when they were almost finished with the meal. Seeing her wineglass was nearly empty, Justin signaled a footman to refill it.

"Ah, no, thank you—please!" said Sabelle, laughing. "Though it is excellent wine. But I fear it has to do with all these . . ."—she indicated her tiny, corseted waist, artificially nipped in to accommodate the narrow middle of the borrowed, pale blue gown—". . . confinements," she finished. "I fear I am quite unaccustomed to such cincturing, you see, and wonder how our mothers and grandmothers endured it. Of course, if she couldn't eat very much while wearing these, it explains entirely why your mother was so slender. Tell me, did your father—"

"Leave it, Sabelle."

The words were curt and clipped, and when her eyes flew to Justin's face, she saw it had gone hard again.

But how rude his tone had been! And here, under the very noses of the servants whose respect she'd hoped to have! He was being utterly unfair. How was she to know the subject of his parents was forbidden? Hadn't he himself ordered his mother's clothes altered for her? It was unreasonable, therefore, not to expect some mention of their original owner to arise in conversation!

Suddenly weary of the repeated efforts she'd found herself having to make at maintaining their tenuous peace, Sabelle's hold on her patience snapped. "Far be it from me, Your Grace," she flung at him as she threw her napkin down and rose from the table, "to tax your civility by my inept efforts at conversation! Perhaps you'll fare better with your supper if you finish it alone!" She headed for the door.

"Sabelle—" His tone held a warning.

She whirled about, eyes flashing. "No, you needn't trouble yourself to show me out. I assure you, I have quite mastered the route to my chambers."

With a flounce of skirts, she quit the room, half expecting him to come after her and drag her back. Instead, she heard his voice behind her before the doors closed.

"Some more wine, Soames," he was saying to the footman in a bored tone. "I fear I'm rather thirsty this evening."

Sabelle was in high dudgeon when she reached the blue-and-cream bedchamber. Only the appearance of Jeannie and the Scotswoman's willingness to let her vent her anger eventually calmed her down.

"Just who does he think he is, Jeannie?" she seethed. "I did not *ask* to be dragged here in the middle of the night, and I'll not suffer his peculiar moods! Why, if he cannot abide my company, did he not leave us alone?"

"Ye maun answer that question yerself, lassie," her friend replied. "Yer duke's a proud, hard mon. His like cuid nae suffer a footloose wife wanderin' the streets o' London, makin' a fool o' him in the bargain."

"Proud?" Sabelle fumed. *"Arrogant,* you mean! And here I'd begun to think—"

"Aye?" Jeannie queried, intrigued. "Wha' *had* ye begun t' think, lassie?"

But Sabelle changed the subject. She was unready to voice, even to Jeannie, those tentative hopes she'd begun to harbor that morning, that somehow this marriage could be rescued from the mess she'd created with its inception.

Instead, she turned to the problem of the poor dogs they'd rescued and what was to be done with them. This latest contretemps with Justin gave her all the excuse she needed to continue her work with abused animals, despite his orders to the contrary. Besides, she reasoned, in the case of these pit dogs, the rescue had already been accomplished. Surely Justin's restrictions did not signify here, did they? The animals were already in her possession!

Resolving to find a way to work with the dogs, somehow,

to regain their shattered trust in humans, she asked Jeannie to pass the word to Michael Kelly. Her friend said she would, and the two women bade each other good-night. Then Sabelle prepared for bed, half expecting her husband to appear at any moment.

Justin never came. Hours later as she tossed and turned, trying to sleep, she thought she heard him enter his chamber, which adjoined hers. But in the morning, when she awoke—much later than was her habit, having dozed off long after midnight—it was to find herself alone.

❖ Chapter 22 ❖

SABELLE SAW VERY LITTLE OF JUSTIN IN THE days that followed. And if the servants thought this odd, not to mention the fact that it was apparent the master and his new bride slept apart—no one gave evidence of it. Mrs. Small did mention to the new mistress, however, that His Grace rode off each morning with his estates manager on Harthaven business.

Twice she encountered her husband briefly, in passing in and out of the house, and on these occasions he merely inquired politely if she was comfortable in her chambers and told her he trusted she was able to amuse herself sufficiently about the estate. Although his words were courteous, Sabelle thought she detected a sardonic edge to them. But not wanting to lock horns with him again, she answered him coolly and politely—and let it pass.

Each morning, after taking breakfast in her chambers, she and Jeannie went down to the stables to meet with Kelly, although she told the housekeeper they were off to look after her wolfhound.

Brendan had recovered swiftly from his injuries and fatigue, and by the second day at Harthaven, he was running about like his former self. Sabelle wished the recovery process was as simple for the poor pit dogs.

Actually, it was determined by Kelly that the dogs they'd rescued hadn't yet been used in the pit, so that gave them a powerful advantage: Dogs that hadn't yet tasted blood would be far easier—and safer—to work with. Nevertheless, the big Irishman took on the initial training himself, relegating Sabelle and Jeannie to assisting. He knew the young women had come to no harm in absconding with the dogs in the first place, but he was "takin' no chances." Privately, Sabelle wondered whether the presence of her husband—always felt in the background there, at his own estate—had something to do with this.

But their work with the dogs—in a remote pasture some distance from the stables—proceeded successfully, if slowly. Mostly it was just a matter of patience—and long, tedious hours of repetition—that began to bring the poor, frightened animals around. But then there was something that Brendan, himself bored with these procedures, did to break the monotony.

It began on their third day in the pasture. Kelly had been working alone with the dogs for a few hours; Mrs. Small had asked Jeannie to stay behind to supervise the unpacking of Sabelle's clothes, which had arrived from London, and Sabelle had decided to remain with her.

The two young women joined Michael in the pasture around noon, and the training continued at its usual snail's pace. Then, about ten minutes later, Sabelle saw Michael shift his attention from the terrier on his lead and look across the pasture.

"Oh, no," the big Irishman groaned, "not again!"

"Not again, what?" murmured Sabelle, puzzled. But then she saw it: Walking across the pasture, his neck arched, his great head held proudly erect, came Brendan.

And in the great jaws was a shocked, befuddled *fox!*

"Again, did ye say?" queried Jeannie.

"I did," said Kelly. " 'Tis the third time since this mornin'! The lad's got it in his head t' rescue foxes!"

"B-but, Michael," Sabelle stammered as the big dog drew nearer with his prize, "it isn't as if Brendan's ill-trained! Why not simply command him to release it?"

"I did," groaned the Irishman, "and, as far as I can determine, he's done this. He's let each o' them go—and then gone t' fetch a new one!"

"A *new* . . . Good heavens, Michael!" Sabelle exclaimed as the hound approached, tail wagging happily. "Do you mean to say that he's caught *three separate foxes?*"

"I do," Kelly replied as he threw the hound an exasperated look. " 'Tis certain, I am, because the first was a vixen and the next was male, and this one"—he peered at the bemused animal hanging, uninjured, from the wolfhound's jaws—"is of a softer red in color than the first two."

"Ach!" exclaimed Jeannie, throwing up her hands. "I remember now. One o' the footmen mentioned there's a hunt in progress t'day at a neighborin' estate. Brendan's merely doin' wha' ye once taught him!"

"But—but that must be *miles* from here!" Sabelle exclaimed. "Harthaven is *huge.*"

Michael nodded. "But not too huge fer the lad, here." The Irishman's tone had changed upon news of the hunt, and he now proceeded to praise the dog, adding, "I was after takin' time away from our rescue beasts t' train him not t' be fetchin' any more o' the poor divils, but now I believe I'll just let the lad be, eh, Brendan?"

The hound's tail thumped furiously, and Sabelle laughed.

"Oh, by all means," she said as the Irishman directed the dog to release this fox, too, in a safe area. "I cannot think of any better revenge on those who train hapless hounds to pursue such quarry—than a hound who rescues it instead!"

And the following day, when the housekeeper mentioned an odd look on the duke's face when one of the footmen spoke of the neighboring earl *whose hunt party had been unable to come by a single fox,* Sabelle merely smiled.

Of course, Sabelle thought, it might have been the footman's remark which prompted a message from her husband the next day. It said he expected her "to join me for a civil meal in the dining hall at the supper hour."

"Humph! Civil meal, indeed!" she groused to Jeannie upon reading his words, yet the Scotswoman noted her taking special care with her toilette as she prepared to join her husband downstairs.

Sabelle relaxed in a perfumed bath after coming back to the house earlier than usual from their dog-training session. She washed her long hair and brushed it until it shone like silken honey before the fire; then she had Jeannie arrange it in a soft, twisted knot high atop the crown of her head, leaving numerous wisps and tendrils to curl beguilingly about her face and neck.

The soft muslin gown she chose was a deep forest green. It had tiny puffed sleeves, and the sheer material fell in a slender silhouette from the high waistline. It was a departure from the soft aquamarines and sea-greens she was accustomed to wearing; but an aquamarine satin sash and matching slippers served as accents, as if to remind whoever saw it that this was still her signature color, reflecting, as it did, the luminous depths of her eyes.

Finally, she was ready—at least in her dress. She wondered if she'd ever be ready to face her arrogant husband when he was in his "Hart the Heartless" phase, as she'd begun to term the cool, distancing mood which had marked the past few days. She nearly jumped back in surprise, then, when she found him waiting for her in the hallway outside her chambers, as she was about to go downstairs.

"Good evening, my dear," he drawled lazily as he ran his eyes slowly over her.

"Justin! I—you surprised me!"

"Did I? I cannot imagine why." He said this laconically, as if to dismiss her reaction, yet he remained for a moment longer where he was when she'd first noticed him.

He was leaning against the wall across from her door, arms folded casually across his chest, and she again had the impression of a big jungle cat, a predator, the cool, pewter light in his eyes as much a part of this as his stance. It was that way about him which cats had, of appearing relaxed and inattentive in their physical posture, giving little indication they had their prey in mind—until they pounced.

Elegantly dressed in an evening suit of dark blue superfine, he was all arrogant masculinity, accoutered in sartorial splendor. A snowy, perfectly tied cravat underscored a deeper bronzing of his face, no doubt acquired from time lately spent out of doors, riding on the estate. And the contours of his broad shoulders and lean, muscular thighs were enhanced by a display of tailoring so fine, nary a wrinkle marred the smooth perfection of that big, lithe body. He was a perfect Corinthian, in the best sense of that fashionable term. Even though she'd collected herself after her initial surprise at seeing him so unexpectedly, Sabelle felt her pulse race at his stark male beauty.

"Shall we dine, Your Grace?" he inquired smoothly. He moved away from the wall in that graceful, catlike way of his and offered her his arm.

Sabelle nodded, placing her fingers on his sleeve, but as they proceeded toward the staircase, she noted his limp seemed much pronounced.

He guessed her thoughts, a habit of his she was beginning to deplore. "I suppose I've overdone the riding a bit lately. My physician was not pleased to learn of it, I assure you, but—"

"You required a physician?" Sabelle hadn't meant to sound alarmed, but there was no mistaking her tone, and he paused, a sardonic gleam in his eye.

"Was that concern for my welfare I detected? I wonder that my *civility* warrants it." Without waiting for a reply, he continued to lead her downstairs.

But if Sabelle was expecting a difficult time at supper, it never came. Justin was the soul of gentlemanly conduct, discoursing amiably on a variety of topics, taking pains, it seemed, to draw her into conversation. He even went to the point of interjecting a bit of wit here and there, complimenting her with his eyes on the speed and cleverness of her responses.

It was clear he was determined to be on his best behavior. When their meal was over, he escorted her back upstairs, and Sabelle suddenly wondered whether this hadn't all been a prelude to getting her back into his bed.

But when they reached the door to the blue-and-cream bedchamber, he merely raised her fingers to his lips, almost in a courtly manner, and murmured good-night.

But he paused a moment and held her eyes. Sabelle had felt a shiver coursing down her spine when she felt his lips graze her fingers, and now it came again, followed by a delicious feeling of something warm curling beneath her belly as she caught the light in his eyes. It was desire she read there; she was sure of it, and her response was a surge of longing so sweet and piercing, she felt faint with it.

But then Justin was heading for his chambers, and she thought she murmured good-night, but couldn't be sure. Her head was filled with images of the night he'd brought her there and made sweet, passionate love to her until dawn.

She felt herself turn somehow and grasp the handle of her door, her knees like jelly; but then, from his own doorway, Justin's voice rang out, bringing her up short: "It seems you out*foxed* them again, Sabelle, but be advised: Had it not been your hound, but *you* who suffered the danger, I should not have been the least amused."

With this he turned and disappeared into his chambers.

In the days which followed, Sabelle saw her husband far more regularly. He invited her to join him on rides about the estate, and once, in the stables when they returned, she showed him how she "talked" to horses, using her gift to charm the lovely little gray mare he presented her with as her personal mount at Harthaven. Encouraged by his increasingly benevolent manner, Sabelle at last divulged what had been going on in the training pasture, though she was careful to imply it had been Michael Kelly, and Kelly alone, who'd incurred any risks with the now manageable pit dogs. And each evening she would join her husband for a supper in the grand dining hall; but always, when it was over, the finish to their day was the same: He would escort her to her door and bid her good-night with that same intense look in his eyes, then leave her to sleep alone.

Sabelle wondered, deeply puzzled, about the celibate state he seemed to be imposing on both of them. If she'd discovered anything about her husband at all, it was that he was lusty and passionate. But then she remembered his arrogance, that overweening male pride he wore about him like a coat of armor, and it all fell into place. On the very evening following the reconciliation which had ended in passion between them, she'd walked out on him, leaving the dining hall in a fit of pique. No matter that she might have had just cause; her overly proud husband would see that as a blow to his pride and was, in all likelihood, determined not to suffer such again. He would never make another overture. If she wanted him back in her arms, it was up to her to make the next move.

Was that what she wanted? She recalled her astounding discovery of the pleasure to be had between a man and a woman, knew she was reminded of it in a hundred little ways during this period of intimate celibacy between them . . . the shiver brought on by a casual touch of his hand . . . the way her limbs turned to water when he looked at her in a certain way . . . and always, always, there was the unvoiced memory of the passion which had passed between them . . .

So Sabelle knew she wanted him, but did she have the courage to initiate what she desired? What if she were wrong and he simply didn't want her anymore? What if he'd grown tired of her? He'd always had a mistress. Who was to say he wasn't seeing one even now? There were hours on end when he disappeared while here at the estate . . . more than sufficient time for a tryst.

Thoughts of Sarah Cavendish flooded her mind, and she was surprised at the sharp, bitter pain she felt. *Oh, God*, she thought then, *is it happening already? Am I to suffer now, the very thing I feared all along and sought to stave off with my revenge? Is he to have the last laugh, after all?*

But then she steadied herself, refusing to succumb to panic. He could only hurt her—really hurt her—if he proved faithless in the face of her *loving* him. *Well*, she thought triumphantly, *that is something he shall never have! All the rest, I can manage. The thing is to get on with him, but not to love him. Surely I can manage that*, she resolved with a flash of her old courage.

But soon thereafter, there came a night that had all Sabelle's resolve fading like mist in the wind. It happened about a week later, when, altering his pattern after supper, Justin invited her to join him in the library for a game of chess. "Or you may wish to avail yourself of some books," he added.

Sabelle looked up sharply at him as he came to escort her from the dining table, clearly caught off guard by his invitation. But she could detect nothing to explain this deviation in those gray eyes—so unreadable when he wanted them to be.

"The—the latter, I think," she managed, trying to recover from her surprise.

Oh, why did he have this ability to affect her so visibly with his unpredictable behavior? Indeed, why was he *so* unpredictable? Must she feel continually off balance?

Pushing aside her annoyance, she added, "While I enjoy a game of chess now and then, I'll admit I've been famished for a good book since we—almost since I arrived."

"Good enough, then." He smiled and led her toward the library.

But what Sabelle couldn't know was that her thoughts had just touched on the very thing that had motivated Justin's behavior.

He was deliberately keeping her off balance.

It had come to him rather suddenly the night she'd stranded him after supper. He'd been about to go after her and press her for obedience and compliance—all those wifely duties he'd long expected of any woman he made his duchess. But then he pictured the angry scene that would in all likelihood ensue, and he'd desisted.

There were other ways to bring her around.

So he'd taken a cue from his experiences in the military, remembering that one of the best ways to defeat a foe was to keep him off balance. It had worked for Wellington; it would work for him.

This little change in the "routine" he'd established was just one more unbalancing ploy. A few more in the next week or so, and he'd have his little independent-minded duchess eating out of his hand.

Justin suddenly frowned to himself as they entered the library. The only problem was, while he was bringing her to heel, how did he keep his hands off her? For he knew the main thrust of his "unbalancing maneuvers" involved keeping Sabelle physically at arm's length. She was such a passionate little creature, he knew she could be set on edge by that tactic. The trouble was, *so could he!* He didn't like to think of all those recent nights he'd spent tossing restlessly in his big bed—the very bed where they'd shared such incredible passion—and she just a few yards away!

By God, he thought as he gritted his teeth and strolled to the shelves to locate a book or two, *how Shelley would laugh if he heard of this coil I've set myself!* And Byron! Byron would be writing him his very own canto in whatever his latest satirical piece was!

But, appeasing himself with the thought that neither poet was a military man, while he was, Justin made himself choose a new translation of Caesar's *Gallic Wars* and settled down to his chosen course of action; he found a chair by the fire, lit to ward off the chill of a June night, and opened his book.

Sabelle wandered along the library shelves that ran floor to ceiling with beautifully bound volumes, enjoying herself far more than she'd anticipated. Her fingers traced familiar titles, as well as many that were new to her. Histories, plays, mathematical treatises, biographies—the variety was endless, and what was perhaps more telling about the man who owned them was that all of them gave evidence of having been read.

Finally, perhaps because her wanderings had brought her close to where Justin was sitting, she made herself choose a book; at that moment, mingled with the woodsmoke from the fire, had come the scent of the sandalwood soap Justin used, and it was sufficient to pull her away from her reverie and remind her of his unsettling presence.

The volume she happened to choose contained works by that strange, mystical poet, Blake. It was not something she'd have selected ordinarily, but the scent of sandalwood, not to mention the play of firelight on Justin's ebony curls, was oddly distracting . . .

Suddenly annoyed with herself, Sabelle headed for the other chair near the fire and, with a flounce of her skirts, settled down to read.

Justin caught the faintest scent of lilac as his wife passed, and swore softly to himself. He'd watched her covertly for twenty minutes, saw her floating dreamily past the shelves, clearly oblivious to him or anything else in the room. So much for keeping her off balance. Devil take it, the chit had been *smiling* to herself! How in hell was he to know a stack of books would have such a calming influence on her? And now that damned perfume . . .

Disgruntled, Justin forced himself to focus on his book.

Sabelle peered cautiously over the top of *Blake's Poetry* and noted the fierce expression on her husband's face. Odd . . . she couldn't recall anything in Caesar's *Gallic Wars* which might produce such a reaction.

But she knew the play of candlelight and firelight on his strong, bronzed hands was having a reaction on her, and it wasn't at all conducive to reading!

Ducking her head, Sabelle made herself focus on the words in front of her: *Tyger, tyger, burning bright* . . . *Damn!* Would everything make her think of *him*?

With a sigh, she turned the page: "The Lamb." There, now, that was better! She began to read . . .

Justin heard the sigh and tried to ignore it, but a few seconds later his eyes were straying toward the chair where his wife sat with her legs tucked under her, feet curled on the cushion. She'd shed her slippers! *Dammit!* he swore silently. This was beginning to be the worst idea he'd ever had!

Tearing his eyes away from the tantalizing view of slender, stockinged ankles, Justin went back to Caesar, grateful that the delectable parts of a woman's anatomy had nothing to do with that noble Roman's account of conquering Gall.

Sabelle heard the movement of a book being shifted and chanced another covert glance. God in heaven, he was handsome! Beautiful, really, yet undeniably male. It wanted decency that such a face should be graced with such long, thick eyelashes!

She released a small gasp as she felt those all-too-familiar tendrils of desire curling below the vicinity of her lap, and bent desperately to her book.

Justin's head came up as Sabelle's lowered, and he stared at her, at her book—*Blake* . . . What the deuce was there in Blake to make her gasp like that? Then, with a smile, he recalled a few erotic passages, rather clearly, as a matter of fact.

Well, well, well, he mused. *Perhaps there was something here after all . . .*

He went back to Caesar, not quite as annoyed as he had been. He read *All of Gall is divided into three parts* for the eleventh time.

The tiniest of frowns erupted on the smooth surface of Sabelle's brow as she dared yet another glance at her husband. He was *smiling.* What in heaven's name was there in Caesar to be cheerful about? All that wretched old Roman ever wrote about was war, war, and more war! Well, she'd known men's minds to be peculiar, her husband's being a notable case in point.

Again, she let her eyes roam upon that handsome face . . . high, angular cheekbones . . . long, perfectly straight nose . . . strong jaw, long and square . . . sensuous, sculpted mouth, and—

And the deepest silvery eyes . . . *He was looking directly at her!* He had caught her staring at him!

Justin was as startled as Sabelle to meet her gaze. He'd thought she was totally absorbed by that damned mystic!

A smile curved the beautifully sculpted mouth as he saw her face grow crimson.

Yet, still, he held her gaze, and the look between them grew . . . and grew . . .

The sensuous thread that held them was gaining in intensity, and Sabelle could feel the heat in every pore. Her breathing became slow, hesitant, and she felt her throat tighten, and a dizzying lassitude invade her limbs.

"Come here, Sabelle," she heard him whisper thickly. Unable to help herself, she somehow found the strength to uncoil her legs and move. Blindly almost, her blood thrumming in her ears, she found herself beside him—

And pulled into his lap.

Justin breathed the lingering scent of lilac as he caught her in his arms. For all its subtlety, it was intoxicating, like the finest wine, and he felt himself go rock-hard. He took his fingers and tilted her chin up to search her wondering face. He held, for a moment, her eyes, which had gone deep, smoky turquoise, then let his gaze drop to her mouth.

Sabelle's lips parted in response, her breathing shallow, her heart beating a steady tattoo beneath her breast.

Slowly, like a person in a dream, she felt her arms steal about his neck, and she thought she saw him smile before his mouth claimed hers.

Oh, it was sweet, that kiss, and Sabelle succumbed to its magic like a drowning woman thrown a life line. All the pent-up longing of the preceding days surged through her, and she twined her arms tightly around Justin's neck, while her lips opened eagerly to his questing tongue. Greedily, like someone starved, she kissed him back and moaned against the moist pressure of mouth moving on mouth as she felt his hand cup her breast.

Justin had intended to keep *her* off-balance, but now *his* head was reeling under the impact of Sabelle's reactions. As he felt the sweet, lush contours of her body settle against his, he savored the heady knowledge that she'd been the one to initiate this passionate embrace. All thoughts of games and tactics seemed to vanish, leaving him aware of nothing save the hungry fire in his loins—and the exquisitely eager, sweetly moaning little creature who caused it.

"Sabelle . . ." he groaned as his lips trailed a burning path to her ear and he felt her nipple tighten to a hard bud beneath his touch. "Ah, Sabelle, you're like a—"

At that moment a door slammed loudly nearby, followed by shouts and the thud of running feet.

Sabelle and Justin broke apart, breathless, and Sabelle

gasped when she realized the commotion was now coming from right outside the library. She had just enough time to note the displeasure on Justin's face when the door crashed open.

Sabelle yelped and scrambled out of her husband's lap. She heard him swear an indelicate oath while she worked furiously to rearrange her gown; at the same instant, out of the corner of her eye she noticed Justin seize the book he'd been reading and slam it, face down, across the telltale bulge in his lap. Then they both stared, she, red-faced, he, furious at the bedlam that invaded the library.

The huge blur of reddish fur that bounded across the carpet was Brendan, of course, and Sabelle groaned to think that her beloved hound was at the center of this.

But Brendan was hardly alone. In his wake rushed several servants—grooms and footmen, by the look of them, though their livery was green and gold, not the duke's colors—and a short, fat, balding man dressed as a lord stood by the door with an apoplectic look on his face. He shouted, "Seize him! Seize that fox-thieving cur!"

Indeed, it appeared the corpulent gentleman was the one who'd dared invade His Grace's library, for his hand still clenched the door's handle as if he would throttle it while he shouted orders to the liveried servants. They made several mad dashes at the circling hound in reaction to each of the lord's furious commands, but drew up short and retreated when Brendan growled fiercely, his hackles raised.

Sabelle's gaze swung to her hound when she heard the growls amid the shouting, and her mouth dropped open. There, hanging from Brendan's jaws, was yet another fox!

"What in the name of hell's going on here?" Justin roared.

Just then Michael Kelly and Jeannie burst into the room, followed by Mrs. Small, who wielded a broom before her as if it were a bayonet.

"They were *shootin'* at the lad, Yer Grace!" Kelly shouted as he thudded to a stop and whirled to glare at the fat one by the door.

Dear God! thought Sabelle.

"Shootin' at a fine Irish hound," Kelly went on, "as if

they meant t' make him take the place o' the poor fox they failed t' come by, and—"

"Poor fox!" shouted the lordly object of Kelly's fury, all three of his chins aquiver. "That fox was supposed to be—"

"Enough!" Justin shouted.

Silence reigned supreme. All eyes turned toward the duke.

"M'lord Brumley," said Justin in a commanding voice, "what is the meaning of this?"

Brumley sputtered indignantly before replying, "I—I should think that would appear quite obvious, Your Grace. That hound has been—been pilfering my foxes!"

"Indeed?" replied Justin, his voice dangerously soft. "And perhaps you would be willing to explain to me how it is that you know these animals"—he gestured toward the unhappy ball of red fur dangling from Brendan's mouth— "to be *your* possessions? I wasn't aware you'd taken up the habit of raising foxes as domesticated animals, m'lord."

Sabelle saw a smile break across Michael Kelly's face as he realized the direction the duke's words were taking, and she thought she heard Jeannie smother a giggle.

Lord Brumley was incensed. "Now, see here, Haverleigh," he fumed, "your hound—"

"My *wife's* hound," said Justin tersely, "and one of her dearest possessions. In point of fact, Brumley, the hound is like a beloved child to my bride—her cherished companion. And I believe I should make it clear, m'lord, that *I* should take it most assiduously amiss if anything . . . untoward should happen to so valued a creature and thereby cause Her Grace any distress. Do you take my meaning, m'lord?"

Brumley stood by the door with his mouth agape, his eyes darting nervously to the petite, elegantly gowned woman beside the duke, and back to the stern visage of her husband. He tried to speak, his mouth working furiously, but no sound came out.

"I believe I asked you, m'lord," Justin said all too softly, "whether we understand each other."

Brumley's beady eyes took in the stark, uncompromising

lines of his neighbor's face, the forbidding features of the man they not only called Hart the Heartless, but about whom daunting tales of battlefield prowess had filtered down, and he knew Haverleigh was the last man on earth he wished to cross. Moreover, in addition to the duke's legendary temper and tales of the retribution it invoked, it was clear the man doted on his new bride. (And who could blame him? The chit was a prime beauty). Who knew what heights Haverleigh's temper would reach if his new duchess's happiness were threatened?

Licking lips all at once gone dry, Brumley mumbled, "We understand each other, Your Grace," and performed a bow. Then, gesturing to his servants behind him, he retreated from the room with a sudden alacrity that belied his rounded bulk.

The entire chamber seemed to breathe a sigh of relief when they'd gone. Michael offered Justin a silent salute, and Mrs. Small lowered her broom. Even Brendan seemed to understand what had happened and began wagging his tail, while Jeannie glanced at the duke and smiled.

In fact, everyone was doing something to indicate overt relief at Justin's handling of the situation.

Except Sabelle.

Sabelle just stood there, a look of profound horror on her face as she internalized her own reaction to her husband's unexpected defense of her beloved hound—and of her.

My God, she told herself in silent agony, *I think I'm in love with him!*

❖Chapter 23❖

I AM IN LOVE WITH HIM! THE SILENT, UN-thinkable words continued to bombard Sabelle's mind as she gazed at her husband in horror.

Justin instantly noted his wife's white-faced stare. Assuming it was from shock at the behavior of his idiot neighbor, he immediately ordered everyone out of the library.

"Except you, Mrs. Small," he added to the housekeeper. "Please help my wife to her chambers and have a bath prepared."

"B-but I've already had a b-bath this evening," Sabelle murmured in a shaky, subdued voice as the housekeeper led her toward the door. Eyes focused on the carpet, she was still in a state of numbness over her painful realization—that she'd succumbed to the very feelings for this man which she'd sworn never to have. It was all she could do to speak, much less look at him.

The tremor in her voice only convinced Justin further of his initial assessment of her behavior. He smiled, finding it somehow pleasant to discover his valiant little bride, with an independent streak a mile wide, had such a patently feminine, vulnerable aspect to her nature.

"That," he said as he watched her accompany the housekeeper on slightly unsteady legs, "was for your toilette. *This* is for your mind's ease."

"That's right," said Mrs. Small as she helped the duchess

into the hallway. "There's nothing like a warm, relaxing bath to soothe a body over a shock, I always say."

Sabelle bit her lip. It would take far more than a bath to help her over *this* shock! And as for her "mind's ease," she doubted she'd ever find that blessed state again!

A short while later Sabelle found herself sitting in the same big brass tub she associated with the beginning of her sojourn at Harthaven.

Her very shattering, impossible sojourn at Harthaven.

How could it have happened? How could she possibly have fallen in love with Justin Hart? The man she'd sworn vengeance on for his casual taking of her virginity. Indeed, whom she'd wed with nothing more than revenge in mind!

Ah, but they'd been all through that on her first night here—was it only a fortnight ago? In some ways it seemed like ages, especially in view of the changes it had wrought between them . . . and of this latest change in *herself* . . . falling in love with a man who had no heart. A man whose stated intention in taking a wife was to beget heirs on her, stuffing her away in the country like a good broodmare while he hared off to London to take his "better pleasures" with mistresses, just as he'd always done. A man who believed himself incapable of love and, at best, thought *married love* an—an oxymoron!

Sabelle stifled a hysterical giggle, knowing it would end in tears if she let it escape. *An oxymoron,* said her grandfather's voice in her mind, to the child he'd been studying poetry with, years ago, *is a poetic contradiction in terms. When the poet speaks of a "cruel kindness," he is using an oxymoron* . . .

The hysterical giggle erupted, after all, and Sabelle clamped her hand over her mouth to contain it. *A cruel kindness,* indeed! She might use just such an oxymoron to describe Justin's act of saving Brendan from Lord Brumley. For in doing so, in letting her witness just one more kind act in a man she'd thought to hate, or at least keep at bay, he'd tipped the balance and—

"Ah, there you are," said a familiar voice from the entrance to the alcove. Sabelle gave a start as Justin's tall, muscular frame filled the entryway. "Feeling any better, sweet?" he queried as Sabelle swallowed audibly and sank down lower in the bath.

He looked, oh, so beautiful standing there in all his masculine splendor. Given her recent acknowledgment of her feelings toward him, Sabelle had never felt more vulnerable in his presence.

He'd removed his cravat and evening coat, and the fine linen shirt he wore was open halfway to the waist, with its sleeves rolled up; this and the tight pantaloons that clung to his long thighs like a second skin gave him a casual, roguish air that was somehow in keeping with the handsome, angular planes of his face. And the hint of satisfied mischief she thought she saw in those quicksilver eyes that missed nothing—

Could he know? Sabelle asked herself in a sudden panic. *Could he possibly have guessed the truth? Please, no, dear God! I'd die if he ever—*

"From the way you look, I'd guess not," said Justin, advancing toward her and producing a brandy snifter she'd been in no state to notice at first.

"Here, love," he added as he hunkered down beside the tub and held out the brandy. "Drink this. It will help you relax."

Relax? Sabelle thought wildly, but she raised a hand out of the perfumed water and took the snifter, her head a jumble of disparate, yet interlocking, thoughts. How could she relax when his very presence unnerved her so? And his ever so casual use of the endearment "love." She knew it meant nothing to him, no more than an affectionate "m'dear" to his grandmother.

At least, she *hoped* it didn't! What if he *had* guessed the truth and was toying with her the way a cat—

Abruptly, Sabelle raised the brandy to her lips and downed it in two quick swallows.

"Whoa!" ordered Justin. He snatched the snifter from her hand as she dissolved into a paroxysm of coughing and choking.

Then all at once Sabelle found herself being lifted deftly

out of the tub and enveloped in a wide sheet of toweling. The familiar scent of sandalwood met and mingled with the florals of her bath as her nose pressed against the texture of fine linen. She felt strong arms surround her, holding her all too close, and yet, also, somehow not close enough. Slowly, her coughing subsided, to be replaced by an odd, giddy feeling.

"Better?" she heard Justin query huskily somewhere above her ear. A strange lassitude had invaded her limbs and dimmed her senses; she couldn't be sure if the throaty timbre in his voice—a quality she felt, somehow, she ought to be recognizing as significant of something—was actually there or had been imagined.

"Mmm," she murmured, dimly wondering how the feel of fine linen had come to be replaced by crisp whorls of chest hair that vibrated against her lips and tickled her nose.

She felt Justin suck in his breath with her reply. Withdrawing enough to tilt her head and look up at him, she thought to spy what was amiss.

Molten silver eyes, their unmistakable message piercing through the brandy-induced haze, met hers. And locked.

"Oh . . ." was all she could manage as inquiry left her face to be replaced by recognition.

Slowly, he nodded, his gaze never leaving hers as a sensual curve shaped his handsome mouth.

And then the swath of toweling was tumbling to the floor about their feet, and Sabelle was clinging to him while he caught her up in his arms and headed for the bedchamber.

Sabelle's brain spun, emotions warring with one another: She loved him . . . She should be resisting him . . . She would . . . She couldn't . . .

But then she heard him murmur in that same husky timbre, "I want you, Sabelle. As I've wanted no other woman, I want you!"

And she was lost, lost beyond help, or hope, or prayer.

He eased her down upon the bed, joining her there after somehow shedding his clothes with lightning speed.

The pent-up hunger they'd shared in the library was back

again, in full measure. They clung together greedily, their mouths crisscrossing in a frenzy of passions too long denied, whetted by their growing awareness and increased knowledge of each other.

But Justin had long schooled himself to be a craftsman in the bedchamber—a master—and after the first few hectic moments of passion had claimed them, he made a mighty effort to slow their tempo. But Sabelle, inflamed with a passion fed by the secret, guilty love she now bore him, would have none of this. It was as if she would take what she could, while she yet had him, and damned be the future and the certain pain she knew it would bring. Justin was here, and for now, at least, he was hers.

"Take me, Justin!" she cried when he lowered his head to nibble and tease the aching peaks of her breasts. "Take me now!"

Justin clenched his jaws, all too ready to comply, knowing he was rock-hard for her, trying desperately to summon up the old distractions that allowed him the control he sought.

"No, love," he murmured hoarsely as she began to twist and writhe beneath him, "you're not yet read——"

"But I am!" cried Sabelle, half on a sob. She reached for his hand, which was circling her belly with maddening strokes, and thrust it high between her thighs.

Justin sucked in his breath, astounded by the moisture there. She was slippery and hot and wet. She couldn't *be* more ready for him!

"All right, you little minx," he said in a shaky laugh as he framed her head in his hands. He felt her eager thighs part for him below. "You win—but for the rest of the night"— he lowered his head, his mouth hovering over her lips— "we'll do it my way." And he kissed her deeply as he thrust into her waiting heat.

Sabelle cried out against his mouth as she felt him drive home. Her whole body welcomed the turgid strength of him filling her, and she felt at that moment as if she could never have enough of him. Wildly, she arched and met each driving, penetrating thrust. Frantic to deny him any further attempts to slow the pace, she arced, and bit, and clawed until she heard him cry out.

"Sabelle! Sabelle, *don't!* You're going to force me to—"

She never heard him finish. Indeed, he never got the final words out. Just as he was damning her for rushing him to completion, before he could bring her to her own, Justin felt her shudder violently beneath him—at the very moment that his own climax raged beyond his control.

Moments passed—or eons—as they clung together in a pulsing, rocking crescendo that swept them out of themselves and into the stars. Male and female in perfect harmony, they found the primal rhythm that made them one with creation, rapture singing in their veins, the universe at their feet.

Untold minutes passed before Sabelle became aware of the reality of the room around them. A log sputtered and cracked in the hearth, and all at once she sensed the slowly diminishing thud of Justin's heartbeat beneath her cheek as he held her close.

Slowly, fearful of jarring the magic that claimed them, she inched her head about, hoping to lever herself into a position to see his face. But even as she began to move, a strong arm drew her tightly to his side.

"Don't!" he said on a breathless whisper. *"Not yet . . ."*

So he felt it, too? But that was silly, her mind protested. Surely this overwhelming sense of wonder she felt was singular—on her part only. It came of physical completion forged in the newly awakened love she bore him, while *he*—

All at once Sabelle felt the hot sting of tears assault her eyes, and she pressed her face against the sweat-sheened plane of Justin's shoulder in a futile effort to stifle a sob.

"What's this? Tears?" Justin was instantly solicitous, shifting his weight to bend over her in the candlelight, smoothing her hair away from her brow to study her face. "Sabelle? What's amiss, sweetheart? Surely you're not still upset over . . ."

His words trailed off as he saw her shake her head from side to side, but he saw, too, the aching misery in the aquamarine eyes that looked up at him through lashes spikey and wet.

"What, then, love?" he murmured with soft concern. He knew she'd shared with him the incredible rapture of completion he'd experienced. Indeed, he'd have sworn it was something he'd only responded to, having come at first out of *her* passion, but sweeping him up in the tide until he'd felt it, too. And, whatever it was, it had joined him to a woman—*this* woman—as he'd never been joined before. He was still reeling under the impact, not even sure of what had happened to them.

But there *she* was, the center of the entire, heady experience, *crying!* Devil take it! He'd never understand women!

Schooling himself to patience, Justin sighed and tried again. "Sabelle . . . sweetheart . . . I know you . . . found your own pleasure just now." A knowing smile curved his mouth as he held her eyes and gently wiped away, with a crooked finger, the trace of a tear that ran down her cheek.

"So what can be amiss, hmm?" he went on, and then a horrifying thought struck him. "You're not one of those females who's been made to feel guilty over finding satisfaction in the marriage bed, are you? Has some priest or relative told you that it's wrong to—"

"No! Oh, no, Justin. Never say so!" As she rushed to deny it, Sabelle saw him relax, but she saw, too, that the puzzled look on his face remained.

What to tell him? Damn these tears, anyway! Now she'd have to invent something, and, as she'd once explained to him, inventing did not agree with her.

But she could hardly tell him the truth. That she was caught up in the pain of a very one-sided love for *him*, her husband, a man she felt could destroy her with that knowledge.

Or perhaps, even without it . . .

But Justin was no fool, and she realized she'd better come up with something plausible. Perhaps the answer lay in telling him only some of the truth. Enough to make him believe her, yet less than enough to give him that unthinkable power over her which he must never have.

Slowly, picking her way with care, she began to speak. "This . . . this marriage of ours, Justin, for all its brevity, has—has not been easy, as you know."

Justin gave her a brief smile that might have been meant to be encouraging, but appeared grim. "Go on," he said quietly.

"My own part in—in the difficulties owing to its beginnings, I have already confessed to you, and—no, please do not interrupt! This—this is difficult for me, as it is." Seeing him nod, she continued. "Suffice it to say I've accepted my own culpability in the matter, and—and I have been gratified to learn—to feel—that perhaps you've forgiven my foolishness and are willing to—to put it behind us?"

A grave nod as his eyes held hers. "And go on from there," he said.

"Exactly," she replied, wetting her lips with her tongue as she broached melding truth with invention. "But, Justin, there is still a—a problem in that, and it is what has me . . . fearful."

"Fearful?"

"Y-yes. Because marriage itself is such a—a difficult thing. I know, you see, because my own, secondhand, experience of it has—has been less than encouraging. My parents . . ."

"Yes?" he prompted, an alert look in his eyes.

Sabelle sighed. "I suppose the *ton* regards a marriage such as that of the earl and countess of Rushton as eminently successful. But I must tell you, Justin, as the only offspring of that union, that for me it was not. *Is* not!" Encouraged by the intense look in his eyes, Sabelle rushed on. "Why, I hardly *know* my parents! I barely encountered them at all, growing up. If it hadn't been for Grandfather, who raised me, I'd never have known any love or nurturing at all as a child!

"And later, when at last my mother and father deigned to take some interest in me, I came to see how hollow and false it all was. I was certain they had nothing to give me because—because there was nothing deep or abiding in their own relationship. They were merely two separate people—"

"Too wrapped up in their shallow lives and the frivolities of the age even to begin to care about a lonely child who desperately needed love," he finished for her.

Sabelle's breath quavered on an intake of air. He'd put it altogether perfectly, in just the right words. And yet, somehow she knew it wasn't *her* parents—or *their* marriage—he was describing.

"Not too desperately," Sabelle said softly, as if they were still speaking of her. "I, at least, had my grandfather."

Justin nodded, but he was looking beyond her, into the flames of the fire as he spoke. "And parents, apparently, who had the decency to keep their distance and not expose you directly to the poisonous trappings of their marriage . . ."

He went on, then, to describe that other example of matrimony they both knew he'd been thinking of. Dispassionately, with a steely hardness to his eyes which was all too familiar, he told her what it was like to have been an only child reared in a great household by servants, while, all along, he only craved the love of two people he doted on. Two people he'd thought of as perfect, as loving each other and therefore, surely, equally capable of loving their son.

Until that day, when he'd been fourteen, and the entire illusion came crashing down around his ears.

Sabelle began to weep softly when he described that devastating moment, but Justin merely gathered her in his arms and went on in the same dispassionate voice.

"It's the age, really," he explained, "the times we live in. Old Royal George may have had a monogamous marriage with that upright German princess he wed, but his courtiers and the bulk of the peerage were another matter entirely." Justin gave a bitter laugh. "And look at the Regent, not to mention the King's other sons—or their uncles! Fat Prinnie won't even allow his wife to be seen with him in public, and if he hasn't gotten a bastard on that mistress of his, it wouldn't be for lack of trying!"

Sabelle nodded soberly. "It—it is said the Prince-Regent is—is the sire of Lady Melbourne's son George."

"There, you see?" Justin said caustically. "If the royal scion and *the* trend-setting hostess of the *ton* are to be the arbiters of what is expected, what hope have the rest of us foolish mortals—in our marriages or anything else we undertake?"

"What hope, indeed?" Sabelle murmured disconsolately.

Her response seemed to shake Justin out of his mood, forcing him to recall his wish to elevate her spirits, not generate more tears.

Sighing, he took her chin and gently tilted it up to study her face.

"We don't have to give in to it without trying, Sabelle. We . . . can at least attempt to make our own marriage different . . . better."

"*How?*" she asked as her tears welled up anew. "By *pretending*, while—while seeking sexual freedom b-beyond the marriage vows?"

Justin's look grew fierce, and his fingers clamped forcefully about her small chin. "Who suggested such a thing?" he demanded.

Sabelle wanted to bite her tongue, to take it back—all back. Dear heaven, she hadn't *meant* to blurt that out!

But there was no help for it now. Justin was looking at her like an enraged cat about to pounce, and she forced herself to respond.

"*Y-you* did. Oh, Justin, don't look at me like that! You *did*, I tell you! It was in a letter to your friend, Thomas Long. I didn't mean to pry, but I stumbled across it. It was lying on your desk the morning after—after you disappeared on our wedding night."

"And the morning before *you* disappeared," Justin added with a ragged sigh as he ran his hand distractedly through his hair.

Suddenly he clasped her by the shoulders, giving her a level look.

"Listen to me, Sabelle. I have no idea what part those casually written words in that letter may or may not have played in what has since occurred between us. Perhaps I shouldn't want to know. But I'll tell you this: That letter was written long before I came to know you as a person—before each of us came to know who the other was. And, what's more, though I penned it, *I never posted it!*"

"N-Never posted . . ." Sabelle stammered.

"Never. It was written on impulse in a momentary attempt to soothe the ruffled feathers of an old friend . . ."

He went on to explain Long's peculiarities, his fanatical devotion to radical ideas, especially regarding personal freedom and the institutions he felt society created to restrict it, even his obsession with Blake.

Wide-eyed, Sabelle sat through the telling, marveling not only at what this told her about Justin's early life, but at the fact that, for the second time that night, he was sharing something intimate with her, a private part of himself he'd never shared before.

"And so," Justin went on, "I cannot imagine what mischief or oversight led to that letter turning up and being so . . . troublesome. And on that, of all mornings!"

He sighed, giving her a wry smile.

"Believe me, love, I never intended it to be read—by anyone, least of all *you*. Perhaps my housekeeper mistakenly retrieved it from the dustbin and set it aside for me, for whatever reason. But I want *you* to set aside what you read there and pretend it never existed.

"In fact . . ." he continued as he eased her carefully beneath him, his mouth tantalizingly near, "I order you to forget it . . ."—he kissed her slowly, thoroughly, summoning the magic—". . . and concentrate on making this marriage . . ."—he drew back slightly and ran a thumb sensuously over her bottom lip—". . . a testament to the fact that those words . . ."—his gaze hovered on her mouth—". . . were a lie . . ." And then he took her in his arms and to the very edge of heaven itself.

The soft, pearly light of dawn was streaking the sky outside the windows as Sabelle rested in Justin's arms, physically limp and replete, yet wide awake. Warm against her skin, amid the tangled bedclothes, her husband's big body relaxed in slumber, his deep, even breathing faintly stirring the hair above her brow. Yet, even in repose, his body seemed to proclaim ownership of the small, slender wife he'd made exquisite love to during the long hours of the night; a long, muscular thigh was thrust peremptorily across her lower torso, and a strong arm held her close, while the opposite hand cupped her naked breast with possessive intimacy.

Sabelle breathed a long sigh, loving the way his embrace made her feel, yet hating it at the same time. She had occasionally overheard snatches of whispered gossip among servant women while growing up, and later, even among women of the *ton*, at parties during the Season. These were to the effect that most men could be counted on to roll over and go to sleep once they'd "had what they wanted" of a woman in bed. That these revelations had made her regard the marriage act as something all too similar to the mechanical couplings of beasts in the field or livestock bred for profit, she now knew had contributed in no small way to her onetime desire to remain unwed. Why would a woman want to surrender the most intimate use of her body to a man whose subsequent act of turning his back and snoring couldn't help but make her feel like some prized broodmare, once the stud was finished with her?

But Justin's lovemaking had never once followed such a pattern. Indeed, his attentiveness during the aftermath of passion was so great, it usually led to a *renewal* of passions! And when he finally slept, as now, it was always with her in his arms.

But there was no denying the possessiveness of those arms. Or of the husband who regarded her as his sole property. *You're mine, Sabelle,* he'd once told her . . . *I'd kill any man who dared touch you!*

Sabelle shivered, despite the warmth of the chamber. She had no doubt he'd meant those words. But where did that leave her if he chose to ignore his own marriage vows, as his words in that letter to Thomas Long had indicated? What if he truly did intend, as Lady Sarah had said, to seek his "better pleasures" outside of marriage, while leaving his wife tucked conveniently away in the country, to breed his heirs and nothing more?

Yet he'd denied the validity of that letter to Long. And, despite the distant voice in which he'd related the horrors of his parents' infidelities, she'd sensed the buried pain that remoteness had conveyed. Would an unwillingness to visit such pain upon his own children—*their* children—goad him into keeping his wandering instincts in check?

And if it did, would that ever be enough for her? Did his fidelity even matter if she didn't have his love? Sweet heaven, did *anything* matter if she didn't have his love?

Justin stirred in his sleep, the movement pulling her even closer to him, tucking her snugly against the side of his body. Sabelle used the brief distraction to force her thoughts away from the treacherous path they were taking.

There were other problems that arose out of his possessive nature, but these, at least, she felt she could handle. Foremost was his demand that she cease her animal-rescue operations—because of the dangers they exposed her to, he'd said.

Warmth spread through Sabelle's body as she savored the caring this implied. He might not love her, but at least he seemed to care enough about her to—

Stop! her mind cried out. He likely cared enough about his horse to keep it out of danger, but what did that signify?

Again forcing her thoughts away from dangerous waters, Sabelle went back to considering what might be done to allow her the freedom to pursue the other passion which had ruled her life—before Justin had claimed her heart: her rescue of the helpless innocents she loved. This was something she'd never abandon—she swore it!

❖ Chapter 24 ❖

WHEN SABELLE SWORE TO RESUME HER RES-
cue work, she had no idea how soon her resolution
was to be tested. The trial came with the unheralded appearance of Sir Jonathan Burke at Harthaven, late the following day.

Sabelle was sitting in the drawing room, talking to Jeannie, when her grandfather arrived. It was after the supper
hour, but the duke had been called away on some minor
estate matter following the meal, so the two women were
alone when the majordomo announced the old baronet.

"Oh, Grandfather, it's so good to see you!" Sabelle exclaimed after her initial surprise and an exchange of hugs.

Jonathan searched her face with canny blue eyes, knowing her open gaze would tell him more about her current
state of mind than any words he might wheedle out of her.
Then the manifold lines of his own worn visage suddenly
creased even further with a small, surprised smile, and he
gave her a nod.

"It is good to see you, too, my dear—especially now that
I can see you have not been . . . unhappy?"

Sabelle laughed and gestured him toward the settee
where Jeannie was seated, hoping to cover the flush she
could feel invading her cheeks. "I . . . have found some
measure of contentment here, Grandfather."

Jonathan's eyes met Jeannie's, and the satisfied nod of
the young Scotswoman allowed him to relax further. He

knew the Highlander to be a cautious, yet pragmatic, sort, and Jeannie's response told him at least that he need not consume himself with worry over his beloved granddaughter's ill-conceived marriage.

But there was much to worry about on another front; and now that he'd assured himself Sabelle was no longer in dire straits, he felt he could broach the second reason for this sudden visit. After Sabelle had sent for tea, Sir Jonathan launched into his explanation while the two women listened intently.

"It seems," said the old man, "that after your pit dog rescues, a plethora of dog thefts—of *valued domestic animals*—has begun to plague London and the countryside nearby."

"Domestic animals?" queried Sabelle. "Do you mean pets? Lap dogs and—"

"Pets, field dogs, even mascots," said Sir Jonathan. "The bulldog mascot belonging to the rowing team at a certain exclusive public school was one of the first to vanish, and—"

"But why?"

Jonathan shook his head in disgust. "According to my sources, the dog pit masters are seeking this as a villainous means of refurbishing their stolen goods. In short, they are stealing dogs to replace the ones *we* have—er—stolen."

"Why, that's outrageous!" exclaimed Sabelle. "We only—"

"The heathen scum!" growled Jeannie.

"Moreover," Jonathan continued, "I've learned the sweeps masters of the city have banded together with these dognappers to discover who has been behind the, ah, removal of their pit stock."

"The sweeps masters! But why would *they*—"

Jonathan gently raised his hand. "It would appear, my dears, that climbing boys have too often been spotted near the, ah, scenes and have been identified with those losses. The pit masters may be cruel, but they are not stupid.

"And, as a result," he went on, with what Sabelle recognized as a quietly burning anger, "a kind of reign of terror has been imposed on the innocent chimney sweeps of the city—to ferret out the guilty parties."

"But that's horrible!" exclaimed Sabelle.

"Vile and unfair!" spat Jeannie.

"Nevertheless, it is happening," said Jonathan. "A certain underworld brigand by the name of Ned Grimsley is thought to be at the root of all this. Notes have been left—barely legible and grossly misspelled, to be sure, but clear as to their message, just the same."

"Saying what?" Sabelle was not sure she wanted to know what such unscrupulous characters might be threatening, yet she burned to know at the same time.

"They say that the sweeps masters will be making the lives of London's climbing boys a veritable hell until those responsible for the pit-dog thefts are captured and handed over to them and their 'dear friends,' the dog pit masters."

"Dear God," murmured Sabelle.

"Ach! I dinna—"

"We have a responsibility in this matter, my dears," said Jonathan, "which goes even beyond our deeply held principles regarding the abuse of innocents. Much as I regret to admit it, it is *our* actions which have placed those climbing boys in jeopardy. Therefore, it is our responsibility to put a stop to it."

"Put a stop to what?" queried a deep, masculine voice from the doorway.

"Ahem, ah, good evening, Your Grace," Jonathan managed as his eyes darted from the tall figure of the duke to his granddaughter. It was clear he hadn't meant to be overheard by Sabelle's husband while discussing their rescue work. He had no idea how much Justin knew of such matters, if anything, and the worry in his glance indicated he was loath to reveal confidences it wasn't his place to divulge.

But Sabelle caught wind of his distress and immediately sought to relieve it. "Justin," she said briskly, "you'll scarcely believe the shocking tale Grandfather has just told us. Do come and join us and let him fill you in while I ring for more tea. And then perhaps we can all have a go at sorting out what's to be done about it."

Sabelle nodded toward Jonathan with far more confidence than she was feeling. She saw her grandfather's brow lift at what her words implied: that Justin knew of—and accepted—their rescue work. That only half of this was true, however, was something she was acutely aware of, and it drove her to the gamble she was taking. Her husband was opposed to her personal involvement in the rescue of abused animals; *but,* she reasoned, *this* was *different! This* had to do with the abuse of *human beings*—innocent children whose only crime was to be poor and thrown upon the streets. She knew there were many people in the world whose compassion didn't extend to *dumb* animals, but who could readily be incited to caring about fellow humans; and, much as she regretted facing such a major shortcoming in him, she felt the duke might be one of these. Surely he would agree with her grandfather, that something must be done to help those poor climbing boys.

And then, she added swiftly to herself, her hopes suddenly kindled by a further inspiration, once thus involved, perhaps Justin could be dislodged from his obtuseness regarding the needs of furred and feathered victims, too!

Smiling with increased confidence as she poured her husband some tea, Sabelle settled down to wait for Jonathan to finish recapitulating.

". . . and so you see how imperative it is that we do something, Your Grace," Jonathan was saying. "Unintentional as it may have been, we cannot escape the fact that it was *our doing* that brought the sweeps to this sorry pass."

Three pairs of eyes were trained on the duke's face in the ensuing silence. It had remained immobile and unrevealing throughout the old man's recitation, and when at last Justin raised his eyes, from the tea he'd been stirring, to address Jonathan, they reminded Sabelle of cold, hard granite.

"Hardly," said Justin. "The fact that they were ever born into the world is what has brought them to 'this sorry pass.' I fail to see how this should concern us."

Something crumpled in the older man's face as he grasped the meaning of what he'd just been told, and his eyes flew to his granddaughter's face.

"You—you cannot—cannot have meant to imply what you just—" Sabelle stopped, unable to articulate further what her spinning brain had just pieced out. *No one could be that cold! That heartless!*

"Of course, I meant it," said Justin as he rose, leaving his tea untouched. He looked down at the small, ashen-faced figure of his wife from his vast height, and Jonathan had the impression of a parent wearily explaining proper behavior to a backward child. "You should know me well enough by now, Sabelle," Justin continued, "to realize I never waste words on things I do not mean. I regard the unfortunate circumstance of the chimney sweeps of London as just that —unfortunate. Beyond that, they do not concern me, and therefore I mean to make it clear that they are not to concern *you.*"

"B-but they *do* concern me—*us,*" Sabelle stammered. "If we hadn't—"

"Disabuse yourself of that notion here and now!" Justin snapped. "I refuse to let you wallow in guilt out of a mistaken notion that—"

He ran a hand distractedly through his hair and sighed, then threw Jonathan a deprecating look before settling his gaze once more on his wife.

"Listen carefully to me, Sabelle," he said, "for what I am about to say, I shall say only once: The world is not a pretty place. It is, more often than not, a cruel, barbaric, unjust, and immensely injurious place in which to live, and the best —*the very best*—I've ever been able to summon to contend with it is to protect myself—me and mine, that is—from the ugly threats it imposes. But, by *me and mine* I mean exactly that: myself and those under my care—no more!

"I see by your eyes that you're thinking this a selfish and uncaring view, but you are wrong. It is merely a realistic one. Do you think me unaware of the human misery out there?" He made a sweeping gesture toward the night outside the windows. "Hardly. I learned of its existence long ago. And I have seen the ravages of war as well, if you'll re——"

"So that's it!" cried Sabelle, jumping to her feet. "You've become so inured to the horrors of war and its destruction that you've allowed it to rob you of—"

"No, madam, that is *not* it," Justin cut in with icy calm. "The realistic view I have came about long before I ever donned a uniform. And, as I said before, it has to do with *keeping me and mine safe!* I refuse to countenance your going off to right the endless wrongs of the world that can only succeed in harming you in the end. In the first place, there are more abuses out there than you could ever hope to correct, and in the second place, it would only be a matter of time until you ran into a danger that proved too much for you. And I refuse to allow you to endanger yourself for such a futile business, Sabelle—now, or ever again. Is that clear?"

Sabelle stared at him, speechless for several seconds, unable to form a reply. *So much for an appeal to fellow human caring! So much for believing he might have a heart after all!*

To her horror, she felt tears choking her throat, and she thrust out a hand to the one person she desperately hoped might help. "Grandfather?" she pleaded on a sob.

Jonathan cast a worried glance at Jeannie, who looked just as helpless as he felt. Then he forced his aged joints to respond and rose from the settee to take Sabelle gently by the forearms.

"Sabelle, my child," he murmured brokenly, "forgive me, but I—I fear I must—must tell you to heed your husband."

Jonathan felt her stiffen under his hands, but he went on before she could respond. "He is your *husband,* Sabelle, and it is clear he has a care for your safety." He lifted gnarled, age-spotted fingers to her chin, tilting her face upward, meeting her brimming eyes. "Perhaps more than I have had—and should have had," he added with a wry attempt at a smile. "No, sweetheart," he went on when she would have protested, "it's true. Sometimes I allowed myself to become so deeply involved in our ideals, I fear I let safety take a hind seat."

"Grandfather, I won't let you—"

"But even if it weren't true," Jonathan continued, despite the gathering outrage in her eyes, "your husband seems to think your safety is of primary importance now, and in that I must defer to his wishes."

"Grandfather, *please,* I—"

"I'm sorry, my dear," said Jonathan sadly as he turned toward the door, "so very sorry . . ."

And then he was gone, leaving Jeannie to murmur awkwardly, something about seeing him out, and she, too, left the room.

Leaving Sabelle to stare at her husband in white-lipped fury.

Justin took one look at the rage blazing in those blue-green eyes and quirked a brow at her. It was a look of inquiry, and yet, while he waited, fully anticipating the storm about to break, Sabelle said nothing.

With a shrug, Justin ambled toward a sideboard bearing a decanter of brandy and several snifters. With an easy efficiency, he poured the golden-brown liquid into two of the glasses, then turned and, eyeing Sabelle as if to gauge her mood, strode toward her.

"Here," he said, holding out one of the snifters, "you look as if you could—"

"Go to bloody hell and take your brandy with you," said Sabelle in a toneless whisper.

Every muscle in her body was trembling with rage, with the need to vent the fury that roiled through her in the face of what he'd just said and done; but she clamped down on it with a strength she hadn't known herself capable of. *Let him see me lose control like the mindless child he treats me as? Never!*

Head held high, eyes straight ahead, Sabelle concentrated on putting one foot in front of the other and walked toward the set of double doors through which she'd seen her grandfather disappear.

"Sabelle, wait!" called Justin. "I know you're upset, but

I don't think it a good idea—*Sabelle!* Damn you, Sabelle, I want to talk to you!" His answer was the rapid patter of slippered feet in the hallway and then the muffled sounds of her ascent on the carpeted staircase.

"Damn!" Justin swore, and downed his brandy in a single gulp. This done, he glared at the brandy she'd refused, then downed that, too.

As he felt the warmth from the fine contraband liquor spread through him, he considered, for a moment, leaving her alone for a while to stew—or perhaps to simmer down until she could be made to see reason.

He certainly had no wish for the fireworks sure to erupt if he pursued the matter now.

But then he recalled just having told her he wanted to talk to her.

And she'd walked out of the room.

And the whole point of what was going on here, as he saw it, was to teach his independent-minded little wife to accept a very necessary thing for a female in a marriage: *obedience!*

A glance at the mantel clock he passed as he headed toward the double doors told him it was almost ten o'clock. It was going to be, he decided with a sigh, a very long night.

But when Justin reached the door to his chambers, it wasn't the length of the night that loomed tauntingly in his disbelieving brain; it was its similarity to their wedding night: She'd locked him out *again!*

Stunned incredulity, that she would repeat such a stupid, futile maneuver, warred with fury at this ultimate proof of her disobedience: *He'd warned her against ever locking him out again!*

With a snarl half directed at his wife, and half directed at a mocking sense of *deja vu* that seemed to jeer at him, he slammed his shoulder against one of the door's raised oak panels. And again, feeling great satisfaction at the splintering sound this evoked.

He was about to assail it a third time when his majordomo appeared from nowhere and held out a ring of household keys.

"Ahem," said the servant with a discreet nod toward the splintered, still-closed door. "I believe His Grace has misplaced his keys?"

Justin took a look at the keys the servant proffered and almost grabbed them. But the satisfying heat of pounding his fury into solid oak was still surging through him, coupled with the strength of the double brandies he'd consumed, and he flicked his hand at the servant in a dismissive gesture.

"No, Haskins, by God, His Grace had *not* misplaced his keys! His Grace is about to take great pleasure in breaking this bloody door down!"

And with a feral grin, the duke resumed his attack on the injured portal.

The bemused Haskins beat a hasty retreat.

Sabelle had her back to him when the door finally gave way and he charged through his own chambers and then through the door that led to hers. Indeed, he noted, she was calmly—*calmly!*—sorting through some clothes hanging in the large armoire she faced; she didn't even deign to look at him as he slammed the interior door against the wall and stalked through.

And that, more than anything else she might have done, brought him up short. He'd fancied, as part of his flash of *dèja vu,* her utter apprehension, if not terror, as he approached, much as it had been on their wedding night. Instead, he beheld this—this calm! How *dare* she not be quaking in her slippers in the face of his wholly justified wrath!

"Look at me, Sabelle!" he demanded from between clenched jaws.

He saw her shoulders stiffen, but the movement was brief, almost imperceptible, before she complied.

And then there was the sea-green ice of her eyes as she regarded him in stony silence.

"I collect telling you downstairs, madam, before your unacceptable departure, that I wished to speak with you."

The sea-green eyes flicked briefly over his features, handsome as ever, but hardened with the forbidding severity of his mien. She had known that face shaped by passion and laughter now, as well as the anger that seemed ever ready to line it with this familiar harshness, yet she was grateful to be facing the latter; it made it far easier to do what she had to do.

"But I do not wish to speak with *you,*" she told him boldly.

"That, too, is unacceptable."

"Nevertheless, Your Grace, that is my position."

"Your position, *wife,* is to accept your husband's wishes and *obey* them!"

"Even when they tear at the very stuff and fabric of my conscience?"

"When they override your idiotic notion that you can save the world, with no thought for your own safety!"

"*Idiotic!*"

"At least. Or would your prefer 'deranged' or 'foolish'? I can think of quite a few terms to describe such stupidity. How about—"

"How about 'heartless' and 'monstrously insensitive' to describe *your* behavior, Your Grace?"

"Sabelle, I warn you—"

"Warn all you like! I'll not be a puppet made to dance on your inhumanely conceived strings. You would jerk me in directions contrary to every concept and value I was raised to believe in! Those poor climbing boys—"

"Are not your concern!"

"They *are!* If I hadn't placed them in their current jeopardy through my rescue ef——"

"And there you make my point exactly, madam! Through your childish fancy to rescue every downtrodden creature in existence, you risk not only your own safety, but *theirs* as well!"

"*Childish!* Oh, I've heard enough!" Trembling, Sabelle swung away from him and made for the door, intent only upon putting as much distance between them as possible. He was not only as arrogant as ever, but utterly brutal in his sensibilities, and the thought had just flashed in her mind that if she'd had a pistol in her hand at that moment, she'd have been tempted to use it on him. Suddenly frightened by this dark side to her own passions, she broke into a run.

Justin had barely taken in the fact that she'd again stalked out on him in the midst of a discussion when the thought registered that she was about to slam the door on him as well.

With a low growl, he was upon her, prying her fingers from the doorknob, picking her up bodily with hands whose hard fingers bit into her waist, setting her none too gently on the carpet before him.

His eyes scoured her slender frame, noting the stiffened arms with hands clenched into fists, the high breasts that rose and fell with each heaving breath, the flush of face, and, finally, the murderous look in her eyes.

But beneath that look was something else . . . Pain? Uncertainty, perhaps? He was so caught by it, he missed the slender arm that rose, pulled back—

And delivered a stinging slap to his face.

"Damn you!" He bit out a harsher oath as her other hand rose to repeat the act, grabbing her by the wrist and, with a downward pull, yanking her off balance.

Sabelle gave a sharp cry as she stumbled toward him, instinctively throwing her free hand forward to brace herself against his chest.

But the damage was complete; she was in his arms, scooped up, off the floor and pressed against the lean, hard length of him as his mouth closed over hers in a ruthless, punishing kiss.

Her hands were trapped between their closely joined bodies, and her feet dangled uselessly above the carpet, yet Sabelle struggled fiercely against this assault. Twisting her head from side to side, she sought to free herself from his mouth, but to no avail. Justin's lips moved against hers with devastating thoroughness, forcing them to yield, preparing them for the invasion of his tongue.

Yet, when it came, she was unprepared for the softness of it. With light, careful probings, his tongue met hers with a sudden gentleness that astounded her, even as she felt her body glide along his to touch the floor; she felt, too, his hold loosen and his hands come up to capture her face and hold it almost tenderly as he continued to explore her mouth with exquisite care.

It was, as always, her undoing. Wildfire raced along her limbs, which responded to this gentler touch as with a memory of their own, embedded in her weak, betraying flesh by the imprint of other days and other nights when he'd plied her so.

With a moan that was half a sob, she felt herself leaning into his warmth, felt her lips and tongue respond as he deepened the kiss; and when he slid his hands along the trembling contours of her body until they cupped and fondled her breasts with intimate knowledge, Sabelle shuddered. She felt something give and melt at the core of her and had all she could do to keep her knees from buckling while her hands gripped the fabric of his coat in an effort to steady herself.

Justin felt her shudder and released her mouth to look down at her passion-drugged face, a smile hovering about his chiseled mouth.

"Do you want me, Sabelle?" he murmured. "Say it. Tell me you want me."

His hands continued their devastating assault on her breasts, testing their fullness, teasing the nipples that had grown erect, pushing against the thin fabric of her gown, and Sabelle barely had the coherence to grasp what he'd said.

"I . . ." She hesitated; every pore in her body cried out for his touch, but something in the back of her brain buzzed a faint warning. "I . . ."

Justin smiled knowingly, and in an instant his deft fingers had loosened the bodice of her gown and then her shift, and she felt his thumbs and fingertips begin to play with the bared tips of her breasts, which were hardened into peaks of throbbing, pulsating desire.

"I want you, Justin," she groaned. "God help me, I want you!"

"Excellent," said Justin, and he released her breasts, abruptly taking a step backward to leave her trembling and confused as she looked at him with bewildered eyes.

Justin's eyes coursed over her half-clad form with insulting thoroughness. Then he swung about and headed for the door.

Sabelle felt a numbing chill envelop her even before he whirled about at the doorway and delivered his parting words.

"Never think to lock me out again, Sabelle—*never!*"

The next morning, when a frightened-looking Jeannie told Justin that his wife had again disappeared, the duke evinced no reaction at all.

"But, Yer Grace, ye dinna understand! *This* time she dinna tell even *me* where she was goin'!"

The duke lowered his copy of the *Morning Post* and regarded her with pewter-gray eyes that revealed nothing of what he might be thinking. "I understand entirely, Miss MacDougal. And when I finish my breakfast, I shall send for my secretary and have him post a message to some Bow Street Runners I've had occasion to employ, instructing them to set about locating your mistress and fetching her home."

With this, he nodded his dismissal to the dumbstruck Highlander and went back to reading his newspaper.

❖Chapter 25❖

THE SWEEP NAMED SAM HUDDLED FOR warmth within the thin, tattered strips of rag that passed for a blanket when they were wound around Sam at night, but it was no use; it was bitterly cold in the damp cellar where Sam and the other sweeps slept, and nothing alleviated the shivering. Or the hunger that had been a constant companion since Sam had come there to work as a climbing boy four months ago.

"S-Sam? You awake?" whispered a small, tearful voice from the other side of the coal bin where the boys bedded down each night.

Sam recognized the voice of Tommy, the newcomer to Lem Tate's crew of sweeps, and felt a surge of pity for the seven-year-old. Tommy had been with them only a fortnight and had spent every night of it softly sobbing out his misery before he finally fell into an exhausted sleep. The eldest of five children, he'd been sold as an apprentice to Tate by his drunkard of a father when his mother died of the wasting sickness in the early fall.

"Don't see 'ow I kin be anythin' but," Sam whispered back between chattering teeth. "I ain't never seen it so cold in October. Doris, the flower mort, tol' me all her bouquets got frost-bit cuz she wuzn't ready fer a freeze on 'em this early on."

Sam waited for a response from Tommy, hoping this bit of casual conversation would take the boy's mind off his misery. It was little enough Sam could do for the poor little tyke, but it had worked before, on other nights when the young sweep's sobbing had threatened to wake Tate—and then they'd all have been in for it.

But Tommy's only response was a wretched sob. " 'Sa matter, Tommy—cold?" Sam asked.

"A-aye," came the plaintive reply, "an' I—I think I 'eard a rat over by the—"

Sam heaved a teeth-chattering sigh. "Come on, then. Over 'ere with ye! I ain't much and ye're even less, but mayhaps we kin keep a mite warm t'gether, an' two o' us'll give the rat somethin' t' think about."

There was a stirring of coals from the other side of the bin, and a moment later Sam felt the nearness of Tommy's emaciated form in the inky darkness.

" 'Ere, now," Sam whispered as the smaller sweep wrapped his thin arms about Sam's swaddling of rags and cuddled close, "Mind ye, don't clamp on too tight, or ye won't get no sleep, an' ye'll be needin' it soon enough, come the morn. An' quit yer snivelin'! Tate's new doxy's a light snorer, so even if 'e don't 'ear ye, she might, an' she's a wicked un, Meg is!"

Tommy muffled what passed for a halfhearted giggle. "She is, ain't she, Sam? An' she sure don't like you none! I thought she wuz gonna go fer Tate's 'orsewhip 'erself when ye tol' 'er ye'd nick a bar o' soap if she promised t' use it an' give all our smellers a rest! Ye should 'ave seen—"

"Stow it, both o' ye!" hissed a threatening young voice out of the darkness. "I ain't 'ad no winks since ye started yer jabberin', an' if ye don't pipe down, I'll—"

"Sorry, Towser," whispered Sam.

"We'll be quiet, Towser," Tommy promised in a fearful voice.

A grunt was their only reply, and Sam breathed a sigh of relief. Towser was the senior sweep among Tate's boys and, after Tate himself, the last person whose anger they'd wish to arouse. At twelve, Towser was a survivor in the climbing business. He'd been at it for almost five years—an unheard-of amount of time among a youthful population that usually succumbed early to lung disease, starvation, or burns. Sam was convinced that Towser's longevity had to do not only with his small, wiry frame, but with another ingredient he had in plenty: unequivocal meanness.

"Leanest an' Meanest," some of the other boys had dubbed Towser behind his back, and with good cause. The twelve-year-old bullied any boy who dared get in his way as he took the easiest jobs, kept the lion's share of the meager food Tate doled out, and generally availed himself of whatever comforts were to be had among their wretched lot.

Lately, Sam was beginning to suspect Towser of being a spy for Ned Grimsley, the underworld brigand whose name struck fear into the hearts of all of them. There was no way to prove it yet, but Sam knew Towser was sporting a sizable bit of the blunt about him—more than any sweep had cause to have; and when Sam had followed him the last couple of times Towser had sneaked out late at night, it had been to see Towser disappear each time, into the same rat-infested building down by the river—a place no honest sweep had any business frequenting.

The thing to do, Sam thought, twisting beneath the rags to try to assume better contact with Tommy's body heat, was to follow Towser into that building the next time. It had to be Grimsley's headquarters; it just *had* to! And all that remained, then, was for Sam to eavesdrop long enough to catch enough names, or places, or other incriminating details . . .

But first it was necessary to determine how Towser gained entry to that building. It had to be by some secret passageway, for Sam knew Towser never used the building's single door.

It was dangerous, to be sure, but someone had to try to follow Towser, and Sam was the only one to do it. So she would, she decided, or her name wasn't Sabelle Corstairs Hart!

Sabelle's breath caught in her throat for a moment as she sounded out the syllables of her name in her mind. It was a luxury she'd rarely allowed herself since coming to London's East End four months ago and successfully passing herself off as a chimney sweep in need of work. A luxury, because she'd soon learned she couldn't afford to think of all the real luxuries she'd left behind in that other life, where warmth and adequate shelter and a full belly were all taken for granted. Where children weren't starved and beaten and driven mercilessly into exhausting labor that lasted eighteen hours a day, seven days a week, with an hour off for "prayer and confession" on Sunday.

If I allow myself to think of it, I'll go mad, and then where will we be? She peered about the darkness, fancying herself able to make out the pitiful, half-starved little heaps that were children littering the coal bin. *I've got to stay strong and cling to my purpose, else I'll never be able to help them! But, dear God, the horrors I've seen! Children coughing their lives away, many riddled with disease . . . running sores all over their emaciated bodies . . . boys smaller than Tommy forced into smoking chimneys to be half burnt alive—*

Oh, sweet Jesus, if I don't stop I shall go mad!

Gathering her self-control about her, Sabelle shifted against Tommy and again tried to sleep, but it was so cold, and—

There! She'd felt it again. That marked the third time this week, and now she was sure. It was all she could do to bite back a wild cry of joy. But the joy was underscored by bitter pain. She bit her lip as she slowly extricated her hand from beneath her armpit, where she'd been trying to warm it, and slid it hesitantly along her belly.

Several seconds passed, and then it came again, a small fluttering beneath her fingertips. There could be no doubt now. She was carrying Justin's child, and it had quickened.

Before this she hadn't been certain, for all those weeks ago, when her courses had ceased, she had attributed it to the hardships and deprivation of her life here in the East End. She'd dealt with animals all her life, and with abused ones long enough to know the females frequently went off their cycles if their nutrition was poor. And she had yet to experience the morning sickness she'd heard of in whispered conversations among female servants while growing up.

She bit back a bitter laugh. How was she to be sick over breakfast of a morning when there was never a breakfast to bring up? The moldy ends of stale bread Tate threw them when they were roused before dawn each day were hardly enough to make a difference to young stomachs cramped with hunger; and Towser kept the best of these for himself, at any rate, greedily dunking them in the mug of ale he always managed to come by, by playing it cozy with Tate's slatternly bedmate, Meg.

In the darkness, Sabelle's lips curved into a rueful smile. She could be glad of her meager diet for one reason, at least: The reduced fare kept her from greatly swelling in size, as she suspected someone of her petite stature might ordinarily do when carrying a child, even as early as four or five months.

And of course, during the late summer and early autumn, things hadn't been as bad as they were becoming now. That had been the season of plenty, when hawkers' carts and produce mongers' stalls in the marketplaces of London had been filled to overflowing with the bounty of the English harvest; there had always been ways for a clever young sweep to come by an overlooked apple, or pear, or some such, and she'd even been shameless and desperate enough to use her way with horses to acquire a steady supply of milk: The butcher's draft mare had had a new foal, and late each night Sabelle had crept stealthily into his small stabling shed and coaxed Dobbin to allow her a generous, satisfying helping of sweet mare's milk—straight from the teat!

But now the plentiful time was over—an early winter, by the looks of it. Dobbin's foal was nearly weaned, and peddlers guarded their wares like brood hens watching their nests.

Sweet heaven, if I don't accomplish my goal and get out of here soon, I may indeed starve, and the child with me! A moment of shame had Sabelle blushing in the dark as the brief thought crossed her mind that she didn't have to stay there and starve; that, any time she chose, she could walk back to the West End and be safe in the life she'd been born to.

And abandon little ones like Tommy and the dozens of others she'd come to know and pity in the four months she'd been there? *Dear God, had it been only four months?*

Her mind drifted back to that awful summer night when she'd stolen out of Harthaven, the memory of Justin's hard eyes a spur to her purpose. It had been her unrelenting vision of those eyes, of the harsh, unyielding planes of his face, that drove her each time she'd faltered. When she'd despaired of securing a mount from the stables without being seen, but had somehow managed to do so; when she'd lost the way back to London, yet found it again; when she'd almost lacked the courage to sell her pearls for money to live on until she could find a young sweep her size who'd sell her his clothes—almost, but in the end she'd done it. Just as she'd done a passable job of assuming an East End mode of speech, though at first this task had threatened to tie her tongue in knots.

And then, later, when the endless hours of drudgery and neglect and cuffings from Tate had threatened to overcome her resolve, she'd again used that vision as a buffer between herself and defeat. It had been the cruelest goad in the world: the bitter knowledge that she'd given her heart to a pitiless monster, a man with no compassion, who would have shaped her life to fit his own heartless mode of existence.

Even now that knowledge stung, made more cruel by the certainty that she carried his child. And where would she go, what would she do, when her current work was accomplished? As surely it must be—soon!—she prayed. She'd steadfastly avoided all contact with those who knew her as the duchess of Haverleigh—even with her grandfather and Jeannie—for she couldn't take the chance that Justin would use them to find her and drag her back.

But when this was over . . . ? What, then? Go quietly back to her husband and submit to his yoke, bearing his heirs like a good little duchess?

And how could she bear to submit to his touch? A touch which burned and consumed her with fire, but in reality was loveless and cold at the root. But did she have any choice? Her child, the tiny creature growing within her, that she'd already begun to love fiercely, with all the pent-up longing she ached to share with its sire—that child would need a father. *A father aptly dubbed "the Heartless."* Did she have the right to deny him even such a one?

Tommy stirred restlessly in his slumber, reminding her that she, too, required sleep if she was to survive another grueling day. Pushing aside the nagging doubts and questions that plagued her, Sabelle stroked the child's sooty curls and tried to sleep.

❧ Chapter 26 ❧

JUSTIN ABSENTLY SIPPED A BRANDY AND stared into the blaze framed by the Adam mantel of the fireplace in his town house library. In the dancing tongues of flame he imagined Sabelle's face and lithe form a dozen times over. Now he saw her whirling gracefully to a waltz beneath the glittering chandeliers at Almack's; now, sharing a clever turn of phrase with a simple tradesman; now, crying his name as she arched beneath him in passion . . .

"Christ! Is there no end to it?" he heard himself swear aloud. He abruptly drained his glass and sent it smashing against the hearth.

That she should plague him so, this creature he ought never to have wed in the first place! Where was the peace of mind he'd thought to purchase in doing his duty by taking a wife? *Duty? Ha!* There was little of duty *or* the dutiful in Sabelle Corstairs Hart! She was a spiteful, disobedient child who ought to have been taught her place and relegated to the backwaters of his responsibilities long ago.

Instead, she'd vexed him, plotted against him, led him on an unmerry chase from the moment he'd met her. And now she was causing him sleepless nights and tense, anxious days, no matter how he tried to pretend it wasn't so.

Where in hell was she? At first he'd been so furious at her disobedience, at her defiance of his entirely reasonable attempt to keep her safe, he'd vowed not to involve himself personally in finding her again; he'd wanted to make it absolutely clear he was not to be expected to drop every-thing and run after her every time she decided to indulge her childish penchant for disappearing. He had, however, hired the most capable professionals to execute the search for him.

And in four months they'd turned up nothing.

Then, when his initial surprise had passed, that the Bow Street people hadn't made short work of locating her, he'd assumed at least her grandfather or the Scotswoman would have had some word. Of her safety, if not her location. But the old man and Jeannie had sworn to him they'd heard nothing when at last he'd questioned them. And from the worried looks on their faces, Justin had had no doubt they were telling the truth.

But, blast it, she couldn't have simply vanished! The tracks of the mount she'd taken from the stables had been lost when they mingled with those of countless other trav-elers, though it was determined she'd been heading north. And when the horse had returned, riderless, to the stables a few days later, it was clear it had traveled a good distance. It was therefore likely she'd gone to London, but even that was only an informed guess.

Where would a young, unprotected woman—

A subdued rapping at the door broke into his thoughts. "Enter!" Justin called in an irritated voice.

The door opened, and his majordomo appeared. "Sir Jonathan Burke to see you, Your Grace."

Justin glanced at the tall-case clock across the room, saw it was nearly two, and only then recalled his wife's grandfa-ther had requested the opportunity to call on him this af-ternoon.

"Show him into the green drawing room," he told the man. "I'll be down presently."

The servant withdrew, and Justin paused a moment be-fore going downstairs to peer into a small decorative mirror hanging above a satinwood side table. His cravat, as always, was tied impeccably, well up to Weeks's outrageous stan-dards. But the face that loomed above it merited little satis-faction. It looked tired and drawn, the year-round tan he normally wore, muddy and faded. And the shadows under his eyes testified to nights spent tossing and turning in his too-empty bed.

"Damn her eyes!" he swore. With a gesture of annoyance, he turned and headed for the door.

He was surprised to see that Burke was not alone when he entered the drawing room.

"I took the liberty of calling these two in from my carriage," said Jonathan after they'd greeted each other, "because they have a part in what I'm about to reveal to you. I hope you don't mind?"

Justin made a dismissive gesture, then nodded in Jeannie MacDougal's direction as she curtsied. But he let his gaze linger for a moment on the thin, pale child beside her. The boy was leaning heavily on a crudely fashioned crutch and bore evidence of recent bruises on his face.

"Davey," said Jonathan to the youngster before they moved to take the seats Justin indicated, "this is His Grace, the man I told you about. Now, what do you think you might say?"

The boy, who looked about nine or ten, stared at the toes of what appeared to be a brand-new pair of boots for a moment, then slowly raised his head to regard Justin with huge, solemn eyes.

"G-good day, Duke, um, Yer Grace," he mumbled awkwardly before returning his gaze to his boots.

Justin quirked an eyebrow on hearing the inflections of the East End in his speech, but replied graciously. "Good day to you, Davey. Please be seated."

Davey hobbled toward the green-and-white-striped settee his host indicated and, with some assistance from Jeannie, perched gingerly on its satin upholstery. From his stiff posture and the way his eyes darted about the room, it was clear he was ill at ease in such a setting.

Justin eyed him a moment longer, then turned to Jonathan. "This has something to do with . . ."—he glanced again at the boy, recalling all the pains his grandmother and Sabelle's family had taken to keep word of the duchess's disappearance from leaking to the public; as far as the *ton*

knew, Her Grace was still enjoying a leisurely stay in Kent
—". . . our search," he finished carefully.

Jonathan nodded, and for the first time Justin noted how
much older and more fragile the man appeared than when
last he'd seen him. The tired lines about his eyes and mouth
seemed heightened by skin that had taken on a pale, translucent quality, and the thin shoulders that heretofore had
been held sprightly and erect appeared to sag under the
weight of his more than three score and ten winters.

"I hope you will allow us to explain ourselves, Your
Grace," said Jonathan. "It may appear to be in a somewhat
roundabout fashion, but I have—"

"Since I assume you have your reasons," interrupted
Justin with a curt gesture, "please proceed."

Jonathan assessed him for a moment with a steady blue
gaze, and Justin noted how the vitality in the old man's
eyes belied the marks of age about the rest of him.

"To begin, let me tell you about Davey," said Jonathan.
"For one thing, you needn't trouble yourself about the
lad's revealing what we discuss here."

Justin raised an eyebrow, and the boy caught this. Seeing
it as a sign of doubt, he blurted out before anyone could
say another word, "I'd sooner cut me tongue out, Yer
Grace—I *swear* it!"

"Thank you, Davey," said Jonathan with a smile, "but
we know that won't be necessary. You see," he went on,
again focusing on Justin, "as of yesterday, Davey became
my legal ward. He is, therefore, you might say, one of the
family."

If the duke was surprised at this, he did nothing to indicate it. "And before he became, ah, family?" he queried.

"He was an orphan—and a chimney sweep."

"Ah," said Justin, beginning to sense some design to the
old man's revelations. "Go on."

"He came into my care several days ago, after Jeannie
found him lying, whimpering, in a gutter near Billingsgate.
He was covered with burns and bloody bruises and had a
broken leg."

Justin glanced at the leg Davey had been supporting with

his crutch and just now noticed how it was thrust out in front of him and that it stretched the material of his pantaloons with far more bulk than the other leg: The boy obviously wore a plaster of some kind underneath.

"He'd been brutalized and left fer dead," Jeannie interjected grimly.

"By whom?" Justin couldn't help asking, although he wasn't sure he liked the way the tale was proceeding.

"Before we come to that, I'd like Davey to tell you something about the events in his life which preceded that monstrous incident," said Jonathan. He turned toward the boy. "Go on, now, Davey. Tell His Grace, just as you related things to Miss MacDougal and me."

The boy eyed Justin warily, then darted a nervous glance at Jennie and his new guardian. He swallowed visibly, but seemed disinclined to speak.

"It's all right, lad," Jonathan murmured in a gentle voice as he leaned forward and gave him a pat on the shoulder. "I've known His Grace for some time, and I assure you, he won't bite."

Davey's look said he wasn't certain he believed him, but at last, in a voice that faltered initially and then picked up strength, he began to speak.

Beginning briefly with his running away from an orphan asylum where he'd been starved and beaten as a matter of course, he described an even more brutal existence on the streets of London. Until, one day, he was "rescued" by a sweeps master who promised him "honest pay fer a honest day's work." That the "honest" day was more than eighteen hours long and entailed dangerous, bone-wearying labor in exchange for less food than he'd had in the orphanage and far harsher living conditions was something he learned soon enough; that he didn't dare run away again was something he learned almost too late. A boy who tried it shortly before Davey had planned an escape was found and hauled back by the sweeps master and then beaten with a horsewhip as an "example" to the other climbing boys. He died two days later. And Davey and another sweep were assigned the task of dumping his corpse into the Thames.

Then Davey told of the routine existence of his days and nights as a climbing boy. He told of scaling rooftops so steep, they could only be negotiated safely without shoes—even in the dead of winter. He told of being forced into chimneys so narrow, he had to be dislodged with a wrenching pull by the ankles, a pull which shredded his clothes against the bricks and took patches of skin off his body. He told of breathing air heavily laden with soot and going to sleep at night with the sounds of other little ones coughing in his ears . . .

Justin heard all these horrors with a stony, impassive silence, but Jonathan began to notice an ominous ticking of the muscles along his jaw as Davey came to the final part of his tale. It involved an incident which, as Davey put it, "made me come a cropper an' near done me in." An incident involving Davey's rescue of a smaller boy named Tommy who'd begun to scream as he was forced down a chimney "wot wuz burnin' 'im alive."

"Enough!" interrupted Justin in an odd, strangulated voice. "I fail to see—"

"Then what happened, Davey?" There was nothing elderly or feeble in Jonathan's voice as it overrode the duke's.

"I got 'im out o' there, but 'e wuz burnt awful bad," said Davey, "an' I could'na done it wi'out I 'ad Sam's 'elp."

"Sam . . . an older sweep among your master's boys—he helped you pull the little one out," said Jonathan, as if this detail was of particular import.

"Aye, an' 'e tried t' stop Tate from layin' into me when—"

"Tate," said Jonathan. "That would be the name of your master, who was furious with you and Sam for undertaking the burnt child's rescue."

"Aye."

"And who then *deliberately broke your leg.*"

"Aye, after Sam started t' yell at 'im t' quit, Towser come runnin' wi' the 'ammer, an'—"

"Towser," said Jonathan, interrupting again. "You mean

the bully-boy sweep who often functioned as a kind of enforcer, or director, of certain punishments of late?"

Davey nodded, then glanced warily at the duke, who no longer seemed to be objecting, who was gripping the arms of his chair so hard his knuckles had gone white. At a signal from Jonathan, the boy continued.

"Like I said, Sam tried t' stop Tate from layin' inta me, but then Towser come runnin' an' tol' Tate somethin' about a Grimsley lesson fer me 'n Sam, an'—"

"And that is when Tate broke your leg," said Jonathan in a tight voice. *"With a sledgehammer."*

"Stop!" shouted Justin. *"For God's sake, stop it!"* His eyes were silver daggers aimed at Jonathan. "Don't you think I know what you're trying to do? That name . . . Grimsley. It was part of the bait you used that night, to lure Sabelle into your dangerous rescue follies, and I have little doubt the pair of you thought to catch me up in them, too. But it won't work. Can't you see? Sabelle is not here to listen, and I—I cannot—*will not!*"

His glance slid to Davey, who regarded him with wide, frightened eyes, but it was not Jonathan's new ward he was seeing in his mind's eye. It was another child, witnessed years ago, whose charred, tortured features he'd long since buried in a forgotten place, along with the other pain of that terrible day when he'd left his own childhood behind.

He dragged his gaze back to Jonathan, and there was a haunted look in his eyes now. "For God's sake, Burke, what are you trying to do to me?"

A look of compassion softened the old man's features, and there was a note of hope as well. Schooling himself to remain calm, he addressed his grandson-in-law. "You will recall I spoke of coming to my point by a circuitous route. If you'll allow us just a moment more, you'll have your answers, Your Grace.

"Davey," he said, turning to the former sweep, "please tell His Grace, and quickly, if you please, what happened to the boy, Sam, after you heard the bully, this Towser, mention Grimsley."

Davey swallowed, still eyeing his host with apprehension.

But at an encouraging squeeze on the shoulder from Jeannie, he resumed speaking.

"G-Grimsley. 'Twere a name t' strike fear in us all, an' I feared it more 'n I feared 'at 'ammer. Sam 'eard it, too, cuz 'e muttered it under 'is breath afore Towser come at 'im . . ."

"Yes?" Jonathan encouraged. "Go on."

"I—I didn' see much more after—after—I blacked out from the 'ammer blows, ye see, an'—"

"But the boy—Sam. What can you recall of him?" Jonathan urged.

Davey shook his head sadly. "Towser took 'im, sir. But Sam fought 'im, 'e did! Gave 'at bully whut-fer an' popped 'im a facer 'r two. I remember 'at much. Ye should o' seen 'im, wi' them odd, blue-green eyes of 'is blazin' an'—"

"What was that, lad?" Jonathan queried with a sidelong glance at Justin. "What was it that was odd?"

Davey paused, seeing the duke suddenly standing and the gray eyes focused intently on him.

"Well, it were Sam, sir," he said to Jonathan. "Th' cove 'ad the oddest-color eyes ye'd ever want t' see. Bright blue-green, they wuz. Ain't never seen eyes 'at color afore."

Justin froze at the boy's words. Closing his eyes, he slowly formed questions in his mind, praying the answers were not what he feared, but knowing, somehow, that they were.

"This—this Sam," he said to Davey in a voice shaken out of its normal cool, "about how tall would you say he is?"

The boy ran his eyes quickly over the duke's tall frame, then nodded. "Sam'd come up t' just under yer shoulder, Yer Grace—'bout 'ere, I'd say," he added, indicating just the spot where Justin could remember Sabelle's honey-toned curls tickling his chin.

Justin closed his eyes as if in pain, but pressed on. "Dark or fair, Davey? Which was he?"

Davey scratched his neck in thought. "Well, Yer Grace, mind, ye kin 'ardly tell wi' sweeps, whut wi' soot coverin' 'em 'ead t' foot, an' I never seen Sam wi'out 'is 'at wuz on

'is 'ead, but . . ."—he met the duke's fevered gaze—
". . . I'd lay blunt 'e wuz fair."

Justin nodded, and his final question came as a strained
whisper. "Would you perhaps be able to tell me anything
about how long Sam—when it was Sam came into Tate's
employ?"

"Aye," Davey replied. " 'At's easy. It wuz 'igh summer,
'ot enough t' roast a—"

An anguished groan from the duke cut him off, but
when Justin turned to Jonathan, there was flint in his eyes.

"I'll not pretend this was all your fault. We both drove
her there," he said grimly.

Jonathan nodded. "But the question remains: Will you
help me get her ou——?"

"Christ, Burke! What do you take me for? She's my *wife!*
And even now she could already be—"

He didn't want to think of where or how she could be.
He didn't even want to contemplate her beaten and
maimed, or burned, or—

"We've sent feelers into the East End"—Jonathan
glanced at Jeannie—"and, thus far, there's been no word of
—of anything befalling a sweep named Sam, except that—
that he's not been seen in a few days. Mr. Kelly heard a
rumor that he's being held by the dog pit masters until
Grimsley returns from a trip upriver for some nefarious purpose. I believe we still have some time."

"Sweet Jesus," Justin murmured, glancing at Davey's
outthrust leg. "I hope to God you're right!"

Late that night, a tall, broad-shouldered figure, wearing a
coarse woolen cape and a slouch-brimmed hat tipped low
over his face, stepped quietly from a barge that had stopped
at the Billingsgate Stairs. Seconds later, the swirling mist
and darkness shrouding the banks of the Thames swallowed
him, and it was as if he'd never been there.

But the big, burly man who awaited him in the dark had
the advantage of having a companion with acute canine
hearing; with the canine's aid, he soon located his contact
in the fogbound blackness.

"Good lad." Michael Kelly praised Brendan in a whisper, then extended his hand to the cloaked figure. "Ye made good time, Yer Grace."

"But I still had to wait until bloody nightfall to move," Justin replied in a testy whisper. Then he added grimly, "Let's just hope it's good enough."

"We've had some luck," said Kelly as he withdrew a piece of ragged linen from his coat. "Davey contacted one o' Tate's boys and was able t' come by this. 'Tis a piece o' swaddlin' o' some sort which he says 'Sam' used t' . . ."—he swallowed hard as he extended the cloth—". . . t' keep warm. Brendan will have a fresh scent t' track the lass by, and though he's no scent hound, I think the lad can do the job."

Justin's fingers closed over the bit of rag just as the fog lifted for a moment. It allowed him to see what he held by the dim light of a quarter-moon, and his mouth tightened into a grim line: The cloth was smeared with blood.

Sabelle huddled in a corner of the filthy kennel that had been her prison for three days and shivered, trying to remember what it felt like to be warm. She wouldn't look at the poor, crumpled thing in the corner that had been a living, breathing dog once—until two nights ago, when they'd dragged it in there to die in agony of wounds suffered in the pit. She couldn't erase from her mind the features of the man they called Oaks. The dog pit master had suspected her anguish and pity for the wounded animal. And he had therefore deliberately ordered it dumped where she would have to see its suffering, but where she couldn't reach it to give it succor; because she was across the room and chained . . .

Like a dog.

Since then, her brain had fastened on an image of Oaks's narrow face and small, cruel eyes, committing it to memory. There were even moments when she felt it kept her alive, that memory . . . because she *had* to stay alive and, somehow, make Oaks pay for what he'd done.

And Grimsley, for what he'd ordered done to poor

Davey—and little Tommy . . . dear God, Tommy! Would she never stop hearing his screams in her sleep?

Yes, Grimsley would pay—she swore it! And Tate, and all the others whose names and faces were etched indelibly into her consciousness—

With an abrupt motion, Sabelle brought her hands up to the iron collar they'd fastened about her neck. She tore viciously at it, then again, and yet again, until the chain linking it to the wall rattled and clanked and her ragged, dirt-encrusted fingernails began to ooze blood. Pain tore through her fingers, but she paid it no heed; she had to get out of there, had to get away before Grimsley came back, as they'd promised her he would, and then—and then—

With a wrenching sob, Sabelle suddenly stopped, her scraped and bleeding hands dropping into her lap as if they belonged to a wind-up doll whose mechanism had run down. Then she heard, dimly, the sound which had somehow broken through her moment of madness. A dog's distant barking.

Now she thought she must be truly mad, after all, because the bark sounded like Brendan's.

Oh, no, don't even think it. Remember? You swore, long ago, you wouldn't let yourself think of such things . . . of sweet, gentle Brendan with his wet tongue and swaying tail . . . of Grandfather's proud smile when you bested him at chess . . . of Justin's arms about you or the fierce protective look in his eyes when he told a fat earl, "My wife's dog"—

Sweet heaven, she mustn't remember Justin. Especially not Justin!

The barking sounded again, and Sabelle pushed the heels of her hands against her ears to shut it out. But images of those she loved swirled in her brain, settling, at last, into her husband's face. It was the face she ran from, in her dreams, but here, now, in the cold and filthy dampness, with her thin body chained to a wall, she could banish it no longer. *Oh, Justin, I never meant to love you!*

The child inside her moved, and she brought her hands protectively to her belly. The face in her mind's eye shifted and became two—both father and son, standing in sunlight and smiling at her, their beloved features so alike, the look in their eyes beckoning, drawing her—

With an animallike groan, Sabelle doubled over and caught her face in her hands. The dam broke then, and her tears became great, heaving sobs that rent her soul and left no room for thought.

And that was how Ned Grimsley found her when Oaks led him there, with Towser close behind.

" 'At's 'im? 'At li'l rat's arse?" Grimsley raised the lantern he carried and sauntered toward the sobbing figure in black. He prodded her with the toe of his boot.

Sabelle choked on a sob and instinctively wrapped her arms about her lower belly, then rolled out of reach—as far as the length of her chain would allow. She jerked her head up to stare at her jailers with burning blue-green eyes.

Grimsley ran his gaze over her, and his lips curled on a sneer. "A right rum one, ain't 'e, Oaks? May'aps we orta call on Mother 'Atcher when we're done wi' th' sneakin' sod. She's got fancy toffs whut'll pay good blunt t' stick it in a boy's arse."

Coarse laughter from all three followed this suggestion, and Sabelle shrank back against the filthy straw in the corner.

God in heaven, they couldn't mean what she thought she'd heard! Life in the East End had familiarized her with much that was sordid and cruel; and she knew this Mother Hatcher he spoke of as the operator of a fancy bordello where certain girls off the streets—the young, pretty ones —were sometimes taken to be trained as whores who catered to the tastes of the aristocracy. But she'd never dreamed—

Towser's voice intruded, bringing her back to the present. "Ye figger 'ere'll be enough left o' th' bleedin' cove t' bugger when ye're done wi' 'im, Ned?"

The amusement left Grimsley's face. "Ye've got a point, Towser, me boy." His eyes, which were small and colorless, studied her from between folds of fat in a gross, fleshy face. Slowly, they narrowed. "Ye're cer'ain 'e's th' one?"

Towser revealed several rotten teeth as his face sported

an evil grin. He nodded. "Shadowed me twice when I went t' yer place, 'e did. "E's th' one, th' bloody sneak!"

"An' 'e jest might be one o' our bufe-nabbers, too, Ned," Oaks put in. " 'As a bleedin' 'eart fer th' pit blighters." He added this with a cruel smile as his eyes slid to the corpse of the pit dog.

The blood drained from Sabelle's face, though it wasn't apparent through the soot and grime covering it. Dear God, the worst had happened! "Bufe-nabbers" was cant for "dog thieves." They not only sought to punish her infractions as one of the sweeps being terrorized through Grimsley's edict; they'd connected her to the rescued dogs!

Frightened, Sabelle ran her tongue across dry lips, intent on pleading a case she already saw as futile. But when she tried to speak, only a pitiful croaking sound emerged. Sweet merciful God, when had she become such a coward?

But she knew the answer. The cold lump of terror lodged in her throat merged with something else and choked off speech. She focused on the child she carried and knew she'd put it in peril with her foolish daring, and the knowledge was bitter. Justin had been right to forbid her this dangerous attempt, and now, for their child's sake, if not her own, she wished she'd heeded him.

Rough hands were dragging her to her feet, breaking into her bitter musings. She saw Grimsley hand the lantern to Oaks, while Towser shoved her against the wall, an obscene grin on his face.

Her eyes widened in fear as she saw Towser step back and hand Grimsley something she hadn't realized he was carrying: Tate's horsewhip.

Stark terror seized her, and something was tearing at the collar at her throat. She suddenly realized it was her own hands. The whip descended with a terrible cracking sound, and she tasted blood as she bit down hard on her tongue to keep from screaming. She threw up an arm to ward off the next lash, while, at the same time, the other stretched across her pelvis and she hunched over to protect her unborn child.

Dimly, through the blood roaring in her ears, she heard

jeering shouts and ugly laughter from the two who watched. She tried to concentrate on keeping her knees from buckling, and then—

And then it seemed the very gates of hell had broken loose.

That same familiar bark split the air. It was followed by a canine snarl, and she felt herself thrown to the floor as a blurred mass of muscle and reddish fur interposed, blocking her from the lash.

At the same instant her spinning brain caught an enraged snarl from a human throat, followed by a man's voice. "Kelly, look to your back!"

Justin? Her disbelieving mind cried out, even as she felt the dearly familiar wetness of Brendan's tongue licking her face.

"Br-Brendan!" she cried brokenly, throwing her arms around the neck of her beloved hound. "Oh, Brendan!"

As Brendan stood over her protectively, she was drawn back to the scene beyond them. The man grappling with Oaks was Michael Kelly, who muttered a string of Gaelic oaths that vied with Oaks's stream of gutter-fed Anglo-Saxon. Yet it was clear from the frenzied pitch of the pit master's voice that he knew he was no match for the huge Irishman.

But it was the grim figure in a coarse cloak her eyes feasted on as he forced Grimsley to his knees from behind. One hand twisted the brigand's arm up high, behind his back, while the other pressed the handle of the horsewhip against his jugular, cutting off his wind. Grimsley clawed frantically with his free hand at the muscular arm supplying pressure to the whip's long handle, but his efforts proved ineffectual. His small, piggish eyes bulged between rolls of flesh; sweat poured down his face, and his complexion began to take on a bluish cast. Grimsley was no match for the man who held him, and Sabelle felt a cheer rising to her throat as she absorbed this, her eyes flying to the victor's face.

Justin. Sweet mercy, he'd found her, even when she'd long since lost hope. *Oh, God, Justin!*

She watched in horror as her tormenter dropped to the floor, all evidence of life gone from his body. She saw Michael finish off Oaks with a smashing uppercut to the jaw, then whirl about and, with a muttered oath, make a wild dash for Towser, who was bolting out the door. She saw her husband grab the lantern Oaks had dropped to the stone floor in his fight with Kelly, nurse its guttering flame back to life, and raise it high as he came toward her and the hound . . .

"Good dog, Brendan," she heard Justin murmur in a strange, raw voice. She couldn't quite place the nature of its emotional tenor, but she knew it hadn't been generated by the struggle with Grimsley; he was hardly winded. "It's all right now, boy. She's safe," she heard him say.

The hound lowered himself to the floor beside Sabelle with a small whine of acceptance. His tail thumped the stones and he administered reassurance of his own with a wet tongue to her cheek.

The hand that held the lantern aloft moved it higher, then checked and brought it closer to Sabelle's upturned face as she knelt in the filthy straw.

"Sabelle . . . ?" Her name on his lips was a disbelieving whisper, and then she saw the hand holding the lantern tremble as Justin's gaze fastened on the collar about her neck.

"Sweet Christ . . ." His voice broke as he dropped to his knees beside her; he set the lantern swiftly aside, then brought trembling fingers to the angry, abraded flesh at her throat. *What have they done to you?*

Hot tears stung her eyes and clogged her throat, stemming the tide of a thousand and one tumbling emotions that begged utterance. *Forgive me,* she wanted to say, *you were right and I was wrong, oh, so wrong, to gainsay you as I did, to jump headlong into danger, to jeopardize our child this way—*

The child! She needed to tell him about the child! And her love for him? Did she have the courage?

The touch of his hands on her shoulders jolted her and she swayed toward him, hating the tears that blurred her vision. Those couldn't be tears in the gray eyes that gazed back at her, but some trick of light, or her own faulty—

Then a movement behind him drew her gaze, despite the mist that veiled it, and she stiffened, pushing a warning past the emotions swelling her throat—

"Grimsley! Justin, he's got a gun!"

Justin released her and spun around, but before he could straighten, Sabelle knew it was too late; already the brigand had him in the pistol's sight. The hammer was cocked and ready to end her husband's life, unless—

With a sharp cry, Sabelle threw herself at Justin's precariously balanced form, sending him sideways, just as the pistol cracked. She felt a searing pain in her chest, and hell itself exploded in her ears: Justin's hoarse cry, Brendan's snarl, Michael Kelly's incredulous shout from the door.

"Die, ye heathen scum!" Kelly roared as he flung Towser's unconscious body aside and dove headlong at Grimsley.

Justin heard the hound's snarls merge with Kelly's, heard the sounds of thrashing behind him, but his only conscious thought was for the thin, crumpled figure in the straw.

"Sabelle!" he cried as he bent to his wife's still form at the end of its gruesome chain. "Sweet Christ, Sa——"

His whole body went rigid as he turned her gently toward him, and Michael heard him moan, a terrible, hopeless sound, as they both caught sight of the dark, glistening wound in her side.

"Sweet Mother o' God," Kelly whispered, "is she—"

But he got no further. The duke of Haverleigh clutched his wife's unmoving body to his chest, threw back his head, and howled his anguish to the heavens—

"Sabellllle!"

❧Chapter 27❧

THE MARCHIONESS OF WINCANTON COMpressed her lips and shook her head sadly as she closed the door behind her. Then she sighed. She was feeling all of her seventy years today, though she was loath to admit it; but what was even more loathsome was the feeling of helplessness which induced that recognition of age that stole over her.

Sighing again, she turned toward the smartly dressed couple across the hallway. They were also, she noted with a quickly discerning eye, looking the full measure of their years these days.

The earl and countess of Rushton rose quickly from their seats on two chairs that had been placed in the hallway for the convenience of those who wished to conduct an inobtrusive vigil.

"No change?" Marjorie queried softly as the earl held her hand and added his questioning gaze to his wife's.

"None in either of them," said the dowager. "He simply sits there, beside the bed, and refuses to speak—or eat or sleep, from what the servants tell me—while your poor child—"

"We know of . . . of Sabelle's condition," Cecil Corstairs managed. "Dr. Campbell told us, I'm sure, as he told you, before you saw him out and went to check at the bedside for yourself."

Marjorie nodded in affirmation at her husband's words,

withdrawing a lace-edged handkerchief from her sleeve and dabbing her eye. "He says, as he's done for the past three days, that the wound is deep, but not necessarily m-mortal, having—having touched no vital organs, b-but—"

A flood of soft weeping overcame her, and her husband patted her shoulder as he took up what had become a memorized recitation for them both. "There's been a great loss of blood, and he cannot say when she may regain consciousness . . ."

If ever. Millicent frowned, hearing in her own mind what had been implied, but which none of them dared say aloud. She forced herself to assume a more cheerful mien. "At least we may take comfort that the child is alive and apparently unaffected."

"It's a miracle," Marjorie sniffled from behind her sodden clump of linen.

"Indeed," murmured his lordship, "and if I may say so, m'lady, His Grace ought to be able to gather some solace from the fact that his future heir lives, and may yet survive this—this entire sordid business."

Millicent nodded, recalling the horrors of that moment three nights ago. They'd brought Sabelle here, to the dowager's town home, because it had been the closest place to that scene of infamy in an East End kennel. She remembered the raw pain lining her grandson's face as he carried the limp form of his wife to the bed she occupied now; his refusal to let anyone else touch her; his stark, dry-eyed silence as he took up a bedside vigil along with that great hound that also wouldn't leave her side; his leaving it to Jonathan and his man, Kelly, to explain what had happened; and to Cecil to deal quietly with the authorities.

The physician's news that the young duchess carried a four- or five-month-old fetus whose heartbeat was encouragingly strong had provided the first glimmer of hope during that initial long night; but Millicent sincerely questioned whether her grandson took it as such.

"I've informed His Grace, of course," Dr. Campbell had said, "but I fear the poor man is distraught. He merely stared at me blankly for a moment and recommenced gazing at Her Grace with that same hollow-eyed aspect we've all observed, I dare say."

What matter the child's strength, if the mother be lost? Millicent found herself wondering.

Marshaling her own strength, the dowager patted the countess's hand and spoke crisply. "I believe a bracing cup of tea is in order right now, m'lady . . . m'lord. Do join me in the—"

She broke off as she saw her majordomo approach from the stairs, his disapproving face alerting her to some problem. Murmuring a brief apology to her visitors, she addressed the servant. "Yes, Willis, what is it?"

"Begging your pardon, m'lady, but there are . . . callers again."

"The same?"

"I fear so, m'lady. I endeavored to turn them away as before, in accordance with your instructions, but the gentleman—"

"That dropface!" The marchioness exclaimed in a disapproving tone, but low enough to miss her guests' ears. Thomas Long's mournful features filled her inner vision, and she had no doubt, if she actually clapped eyes on them, they'd have her feeling *more* than her seventy years.

The lackjoy had been calling repeatedly each morning and afternoon since Justin's arrival and, as of yesterday, with Lady Sarah Cavendish in tow. She'd had Willis inform them, as, indeed, he was to inform any callers outside the family, that Her Grace had been taken ill suddenly, while visiting. He'd told them, too, that the duke had rushed to her bedside, and that neither was, therefore, receiving callers—as, indeed, she herself was not.

But had that satisfied Longface? Apparently not, and she wondered if the excesses of the age, coupled with the exigencies of wartime living, hadn't begun to strip it of common decency. Of course, the sourpuss tutor, for all his scholarship, hadn't the breeding which fine-tuned someone of the *ton*'s sensibilities to respecting a family's privacy. But *Lady Sarah ought to have known better!*

Well, she supposed there was no help for it but to set the

pair straight herself. Moreover, she added to herself with her ever-present eye to circumspection, she could use the opportunity to feel them out, regarding how much of this crisis had leaked to the *ton*, if any.

Pray to heaven, none, she added silently. She instructed the majordomo to show the callers into the drawing room, where they were invited to join her and her other visitors for tea.

Justin gazed at the still, pale features of his wife as she lay on the bed that seemed much too large for her small, fragile frame. One part of his brain told him he was seeing her here, as she'd remained, unmoving, for three days and nights. But another part was seeing her chained like an animal to a damp stone cell.

Sweet Christ, would he ever wipe that image from his mind? From his soul? And would he ever succeed in living with the certain knowledge that it was because of him she'd been there? Because he knew the truth as surely as he knew his own name. He'd denied her the right to act on behalf of innocents and driven her to the desperate acts that put her in that cell, as surely as if he'd fastened that chain or wielded that whip himself.

Sweet Christ, the courage it must have taken to do the things she'd done! What selflessness! While he'd sat at home in comfort and done nothing but curse the inconvenience she caused him. While he'd refused even to rouse himself to search for her. *While he'd refused to become involved.*

She put him to shame! Her very strength unmanned him.

And now she lay near death, again because of him. Because she'd deliberately taken a bullet meant for him, and saved his life.

His eyes drifted over her delicate, fragile features, beautiful even in their pallor, with the faint mauve shadows beneath her eyes. He took in her slender length, saw how thin she was, and swallowed against the lump forming in his throat.

Such a small, tender package to contain all that courage and love! All that caring she seemed bent on pouring out to the world . . .

And to him? Could he deny that Sabelle's act of putting herself in the way of that shot was evidence of the deepest kind of caring, and perhaps even—

"Christ!"

The explosion of sound roused the hound at his feet, and the great dog whined questioningly, as if to ask what was wrong.

"Stay with her, boy," Justin managed as he staggered to his feet. He had to get out of here, away from the sight that drove guilt through his heart like a knife. He had to get away and think. Sweet Jesus, there had to be time to think!

Thomas saw Lady Sarah into her carriage, where her ladies' maid waited patiently. The servant would provide adequate chaperonage to prevent *ton* tongues from wagging while he took a hackney, as he had on the way over.

"I'm sorry for this waste of your time, my dear," he told her while her groom held the carriage door ajar. "I had no idea the chit would remain indisposed so long."

"Indisposed? *Indisposed?*" Sarah sneered. "She's no more indisposed than I, if you ask me. That old dragon in there has been fobbing us off with a Banbury tale, I tell you! There's something that reeks of day-old fish in this entire business. There's more than meets the eye in the duchess of Haverleigh's curious lack of visibility, Thomas, and you know it! Why hasn't she been seen at balls and parties since the wedding, hmm? And don't tell me, as you had me believing at first, that Justin has merely been shutting her safely away in the country! I was willing to believe that at first and would have continued to do so, had he hurried back to town to enjoy his former . . . pastimes. But you know as well as I that he's made himself as scarce as soil on Brummel's linens since—"

"My dear Sarah—"

"Lady Sarah, and don't take that patronizing tone with me! You promised—"

"And I intend to keep that promise . . . *m'lady*. But you must allow me time to do my part. I shall then make it possible for you to do yours."

The brunette's eyes narrowed, and she gritted her teeth. "See that you do, then, but I warn you, I am swiftly running out of patience!"

Motioning the groom to shut the door, Sarah settled against the plush squabs of the carriage seat with a haughty lift of her chin, staring straight ahead, as if Thomas no longer existed.

The driver snapped his whip, and the carriage lurched forward.

Bitch, thought Thomas as he watched it move away. *But a useful bitch, if I play my cards right.*

He turned and began walking away from the dowager's house. It was a fine October day, the bitter cold spell which had gripped the city for a fortnight having given way to warm autumn weather; he would walk home and save the cost of—

A movement in the side yard of the marchioness's mansion caught his eye, and he paused in mid-stride to peer through the ornate wrought-iron fence. A tall male figure in a disheveled state of attire—wrinkled shirt-sleeves, minus a cravat, faded breeches, and scuffed, dirty boots—strode to a small garden bench beside a fishpond and slumped down on its seat.

Justin, by God! It's Justin! Pivoting about, Long hurried back to the front gate and found his way quickly from there to the side garden. Slowing his steps as he approached his former pupil, Thomas had a moment to study him, and his eyes widened at what he saw.

Not only was the normally fastidious attire of the duke lacking; there was at least a few days' growth of beard on his face, and his hair was equally untended, tangled about his head in an unkempt jumble of wild black curls.

"Justin! What in the name of—"

The duke's head snapped up and he stared at the tutor for a moment, as if unable to place who he was. Then he

brought a hand to his brow and rubbed it before gazing
again at his longtime friend.

"It's you, Thomas." Justin shifted on the bench and motioned wearily with his hand. "Come, sit down."

Thomas did so, then met the grave gray eyes and at-
tempted a smile. "I've . . . we've missed you, you know,
those of us who—"

"She's very bad, Thomas . . . perhaps even—perhaps
even dying, and I—*Christ*, I feel so weak and ineffectual!"

"She . . . ? You mean your wife? She—she really is ill,
then?"

Justin went on as if he hadn't spoken, his eyes staring,
unseeing, at the fishpond, where several carp swam lazily.
"Oh, Thomas, you cannot imagine the guilt! And what I
wouldn't give to make it up to her. If only there were a
chance—that she might recover, and I could have the opportunity to try to—"

He broke off, his breath catching on a gust of dry, empty
laughter.

"Justin, get hold of yourself. I can see you've been under
a strain, but—"

"And most of all," Justin cut in as the laughter abruptly
ceased, "most of all, Thomas, if she lives, I'd beggar myself
for the chance to earn the right to tell her . . . God's
mercy, I might never even get the chance to *tell her!*"

"Tell her? Tell her what, for the love of heaven?"

The duke slowly raised his head, and Thomas gasped at
the raw emotion he saw in Justin's eyes. Unbidden, an image of a far younger version of those eyes flashed across his
vision, and he knew that had been the last time they'd revealed such feeling.

He'd wanted to weep, then, at that child's walling up of
all the deeper emotions, just as now he wanted to weep for
joy at their return.

Until he heard Justin's next words.

"You see, I love her, Thomas. I love her, more than my
own life, and I've only now realized it—because I was too
stupid, blind, and proud to figure it out! Oh, how the fates
must be laughing at me—the great duke of Haver-

leigh . . . Hart the Heartless—in love with his own wife, and she, lying up there in that room—

"Christ! I've got to go to her! At this moment, she could be—"

"Sit!" said Long, pushing him back onto the bench from which he'd half risen.

The duke's expression changed at this impertinence, and Thomas quickly softened his tone. "Forgive me, Your Grace, but I was only thinking of your needs. If you could see yourself in a mirror, you'd know you're in no condition to resume a bedside vigil without rest. And perhaps a bath and some food. Your wife—"

"*May be up there dying, man,* with no one save a loyal hound at her side! How can you speak of—"

"She may also be taking a turn for the better, my dear man, and what do you think she'd do if she awakened and saw you like this? Why you'd scare her out of her wits!"

"Thomas—"

"I shall take up your vigil for you—that is, if you like. Just help me enter through the side door—no need to disturb her ladyship—and point the way to Her Grace's chamber. Then, when you've rested, or at least refreshed yourself, I'll relinquish my post, and you'll be much better equipped to carry on, won't you?"

Justin ran a hand over the stubble on his chin and nodded wearily. "Of course, you're right, Thomas. You always were one to see things clearly when we attacked a problem."

He rose slowly from the bench and offered the tutor a ghost of a smile. "Don't suppose I'd be of much use to anyone right now. My thanks, and I accept your offer, but I want your promise that you'll summon me at the slightest change—whether for good or—My chamber's across the hall from hers. I'll post a footman and—"

"Consider it done," said Long.

"Come, then, quickly."

Thomas saw the duke to his door and into the care of his valet after they'd peered briefly into the duchess's chamber and determined she was as she'd been when Justin had left. Then he stepped across the hallway and entered her chamber, closing the door quietly behind him.

The wolfhound raised his head, and a low warning rumble issued from his throat.

Long hesitated. He'd forgotten about the dog.

Suddenly his palms felt sweaty and he wiped them against the sides of his pantaloons, forcing himself to reconsider that dark flash of inspiration that had come to him in the garden.

When Justin had voiced his love for *her*.

His eyes skimmed over the pallid figure on the bed. It would have been so simple, so easy to—

He met the keen, intelligent eyes of the hound and discarded the idea. It wasn't really his style, anyway.

But Sabelle Hart had to be dealt with. He'd merely have to carry on with his original plan.

Because now the worst had happened. Justin believed he loved her, and there was no room in Thomas's life for that.

Because Thomas was in love with Justin Hart.

He wondered how he'd managed, sometimes, during the long years of their acquaintance, to keep the young duke from guessing how he felt about him. There'd been times when he ached with the need to blurt out his feelings, catching himself at each such desperate moment, just in time, knowing the son was not like the father . . .

Thomas smiled, recalling his years of secret passion with Derek Hart. Oh, he knew that the late duke of Haverleigh had not been a true homosexual like himself. Derek Hart had been a man of jaded appetites, always searching for a newer experience when his current interest began to pall. And so it had been only a matter of time before he tired of pursuing one beautiful woman after another, and went after an entirely different sort of game. And Thomas had been waiting.

But Thomas had been young and callow in those years, and he hadn't been emotionally prepared for the consequences of falling in love with the older man, who was using him only as a novelty to stimulate his dulled palate.

He'd panicked when the duke evidenced signs of boredom with their affair; and when Derek began to show a renewed interest in Vanessa, his own wife, Thomas had acted with a vengeance—a vengeance peculiar to those who feel threatened in their love relationships.

He'd begun a secret affair with Vanessa Hart to keep her out of her husband's bed.

Oh, it had not been easy, pretending passion for a woman when he craved the clean, hard lines of a man's body. But through a heroic effort of will and the useful trick of pretending—imagining Derek's body beneath him as he drove into hers—he'd managed to hide his distaste for the duchess's soft curves and—

A moan from the bed drew Long's attention. He saw it had claimed the wolfhound's, too, and he used the opportunity to move a few steps closer before the warning growl came again.

He noted the dog's control, that it made no overt move to attack, or shift from its position of wary alertness; but the animal's message was clear: *Keep your distance,* it said, *and I shall tolerate your presence in this chamber, but only to a point; if you make any move to harm, or touch my mistress without leave to do so, I am here to stop you.*

Sabelle moaned again, and then she began to toss restlessly, her pale features showing signs of acute distress.

" 'E's jest a wee thing! Goddamn you, Tate, 'e's jest a child! Tommy! Oh, sweet God, Tommy! 'Old on, sweet'eart! We're comin'!"

Thomas started and blinked in disbelief at the East End accents issuing from her mouth. *What in the name of—*

A sob from the bed drew him back to Sabelle, and he saw the wolfhound was standing now, his obvious distress paralleling that of his mistress.

"Oh, Justin!" Sabelle cried. "I never meant to love you!"

Thomas glanced over his shoulder at the closed door, wondering if she'd been heard outside the room, hoping she hadn't; it would indeed make his plan difficult, if not impossible, should the pair of them—

"Sweet merciful God, he's going to kill him! *No! I-ahh . . .*" Sabelle's sharp cry filled the room, and then all was silent as she lapsed into a deep stillness, much as she'd been when Thomas had first spied her on the bed.

A door banged open across the hallway, and Long acted quickly. Spinning about, he lunged for the door he'd shut earlier and pulled it open, just as he heard the duke shout his name.

"Your Grace, I was just about to call you." As he spoke the lie Thomas took in Justin's valet in the hallway, as well as the neatly groomed figure of the duke. "She stirred briefly and cried out something in her sleep."

"What—what did she say, Thomas?" Though the question was put to the tutor, Justin's eyes were only for his wife as he strode toward the bed.

"I . . . ah, it was of a private nature, Your Grace." Long cleared his throat meaningfully and darted a glance at the servant.

There was no response from Justin, who was bending anxiously over the bed, clasping his wife's hand. Mr. Weeks bowed deferentially and withdrew, pulling the door closed behind him.

With a wary glance at the wolfhound, Long approached the bed. The dog seemed to accept this and slowly lowered himself to the floor.

Justin turned as he felt the tutor's presence, but Thomas noted he continued to hold his wife's hand.

"You said she spoke?" Justin queried.

Long seemed to hesitate, then nodded gravely. "She cried out the words, actually."

"Well? Dammit, man! What did she say?"

Thomas sighed heavily. "I'm truly sorry, Justin, but her exact words were: 'I hate you, Justin! I loathe the very sight of you!' "

Justin winced and turned slowly back toward his wife.

Behind his back, the tutor smiled.

❖ Chapter 28 ❖

ANOTHER DAY WENT BY, AND STILL SABELLE did not regain consciousness. Justin continued his bed-side vigil, more terrified than ever that he might lose her; the acrid words of her unconscious ramblings, revealed by Thomas, haunted him through the long hours of his watch, and he became a man driven by a single thought: *She must not die!*

That she hated him, he did not doubt, for he knew he'd given her cause. But instead of letting this knowledge defeat him, Justin used it as a rallying point for his love. If she lived, he'd do all in his power to banish her hatred. He'd court her, cherish her, respect her ideals; and he vowed to spend a lifetime loving her and making up to her for his blindness in the past. But first she had to live—she had to!

As the hours ticked by, the members of the duchess's family and those closest to her passed in and out of her chamber like silent wraiths. Her parents looked so worn out from their concern, the marchioness feared for their own health; and so she insisted they lodge with her, in one of her dozen guest chambers, to be spared the effort of traipsing back and forth. Jeannie MacDougal had already been given a chamber in the servants' quarters, and Michael Kelly was treated to a splendid guest chamber just down the hallway. He had become something of a hero to those trusted members of the dowager's staff who were made privy to the duchess's tragic mishap, indeed, to the dowager herself, and nothing would serve but that he be treated with due regard.

Only Sir Jonathan continued to come and go from his own town house several blocks away, usually with Davey Fields, his new ward, at his side. The old baronet steadfastly resisted Lady Strathmore's efforts to coax him to be her guest as well, insisting the walk would do him far better than her mollycoddling. And, besides, he said, his new ward needed the feeling of some stability in his life. Jonathan was bound to see he got it; he'd be spending as much time as possible with Davey in his own home.

Of course, what Jonathan wouldn't tell her was that he needed to cram his own fear-filled days and nights with as much activity as possible; if he were to spend them waiting in dread, under the same roof as his beloved grandchild, he feared he'd go mad.

For Justin was not alone in his feelings of guilt over the tragedy; but what made it worse for Jonathan was his suspicions that, had he to do it over again, he would do exactly the same thing. He'd searched his conscience and found he had little to regret over the manner in which he'd reared his granddaughter. Sabelle was a compassionate idealist patterned on himself, yes, but he truly believed she had reached that state of her own free will; he had merely made it easier for her to act on her choices.

Of course, in the matter of the terrorized sweeps, he had been the initiator, and that troubled him. It didn't signify that he'd *unwittingly* placed her in the terrible position of being caught between their mutually held ideals on the one hand, and her husband's implacable will on the other. He ought to have sounded out the duke first, before approaching Sabelle.

And, above all, he ought to have realized that Sabelle had an implacable will of her own. But he had failed to do so— *failed her.*

And so it was that on the fourth afternoon following Sabelle's injury, Jonathan arrived at the dowager's house, still trying mightily to keep his guilt-ridden doubts at bay. He had just sent young Davey off to the kitchens with

Willis, in search of some biscuits and milk, when the marchioness came down the stairs and spied him in the vestibule.

"You look terrible," she told him.

"I see you are in your usual inimitable form, Millicent," Jonathan replied acerbically, "and good day to you, too."

"I mean it, Jonathan. You're ruining your health with all this haring off and back again, and your appearance proves it. You look a fright, I say."

"Thank you, my dear." He ran his eyes impudently over her, taking in the regal pile of silver hair, the proud, erect carriage. "I wish I could say the same of you."

"Nonsense. I look a fright, too."

"Excellent. Then we shall deal well together, I have no doubt."

"We never deal well together. We are constantly at tops and bottoms."

"I own that to be true enough," said Jonathan, but he added, as his face softened, "although I collect a time when it wasn't."

Millicent's features softened for a moment as well. She was plunged back to those days, more than half a century before, when he'd courted her, and she'd had eyes and thoughts for no one but him.

Why had it all had to end, that blissful time when they'd both been truly happy? Her mouth tightened, and the soft look was gone as she recalled why.

They'd gone riding with a small group of other young people, all of whom were down with their families for a house party at her cousin's estate in Surrey, when a sudden squall had erupted. The rain had been so dense that they'd not been able to see two feet in front of their mounts' noses, and she and Jonathan became separated from the others. Familiar with her cousin's lands, she'd led them to shelter in an abandoned woodsman's cottage, where Jonathan built a fire; there had followed the most delicious of interludes.

But when the storm finally ended, both had known her reputation would be in shreds if they returned to the house together after a few hours' absence. Jonathan's solution had been to escort her safely back by a circuitous route, but then to send her into the home of her cousin alone while he rode on to the village, pretending to have found shelter there all along; she would pretend to have taken shelter in the abandoned cottage alone.

She had agreed to this plan, although by then she was so completely in love with Jonathan, she'd have risked her reputation to ensure the immediate marriage between them, which her family would have demanded. But Jonathan had been adamant about keeping her name free of gossip, and he'd made her promise never to reveal how—and with whom—she'd spent those hours.

"But if I should be with child?" she'd questioned worriedly.

He'd smiled. "Then you've but to send word, and I shall wed you willy-nilly, because I love you, you goose. But I pray that will not be the case, and I intend to court you for a proper time before we engage to wed—that is, if you'll have me?"

"Oh, yes—*yes!*" she'd cried, falling into his arms again.

And so they'd pledged their love and proceeded with the plan that was to keep Millicent's reputation safe from wagging tongues.

Unfortunately, neither had reckoned with her family's far greater fear of those tongues. Saying she'd waited out the storm alone had not been sufficient—"You are ruined unless we can produce a witness to account for your unseemly disappearance for such a length of time," her father had said. "But how can we produce a witness to the fact that I was *alone?*" she'd countered, to no avail.

A male cousin had been summoned to invent a tale of having seen her leave the cottage, quite alone, but to ensure her name would remain unsullied, a hasty betrothal was also arranged—to the marquess of Wincanton, the son of her mother's best friend.

Millicent had wept and protested, but also to no avail. Then, while the banns were posted, she'd written secretly to Jonathan, begging him to release her from her promise, and to come forth and proudly announce with her that they'd been lovers. "It will put the finish to my betrothal, my darling," she'd written, "and I dare say my name will be ruined, but what care I for that? Father will be forced to insist on our immediate wedding, and I shall have you to console me for my lost reputation."

Jonathan's reply had been swift and brief; it had also left her stunned: "Forgive me, my love," he had said, "but I cannot. I release you to marry your marquess and *'in this way allow your court no decline, but life in honor and in pride.'*"

The quotation was from *Le Morte Arthur,* in a prose translation of the Arthurian legend which they had once read together. Upon seeing it, she'd known there would be no changing his mind. Jonathan Burke, romantic idealist that he was, would steadfastly relinquish his heart's desire rather than see the impugning of her good name. To him, honor was all—Damn his idealistic hide!

A large, orange-striped cat padded into the vestibule, and Millicent eyed its progress, glad of an excuse to avoid Jonathan's gaze.

"Well, well," said Jonathan, bending to inspect the feline, "and whom do we have here?"

The cat ignored him and began purring and brushing against Millicent's skirts.

"His name is Hortense," replied the marchioness with a challenging look as she stooped to pick the cat up.

"His . . . ?" Jonathan questioned carefully, for he knew that look all too well.

Millicent managed a shrug while holding the happily purring Hortense. "It was impossible to vouchsafe for his being male or female when he was a kitten, so we hazarded a guess. And by the time we learned the truth—" She shrugged again.

Jonathan scowled, clearly offended at such high-handed treatment of a fellow male. "I believe I shall address him as Henry," he told her.

Millicent scowled back. "That will not suit, Jonathan. He will merely become confused."

"And so should I be, if I were uncertain of my gender!" he snapped.

The marchioness bristled while Jonathan ignored her and reached out to stroke the cat; but he received a feline hiss for his reward.

"Hortense does not care for gentlemen overly much. He prefers the ladies," Millicent sniffed.

"Aha! *There*, you see? His confusion has already infected his disposition. How can he deal well with his own gender when he doesn't know what it is?"

"Perhaps," Millicent sniffed again before glaring at him, "his preferences signify because he knows entirely too *well* what that gender is!"

Jonathan glared back at her, but at that moment they were interrupted by the earl and countess of Rushton descending the stairs. Greetings were duly exchanged, and Marjorie tearfully reported a lack of progress with her daughter, from whose chamber they had just come.

Her father nodded somberly, then used the occasion to extricate himself from Millicent's barbs, announcing he would go up and check on Sabelle for himself.

"Good afternoon, Henry," he bade the cat after taking leave of the three family members. He actually found himself grinning as he felt Millicent's eyes boring into his back while he ascended the stairs.

But Jonathan's grin was long gone by the time he neared Sabelle's chamber. He fully expected to see the duke there, as he had each time he'd come, and this reminded him of yet another worry: Why had that young man bottled up all feeling early in his life? (That it had been early, he had no doubt, for the duke had long ago earned the soubriquet "Hart the Heartless.") And what would happen to that spark of emotional involvement he'd glimpsed that fateful moment, four days ago, should his wife and unborn child—

Muttering a rare oath, Jonathan glumly swore off thinking and walked to the door of his granddaughter's chamber.

But when he reached it, he paused. It had been left

slightly ajar, and he could hear an emotional male voice resonating from within the chamber.

"Sabelle, don't die, I beg you!" Justin cried, and there were tears choking his speech. "She must live, do You hear? If she dies, it will rob me of my own will to live! Oh, God! Don't let her die!"

Jonathan heard the broken sounds and felt moisture gather in his own eyes. Moved beyond speech, he retreated down the hallway; but as he neared the stairs, he knew what else he felt, besides pain at Justin Hart's anguish: Relief—and hope . . . *the iron duke had learned to feel again!*

With a lightness he hadn't felt in years, Jonathan descended the stairs.

And an hour later, Sabelle regained consciousness and spoke her husband's name.

⸎ Chapter 29 ⸎

"JUSTIN?" SABELLE'S VOICE WAS A WHISPER
in the quiet chamber.

Justin started, then savaged his lip with his teeth, sure it
was only his imagination taunting him again. He'd fancied
hearing her voice so many times these four days, he—

"Justin, what's wrong?"

Ever so slowly, he looked up from where he'd been focusing on his hands, which were clasped in front of him as
he hunched forward, elbows braced on widespread knees.
Slowly, very slowly, hardly daring to hope, but still unable
to keep his heart from pounding in his chest, he raised his
eyes.

"*Sabelle?*" His voice was disbelieving, though his eyes
told him she had at last opened hers, that they were regarding him lucidly—two deep pools of incredible aquamarine.

"Justin, is there something—?" she began to ask again,
but her husband's shout of mirth cut her off as he reached
eagerly for her hands.

Sabelle frowned in bemusement, wondering why she
thought she'd heard a sob through his laughter.

"Justin, are you all right? Because if—"

Another burst of laughter; but this time he sounded genuinely amused. He released her hands and placed his on the
pillow, to either side of her head, while bending over her
and gazing merrily into her eyes.

"Am *I* all right?" he questioned with a grin. "Madam, that is the ironic question of the century!"

"Justin, I fail to see—" Sabelle gasped; moving her arm to his forehead to feel for a fever had brought a sharp pain to her rib cage.

"Christ!" Justin swore, and then his face grew deathly pale as he saw her wince. "Don't move, Sabelle. For Christ's sake, *don't move!*"

"You needn't blaspheme, Justin," she told him grumpily, but her features lost their look of stress when she obeyed him, and the pain eased.

"What . . . ? What's happened to me, Justin? I cannot—"

"You don't remember?"

A frown knitted her brow for a moment, while her glance slid to the side and she tried to recall. "No," she said at last, her eyes returning to his. "Except that . . . how long have I been here, and whose bed is this?"

Justin sighed, but the clear, sane quality of her gaze and the cool hands he'd held to assure himself, among other things, that she was not feverish, told him she was in no danger of raving. So he attributed her loss of memory to shock, much as he'd witnessed in wounded soldiers on the battlefield. Then, sitting back in his chair beside the bed, he carefully related what had happened four nights earlier.

When he'd finished, Sabelle remained silent for several long moments, scanning his face. She was trying to put together the emotional blocks—the inner life—of those missing pieces of time, as he'd just supplied the external ones for her.

What else had happened during the past four days? Four days! She could scarcely believe she'd been lying there that long. And what about the events prior to that? Why wasn't he sitting there, scowling and admonishing her until it was the outside of enough, that she should have done what she did? As she had every right to expect him to do.

True, she'd given him—given them all—quite a scare, and it was clear he was relieved to see she was not about to succumb to her gunshot wound. *A gunshot wound! Imagine that!*

Nevertheless, the Justin she knew ought to be evidencing signs he was furious with her . . .

For disobeying him . . .

For endangering herself . . .

For disturbing his peace, forcing him to search for her and come to her rescue . . .

Indeed, he should, by all rights, be dressing her down one side of beyond and up the other . . .

But he was not.

Why?

He was looking straight at her . . .

And *smiling*.

"Does it all fit together now, little one?" he asked softly. Still the warmth in those eyes . . . old pewter in candlelight . . .

Suddenly Sabelle felt a warm, curling sensation invade her flesh, obliterating even the dull ache she'd become aware of in the area of her wound.

"I . . . I believe so," was all she said aloud to him. Then, in the next instant, her eyes widened as she felt a fluttering sensation in the lower region of her belly.

The child! The one thing neither of us has mentioned is the child! Oh, heaven, does he know? But he couldn't possibly, else he'd be raging at me for—Oh, God, the danger I placed it in!

But the babe had *moved*. She'd just felt it move, and that must mean it was all right. *Oh, thank God I haven't lost it!*

Justin watched as a range of emotions passed across her face. At first he grew alarmed, then puzzled, by them— until he saw where her hand had strayed, seemingly without her even being aware of it—to her pelvic region.

He smiled and covered that hand with his own. "Our child lives," he said, meeting her eyes.

"You . . . *know?*"

He nodded, though he could have told her how he'd pushed that knowledge to some nether region of his mind during the long, hellish hours of his vigil. How he'd needed to separate it, somehow, from the single force which had driven him during the waiting—that Sabelle, and Sabelle alone, was all that mattered while she lay suspended between life and death.

That if she died, nothing else mattered . . . nor would it ever matter again.

But he schooled his emotions and kept these thoughts to himself. Because, first, he had to travel the long, delicate road of winning back her respect—and then, God willing, her love.

He realized she'd spoken his name, and he snapped out of his reverie to give her his full attention.

". . . you're—you're not *angry* with me?" she was saying.

"For what, sweetheart?" he responded quite casually. He noticed she was beginning to tire, and he began tucking the covers tenderly about her, much as if he were bedding down a child for the night.

"For . . ."—she yawned, and her eyelids began to droop—". . . for vexing you sorely and . . . disobeying, and . . . risking so much . . . my own life . . . the child . . ."

Justin watched her eyes close, watched the steady, even breathing that indicated sleep, before he answered.

"No, love. For all those things, and more, I love you beyond measure."

Sabelle rallied quickly with her return to consciousness, and the members of her family and friends who'd waited near her bedside were overjoyed. But none was more joyous than Justin, whose ready laughter rang about the chambers and hallways of his grandmother's house like a young boy's.

And perhaps, in some ways, that was exactly what it was. Decades earlier, a fourteen-year-old child had cut himself off from all deep caring to avoid any sense of loss, and the pain it could bring; and now, all these years later, a head-on encounter with pain, with the threat of an unbearable loss, had released him to feel again. Now the child in him would teach the man how to live.

And love again.

On the latter, Justin spared no expense of energy or patience or hope. Lavishing care on his convalescing wife like some doting nursemaid or parent, he couldn't do enough for her. He read to her, sang to her, joked with her, spending hours at her bedside, even when she slept the healing sleep which would make her body whole. And when she grew restive, fretting at the boredom that often threatened, he cajoled and coaxed her out of these pets of temper, digging into his memory for funny stories or, when that supply grew thin, inventing his own. In short, he was a man committed to his wife and letting her know he loved her—long before he told her so in words.

As for Sabelle, there was much she wondered at in this time. Not at the delight she took in her husband's buoyant presence in her daily life—oh, no, never that. For she knew she loved him, and who that loves does not delight in the presence of the beloved? But she wondered at the delight *he* seemed to take in every moment they shared. She feasted on the humor and vibrancy in the mercurial silver eyes that met hers so readily these days; but she wondered, too, why they no longer held storm clouds or, worse, that immutable coldness of before.

What was on his mind? she found herself thinking one morning at the end of October. She had been allowed out of bed by Dr. Campbell, to take a few shaky steps two days before. She was now sitting in a chair by the window, where Jeannie had just dressed her hair and then left her to fetch a ribbon to match her new rose gown.

Justin's behavior toward her had changed so, he was like a different person. Why, it was almost as if he *cared* for her, cared deeply, in a way that—

No, she wouldn't think it. She had lived for so long with the futility of even hoping Justin could come to love her, she didn't dare let herself think it now.

I truly believe that idealized emotion beyond me, she recalled him writing about love in that letter to Long—*or any thinking, rational man.* Well, whatever his current state of mind, she could not think its rational quality had altered;

the depth of thought and quality of his wit in their many long bedside conversations testified to that. In such matters he was the same Justin as before, so whatever—

A rapping at the door interrupted her thoughts, and she called permission to enter, thinking it was Jeannie.

The door swung open, and Justin came in, wearing a grin that emphasized those deeply grooved male dimples which had the capacity to make her go weak all over . . . like now.

"Good morning, Your Grace," he said, making her a playful bow that ended with a flourish of his arm. Then he ran his gaze over her so thoroughly, Sabelle flushed.

She blushes so prettily, I find myself thinking her a virgin, Justin mused. *Yet she carries my child, and I can well recall the woman's passion she brought to our bed. Oh, Sabelle! You're so lovely, I can't take my eyes off you! And I love you so much it hurts!*

"Good—good morning to you, Your Grace." Sabelle tried to match his playful air, but she found herself stammering under that gray-eyed gaze.

"Well, what's this?" Justin queried as he came forward and lightly touched her hair. "A new coiffure? And a new gown, too, or I'm greatly deceived. There must be important business afoot today, hmm?"

Sabelle laughed, pleased he had noticed the changes. In fact, she'd been allowed to exchange her negligée for a proper morning gown only yesterday, when the heavy bandages on her rapidly healing wound had been removed. The rose gown was a gift from her mother, who'd been in a taking because her old ones had all proved too loose as a result of the weight she'd lost during her ordeal.

"You know very well what's afoot today, Justin Hart," she told the duke. "I'm to have my first outing, and I am at sixes and sevens with anticipation!"

"But only to take a brief airing in the garden," Justin admonished with a wagging finger. "And that, only because the weather continues so remarkably fine and—Ah!" He made a sudden show of peering out the window. "Do you suppose it might rain?"

"Justin, don't you dare tease me!" Sabelle cried. She nevertheless cast a reassuring glance at the sky through the window. "There's not a cloud in sight!"

Justin chuckled. "Sorry, pet, but I simply couldn't resist. Teasing brings such a fascinating flash of green to those incredible eyes of yours."

It was true, he thought as he braced his hands on the arms of her chair and leaned over her upturned face to capture her gaze. As blue as they were green, Sabelle's eyes resembled a tropical ocean on a sunny day, at once deep and clear and shot with a light that made his breath catch in his throat . . . as now.

"Justin . . . ?" Sabelle managed to whisper as the nearness of him, the familiar scent of the sandalwood soap he used and the visible texture of his skin, threatened to unnerve her. "Is . . . is there something amiss with—with my eyes?"

Slowly, Justin moved his head from side to side while his eyes continued to hold hers. "Not a thing, sweetheart," he murmured huskily, ". . . not a damned . . . solitary . . . thing . . ."

His lips, when they claimed hers, were warm and firm, and the feel of them plunged her instantly back to other times when their mouths had touched, when they'd let their bodies speak where words left off.

Justin felt the tip of her tongue meet his, hesitantly at first, and then with a quick, eager thrust that sent him reeling. She was so ready with her responses! How could he have forgotten that? He'd only meant to taste the sweetness of her lips for a moment, helpless to deny their lure when he'd suddenly found them so near, but now—

A knock at the door crashed into his thoughts, and he pulled away sharply. He groaned as Jeannie's Scots accent intruded.

"Sab—er, Yer Grace, I've found it! Shall I come in?"

Sabelle pulled in a shaky breath and then flushed. She'd seen Justin straighten, but then he'd touched his eyes to the swell of her breasts above the square décolleté of her gown. Now he met her gaze and grinned.

"You'd better give us a minute, sweetheart," he whispered, so Jeannie might not hear. "Your charming blush is telling enough, but I fear these breeches leave little to the imagination."

Sabelle dropped her gaze without even thinking, then felt herself go crimson.

"One—one moment, Jeannie," she stammered. Suddenly she felt herself pulled out of the chair and enfolded in Justin's arms.

"Shh!" he murmured into her hair, when she seemed about to resist. "Just let me hold you for a moment. I promise I'll behave—for both of us!"

Sabelle muffled a giggle against his chest, where she could feel the rapid thudding of his heart. Oh, but it felt so good to be enveloped in his arms like this!

But in the next instant reality intruded, and she sighed and pulled away. *What must Jeannie be thinking?*

Justin sighed, too, and offered her a lopsided grin. "Better fetch the ruddy Scot in," he told her with a wink.

Sabelle smiled, despite herself. "Ruddy" constituted not only a barely acceptable substitute for "bloody," but an apt description of Jeannie's Scots complexion.

Jeannie was admitted, and her keen eyes seemed to assess at once the situation that had developed and kept her waiting. She said nothing, however, but curtsied to the duke and went straight to work threading a narrow rose ribbon through the curls at the top of Sabelle's head.

"Thank heaven you didn't find it necessary to shear your hair for that impersonation," Justin said as he let his eyes roam across her shining curls. "I know some women are bobbing and frizzing theirs lately, but I should sorely miss these silken tresses if they were gone."

Sabelle's brow rose a fraction at this. It was the first he'd alluded to any particular of her time with the sweeps. Oh, they'd discussed the nature of what had transpired in general terms, and she'd had the satisfaction of learning that Grimsley and Oaks and their lot were suffering the most severe punishments for their crimes. But that was all. She'd gotten the impression Justin purposely avoided hearing the specifics of what she knew he suspected: that her life as a climbing boy had been hard and brutal—and obviously fraught with danger. Was it that he didn't care to hear about such sordid business, just as he'd not cared enough to become involved with her grandfather's proposal that night?

Biting her lip at this reminder of what she regarded as the huge missing piece in Justin's character, Sabelle was relieved when Jeannie responded for her.

"Davey told me most o' the laddies wore their caps at all times—even whilst they slept. 'Twas guid protection fra' the cold and dirt and the like, ye ken."

Justin nodded, almost pensively, Sabelle thought. But before she could begin to analyze his mood, Jeannie was giving her curls a pat and stepping away.

"There," pronounced the Highlander. "Ye look all the crack, Yer Grace, even if ye aren't shorn like the blasted duke o' Sutherland's sheep!"

"Indeed," echoed Justin, motioning Sabelle to turn about. "Come, let's have a good look at you, Your Grace. We shan't want the robins in the garden to fly into the boughs over your appearance."

Jeannie chuckled at his wit and took her leave, while Sabelle slowly turned for his inspection.

He ran his eyes appreciatively over her lithe form, noting her breasts were fuller. And, given the current high-waisted fashion, her pregnancy was not the least bit in evidence. Of course, judging from the increased prominence of the cheekbones in her *gamin* face, he suspected she was still entirely too thin; and he made a mental note to speak to cook personally about fattening her up a bit.

Beyond all this, she was entirely the loveliest creature on God's earth, and he feasted on her beauty like a starving man before a banquet. Her shining mass of honey-toned curls was piled atop her head with an air of insouciant elegance, with curling wisps and tendrils left here and there to grace the elfin beauty of her face. And, huge in that face, were those eyes he could get lost in . . .

His gaze traveled the length of her, caressing the graceful

lines and delicate curves of her body like a lover. That he was that lover, *the only lover,* who had known that body was a thought that had once filled him with fierce, possessive pride; the pride was still there, he acknowledged, but it was tempered now with a deep humility—that he should be the one chosen by fate, by heaven, by whatever moved the sun and stars, to have such bounty entrusted to his care.

Now only let me be worthy of her, he reminded himself as Sabelle came about and met his gaze with shining eyes. *Let me earn the right to love her.*

"Well, sir, do I pass inspection?" The question was pert, and Sabelle's eyes twinkled mischievously, for she recognized the gleam in his eyes.

"You know you do, minx," he told her with a grin, "but not merely do you pass—you exceed!"

She dimpled and offered him a low, sweeping curtsy, at which Justin felt his mouth go dry and his loins suddenly tighten: He'd just been treated to a more-than-generous glimpse of the lush, ripe curves her bodice hadn't managed to conceal—though he doubted she was aware of this.

Knowing this was neither the time nor the place to pursue such matters, he raised her from the curtsy with one hand; then he swept her off the floor and into his arms.

"Justin, are you mad? Put me down, for heaven's sake!"

"No," he said, smiling, and kissed the tip of her nose.

"But I can walk! I've been practicing!"

"I'm sure you have, sweet, but there's no sense tiring yourself before we get to our destination. You shall have your walk in the garden—and in the meanwhile allow me the pleasure of . . . assisting you."

"Humph!" was all she said, but she smiled all the way to the garden while she drank in her dark and handsome husband's looks and savored his strength as he held her.

The day outside was as warm and beautiful as the view from the window had promised, and Sabelle hugged its loveliness to her like a child who'd just escaped the schoolroom. Justin stayed by her side, watching as she took pleasure in the simplest things . . . the flight of a sparrow . . . a clump of Michaelmas daisies hidden in a corner . . . the footprints of a rabbit . . .

How she delights me, he thought, smiling at her happy chatter, *this fragile-seeming, elfin creature I never took the time to really know—until it was almost too late. Oh, Sabelle, I want years for us to grow together, you and I—and worlds to discover, too . . . but together . . . only together!*

After awhile, Justin suggested they rest on the garden bench, lest she tire, and she agreed. The puckered scar over the side of her rib cage no longer even itched, thanks to some salves and simples Jeannie had constantly applied, procured from a Scottish "wisewoman." But the dull ache in her legs told her how out of condition she was from lying abed for so long.

They were sitting there only for a minute or two, talking quietly, when she noticed Justin appeared distracted. He kept glancing in the direction of a gate to the side of the garden, and he seemed mildly apprehensive as well. Was he looking for someone?

And then she saw he was. Through the gate, now, came her grandfather with little Davey in tow and, bringing up the rear, Jeannie, holding hands with Michael Kelly; and then a small figure she couldn't quite get a good look at yet . . .

Justin gave her hand a squeeze before leaping up to greet them. He ushered them toward the bench where she was sitting, having indicated she should remain there, and Sabelle saw they were all grinning—except Justin, who looked as near to nervous as she'd ever seen him.

Greetings were enthusiastically exchanged, although she'd seen these people she loved almost daily during her convalescence.

"We brung ye a surprise!" Davey piped amid the clamor.

" 'Brought,' not 'brung,' " Jeannie corrected affectionately.

"Aye, well, we brought 'im, but 'e's the *duke's* surprise, really!"

"What . . . ?" Sabelle began to question, but then

Jeannie and Michael stepped aside all of a sudden, and there, behind them and open to her gaze, was—

"Tommy!" Sabelle cried. She lurched off the bench and flung herself forward, then stopped just short of the shyly smiling child, hardly willing to believe her eyes.

"Oh, Tommy, I thought you were dead!" The words came out in great, choking sobs, and she felt her husband's arm go around her, supporting her.

"Sam!"

The seven-year-old's face screwed up, and with a sob, he flung himself into Sabelle's outstretched arms. "Oh, Sam, it *is* you, ain't it?"

And there, in that circle of happy onlookers, the two of them wept, while the duke wrapped his strong arms around both and held them close.

"Well, here, let me look at you," Sabelle murmured in watery tones when at last she could speak. She sniffled and held the boy gently at arm's length. Tommy began to wipe his nose on his sleeve, then sheepishly accepted a handkerchief from Justin. It helped that the duke's eyes looked suspiciously moist, as well, to the child.

Sabelle noticed that Tommy had a burn scar on the side of his face, and one of his hands had a bandage wrapped about it, but, other than this, he looked rested and well fed. Moreover, he was dressed in fine clothes—like a little gentleman.

"Ye're lookin' a right rum swell these days, Tommy," she told him in the accents he remembered.

Everyone laughed, though there was still much blowing of noses as handkerchiefs did prodigious service.

Sabelle glanced at Davey, whose attire was every bit as smart as Tommy's, and then her eyes sought out Jonathan's.

"I take it you're also responsible for—"

"Ahem. Ah, not exactly, my dear," said her grandfather. "Fact is, the only part I played in Tommy's rescue was a small one, for I merely offered the services of my solicitor, who was already familiar with the adoption procedure because of Davey, here."

Sabelle glanced at Davey and then looked about in bewilderment. "Then, who . . . ?"

Tommy laughed and caught her hand, turning her toward her husband, who was standing there looking at her with an odd, unreadable expression on his face.

" 'Twas *'Is Grace* done it, Sam! Yer own rum duke. 'E's me new ger—gar—"

"Guardian," Justin supplied quietly.

"Aye! 'E's me guardian now," Tommy echoed proudly.

Sabelle's eyes flew to Justin's face, and she thought it might even be true. He was regarding Tommy with a soft smile as he ran a hand affectionately over the boy's curls.

But when, in the next instant, his gaze lifted to meet hers, she *knew.* Justin's eyes held all the tenderness and warmth she'd ever dreamed of seeing there, and not just for Tommy, she realized, but for *her.*

Her vision blurred suddenly by tears, Sabelle opened her mouth to speak, but nothing would come. *Oh, Justin, I love you so!* her heart cried out, but still she couldn't say the words. So she just gazed at him through shimmering tears, her heart in her eyes, until he caught her to his chest and held her without words.

✤Chapter 30✤

SABELLE STOOD BEFORE A CHEVAL GLASS IN the master bedchamber of the ducal town house, eyeing her reflection. Yes, it would do, she thought as she gave her stomach a pat. The heavy, green velvet folds of the slightly high-waisted medieval costume concealed her pregnancy as well as any gown of the current Empire mode.

She certainly had no wish to create gossip by appearing visibly *enceinte* on this, her first public appearance since her recovery. The occasion was a Guy Fawkes Day ball being hosted by none other than the Prince-Regent himself, at Carlton House. And, since it was Guy Fawkes Day, nothing would serve but that the ball be a masquerade affair, complete with the little masks called dominoes and other concealing costumery.

Sabelle smiled as she thought of the vast changes in her life since the last Guy Fawkes Day. And she wondered, for a moment, that she could look back on those unsettling events of a year ago and smile at all. She had come away from that evening hating Justin with a vengeance—literally.

And now she loved him—deeply.

Her smile faded as she turned from the mirror and glanced about the chamber where she'd spent her wedding night. It looked as it had then; every detail, down to the expertly repaired hinges on the outer door, was the same.

Except that Justin wasn't using it.

After taking leave of his grandmother the evening after

Tommy's "return from the dead," as Sabelle had called it, the couple had come here to settle into their own household, bringing Tommy with them. That had been two days ago. But after Justin had escorted Sabelle to the master suite, with the admonition to rest and gain back her strength, he'd promptly given her a good-night kiss on the forehead and announced, if she needed him, he'd be across the hall!

If she needed him? She fairly quaked with needing him! She was convalescing, not *dead!* Now that she'd witnessed the blessed miracle of her husband's moral transformation (she could think of his compassion for Tommy as nothing less), Sabelle felt her love for him grow to brimful and overflowing. She could scarcely contain the depth of emotion that welled up in her every moment she thought of him, which was almost always.

And when he was near! God help her, was she so wanton that all she thought of in his presence, all she craved, was melting in his arms and having him make sweet, passionate love to her? And if a wanton, did she advertise it by her looks and gestures, and thereby put him off?

But they were a wedded couple, for heaven's sake, and she knew, firsthand, her husband had a lusty nature.

A distressing thought struck, and her hand moved quickly to her belly. Was it the child that put him off? Or held him back? She knew little of these things, but she certainly thought Dr. Campbell would have said something to her if she wasn't supposed to—

A blush stained her cheeks, visible in the mirror she again regarded, but she ignored it, turning herself sideways to observe her profile. No, there wasn't a hint of swelling, but what if Justin didn't require actual evidence of pregnancy? What if just the *thought* of—

An energetic rap on the door broke into her thoughts, and Justin's voice called out. "Is my damsel in distress dressed and tressed?"

Despite her gloomy musings of a moment before, Sabelle chuckled and bade him to enter.

The door opened, and Justin struck a playful pose in the

aperture, his gray eyes gleaming with amusement and something else she couldn't quite define. His dress was more reminiscent of a medieval troubadour than the knight she'd imagined; for after they'd explored ideas for a costume theme, they'd settled on the period when knighthood was in flower. He was more handsome than ever in the blue braies, or fitted breeches, and hose called chausses, but the red tunic he sported was of a simpler design than that which might have been worn by the aristocracy; and slung across the back of his short blue-and-silver cape was a lute, not a sword.

No courtly knight, this, she thought, *but a rascal and a rogue, right down to the gleam in his eye!*

And now, suddenly, Sabelle recognized that gleam's import well enough. Her husband was looking at her as if he would swallow her up whole.

But, if that's the case, then why doesn't he—

"You, fair lady, are the most delicious-looking creature God ever wrought," Justin breathed as he came forward to take her hand and graze it with his lips.

Sabelle shuddered involuntarily, a spasm of delight coursing through her with even this lightest touch.

"Are you cold?" The laughter in Justin's eyes vanished, replaced by concern. "You've not overdone things, have you? Is the babe—"

"Heavens, no!" Sabelle laughed, eager to dispel the worry he'd been all too prone toward displaying during her convalescence. He'd been solicitous to a fault, and she loved the care this showed; but she'd also been dying to resume a more active life, and tonight was a beginning she wouldn't miss for anything. "I'm in the pink of health, Justin, really I am!"

"I'm glad to hear you say so," he told her in a serious voice, "but come here and let me warm you, just the same."

Before she could respond, he caught her hand and pulled her gently against his chest, wrapping her in his arms while his cape fell around them.

"There," he murmured against her hair. "Better?"

Sabelle nodded, hardly daring to breathe. His chest felt warm and solid against her cheek, and the familiar, masculine scent of him had her light-headed and giddy.

Justin swallowed, a constriction in his throat, and then in his loins, threatening his control. He wanted her with a longing that was almost palpable, but he didn't feel the time was ripe for it. It was clear, from the way she looked at him since she'd learned about Tommy, that she'd forgiven him much, and perhaps was beginning to see him in a new light.

But now he knew that wasn't enough. Now he yearned for her love as well as the sweet flesh he'd claimed in the past. And he stubbornly held to the notion that, somehow, now that he knew what love for a woman was, it would be wrong to claim the one without having the other.

He would have Sabelle's love, and nothing less. But for that, he needed time—and patience.

With these thoughts in mind, then, Justin kissed the top of her head and, with a fond squeeze, released her.

"I almost forgot to tell you," he said. "Thomas and 'La Cavendish' are waiting in the drawing room. Are we about ready to join them?"

Sabelle hid a moue of irritation as she turned and reached for her peaked medieval headdress and veil. She'd forgotten the dour tutor had managed to procure an invitation and asked to join them for the evening. And Lady Sarah, no doubt, had been the source of that procurement. According to Lady Corstairs, the beauteous brunette was being seen in the "upstart's" company quite frequently these days, and the *ton* was shocked by it; they could, apparently, forgive one of their own any number of discreet liaisons, but never the indiscretion of hobnobbing with one of such baser origins.

Yet none of that had to do with Sabelle's irritation. But the presence of Lady Sarah Cavendish in Justin's life did. And Sabelle found herself surprised to realize she didn't even mind admitting she was jealous. Cavendish was a prime beauty and had been Justin's mistress for ages. Moreover, it did not signify that she was reentering the duke's

life on Thomas Long's arm; they'd dropped in for tea yesterday, and if the way the brunette looked at Justin was an
indication she was smitten with another, Sabelle was a Guy
Fawkes firecracker!

As for Long's interest in the matter, Sabelle hadn't had
time to ponder that yet; but yesterday she'd glimpsed a
calculating look in his eye in a mirror, when he hadn't
known she could see him studying her.

Yes, Cavendish and Long were trouble, she had no
doubt, and the last thing she wanted was their presence on
what promised to be a splendid evening. But Justin seemed
oblivious to the source of her irritation, and she did not
wish to appear the carping wife who was always ready to do
battle with remnants of her husband's bachelor past.

"Let us join them, by all means, Sir Troubadour," she
said with the brightest smile she could manage.

Justin eyed with approval the charming picture she made
with the green hennin and diaphanous veil in place, then
led her downstairs. And when he lightly murmured
snatches of a *chanson d'amour* along the way, Sabelle
shoved her irritation completely aside.

Carlton House was ablaze with light when they arrived.
From the torchlit portico they were ushered into the grand,
high-ceilinged entrance hall lined with columns of por-
phyry marble, where dozens of liveried footmen waited to
take their wraps.

Sabelle had time to look around her as they were directed to make their way through the suite of rooms beyond. She saw all manner of elaborate costumes, including
at least three Julius Caesars, an Elizabethan shepherdess,
several caped dominoes, and no less than four Helens of
Troy.

That one of these was Lady Sarah seemed not to annoy
the smug brunette at all, and Sabelle knew why. Of all four
costumes, Cavendish's was outrageously unique; it con-
sisted of a sinuously draped swath of sheer white fabric,
wound to resemble a classical garment. But Sarah had then

dampened it with water to make it cling to her body and enhance the material's diaphanous qualities.

Glad her domino mask hid her distaste, Sabelle kept her fingertips firmly on Justin's arm and walked on.

The impression of grandeur and spaciousness increased as they entered the Regent's audience chamber, called the Blue Velvet Room. Bathed in a tender gray-blue, from its thick carpet to its graceful settees to its painted ceilings, it was a study in elegance; and a three-tiered crystal chandelier fringed in gold reflected the same hue in its sparkling depths.

They followed the crowd through the Throne Room, with its curtained Romanesque bays flanked by gilded Corinthian columns; it was rich with red brocade and carved, painted furnishings of the finest quality.

Then came the Circular Dining Room, all mirrors and silver walls, and then the famous Rose-Satin Drawing Room, which shimmered in warm pink touched with gold.

Each room brought new wonders: the ceilings, works of art on their own; the doors elaborately painted; the richly appointed furnishings chosen to blend perfectly with their ornate settings. There were Gobelin tapestries, Aubusson carpets, Sèvres vases, and delicate wooden furniture with inlaid designs.

The Regent had beggared the coffers of the Royal Treasury, it was loudly rumored by his political opponents, to assemble all this, and to top it off, he'd adorned it with one of the finest collections of paintings in the world. They noted a number of Dutch and Flemish masterworks among the couple of hundred that adorned Carlton House. And when Lady Sarah pointed out Rembrandt's *The Shipbuilder and His Wife*, remarking that it had cost five thousand guineas, Justin spat under his breath, "And climbing boys get moldy bread to eat—if they're lucky!" Only Sabelle heard him, and her eyes shone with emotion as she gave his arm an answering squeeze.

Throughout this earlier part of the evening, as guests continued to arrive, they crowded into the assembly rooms by the hundreds, all pressing toward the grand ballroom, where the Regent would be found. The air quickly became hot and stuffy; the competing scents of perfumes and various toiletries grew cloying and stifling while warm, richly costumed bodies pressed ever closer.

Vials of vinaigrette began to make an appearance at regular intervals as ladies grew faint from the crush. They had just seen an earl's daughter helped to a divan under such circumstances when Justin glanced down at Sabelle and detected a pallor on the part of her face unobscured by the domino.

"Christ!" he swore as he felt her falter and clutch his arm. "Thomas, Sabelle's in no condition to withstand any more of this nonsense. Will you be so kind as to fetch her a glass of water while I get her to that alcove over there?"

Even as he spoke, he had his arm about his wife and half carried, half walked her toward a corner. There a tiny island of cleared space, framed by a pair of gilded, arched columns, seemed to have gone unnoticed by the crowd.

Long nodded and went off in search of a footman, while Sarah made a great show of searching her reticule for her vinaigrette while she accompanied the duke and duchess.

"I don't appear to have brought it," she told Justin as he settled Sabelle onto a marble bench behind the columns. "Why don't I stay with Her Grace while you try to locate some, Justin, darling? She looks ghastly pale," Sarah added uncharitably as Justin removed Sabelle's mask and gazed worriedly into her face.

"I—I shall be just fine, really," Sabelle protested. "No need to make such a—"

"You're sure it's not the babe?" her husband interjected. "You're not feeling the morning sickness in the evening, are you?"

Lady Sarah's hands froze on her reticule strings as Sabelle's reassurance cut him off. "No, Justin, I'm certain the —the child is quite uninvolved." She chuckled. "In fact, it may be better off than its parents, for I dare say, where it resides, I'll wager it is far less crowded than where *we* are!"

Sarah gestured impatiently. "Now I *do* insist you go after that vinaigrette, Justin—or perhaps hartshorn, if Thomas ever returns with that water. Now, run along, darling. We women know how to deal with these things, and Her Grace will be just fine with me until you return."

Justin looked undecided for a moment, but another look at Sabelle's face, which now seemed flushed, convinced him.

"I'll be back in a trice," he said, giving her hand a squeeze, and then he melted into the throng.

He had barely disappeared from view when Sarah lowered herself to the bench beside Sabelle, ripped off her own mask, and eyed Sabelle with unveiled hostility.

"So, the little duchess is breeding, is she? How very interesting!"

Sabelle checked the urge to flinch at the supercilious tone, the open antagonism in the dark eyes. "It is, *to us,*" she heard herself say.

"Us," Sarah repeated on a hiss. "Ah, yes, Justin would be extremely interested if you should produce an *heir,* I have no doubt. And, of course, *your* interest, as the *breeder . . ."* She shrugged as if to say that was the nature of things.

"Lady Sarah," Sabelle said as she felt her anger rise, "I am growing weary of your innuendo. You obviously have something to say to me, so come to the point before I decide to faint after all—as a means of avoiding your nasty tongue!"

Sarah sucked in a breath through her teeth, then leaned forward, her eyes narrowed into dark slits.

"Listen to me, you pathetic little country mouse. Justin Hart had only one aim in wedding the likes of you, and now you've served it—*if* you produce a male offspring, that is! If not—" She affected an insouciant shrug. "I suppose he may yet ride you a time or two, until he gets an heir on you.

"But beyond that, he'll be mine—*mine,* do you hear? For he never *was* yours, but for the purpose of breeding sons, and once you've done your"—her eyes traveled down, insultingly, to Sabelle's belly—"duty, I've but to crook my finger and His Grace will come running.

"And, believe me, my not-so-dear duchess," she finished with a smug smile, "I intend to crook it!"

Sabelle felt all the old fury returning, felt it as she had that night outside the retiring room at Almack's, even as she tried to deny Sarah's spiteful diatribe. Justin was no longer the hard, compassionless man he'd been then, she reminded herself, desperate to put the lie to the brunette's words. He had changed and so had she, for she'd grown far beyond the naïve child who'd thought to wreak a harsh revenge and remain untouched herself.

But you still haven't the one thing that would counter her claims, a small voice inside her cried. *He's never told you he loves you, and who is to say his present solicitousness is not for the child you carry—and nothing more? Even Justin's new-found capacity for compassion guarantees nothing. You crave his love, not his pity!*

Swallowing to moisten a throat suddenly gone dry, Sabelle banished the voice with a will and fastened on the one thing she could think of to daunt her antagonist.

"I have no doubt you will crook it, Lady Sarah, but do try to remember"—she placed her left hand in plain view, over the place where Justin's child rested—"it is *my* finger which wears his *ring!*"

Lady Sarah bared her teeth and would undoubtedly have hissed a retort, but a mature female voice intruded from behind her.

"I have both hartshorn and vinaigrette in my reticule, my dear, though I've never required either in my life," said Lady Strathmore. "But it is indeed fortunate that I have a ladies' maid who is given to fits of the vapors, for I always come away prepared, whether the ninny is with me or not. Now, which do you require?"

Sabelle had torn her gaze away from Sarah's face with great relief during this speech, and she now beheld not only the marchioness, but, behind her, Sir Jonathan and Justin, each looking at her with concern.

Suddenly feeling her mood lighten in this supporting company, Sabelle offered them a bright smile, though she spoke to Justin's grandmother as she rose briskly from the bench.

"Neither, m'lady, though I appreciate your concern. But I am feeling quite restored now, and I should be pleased if you would all join us in paying our respects to His Royal Highness."

While Justin and her grandfather inquired solicitously as to the certainty of these assurances, the dowager's quick glance took in the high color in Lady Sarah's face and the way her eyes raked Sabelle's petite figure before quickly shuttering. *Hmm, the she-cat has been unsheathing her claws, unless I miss my guess. This bears watching!*

Thomas appeared at that moment with a goblet of water, which Sabelle drank obligingly, although she again declined the hartshorn. Then they all made their way slowly to the ballroom. There the Regent, dressed, according to one of his stewards, as the god Apollo, held sway over his guests.

The Prince's costume immediately put the duke in mind of the lamentable fate of his friend, Leigh Hunt; the poet and critic was languishing in prison for two years for calling Prinny a "fat Adonis of fifty," and Justin remarked on this in a whispered aside to Sabelle.

Sabelle managed to contain a giggle upon hearing it, for, accoutered as he was, that was exactly what the Regent looked like.

Grossly overweight and florid-faced from his many excesses, the future king of England cut a ridiculous figure in the purple silk toga and golden laurel wreath he wore. He had a round, cherubic face that was set off by what was, perhaps, his best feature, a fine head of light brown hair. Yet, when they drew closer, Sabelle recalled some other redeeming qualities in his aspect which she remembered from the two or three times she'd encountered him before, during her Season. Despite his age, the prince was still boyish. There was a puckish quality to his face, a hint of mischief and even of innocence that was greatly at odds with that almost repulsively corpulent body.

So it was the Regent's face she made herself focus on when the prince raised her from her curtsy.

"My dear Haverleigh," he remarked to Justin after bestowing greetings on them both with an infectious smile, "how courageous of you to suffer your beauteous wife to attend *sans masque.*" Then, turning back to Sabelle: "But how fortunate for the rest of us!"

Sabelle felt herself flush as she murmured her thanks, but the Prince went on as if he hadn't noticed; he conversed amiably with Lady Strathmore and Sir Jonathan, greeted Lady Sarah and even the tutor with a graciousness that was worthy of his royal station. It was clear Prinny was in one of his more convivial moods (for he could be petulant and sulky when he chose), and they were all treated to a sample of the rare charm that had seen him dubbed the "First Gentleman in Europe."

The orchestra struck up a stately minuet as more guests claimed the Regent's attentions, and Justin offered to lead his wife on to the floor if she promised not to tax herself.

"You'd think I was made of the most precious glass!" laughed Sabelle as she gave him her promise.

"Not glass," she heard him whisper in her ear before they broke apart to take their positions, "but I own the rest is apt."

Jonathan and the dowager were standing to the side, watching their second-generation offspring during this exchange; and upon noting the color staining Sabelle's cheeks when her husband bent to whisper something in her ear, Jonathan murmured a comment Millicent didn't quite catch.

"What was that, Jonathan?"

"I said, it's clear the child's smitten, but there's such a thing as loving too much."

"Too much! How can she love too much?" the dowager snapped.

"When it isn't returned in kind, of course."

"Fiddle! It's entirely obvious to me, my grandson's besotted with her!"

"Millicent! Are you *certain?*" Jonathan's face held a radiant smile.

"Of course I'm certain. I had them both under my roof for weeks, hadn't I? And you would have seen it, too, if you hadn't been such a stubborn ninnyha——*Oh-oh!*"

"What is it, my dear? What's amiss?"

"A she-cat and a lemon-face who deal uncommonly well together, for such an odd pair."

Jonathan followed her gaze to where Sarah Cavendish and Thomas Long had their heads together as they slipped into one of Carlton House's many alcoves—this, a curtained one on the far side of the ballroom.

The dowager described what she'd witnessed between the earl's daughter and "our Sabelle" earlier, then went into a history of her reservations about Long.

"And the pair of them have been hovering about our ducal grandchildren like jackals about a pair of wounded deer," she finished while the baronet frowned uncertainly in the direction of the alcove.

"That does it!" said Jonathan as he hurriedly raised the Greek comic mask that had served as his costume before he'd lowered it to converse. "Wait here for me, my dear."

"But where—"

"When you appeal to me with such a simile—connected to the animals I cherish—I see it is time to act. In short, I am about to *spy* on that pair of jackals, dear Millicent, so stay put until I return."

With that, he hefted his cane and moved off in the direction of the alcove.

And several minutes later, he was infinitely glad he had. Standing near the alcove amid the crowd that thronged that side of the ballroom, Jonathan appeared to be watching the dancers while sipping some punch; instead, he listened intently to a conversation that had him scowling over those snatches he could make out amid the general noise.

". . . and how am I to secure enough time alone with Justin to . . ." Lady Sarah's voice.

". . . me to distract her . . . you pretend to faint . . . breath of air." Long's response.

". . . up to you to make sure she discovers us to-gether . . ." Again, Lady Sarah.

". . . at the end of the hallway in that . . . chamber," said Long.

Jonathan moved away as Sarah said something about "that little bitch duchess" and "bilious with jealousy." He had heard enough. The jackals were planning a bogus tryst between the duke and his former mistress to hurt Sabelle and discredit her husband in her eyes. Oh, he had to find the children and warn them!

But as the old man moved off in search of the couple, the crowd in the ballroom seemed even thicker than before. He could no longer even see the dance floor beyond the masked and bewigged heads that thronged close. Slowly, far more slowly than he wished, he inched his way through the revelers, hoping for a glimpse of a green medieval gown or a troubadour's cape.

Millicent began to grow impatient when Jonathan failed to return. He'd been gone for nearly twenty minutes, and the crowd had grown so thick that she could no longer see the alcove. In fact, she could see little of the entire ball-room, her field of vision having been narrowed to that small portion of the dance floor directly in front of her.

"How these imbeciles can pretend to dance in such a crush is beyond me," she remarked to Lady Bessborough, who was standing beside her.

"I do hope," said Bessborough with a smile, "that your intent was not to include His Grace, your grandson, in that attribution . . . nor his lovely wife and their friends, for that matter."

"My grandson? Where?"

"Why, I saw him waltz by a few moments ago . . . with Cavendish," Lady Bessborough added slyly.

The dowager frowned. Bessborough knew, of course, of Justin's former liaison with Sarah, as who did not? And the woman was not above carrying on a dalliance or two of her own, the most notable being a heavily rumored alliance with the Regent. But Cavendish's dancing with the duke, in light of what she'd glimpsed earlier, began to sound like the outside of enough! Oh, where *was* Jonathan, anyway, and what had he learned?

Sarah Cavendish smiled smugly to herself as Justin led her expertly through the waltz she'd coaxed out of him, despite the crowded floor. This press of whirling bodies was just the excuse she needed to engineer her ruse.

Suddenly Sarah seemed to stumble, and she clutched the duke's arm.

"Sarah, what is it? Are you—"

"Oh, Justin! Please, I feel . . . faint. Can—can you lead me—lead me away . . . somewhere? I need . . . I require some air!"

Justin nodded, beginning to think a knight's costume would have been more fitting, after all. It seemed to be an evening of rescuing beautiful women in danger of fainting.

As he led Sarah out a side door she indicated, his mind was not on his former mistress, however; it was on the miffed features of his wife, as they'd appeared when Sarah had maneuvered him into that dance. He'd have sworn the minx was jealous! Perhaps the time was near when he could tell her why she need never be—why his fidelity and his love were hers for a lifetime.

"I . . . there's a small chamber at the end of this corridor," said Sarah, "a—a small music room of some sort, as I recall from a previous visit. Could—could you help me to it, Justin?"

The duke hesitated, then nodded. He'd been raised as a gentleman, and the code of a gentleman involved seeing to the comfort of a lady. Even if that gentleman would rather be rescuing his wife from the company of a melancholy tutor, which was where Sabelle was right now.

Dammit! He hoped Sabelle's mood wasn't down to the ground by the time he got back to her.

Sabelle ran her eyes over Thomas's costume and, in an effort to make conversation while they waited for their partners' waltz to end, complimented him on it.

"That is a very excellent Richard the Lionheart, Mr. Long. What made you choose it, if I may ask?"

Thomas evinced a thin smile, wondering how many there tonight, including Her Grace, were aware the medieval English king had been one of history's confirmed homosexuals.

But to Sabelle he merely said, "The Lionheart cut a glamorous, kingly swath through an age that was really, for all its being written up as glorious, a dark and dreary period."

"Hmm," mused Sabelle. "I suppose so, yet by dying without offspring, he left our country at the mercy of his brother, wicked King John."

The scholar's brows rose a fraction. He'd forgotten Justin's wife was well read and better educated than most women. Did she guess, then, at his reasons for the costume? The little reference to Richard's lack of heirs of the body could mean she knew why he hadn't been able to sire any. If she was as bright and perceptive as Justin claimed— Bah! She was only an insignificant female, and his business with her right now was to eliminate her from Justin's life!

"Oh, speaking of medieval figures, His Grace does very handsomely as a troubadour, does he not?" He gazed pointedly at a pair of figures on the dance floor.

Sabelle smiled as she thought of her husband and the handsome figure he cut—in and out of troubadour's garb! —and followed Long's gaze to the floor.

The smile faded as she saw Sarah Cavendish dancing in Justin's arms, a flirtatious look on her face as she gazed up at him.

"A pity you weren't up to the crush of the dance floor, Your Grace," said Long. "But I do think Lady Sarah and His Grace do well together, don't you?"

"They—they dance very nicely."

"Indeed, and His Grace seems to have gotten over his war injury completely. I wonder if it was all that exercise he took with Lady Sarah while you were, ah, ill."

"With *Lady Sarah?*"

The tutor glanced at her, a look of pity evident on his dour features. "Why, yes, as I'm certain His Grace explained to you. Yours was a lengthy recovery, you know, and there were times when those walks, or rides in Hyde Park, with Cavendish were the only release your husband had. Awfully tedious, sitting by a sickbed day after day, after all."

"I see," said Sabelle in a small voice, though her heart was hammering and there was a constriction about her chest that felt like pain. He'd *stayed by her side, day and night,* they'd all told her. Had they all lied to her? Had *Justin* lied to her? Oh, God, if—

"Now, that's peculiar," Long's voice interrupted.

Dully, Sabelle followed his gaze again. "What is?" she replied automatically, not really caring.

"Well, His Grace and Lady Sarah have left the dance floor . . . too crowded, I suppose . . . and I naturally thought they'd be coming our way . . ."

"Yes?" Sabelle urged as his words trailed off on a note of innuendo.

"Something must be amiss, Your Grace. They've just left the ballroom by that doorway there," said the tutor in a puzzled voice.

"What—what could be a-amiss?" Sabelle stammered. But she knew . . . Justin and Sarah, gone off alone together—that's what was amiss!

Long was very solicitous as he took her hand and patted it. "There, there, Your Grace. I'm sure it's nothing. But if you like, we can follow them . . . just to be certain . . . ?"

Swallowing back the tears that threatened, Sabelle nodded bleakly and allowed him to lead her through the crowd.

Sarah smiled up at Justin as she leaned against a pianoforte in the small music room.

"Yes, much better, Justin, darling," she murmured. "So good of you to be concerned."

"My pleasure, m'lady. Now, shall we—"

"I recall a time when it was always your pleasure, you know." Sarah's eyes were sultry as she gazed up at him through half-lowered lashes.

Justin stiffened. "A long time ago, and well in the past, Sarah."

Her eyes opened fully, and Sarah studied his face. This was not going at all as she'd intended. Justin didn't seem the least bit susceptible to her charms, and the plan—Dammit! She'd have to engineer something quickly, or lose this chance!

"I understand, Justin, darling," she told him, "but I do hope—Oh, dear! Oh, God, I've a cinder or something—Justin, I've something in my eye, and it hurts like the devil!"

Sarah collapsed toward him, one hand braced against his chest, the other covering her eye.

Justin sighed with exasperation, then took Sarah's head between his hands to see if he could discover the offending cinder. Carefully, he studied the eye she'd indicated . . .

And that was how Sabelle and the tutor discovered them as they burst into the room.

❖Chapter 31❖

SABELLE STARED AT HER HUSBAND AS HE held Sarah's head and gazed into her face. She saw his former mistress's thinly clad body pressed intimately against his; and she saw, too, that she ought never to have followed Long into this chamber.

"Let me go!" she demanded of Thomas when he held her arm.

Justin's head swung to the doorway as he tore his hands away from Sarah. "Sabelle! What—"

"Have we done something wrong?" Sarah inquired in tones that stretched credence.

Long stepped aside to allow the ashen-faced duchess to depart, but at that moment two white-haired figures rushed in from the corridor, nearly knocking Sabelle and the tutor off their feet.

"It's all a sham, Your Grace!" Jonathan shouted.

"It's a wicked plot!" cried the dowager.

Justin's eyes darted to his wife as she fell into a chair by the door, then went back to the two older people who stood glaring at the tutor. "What the deuce is going on?"

"A plot," said Jonathan with something akin to murder in his eyes as he continued to glare at Long.

"She's in on it!" cried Justin's grandmother as she walked toward Sarah and pointed a finger at her.

"And so is he!" Jonathan pulled Long by the arm until

they were both standing in front of the duke. "Your Grace, this man who claims to be your friend—"

"I *am* his friend!" snapped Thomas.

"Such friendship would make me cautious, indeed, of my enemies!" spat Jonathan.

"Of which you are one, no matter what you say!" accused the marchioness. "And so is this—this *baggage*, here!" She gestured angrily at Sarah.

"I overheard their entire scheme," Jonathan said, and he went on to explain everything he'd learned of the contrived tryst plotted in the alcove.

"Thomas?" Justin questioned, stunned. "Is this true? I mean, Sarah's involvement, I can see, but I find it hard to—"

"Of course it's true!" shrieked Sarah. "Because neither of us could bear to see you throwing your life away on that little—"

"But, *why?*" asked Justin, his eyes still on his old friend. *"Why, Thomas?"*

Thomas shook off Jonathan's clasp on his arm with a gesture of contempt; then he straightened and looked at his former pupil, his eyes clouded with pain.

"You really don't know, do you?" He paused then, the silence in the room punctuated only by intermittent sniffles from Sarah, who clutched a handkerchief.

"Can't you guess?" Thomas went on. "Look at me, Justin! *Can't you guess?*"

Justin searched his eyes and then wished he hadn't. "Thomas . . . I don't—"

"I've loved you for years!" the tutor cried, at last breaking down. "Oh, yes, *years,* and you never knew! I couldn't let you know, could I? You, the austere, virile duke of Haverleigh—military hero and virtuoso in the bedchamber—but only *ladies'* bedchambers, isn't that so?

"But all these years, I've loved you just the same, loved you and wanted y——"

"Stop it!" Justin shouted. "Thomas, for God's sake, please stop! Isn't it enough that you've cheapened your—whatever feelings you bear me by this tawdry little game, which you had to know would hurt Sabelle? Must you now also—*Christ!*" Justin's eyes flew to the chair by the door. *"Where's Sabelle?"*

"Good God! She's gone!" murmured Jonathan as the duke leaped past him.

"That's it, my boy!" the dowager called after him. "Go and find her, and tell her the truth. *We'll* deal with these jackals!"

Sabelle ran blindly past the marble columns of Carlton House's entry hall, her eyes blurred by tears. Whatever was taking place back there in the music room, she didn't want to hear it or see it. She'd had enough!

She swiped at the tears coursing down her cheeks with an angry hand and asked a startled footman to summon their carriage. As she waited, again a tear trickled, and again, she wiped it away. It was as if, with each swipe, she could rub out the image that savaged her mind. *Justin and Sarah— Oh, God!*

Presently the duke's carriage arrived, and Sabelle stormed toward it in a fury. If she could just keep the pain at bay with anger, then she'd be all right.

"Where to, Your Grace?" The driver's question startled her. In the distance she could hear firecrackers, and the noise of a crowd. Of course, it was still Guy Fawkes Day!

But not the happy one you expected, said that small voice inside her head.

All at once Sabelle smiled, though bitterly, as some perverse sense took over. "Take me to the Shakespeare's Head Tavern," she told the driver.

Justin reached the portico nearly out of breath. He was just in time to see his carriage pass through the gates and into the crowded street.

"Damn!" he swore as his eyes raked a pair of young footmen. "Bring me my grandmother's carriage—you know it . . . the marchioness of Wincanton's . . . blue and silver . . . finely matched bays. Fetch it quickly, please!" He tossed some coins at them.

One of the footmen leaped to do his bidding, while the

other ran for the greatcoat he'd brought to the ball with him.

The carriage and coat appeared in short order, and as Justin made for the vehicle, wondering where to begin yet another search for his wife, the immediate problem was solved for him.

"Er . . . Yer Grace?"

He looked back to see one of the young footmen fidgeting nervously with some gold braid on his livery. "Yes? What is it?"

The youth glanced at the three guineas in his hand—more than he'd ever hoped to see as a gratuity in a month of balls—and swallowed past the lump that had formed in his throat on encountering the duke's stern visage. "I'd 'urry if I wuz you, Yer Grace. Th' Shakespeare's 'Ead ain't no place fer a lady, 'specially one alone."

The duke's brow rose a fraction, and then the servant saw him frown. Digging into his pockets, Justin extracted a fistful of gold sovereigns and showered them over the speechless footman's boots.

"My thanks," the duke added as he bounded into his grandmother's carriage. Then he called to the driver, "The Shakespeare's Head, and there's some good coin in it for you if you know a shortcut!"

Sabelle clutched her reticule tightly in her lap as she felt the carriage sway and roll, then come to a stop, then roll again. The crowds along Piccadilly were so thick, the vehicle could advance only in stops and starts, a few yards at a time. And the noise outside was close to deafening, the shouts and laughter of the holiday revelers punctuated by neighing horses and fireworks exploding in the background.

Yet none of these accounted for her tightly gripping fingers or the way her small jaw clenched below the contours of her mask. Rather, it was her determination to avoid thinking about the incident which had promoted this trek across half of London, or the nature of the impulse which had launched it.

She decided to focus on her destination as a means of

keeping unwanted thoughts at bay. What, in heaven's name, did she intend to do when she got there?

You can have a late supper, a small, practical voice answered.

But, a woman, unescorted? She recalled Covent Garden wasn't the most savory part of town.

But you're costumed and masked, said the voice. *No one will ever know who you are. And if you're clever, and affect the right accent, and act as if you belong there . . .*

There, it was settled. She would leave the carriage a bit of a distance from the tavern, blend in with the revelers along the way, and have a quiet supper in one of the private rooms. Then, perhaps, with a full stomach, she could see her way clear to thinking about—

Not now! said the practical voice. *You're in no mood to think of it now.*

Settling back against the squabs of the carriage seat, Sabelle was only too glad to comply.

It took another half-hour to reach the western end of Covent Garden Market; there she had to use the full authority of her position as the duchess of Haverleigh to persuade Justin's driver and groom to let her alight and then promise to stay with the carriage until she returned. In the end they only acquiesced when she threatened not to return at all, but hire a hackney to go home.

Then she made her way slowly through the densely packed crowd. But at last she found herself standing before the building bearing a large wooden sign with the head of William Shakespeare painted on it. Merrymakers jostled her from every direction, many of them not in costume at all, but clad in the plain garments of their trades. Garishly painted whores laughed with aproned butchers' apprentices, and ragged beggars cried their need in the midst of rough-looking characters. Her months as a climbing boy stood her in good stead here, for she had no doubt these were flash coves, pickpockets, and other highly specialized thieves.

Squaring her shoulders with confidence, she entered the tavern.

Inside, it was smoky and even noisier than outside. The common room's low, heavy-beamed ceiling trapped the smoke given off by dozens of lamps and candles. The thick stucco walls did little to dampen the sounds of numerous conversations interspersed with raucous laughter and the shouts of barmaids and waiters.

She was about to try claiming the attention of a harried-looking barmaid when she felt a tug at the green-velvet cape she'd flung over her shoulders as an outer wrap.

"Well, wot 'ave we 'ere?" asked a crude male voice as the cape slid off her shoulders.

Sabelle gasped and whirled about to face a table seating four disreputable-looking men, the nearest of whom was holding her cape, while they all hooted with laughter.

The one who held her cape gave a low whistle when he found himself at eye level with a pair of ripe breasts swelling above the square décolletage of the medieval-style gown.

"Blimey, coves!" he said to his companions. "But if this don't be a rum blowen fit fer tuppin'!"

More laughter, and one of his fellows called out to the barmaid, " 'Ere, Meg! Fetch us a pint fer th' rum moll!"

By now the first one had shoved his chair back and placed a huge, callused hand on her arm, clearly intent on pulling her into his lap.

Sabelle stiffened, and was trying to extricate herself, when, out of nowhere, a flash of red velvet interposed, and the ruffian's hold on her was broken.

"Touch her again, and you're finished," said a voice cased in steel.

Justin! Even as recognition flashed into her conscious-ness, Sabelle's head snapped about and she beheld the handsome, forbidding visage of her husband. His eyes were silver daggers aimed directly at the man who held her cape.

"I believe you have something that belongs to the lady," Justin said in a voice that was dangerously soft.

Resentment flashed across the man's coarse features, while around them, Sabelle noticed, the common room had grown quiet.

"Wot if I 'ave?" the lout sneered.

"Take more than five seconds to return it, and find out," came the softly menacing response.

The man gathered a breath as if to speak, then for the first time looked into the duke's eyes—really looked—and saw death. Swallowing convulsively, he quickly handed over the cape.

Justin took it and, without a word, wrapped it around his wife, the gesture undeniably possessive.

The men at the table relaxed visibly as he led her away from it, but Sabelle felt her tension mounting, especially when she saw they were not heading for the door.

"Where—where are we going?" she questioned uncertainly above the noise that had resumed about them.

Her husband offered a sardonic grin. "What? Lost your taste for intrigue, m'lady? Or should I call you *Samantha* again?"

Sabelle sucked in her breath at the reference to what had happened there a year ago. But before she could concoct a response, he was ushering her up the stairs and into an all-too-familiar private chamber.

Sabelle froze in place, while, behind her, Justin shut the door. He had obviously anticipated this! A fire was burning pleasantly in the grate, and, on the central table she remembered all too well, stood an array of food, a wine bottle, and two goblets.

"You—how did you know I'd be here?" she asked as she whirled to face him. "And how did you manage to arrive before me?"

Justin gave her an offhanded shrug, then closed the distance between them. He began to remove her mask and headdress.

"It wasn't really that difficult," he told her as he tossed the articles of concealment aside and met her eyes; she saw that his had all at once grown serious. "What *was* difficult was trying to figure out *why you'd chosen to come here.*"

Sabelle tried to look away but couldn't. It was the question she'd been evading since she decided to go there. Now, gazing into those compelling gray eyes, she knew she had to answer.

"I . . . I wished to go to the one place I knew would—would remind me of why I ought to hate you."

"Ought?" he asked softly.

Dropping her gaze, she nodded, but Justin had already caught the hurt in her eyes.

"Sabelle, I know what you thought you saw in that music room, but, had you remained long enough to hear, you'd have learned the truth—and perhaps realized something I've been trying to show you with my every action for weeks.

"Sabelle, women like Sarah Cavendish no longer have a place in my life. They are all a part of the past, and no piece of the future I envision. Can you understand that?"

"She—she spoke to me earlier and—and said that—it was the thing you once wrote to Thomas Long—that you wed me for the sole purpose of breeding heirs—no other!"

Justin heaved a ragged sigh, then took her chin and cupped it, forcing her to meet his eyes.

"When you were lying in that bed, unconscious, the physician gave me the news that you carried our child—and that it appeared unharmed. He thought to cheer me, I suppose, with the thought that my future heir had survived, even—even though we both knew the mother might not.

"And do you know what I did, Sabelle? *I dismissed it from my mind.* Utterly! Because I'd suddenly realized that the only one who mattered was you. In my blind, stumbling, all-too-slow journey to the truth, I'd found out who mattered to me, and I was terrified it was *too late!* Sabelle, don't you realize what I'm trying to say? *I love you!* Not for the child you carry, not for any reason a hundred Sarah Cavendishes can threaten, but for *you* . . . willful, independent, maddening, and adorable creature that you are—*you!*"

Hot tears stung Sabelle's eyes as she heard the words she'd never dared to hope for. She blinked them aside, intent upon her husband's face as she searched it for the truth.

It was there, along with a look of love so profound, it shook her to her toes.

"Oh, Justin!" she cried, her voice catching on a sob. "I've loved you for ever so long!"

Justin closed his eyes as he drew her against him, emotion clogging his throat. She loved him! Miracle of miracles, she didn't hate him, she—

"Sabelle?" He murmured her name in a voice none too steady. "Did you say 'for ever so long'?"

Blissful in his arms, she nodded, then drew partly away to gaze shyly up at him. "Ever—ever since Harthaven."

Justin looked stunned. "Harthaven? Not when—not after I rescued Tommy and . . ."

His disbelieving words trailed off as she slowly moved her head from side to side, her eyes shining with love.

"But I'd done nothing to merit—"

Her fingers stilled his lips, and she smiled up at him through the drying tears. "Merit has little to do with the heart's choices, my darling."

"But I was a heartless bast——"

Again her fingers touched his lips. "So you seemed to us all, and it was thinking that which made me run away. My *mind* told me to flee, Justin, but my *heart* was already yours. Perhaps . . . perhaps it already knew who you really were . . . what you've since become. Oh, Justin, please, don't stand there gaping at me as if I've gone mad! I felt I *ought* to hate you, but—"

All at once she was in his arms as he held her tightly, his lips against her hair. The softness and fragrance of it permeated his senses, and his very soul was caught up in the sweet, painful joy of the moment.

Presently, but ever so gently, he loosed her and brought his hands to cup her face and look at her. He read the love residing deep within her eyes and moved his lips to breathe her name—

"Sabelle . . . beloved . . ."

She gave a small ecstatic cry, and then their lips met in a kiss that held all the joy, and hope, and love in their hearts, healing the long months of separation and doubt, making them whole.

At last Justin raised his head and, never taking his eyes from her face, led her to the bed by the wall.

"Once, in this room," he told her, "I took from you something of great value, something that could never be restored. Now, on this night, I offer you the only thing I can, in its place—my heart. I love you, little one . . . I love you."

And as he murmured words of love and praise, he began undressing her. Tenderly, almost reverently, he removed the pieces of costume and set them aside.

But when at last she stood in her shift and he began to untie the ribbons fastened below her breasts . . .

"No," she whispered.

Justin stopped immediately and touched the side of her face with a gentle hand. "Sabelle . . . ? What is it, love?"

There was a pause as Sabelle looked up at him with huge, uncertain eyes. "I . . . I wouldn't have you find me . . . displeasing, Justin. The scar . . . from my wound—"

It was Justin's turn to still her lips. "Never say so, Sabelle. That wound—this scar," he added as he slipped the shift off her shoulder and downward, until it fell at her feet —"is a badge of honor . . . and courage . . . and perhaps the most beautiful thing about the loveliest creature on earth . . ."

Kneeling before her, he ran his hands lightly down her unclad body until he reached the small, puckered scar below her ribcage. Then, ever so tenderly, as if it were an act of homage, he pressed his lips to the ravaged flesh while Sabelle closed her eyes and whispered his name like a prayer.

Justin rose and took her in his arms. "Never, never say so," he whispered. And then he claimed her lips in a kiss that was at first gentle, but soon began to grow into something more.

Justin felt her warm flesh under his hands, felt her arms slide eagerly around his neck, and suddenly knew a hunger so great, it left him reeling. His hands moved to her breasts; tip-tilted and proud, they seemed to seek his touch, and he felt the heat build in his loins. "Sabelle . . ." he whispered raggedly as his lips slid to her ear, "Sabelle, it's been *so long*. Sweet love . . . ah, woman, how I want you!"

Giddy with need, Sabelle began to pull and tear at his clothes, frantic to remove this last barrier between them. "Justin . . . Justin, I want you, too! I want to feel—oh, help me, please!"

Justin laughed, a deep, throaty chuckle, stilling her hands while he began to shed the garments himself. "So eager, love? Ah, but that was always something I loved about you . . . your response to my slightest touch. . . ."

The last of his clothing hit the floor, and he demonstrated by lightly grazing the tips of her breasts with his thumbs.

Sabelle shuddered, feeling the familiar curling sensation deep in her belly.

". . . and your readiness so soon after we begin. . . ."

Again, he showed her, trailing a finger downward, until it slipped into the cleft where she was already hot and wet—

—and quivering with need: "Justin, please!" she cried. "Don't make me wai-"

But he had dropped, suddenly, to his knees again, and before she could guess what he intended, she felt his mouth on her.

Shock was her immediate reaction, but before she could pull away or think, he clasped the rounded curves of her buttocks and held her to him, and then—*and then!*

Sabelle cried his name as a spear of pleasure shot through her—once, and then again—

"Justin," she sobbed. *"Justin!"* His tongue passed deftly over the tiny bud above her nether lips, and with each stroke, her pleasure broke anew. . . . thrice . . . a fourth time, until her knees began to buckle, no longer able to support legs that had turned to jelly while ecstasy sluiced through her body.

Justin felt her grip his shoulders for support and guessed the cause. He stood, taking her with him, and a moment later they were on the bed, their mouths locked in a kiss as fierce as it was sensual. Sabelle tasted herself on his tongue, and this reminder of that intimate act renewed her hunger. She became a wild thing, arching against the hard male length of him, until there could be no doubt what she craved.

Again, Justin laughed, but it was a ragged, breathless sound, for his own need was great. But when he'd risen above her, his manhood poised between her parted thighs, he summoned the last of his control and forced them both to pause.

"Hush," he whispered, stilling her frantic body and sweeping her hair back from her face to frame it with his hands. "Sabelle . . . look at me."

She complied, though her breath came in gasps and she quivered beneath him.

Justin gazed into two limpid pools of deep aquamarine, and a shudder ran through him, forestalling speech.

His words, when they came, were an echo in the still chamber. "This," he murmured thickly as she felt his shaft press against the place where his mouth had been, "is for love, Sabelle. . . ." He let the first penetrating thickness spread her lips. "Now, love! Take me home!"

And she did, welcoming the thick, hard length of him as he drove into her, and she heard herself crying his name aloud. His own harsh cry echoed hers as he thrust again, deeper, harder, claiming her with his body as he'd claimed her with his heart.

Together, they pulsed and moved, finding the rhythm, sustaining it, until their bodies blended into a single spiral of white-hot passion that strained toward impossible heights.

"Yes!" Sabelle cried as they reached those heights and the final release came. "Ah, Justin, *yes!*"

Justin answered her cry with a shout that was her name, while his seed spewed hotly into her and they reached the peak as one.

Then, their love shimmering in the air, they collapsed in each other's arms.

❖Chapter 32❖

$\mathcal{T}$HE FIRE BURNED LOW IN THE GRATE, AND A guttering candle on the table sent shadows leaping against the wall, but Sabelle and Justin paid these no heed as they conversed desultorily on the bed.

"When did you begin to love me?" Sabelle inquired softly as she lightly traced a whorl of dark hair on her husband's chest.

Justin ran his fingertip along the full curve of her breast and slowly circled the pink crest before answering with a lazy smile. "I think it was the day I saw you absconding with a fox beneath the very noses of—"

"*But that was—!*"

"I know."

"But I thought you said that when you—"

Justin reached down to capture her mouth with an unhurried, thorough kiss. When he had finished, he held her adoring gaze and grazed the fullness of her lower lip with his thumb as he spoke.

"I said it was my fear of losing you, during your convalescence, that made me *realize* I loved you. But when you ask me to think back, now, to its beginnings . . ."

He sighed deeply, with pleasure, and drew her even closer against him.

"All it wanted was to ask myself when your appearance in my life began to change it forever—and that, my love, had to be answered: On the first day I saw you standing there in that meadow with your beloved dog and that poor, befuddled fox.''

Sabelle chuckled, but there was a note of curiosity in her voice, too. "And here I thought you believed me to be the more impossible sort of hoyden—or worse—an incorrigible child.''

Justin laughed. "That, too, but a child who touched me in a way that allowed me to reach into the best part of my own childhood . . . and find my way back.''

"Back?" she questioned softly.

He shifted until he was leaning on one elbow, looking down at her. The gray eyes were clear and unwavering as they met hers.

"In each of us," Justin said, "if he is allowed to develop fully, the clear, simple truths and perceptions of childhood provide a foundation that underlies the adult he becomes. Do you recall a poem by Mr. Wordsworth, one we read together once, wherein he begins, 'The child is father to the man'?''

Sabelle nodded. "The 'Ode on Intimations of Immortality—' ''

"—'from Recollections of Early Childhood,' '' Justin finished.

Again, Sabelle nodded. "I remember thinking, when we finished reading it, that I was so awfully lucky to have had Grandfather beside me as I was growing up, because he taught me to explore and hold on to the wonders I saw as a child and use them to nurture my view of the world as an adult. It's—it's what feeds my idealism to this very day, I fear.''

A strong male finger came up and stilled her lips. "Never say you *fear* it, sweetheart. Because there you have the very essence of what that little hoyden—and this little duchess,'' he added as he playfully tapped her nose, "had, to make her a truly whole human being. And which a fourteen-year-old boy lost once, long ago—and found again only when you showed him how.''

He went on, then, to tell her what had happened on that day after he'd discovered the sordid truth about his par-

ents' marriage and allowed it to rob him of the innocence
and wonder he now believed were a child's legacy to take
with him into adulthood.

Wide-eyed and solemn, Sabelle listened to the account,
which ended with his description of the tragic death of a
young sweep, from burns suffered under cruel conditions
with which she was all too familiar.

"And so, you see, it was *fear* which kept me from allowing myself *to feel what was mine, by right, to feel*, Sabelle.
I hadn't the courage to take the chance I might be hurt
that way again—and no Jonathan Burke to show me a better way. The two people I'd depended on to do that were
my parents—and they were the very root, the source, of the
pain that drove me from it."

Sabelle's hand went out to smooth the furrows etching
his brow, then moved to cover the barely discernible swelling of her belly. "This little one," she whispered as emotion clogged her speech, "will benefit from that loss you
suffered, my darling."

"He *will*," Justin said fiercely. Then, just as fiercely, he
pulled her beneath him, gazing intently into her eyes. "I
love you, Sabelle—more than my life—*I love you.*"

"And I, you, my darling," Sabelle murmured through
joyful tears.

She felt herself clasped, then, in an embrace that was as
tender as it was fierce, and they both knew it would be a
long time until they slept . . . *a long, long time* . . .

It was late morning when they left the Shakespeare's Head.
Their clothing and toilettes had been refreshed through
articles delivered by a footman in a portmanteau the duke
had sent for the night before. A message had been sent to
their family via the same footman, that all was well. So,
between their immaculate grooming and these written
words of reassurance, it was hoped no one would guess the
duke and duchess of Haverleigh had spent the night making love in a Covent Garden tavern.

Of course, that supposed no one noticed the way they
looked into each other's eyes . . . or the way the proud

duke seemed unable to keep his hands off his wife, finding reasons to touch her hair, her hand, her arm, even in public . . . or the way Her Grace gazed adoringly at her husband with dreamy aquamarine eyes . . .

When they finally arrived at their destination—the dowager's house, to determine what had become of a pair of "jackals"—it was nearly noon, but, again because of a messenger, the family was expecting them.

As Sabelle followed the majordomo into the drawing room on Justin's arm, her thoughts centered on the astounding things her husband had told her, of what had happened in that music room at Carlton House the night before. She had readily accepted the fact that a plot had been afoot to discredit Justin's allegiance to his wife, not to mention her perceptions of the duke's feelings toward her; it was enough to know Sarah Cavendish was involved, and then to see the love residing deep in her husband's eyes, to know that what she'd witnessed had been a sham.

But to be told of Thomas Long's involvement! That it arose out of a secret, unnatural—She couldn't even think the word *love*, in connection with Long's motivation; it was too unsettling and alien a concept for her to grasp . . .

An image of some ugly things hinted at by her captors in the East End kennel came to mind, and Sabelle shoved it hurriedly aside as they reached the drawing room and a chorus of greetings welcomed them.

"My dears!" Jonathan Burke's eyes held warmth and tenderness as he arose from a settee beside the fire and met them before they could cross the room. "I won't ask how you are," he added as he clasped his granddaughter's hands and swept their faces with a shrewd, canny gaze. "The looks on your faces speak for themselves."

"And about time, too!" said the dowager as she came forward to bestow a warm embrace on each of them. "Playing Cupid's assistant over such an extended period of time has proved no easy task, I assure you, and at my age— Oh, Henry, do behave yourself!"

They all glanced down to see the marchioness's orange-striped cat insinuating itself between her skirt and Jonathan's boots.

"Henry?" Justin queried as Jonathan held out his arms and the cat sprang into them.

The duke was astounded to see his grandmother blush before she turned and motioned them all to be seated. "Just a minor correction that was long overdue," she murmured as she swept to one of the pair of settees by the fire.

"Along with a rather major one," Jonathan added cryptically, with a wink for the duke and duchess as he joined her and settled Henry on his lap.

But as she and Justin took their seats across from them, Sabelle noticed her grandfather had taken the dowager's hand and was cradling it tenderly, along with the cat on his lap.

"Now," said the marchioness, her tone suddenly brisk and businesslike, "before we enjoy the luncheon I've arranged—"

"To celebrate," Jonathan interrupted with a twinkle in his eyes, "the successful conclusion to the efforts of that 'upstart bungler, Cupid,' I believe you said, my dear."

"Indeed," said the dowager, "but before I—Oh, bother! I suppose there's no help for it but to tell you the agreeable news first." She slid a sidelong glance at Jonathan. "It seems Miss MacDougal and Mr. Kelly are to be wed, and—"

"Oh, but that's splendid!" exclaimed Sabelle, clapping her hands.

Justin added his approval, and there followed a brief discussion of the date and timetable for the wedding, as well as the dowager's news that the engaged couple would be joining them shortly for the celebratory luncheon.

"Now, then," said Millicent briskly when this had been concluded, "I think we need to—"

"My dear . . ." Jonathan interrupted with an arch look at the dowager.

For the second time in his life Justin saw his grandmother blush.

"Really, Jonathan," she said with only the briefest of

glances at the man beside her, "can it not wait? I would so like to put this other, awkward, business behind us."

Jonathan patted the hand he'd been holding and nodded, an odd warmth in his eyes. "Of course, my dear . . . something like a good-news sandwich, with a bit of bitter relish in between, eh?"

Millicent's blush seemed to deepen. But she offered Jonathan one of her rare, warm smiles before clearing her throat with a loud "Harumph!" and beginning again.

"I take it Justin has enlightened you as to what transpired between those jackals at Carlton House," she said to Sabelle.

Sabelle nodded, and the dowager's gaze shifted to her grandson. "But what you were unable to tell her, Justin, because you were as yet unenlightened yourself, was the true extent of the villainy of that—that catamite dressed in tutor's clothing!"

The marchioness shuddered suddenly, unable to fend off the thought of how much worse it could all have been, had Long's appetites been directed toward children . . . toward the boy her grandson had been.

She recovered quickly, however, and put a question to the duke. "How goes it with the Bow Street contingent?"

Justin's brows rose a fraction at this apparent change in topic, but he answered easily. "No news that I'm aware of, though I'll admit I've been otherwise . . . preoccupied of late." He pulled Sabelle's hand from her lap and held it against the hard plane of his thigh as his eyes coursed warmly over her.

"Exactly," said his grandmother, "and for the same reasons, I have not had the opportunity to tell you that *I did* receive some news regarding that business of mutual interest to us both."

"Go on," said the duke, more alert now.

"Upon a suspicion which was aroused by some odd behavior exhibited by that dropface of late, I took the liberty of having his rooms searched."

"And the result?" She had Justin's full attention now.

"A miniature bearing the likeness of someone we both

knew turned up, tucked away beneath a stack of small-clothes in a chest of drawers."

"A likeness—of whom?" Justin's voice was barely audible.

"Of Vanessa Hart, the late duchess of Haverleigh and your mother." The clipped response indicated how thoroughly his grandmother was holding her emotions in check.

Justin blinked as he tried to digest this news, but it was Sabelle who voiced confusion. "But how does that signify when we now know Long to be—"

"Nevertheless, he somehow contrived to become my daughter's lover," the dowager cut in, "and to impregnate her as well. In short, he was responsible for . . ."—briefly, her voice faltered, but Millicent forced the strength back into it and continued—". . . for the botched termination of a pregnancy that ended her life."

"*Thomas* was the unknown lover who demanded the abortion?" Justin queried incredulously. *"Thomas?"*

The dowager nodded. "Although I didn't readily comprehend why, myself—until I questioned the jackal last night.

"You see," she went on, "when he'd admitted to carrying a certain . . . *tendre* for you, my boy, it all began to come together. I forced myself to examine him—thoroughly . . . the look in his eyes as they focused on you . . . the way his voice sounded when he spoke to you . . . Ah, yes, I told myself: Millicent, you have seen these things before—decades ago, when the object of that creature's affections was not my grandson, but my daughter's husband!"

"My father?"

At Justin's dumbfounded query, Jonathan, who'd felt Millicent's hand begin to tremble in his, took up the telling. In a few succinct sentences he explained how the dowager had questioned Thomas on the circumstances of his relationship with the late duke and duchess, and how the tutor had broken down and confessed everything to them —his homosexual affair with Derek Hart, the affair with

Vanessa to keep Derek from his wife's bed, the forced abortion that ended in Vanessa's death; all of it.

And when he'd finished, he took his handkerchief and gently wiped away the single tear that coursed down the dowager's cheek: her one concession to a lifetime rule of never venting one's "maudlin emotions" for others to see.

Missing none of this, nor her husband's grim-faced silence in the face of such shattering revelations, Sabelle was the first to speak. "That poor, tortured creature . . ."

Millicent glanced at her sharply. "My daughter?"

Sabelle sighed. "Her, too, of course, but I was speaking of Thomas."

The dowager frowned and drew a breath as if to argue, but Justin's voice claimed their attention first.

"Sabelle is correct, of course . . . as usual," he added as he turned to bestow a tender smile on his wife. "In matters of compassion, my love, I suspect you'll always be the first among us to see into the heart of things."

Justin sighed wearily, then met his grandmother's eyes. His own held more than a hint of sadness.

"Forgive me, m'lady, if I no longer seem to have a stomach for the vengeance, or even the justice, we spoke of when we agreed to pursue this matter years ago.

"But, now that I know the truth, I fear I can no longer summon up a desire to see the man punished—no matter what his crimes. Because I think"—sadly, he shook his head—"Thomas has been punished enough already—perhaps for years . . .

"Poor Thomas . . ." he went on. "It all begins to make some sense now . . . the fanatical idealism that sent him chasing after rainbows he couldn't hope to hold . . . caught in the prison of his own mind, just as, perhaps, he was caught in the prison of his own body—neither his ideals nor his physical desires were within the realm of the attainable, given society's restraints, and so he was destined to fail in each of these spheres."

Jonathan nodded. "I spoke to him at length at your wedding and quickly learned of his passion for social reform. At first, I began to think I'd found a kindred spirit. I cannot deny my own idealism and the passion it has inspired.

"But the differences between us quickly became apparent," Jonathan went on. "Where Long became an ineffectual extremist—chasing after rainbows, as you put it, I simply sought to do the things I was able to do—in my own small way—to make some difference in the world."

"And taught me to do the same," said Sabelle with a warm smile for her grandfather.

Justin's smile was for both of them. "And now it has become my turn, as well, and I only regret I've come to it so late."

"Better late than never, my boy!" exclaimed Millicent with an indecipherable look at Jonathan. "But I think you haven't yet told Sabelle what Jonathan has told me it is you plan to do in your newly acquired, ah, *practical* idealism."

Sabelle turned to her husband with surprise. "Told me?"

"I haven't had the chance, love," he replied with a smile. "But what my grandmother is speaking of is something I discussed with your grandfather at the time I made the arrangements to adopt Tommy."

He paused and grabbed both her hands, turning her toward him on the settee. There was a look of barely contained excitement in his eyes, along with the warmth that was always there these days when he looked at her.

"What would you say, love, if I told you that, right now, at Harthaven, I've men working on expanding the facilities of a small farm which was no longer in use since its tenant passed away a year ago—to turn it into a home for rescued . . . innocents, I suppose we might call the—"

"Justin!" cried Sabelle as an incredulous joy lit her face. "You cannot mean—"

"I mean a place which will be a haven for those poor, abused animals you seem so fond of picking up, as well as a home for children who've suffered—"

"Oh, Justin!" Sabelle flung herself into his arms, nearly toppling them both over the carved rosewood arm of the settee. "I think I shall explode, I love you so!"

Justin laughed as he caught her to him, and there was laughter from the other settee as well.

"Well, Millicent," said Jonathan when their mirth had quieted, "it appears this good-news sandwich is to have three layers."

"Jonathan," said the dowager, "your odd metaphors are in danger of becoming depressingly ornate."

"Fiddle!" he replied, picking up one of her own expressions with a mischievous look in his eye. "But I fear it is you, and not I, who's been shilly-shallying, my girl, so I suggest you tell them outright—or shall I?"

There was a pause.

"Well . . . ?" said Jonathan, grinning at her with what Sabelle thought was a decidedly wicked gleam in his eye.

The dowager shot him the look that had had many a lesser mortal quaking in his boots, but the old baronet merely chuckled, and he gave her hand an affectionate pat.

"Jonathan and I," she said at last, "are to marry."

And as Sabelle squealed with delight and he offered his own congratulations, Justin noticed his grandmother blush for exactly the third time in his life.

❖Epilogue❖

THE DUCHESS OF HAVERLEIGH STOOD BESIDE a horse paddock on the piece of property her husband had named Sam's Farm and smiled at the two dark-haired figures at the far end of the enclosure. Three-year-old Lord Jonathan Hart listened attentively to his father as Justin squatted on the ground beside him and endeavored to explain the nuances of "talking" to the week-old foal that eyed them curiously from the opposite corner.

Beside the foal, gently stroking the neck of its dam, their adopted son Tommy nodded his encouragement, while five youngsters of a slightly lesser age looked on as they perched on the top rail of the fence. The three boys and two girls comprised the latest batch of children rescued from the slums of London's East End, and although they'd been at Sam's Farm only a fortnight, they already regarded the duke and duchess as their absolute heroes, and Tommy as an older brother whose example they longed to follow.

Tommy had come a long way since that day Justin had rescued him from hell. Her grandfather vowed he and Davey Fields were lacking only in a dozen or so inches and a few stone in weight before they became the equals of Michael Kelly in handling horses. And Michael had already put Davey in charge of all but the most ferocious of the canines they had brought to Camelot Downs for succor.

But Tommy's specialty seemed to be knowing how to treat with the often fearful, sometimes lonely, always hurting children when they first came to the farm. Justin had asked him once what his secret was in helping these abused little ones to settle in. "Oh, it's easy, sir," Tommy had replied. "I just hug 'em a lot, the way Sam did me once." Justin's eyes had been suspiciously moist when he'd held Sabelle tight and told her of it that night.

A pair of huge, shaggy forms, one dark and one reddish brown, came bounding into view from the crest of a hill behind the barns, and Sabelle waved to the small group on horseback that followed.

The duke and duchess of Ravensford and the couple's two children were their guests for a few days at Harthaven. Justin had known the strikingly handsome Brett Westmont casually in London, but Jonathan had recently made a point of reintroducing the duke, as well of his exquisite wife, Ashleigh, to Justin and Sabelle, and for a very particular reason: The Westmonts, it seemed, were also involved in the business of rescuing innocents—in their case, the orphaned or foundling children left by the war in Europe, though it was clear that any poor child in need of a home and lots of love would find a welcome at their country estate in Kent.

The pair of shaggy figures came closer, and Sabelle marveled at the fact that the Harts and the Westmonts had something else in common: Except for the grayish black color of his coat, the Westmont's Irish wolfhound, Finn, was the spitting image of Brendan!

Justin spied their guests' return from their ride about the estate. He swung young Jonathan onto his shoulders before joining Sabelle in walking over to greet them.

"Did you enjoy your ride, m'lady?" the gray-eyed duke asked four-year-old Lady Marileigh, the Westmonts' daughter.

"Oh, yes, Your Grace!" the vivacious little raven-haired beauty replied from her pony. "But it was too famous when your Brendan showed our Finn how to capture a fox kit which had wandered away from its den—and take it back to its mama!"

Everyone laughed, and then young Jonathan piped up in

a precociously authoritative voice, "Well, that's the point, isn't it? We're in the business of rescuing animals, not hunting them! Your Finn had best learn that lesson, and the sooner the better."

Lady Marileigh's turquoise eyes flashed as she swung down from her saddle and stood looking up at him, arms akimbo. "My dear Lord Jonathan, you have much to learn about our Finn. *He* succeeded in rescuing a pig from a butcher's cleaver before you and I were even born!"

Sabelle watched her son's gray eyes darken into storm clouds for a moment and then, at a surreptitious signal from Justin, focus on the large pink pig just now making its way over the hill toward them.

Young Jonathan's eyes widened when he saw the pig wore a *bonnet* on its head. His father lowered him to the ground, and the young lord turned toward Marileigh with a new measure of respect in his eyes.

"That pig, m'lady . . . do you mean to say you've trained it to—to enjoy civilized company?"

"Of course we have, silly," said Marileigh as she took his hand and led him toward the porker. "Now, do come along and I'll introduce you. Her name is Lady Dimples, you see, and . . ."

Ashleigh Westmont's deep sapphire eyes met Sabelle's, and she winked as their children strode off, deeply immersed in the kind of conversation only another generation of people such as they could enjoy.

Sabelle's gaze shifted, and she found herself mesmerized by the look of love abiding deeply in her husband's eyes. And for a moment she was taken back to a day in early November, a few years before, when she'd vowed a bitter promise of revenge, never realizing where it would lead.

But now, in this place they'd carved out as the best they could devise in an imperfect world, Sabelle felt a sense of awe. Instead of the disaster she might have reaped, she saw the splendid realization of a miracle . . . a miracle beyond her wildest imaginings.

Dominic and Catherine walked along the moonlit road, then disappeared into the trees, where the rest of his horses were tied. Dominic unsaddled and tethered the gray, then walked back to where Catherine waited beneath a thin-branched poplar.

He laced her fingers through his, but didn't start walking. "Since I've promised to take you home, it seems only fair that you should thank me properly."

Catherine's look turned guarded. The woman was surely no fool. "And just, pray tell, how might that be?"

"I ask only the price of a kiss."

Green eyes fixed on his face, searching for the truth.

"Just a kiss," he repeated. "Surely that's not too much to ask."

"If your promise is true, I don't suppose it is." She leaned over and kissed his cheek.

Dominic couldn't help but smile. "That isn't exactly what I had in mind." How could she possibly be so fiery and at the same time seem so innocent? But then maybe, in a way, she was. It was one thing to be used, another to be seduced. Dominic intended the latter.

"The kind of kiss I want takes a little more effort," he said. "Just close your eyes and I'll do the rest." She hesitated a moment, and he read her uncertainty. "You're sure going home is what you want?" he prodded.

Catherine squared her shoulders and her eyes slowly closed. Dominic admired the perfection of her features as she stood in the moonlight, but only for a moment. Cupping her cheeks with his hands, he slanted his mouth across hers, gently at first, then with an insistence that sent a fresh flood of warmth to his loins. Catherine's big green eyes flew open, and she tried to push him away, but he only increased his assault. When she opened her mouth to protest, his tongue invaded the warm interior. She tasted as sweet as her scent, he thought fleetingly, wishing he could taste her all over.

Catherine tried to break free, but something seemed to war with her will. From the moment of their first meeting, she had been drawn to Dominic's dark good looks. That he had come to her rescue had increased the attraction, and in the short time since, she had felt his powerful masculinity as she never had another. She felt it now as his lips moved gently over hers, his tongue tasting, invading, compelling her to accept him.

As if her heart lay just beneath her skin, Catherine felt every too-rapid flutter, the blood that seemed to pound through her veins. She couldn't think straight, could barely remember to breathe . . . She moaned. Dear God, this couldn't be happening! Could not possibly be allowed to happen. And yet some little-known feminine part of her wanted it to . . . .

GYPSY LORD—A NEW HISTORICAL ROMANCE FROM BESTSELLING AUTHOR KAT MARTIN— A SEPTEMBER 1992 ST. MARTIN'S PAPERBACK!